BEHOLD
THE DAWN

BEHOLD
THE DAWN

K.M. WEILAND

SCOTTSBLUFF, NEBRASKA

Published by PenForASword Publishing
P.O. Box 448
Scottsbluff, Nebraska 69363

Printed in the United States of America.

ISBN: 978-0-9789246-1-4

Dedicated to my beloved Savior, who has given us a fresh beginning in each new day. May we always have the strength to reach out and grasp that perfect gift.

And to Adrie, who lets Annan live in her closet.

Also by K.M. Weiland:

A Man Called Outlaw

Acknowledgments

MANY PEOPLE HAVE been instrumental in helping this project to publication. I am deeply humbled by the time and encouragement they lavished upon me while I was writing and editing this story. Without them, this book might never have made its way into your hands, and it certainly wouldn't have been anywhere near as good a story. In no particular order, those people are:

My #1 fan, my unfailing encourager, my sister: Amy.

My writing buds, critters, and proofreaders: Linda Yezak, Adrie Ashford, Laiel Upton, April Upton, Molly LoGalbo, Sterling Woomert, Daniel Farnum, Anna Naylor, Michael Snyder, Paul Chernoch—and everyone else who took the time to read any part of *Behold* and offer their criticism and support.

My family: Ted, Linda, Derek, and Jared, for putting up with me and all my writerly craziness and for supporting me and my work unswervingly.

Thank you all. May you be blessed as you have blessed me.

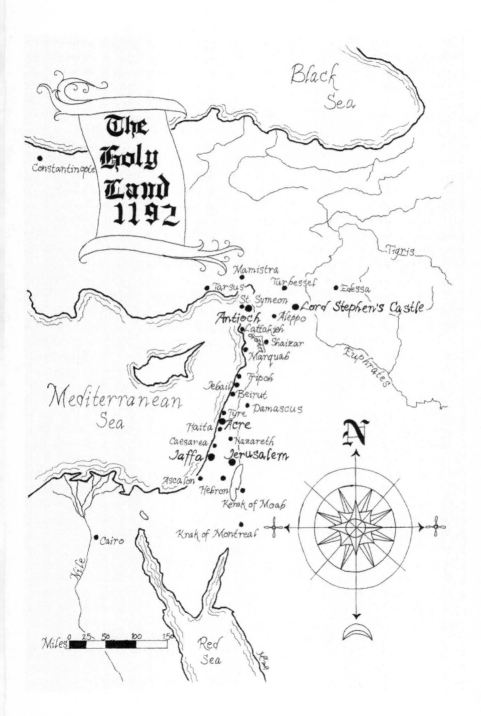

Heroes are forged on anvils hot with pain,
And splendid courage comes but with the test.
Some natures ripen and some natures bloom
Only on blood-wet soils; some souls prove great
Only in moments dark with death or doom.
                                    —*Ella Wheeler Wilcox*

Chapter I

1192—*Bari, Italy*

 ARCUS ANNAN HAD killed before. He had killed so many times he could no longer remember them all... so many times he had become inured to the ache of sorrow as he stared into the faces of the dead.

Some had deserved to die; some hadn't. It mattered not. They were all dead, and he could not bring them back. Unlike himself, they would never have to wonder if the end would ever come, if life would go on and on forever, taunting in its gaiety, tormenting in its bleakness.

As he reined his horse back amidst the chaos of a southern tourney and watched his allies crash into the opposing line of horsemen, he wondered if perhaps he had traveled this dark path beyond his ability to return. He watched through the barred vision of his great helm, concentrating on the steady rhythm of his breathing, forcing down the fire of battle that coursed through his veins as he waited for his quarry to extricate himself from the clangor of battle.

Today, Marcus Annan—tourneyer, soldier, and wanderer—would bring the tally of deaths yet a little higher as he played one more round in this bloody, accursed game of mock battle that had become the only pursuit of his shattered life. The legend of his name would grow, and the burning flash of battle fire would once more blind the sorrows of his heart. He would end one more life, even as his own hurtled onward, unable to escape the demons that wailed as loud on this day as they had upon their birth almost a score of years past.

Only two horses' lengths ahead, a knight in a purple surcoat freed himself from the roiling knot of iron and flesh, sword lofted in victory. Annan exhaled. This would be his last conquest of the day, chosen from among the dozens of other competitors because the knight in the purple surcoat was one of the few who could possibly challenge his strength.

Annan released his hold on his destrier's mouth, and the horse leapt forward. Long strides devoured the distance between him and the purple knight. Lifting his sword, he felt the familiar swell of his muscles beneath their covering of mail.

A knight from the opposing side swung his sword as Annan galloped past, his blow ringing against Annan's buckler. The arm behind the blow was strong, and Annan felt the ache all through his bones. He afforded his attacker a glance, swinging hard with his sword and catching the knight full across the chest, not even touching his shield.

From the corner of his left eye, he saw the descent of another knight's blade. His horse wheeled at the touch of his leg, and he smashed his opponent's sword from his hand. The man lifted his metal-sheathed gaze in panic.

But Annan left him. He had more pressing matters to deal with than an unarmed opponent: The purple knight had seen him.

The man reined his destrier around, sword leveled at Annan's chest, a wordless battle cry echoing inside his helm.

Joy of the fight—his only joy—swelled in Annan's heart, and he drove his spurs into his blood bay's flanks. The horse leapt forward, grunting through its nostrils.

The purple knight's sword struck Annan's with all the furor of a young body and determined mind. With a flick of his wrist, Annan separated the blades even as he thundered past. The knight turned back to confront him, and he brought his sword before his face in a salute, perhaps recognizing Annan as the famed Scottish tourneyer. Then he sheathed the sword and drew, from beneath the purple brocade of his horse's caparison, a new weapon. The setting sun, burning gold through the dust of the field, glinted against the iron tip of a war hammer.

Annan's blood pumped heat into his muscles. The rules of this tourney banned the war hammer from competition; its lethal heft would crush armor and shatter flesh and bone alike. His fist tightened on his sword hilt, the leather finger of his gauntlet creaking against the steel of the crossguard. Marcus Annan wasted no mercy on duplicitous knaves.

The purple knight laid his spurs to his horse. The war hammer rose above his head, its point flashing once across the face of the dying sun. Annan charged to meet him.

The war hammer caught his blade, and his horse, wearied from the long day of fighting, stumbled in the mud and fell almost to its knees. The hammer skidded down Annan's blade, toward his crossguard, and the purple knight jerked hard, trying to wrench the hilt from Annan's hand. The sharkskin wrap on the hilt skidded against the leather palm of Annan's mail glove. He was losing his grip; another moment and he would be defenseless. The knight's mount smashed into Annan's knee, and the destrier staggered yet again.

Dropping the reins, Annan heaved all the strength of his sword arm against the unfair leverage of the war hammer and clamped his other hand on the hammer's back spike. With a roar, he ripped it free of his blade and spurred his horse.

The destrier scrambled, mud splattering in wet clods, and Annan twisted in his saddle to strike his opponent's vulnerable back. From the depths of his helmet, he could hear the knight's cry of pain, and he wheeled his destrier in time to see the recoil of his opponent's body against his saddlebow.

He waited, hilt resting against his thigh, as the man pushed himself aright and straightened his contorted body. Again, the knight lifted his luckless hammer and bloodied his mount's sides with his spurs.

Annan remained as he was, his only movement that of his sword swinging away from its resting place on his hip. He cast one glance at the waning tangle of battle to his right, and his fingers tightened on the reins. The purple knight lifted his weapon high above his head, a scream upon his lips.

Annan foresaw the moment of the blow, sensed it in every taut line beneath the purple surcoat. With the grace and strength of a man who had spent more than twenty years in the armor of a professional soldier, he hurled his weight into a stroke that deflected the war hammer and pierced the mail above the purple knight's heart.

The knight froze. His limbs yanked tight, his sword arm falling to his side. Annan waited as the body slumped forward onto the saddlebow and, at last, tumbled from the skittish destrier's back. The war hammer, its gleam still unmarred by the blood of a first kill, crashed to the trampled sward, inches from its owner's outstretched hand.

Annan raised his head. Shouts and the clatter of arms echoed in the heavy dusk. Against the horizon, framed by the dirty huts that bordered the field, men fought on to claim the last ransoms of the day. Annan's arm fell to his side, and he reached to take the purple knight's reins. The horse would be his only gain from his victory. No one ransomed the dead.

He touched his rein to his destrier's neck, ready to return to camp. The battle fire had fled, draining his veins to emptiness. Another battle won, another tourney at an end. Another day he would never have to live again.

Against the backdrop of the encroaching woods, a stranger in the dark robes of a monk stood, watching him. Annan's brows came together. Holy men did not frequent the fields of a tournament, save to spit in disgust or cross themselves in horror.

Faceless beneath the shadow of his cowl, the monk stood with his hands hidden in his broad sleeves. He was not a tall man, but his shoulders were broad, his chest deep. He said nothing, and he did not move. He only watched.

The monk's head shifted away from Annan, and he seemed to stare at the fallen knight. Then he turned and staggered into the forest, every step warping his body as he struggled to move his crippled feet.

As the shadows swallowed the monk's ragged limp, Annan's heart beat a strange rhythm. He did not believe in superstitions, the guidance of the saints, or the power of visions. Indeed, he believed in little at all, save the strength of his own arm. But something about the sight of this crippled monk whispered a chill across his skin and prodded him to flee.

He turned his horse's face and spurred hard. He didn't look back to see if his allies were bending to gather their spoils, or to see if his opponents had noticed and reacted to their dead confederate.

And he did not turn to see if the monk had resurfaced to watch him retreat.

_____

After collecting the day's ransom money and selling the purple knight's horse and accoutrements, Annan returned to camp. As he entered the maze of tents spread beneath the city walls like the parti-colored cloak of a minstrel, he reined his destrier to a walk. The camp and, beyond it, the city of Bari bustled with all the color and noise of a foreign tourney. Even here, so near the earthly domain of the Popes, after almost two score years of threatened excommunication, the tournaments thrived.

In front of a wedge tent striped in green, he drew to a stop and dismounted, his bones creaking. Somewhere in the back of his mind, he had hoped the mild southern air would ease the pain of old wounds. But some things went too deep for healing.

He ducked to peer into the tent but could find no sign of Peregrine Marek, the Glasgow lad indentured to him after he had rescued the little thief from an irate shopkeeper three years before. He wasn't surprised. Marek had the bothersome habit of never being anywhere Annan wanted him when he wanted him. He growled, out of habit more than anger. Tossing his heavy purse into the tent, he turned to untack his horse.

He had already unbuckled the muddy caparison and stripped it from his mount by the time Marek finally trotted around the tent at the end of the row.

The lad's quick eye found Annan in a moment, and he slowed, pushing through the crowd with the stiff stride he invariably used when trying not to attract attention or appear in any haste. Even from across the camp, Annan could see the darting of Marek's eyes. He was fidgety about something.

Marek managed to dodge squires and knights alike and duck beneath the necks of a dozen skittish chargers without tripping himself or anyone else. At last, he stopped next to the tent pole and planted his hands on his belt. "Well. And how'd it go?"

Annan glared at him.

Marek huffed a breath. "And how'd it go, *sir*?"

Annan tried to ignore the inevitable sourness in his stomach as he tossed the caparison into the lad's chest. Crowing about the blood on his hands had never brought him much joy. "Mayhap you'd like to be explaining why you weren't waiting here when I told you to be?"

Marek shook out the heavy green brocade, dragging the edge in the dust at his feet. "If you'd any idea the fuss that's about to befall that fair city, you wouldn't waste time wanting explanations."

Annan turned away and slung his horse's reins over a tree branch. Marek's theatrics were rarely worth the effort of playing along. "It's a tourney town today, laddie. When isn't there a fuss?"

"It's a wee bit more'n a fuss this time. More like an unholy uproar. Didn't you hear anything about it when you was picking up your prize money?"

Annan glanced at the city's walls. Beyond the workmanlike clamor of the camp, he could hear only the shouts of knights galloping into town to drink their own health. "No."

"That Count Heladio—or whate'er his name is—you know the bucko in charge of this here tourney thing. Well, appears his nephew got himself killed out there today. In the last hour or so, they say."

"They can't know that. The bodies won't be collected 'til morning light."

"Well, all I know is this count person seemed to know what he knew. And he's none too rejoiced over it, neither. He's got him about half a score o' men-at-arms, and he's riding out to find the man what did the deed."

"It's a tourney. Men die all the time." Annan looked down at the dirt and blood crusted in the mail links on the back of his gauntlet, and he flexed the stiffness in his sword hand. "Matters not to us, anyway. Unsaddle the horse and rub him down before he binds up."

Marek made a face. "How many'd you kill today?"

"A few." He tugged the glove from his hand. "One for certain."

Marek lifted both eyebrows, and Annan knew what the lad was thinking before he could give it voice. "Master—"

"Crusade. I know." As if a Crusade could be enough to ransom him. He yanked the glove from his left hand. The leather underside had ripped earlier that day, and a dark bruise filled his palm.

Marek tossed the caparison over the destrier's flanks and flopped the stirrup onto the seat of the saddle. "I've said it before, and I'll say it again. All the priests swear it's true. Take the vow, kill a few infidels, and the name of a tourneyer becomes as good as that of a saint."

Annan stared at his palm, at the deepening shadow of purple. "The priests delude themselves."

"How would you know?"

"I know. Let us leave it at that."

Marek loosened the girth with a grunt. "Well, I'll tell you something else *I* know."

"And what's that?" Annan unfastened his belt with one hand and, with the weight of his sword in the other, joined both ends behind his back. He turned for the shade of the tent. Tomorrow, he and Marek would be traveling on to another tourney somewhere. But for tonight, all he wanted was meat and wine and the abyss of sleep.

"Count Heladio has other reasons to be unhappy." Marek yanked the saddle from the horse's back. "The Baptist is here."

Annan stopped and flicked his eyes to where the sunset backlit the city walls. "The Baptist—" The habitual lines in his forehead etched themselves deeper, and the dark-robed figure who had watched him from the edge of the tourney field flashed across his memory.

In the last year, the mendicant friar known as the Baptist had seemed ubiquitous. Everywhere Annan's travels had taken him, this fire-breathing monk, who preached against the excesses of the Church with the assurance of the Devil, never traveled far behind.

Marek dumped the saddle next to the tent pole. "Ever get the feeling he's been following us?"

"Why should he?"

"I dunno, maybe he likes tourneys. They say he's a heretic."

The Baptist's railings against the Church, against the Pope, against the Holy War that even now raged in the East, were enough to bring anathema down on him from every quarter. But what made Annan's skin burn cold was that the Baptist also raged against Roderic, bishop of Devonshire, the one-time prior of St. Dunstan's Abbey—the man and the place that had hurtled Annan down the sunless path he now trod. Despite the sins of his past, Roderic had risen in the circles of English royalty until he counseled the king himself, an honor he little deserved.

Marek pulled a water bucket from a tree limb and lugged it to the destrier. "Mayhap we should catch a glimpse of him before we head our own way again. The count'll throw him out sooner or later, and I never was one to oppose a good show. Eh?"

Annan unclenched his teeth. "I've seen him already."

"What?" Marek stopped short and water sloshed against his chest. "Already?"

"He was on the field, watching."

"So he does like tourneys, then." Marek shoved the bucket beneath the destrier's outstretched muzzle. "Can't tell me this isn't a ruddy sad world, when even monks are chasin' after the tournaments."

"It isn't the tournaments." Realization razored across Annan's mind. "It's me." Without looking down, he buckled his sword back on. This monk knew him. When they had stared at one another across the tourney field only an hour before, the intensity beneath the man's cowl hadn't been mere curiosity. Somewhere in the shadows of the past, the Baptist had known him.

Annan caught his saddle up from the ground and lugged it to where Marek's palfrey stood stomping at flies.

"Hey. Where is it you're off to?" Marek craned a look over his shoulder.

"To find out what he's after."

"How about me? Don't you think I want to see the count throw him out on his ear?"

"You'll wait here." He tightened the girth and drilled Marek a look. "And when I say wait here, I mean wait."

"You always say that. But what if there's extenuatin' circumstances you're not foreseeing?"

"Your extenuating circumstances always end up sounding like excuses." He took the reins and swung aboard. "Just stay here. I'll be back before night falls."

Marek huffed. "Well, when Heladio does decide to throw Master Gethin the Baptist out of town, please don't go trying to rescue him and get us all into trouble."

Annan's heavy hand on the reins choked the palfrey back to a halt. In his veins, his blood grew thick. "Gethin?"

"Gethin the Baptist. That's what they're calling him back in the town." Marek shrugged. "You weren't thinking his name was John, now were you?"

Annan let his breath out. "Stay here," he said and spurred the palfrey.

The name rang in his ears. Wasn't it one he had once known as well as his own? For sixteen years, it was a name he had believed belonged to a dead man. Had Marek told him John the Baptist had indeed walked across the centuries to resume preaching, the numbness in Annan's soul could have left him no colder.

At the city gates, Annan found him. The tourney crowd swarmed around and beneath the gate arch, laughing and yelling. Filmy twilight was falling over the city, and the gay festival colors had reverted to everyday grays and browns. A few men, already deep in their cups, staggered and swore, looking for one more fight before the day ended.

Just outside the gate, his back against the sand-colored bricks of the wall, the dark-robed monk stood atop the overturned half of a barrel. The shadow of his cowl hid his face, and his hands buried themselves in his opposing sleeves. At his feet, a score of people had gathered, faces upturned to hear him speak. His voice, deep almost to the point of hoarseness, rumbled across the distance, audible in tone, if not in word. He stood as if cast in stone; he did not move, did not gesture. Only the rise and fall of his voice held in check the throng that surrounded him.

Annan reined the palfrey to a halt just beyond the crowd. As the monk had watched him at work on the tourney field, he now watched the monk. His heart thudded against his breastbone, swelling until his chest seemed to hold nothing but its beat.

This monk, this Gethin the Baptist, could not be the man he had known. The Gethin he had once loved as a brother had died. He had been killed, murdered, cast out to feed the ravens and the dogs. For sixteen years, Annan had known this as certainly as he had known the weight of his sword in his hand. It could not be him.

He dismounted and led the palfrey to the edge of the crowd. He towered over the townspeople, the line of vision between himself and the Baptist unimpaired as the Baptist's growl floated through the crowd to reach him.

"Thus saith the Patriarch, 'By thy sword shalt thou live, and shalt serve thy brother; and it shall come to pass when thou shalt have the dominion, that thou shalt break his yoke from off thy neck.'" A white scar slashed the Baptist's dark lips, twisting them into perpetual mockery. "And thus saith the Prophet—" The shadow of his hood tilted across his face, flashing a glimpse of shriveled, waxen horror. "'Hear ye this, O house of Jacob, which swear by the name of the Lord and make mention of the God of Israel, but not in righteousness, not in *truth*.'"

The Baptist looked up, his eyes blazing with all the furor of a hunting falcon's, and Annan's blood stopped pumping. He knew these eyes. He knew this man.

The scar across the Baptist's lips twisted harder, carving a serpentine into the albescent flesh. He stretched out his hands, and two young men lifted him to the ground. The crowd parted before him, scrambling out of his way, opening a path down their midst.

At the end of the path Annan waited. He had come to this country with the hope that his old wounds might find relief. Now, the oldest of his wounds ripped open before his eyes.

The Baptist limped toward him, every step contorting his body, his left hip collapsing beneath him, his toes dragging, then lifting, then dragging again.

"Gethin," Annan whispered.

He knew now why, back on the tourney field, he had felt the urge to flee. Standing before him was the greatest enemy he had ever faced.

His past.

CHAPTER II

"SO YOU KNOW me after all." Gethin the Baptist's smile leered from the lower half of his face, somehow detached from the intensity of his eyes. "For more than a year, I've followed you, and yet you have never sought me out. Surely you heard my name."

"I thought you dead." Annan's tongue cleaved to the roof of his mouth. Phantom images of long ago flitted through his memory:

Himself—as a young penitent in the Abbey of St. Dunstan's, bowed down beneath the grief of his sins, face against the cold stone floor.

Gethin—kneeling beside him before the altar, praying the words Annan could not say for himself.

And then followed the images he had never seen with his own eyes, but which had, at one time, burned deeper within his brain than all the rest:

Gethin—the skin flogged from his body, his bones broken into pieces, cast out as dead, because he had dared to believe in a cause.

"The years have changed you." Gethin laughed, a single grating note. "But the strength of your arm and temper remain the same. Indeed, I am not surprised to find you chasing battles. Why have you avoided me all these years? Have you been running from me?"

"They told me you died at St. Dunstan's."

Gethin came nearer, and his twisted face glared up into Annan's. "St. Dunstan's. Now there is a name I am happy you remember. Tell me, do you recall any more names?"

Annan raised the fist that held the palfrey's reins and clasped it in his other hand. The bruise in his palm throbbed. "You are much altered. Have you abandoned the quiet piety of a monastery to monger glory for yourself?"

"And you haven't, *Marcus Annan?*" He spoke the name as if it were a curse. "Do you know why I have sought you out through all the kingdoms of Christendom? Why I have delayed my journey to Jerusalem, despite the desperate need of my presence to combat the enemies who gather there even now? Do you know why I sought *you* out first that I might warn you of what will soon come to pass?"

"I know not."

Gethin snorted. "Indeed, you do not. There was a time, long ago, when you would have already snatched up the arms of truth and joined my battle against the hypocrisy of the Church. But no longer."

The crowd shifted, their murmurs whispering at the edge of Annan's hearing. Far away, down the road, hoofbeats rumbled. The palfrey nudged his arm with its muzzle, then shook its head, and the reins clanked against the bit. Annan stared at the Baptist, the evening's warm breeze turning chill against his face.

Gethin stepped nearer, and his voice dropped to a croak, his words meant only for Annan. "If you know who I am, then you also know that what happened at St. Dunstan's Abbey has not found its end. Father Roderic has yet to pay for his sins."

Annan's skin tingled. His backbone hardened into a spear haft. "I have left what happened at St. Dunstan's in the past."

Gethin scoffed. "You think you can bury St. Dunstan's in the gore and glory of the tourney field, but you are mistaken. Bishop Roderic must die for his sins. Sixteen years ago one man attempted to exact the price in blood from Roderic. It is he who must end this now. A man named Matthias of Claidmore. You do remember him?" His eyes flashed with an anger that was only a blink away from hatred.

Annan stared at him. His hand fell to the hilt of his sword, his knuckles turning cold. He had not wanted this. He would much rather have grieved for Gethin the rest of his days than see him resurrected in such a form. He had spent the last sixteen years forgetting. To ask him to remember now was asking far too much.

Gethin dragged himself back a step. He looked behind Annan, beyond him, and the specter of a smile crossed his lips. Running footsteps slapped the ground, scarcely discernible above the hoofbeats that thundered yet nearer.

"Master Annan!"

Annan broke his gaze from Gethin's and turned to see Marek running madly, arms and legs pumping, barely keeping ahead of the troop of knights galloping behind.

Marek veered off the road, and the Baptist's crowd scattered before him. "It's Heladio! He's coming for you!"

At the head of the troop rode a swarthy man clad in a purple tabard. Annan stiffened, realizing a second too late that Heladio's surcoat was the same as that of the dead young knight with the war hammer.

Marek scrambled to a stop. "In the name of St. Jude, why didn't you tell me you'd killed the bloody nephew!"

Heladio flung one hand into the air, signaling his men. "*Nessuno se ne vada! Sto cercando l'uomo chiamato* Annan!"

Annan faced the count, squaring his shoulders, making himself relax. Beside him, Marek straightened up and forced an innocent smile. He was either unable to control or just entirely unaware of the fidget in his leg.

The crowd fled despite Heladio's warning. From beneath his cowl, Gethin watched Annan, the scarred twist of his lips almost contemptuous.

Heladio dragged his horse to a stop. His small nostrils flared with every breath. "I seek a man called Annan. You are Annan?" His guttural accent all but buried the words.

"Aye."

"And you are a competitor at our esteemed tournament?"

"Aye."

"I am astounded the renowned Marcus Annan deigns to compete at such a humble tourney." He unsheathed his sword and jerked his

head at one of his men-at-arms. "Renowned or not, this is the last tourney in which you will ever fight."

The man-at-arms, joined by one of his comrades, kneed his horse
forward and advanced on Annan.

Annan held his ground. "Why?"

Behind him, Marek uttered a pained noise and crossed himself.

"You dare to ask? My nephew Giulio is dead! I have a witness who
swears you committed the murder. For the honor of my family, you
must be punished for this!"

"He attacked me with an illegal weapon, a war hammer. Apparently, your nephew didn't take your family's honor as seriously as
yourself."

"He was a boy fighting against the great Marcus Annan! You
expected him to give you the benefit of the battle?"

"I expect an honest fight from every man. The world is not the
worse for one less knave."

"You dare insult me? You, the most infamous of tourneyers? You
are covered in blood!" His gaze darted past Annan to where Gethin
stood in silence. "And you consort with heretics!"

At the edge of the road, the men-at-arms dismounted and propped
their lances beneath their arms. One after the other, they drew their
swords. Annan opened his fingers, and the palfrey's reins fell to the ground
behind him. His right hand reached across his body to pull his sword
free of its scabbard, and he clasped the hilt with both hands. The two
young knights wavered, no doubt measuring their combined strength
against his.

With Marek at his back, he could dispatch the two unmounted men-
at-arms with little enough trouble. It was Heladio and the remaining
men on horseback who would present a problem. Already, they were
closing in to surround him, to cut off his escape should he fight his way
past the first attack. A man on the ground was nigh defenseless against
a mounted knight.

With Gethin depending on his sword for protection, Annan would
have no chance of retreating on foot fast enough or far enough to escape a charge. He must work quickly, and then regain his saddle.

Heladio's eyes bored into Annan's face. "Even the saints cry out for
justice, *Signore*."

Annan widened his stance and raised his sword. "Let them cry."

The knight on Annan's left struck first, using both hands to swing his blade at Annan's upper body. Annan met the stroke before it had gone two feet and hammered his own sword into the other's. The knight reeled, flailing. Behind him, the two riderless horses spooked and ran, dodging onlookers and charging through the gates. Without altering his stance, Annan swung again and caught the second knight full across his mail-clad chest.

Heladio charged. Men and women shrieked and scattered, and the handful of louts and drunken knights who had been lounging about snatched up their swords. Who or why they fought probably wasn't something their ale-fogged brains paused to ponder. Annan didn't care. The bigger the distraction, the longer he and Marek had to get free.

Heladio pounded the distance that separated them into a hundred dusty fragments. Annan flung aside an incapacitated knight and spun around to snatch the palfrey's reins from Marek's hand.

"Take the Baptist and leave! Get into the city before they shut the gates!"

Marek ducked a flying three-legged stool and staggered back to his feet, his short sword clenched in his hand. "What about you?"

"I'll find you later!" He leapt onto the palfrey.

"Why do you always have to say that?"

Heladio's thunder grew in Annan's ears. "Because you haven't yet learned the art of watching your own back during a retreat!"

Marek gave no argument. Someone threw a dirt clod that smacked him in the back of the thigh. He uttered a yelp and scrambled away. A few paces back, the Baptist stood amidst the chaos, so motionless he could almost have been praying. Only the glitter of his eyes, as he stared at something beyond Annan's shoulder, betrayed him.

Annan spun the palfrey around, sword before his face, barely in time to catch Heladio's ringing blow. He shoved the man away and almost toppled him from the saddle.

The palfrey jibbed sideways, head high. Annan dragged the horse's muzzle almost to its chest. "You've struck your blow for honor, Count. Best call an end while you still can."

"Honor me by your death, tourneyer!" Heladio drove his spurs into his horse's sides and charged once more.

Annan reined aside, and the count's blow sliced past his face. "If I kill you today, who will mourn your nephew tomorrow?" He dared a glance at the gates, where Marek had tangled with a drunken squire. Gethin was nowhere to be seen.

Beneath the purple surcoat, Heladio's chest heaved. "I find your courage overestimated, *Signore Cavaliere*. Do you run from the blade of a man with gray hairs?"

Annan's muscles stilled. Fire crackled beneath his skin, and the world faded to gray around Heladio. "I do not run, Count. I simply wait." He lowered his sword, exposing his chest in invitation.

Heladio dragged his horse around for another pass. "*Sputerò sulla tua tomba!*"

Annan waited as time stretched into forever and disappeared into nothing. Heladio dropped his reins to his horse's neck and twisted both arms behind his head, every sinew strained with the effort of the stroke. His lips parted in a scream, but the sound of it disappeared in the rush of Annan's blood.

Annan whipped his sword up to meet Heladio's. Iron crashed against iron. Heladio's dark eyes widened as Annan's blade tore his sword from his grip and smashed into his mail-clad arm. The bone buckled and broke. Heladio plunged to the ground, and his horse galloped over the top of him.

Pivoting the palfrey to face his fallen foe, Annan choked back the heat of his blood. "Mourn your nephew, old man, and host no more tourneys."

Moaning like a woman in childbirth, Heladio pushed to his knees. "Isidorio! *Fermatelo! Fermatelo, lui e il monaco!*"

Across the street, the men-at-arms shoved through the flailing crowd at a redoubled pace, trampling underfoot those who did not clear the way. One of the men pointed and snapped commands.

Annan spun the palfrey toward the gates. If these men craved a meeting with Death, they would have to find the point of someone else's blade on which to throw away their lives. He had given Heladio and his honor fair enough play for one night.

To his left, just outside the long shadow of the wall, the tottering figure of a monk broke the plane of his vision. Gethin the Baptist held someone's forgotten quarterstaff in his hand. He leaned against it like a shepherd who had dried up his life beneath the Mediterranean sun. But even at a score of paces distant, Annan could see the tension in his body: every muscle stretched, every ligament a bowstring drawn to breaking, ready, waiting, begging to be released.

Behind Annan, Heladio shrieked, "If I cannot have the tourneyer, I shall have the heretic!"

Annan stabbed his spurs to the palfrey's sides, and the horse leapt forward. Gethin leaned upon the staff 'til Annan was almost upon him. Then, with a flash of energy that nearly eliminated the crippled stride, he sprang forward. Annan caught his outstretched hand and swung him up behind the saddle. The palfrey staggered a moment under the new weight, then leapt forward as Annan laid the flat of his blade to the animal's haunch.

One of the few unhorsed men-at-arms scrambled to close the gates, and the palfrey clipped him with its chest and sent him sprawling. Annan galloped through the gate arch, scattering brawlers like seed for the sowing. Shouts echoed behind them. Hoofbeats pounded.

He gouged the horse again, demanding speed the animal could scarcely muster. Ahead, in the distance, a slender lad of some score years tore through the crowded street, headed back toward the gate, sword flashing in one hand. *Marek.*

The youth looked up, stopped short at the sight of his master's flight, then spun back around and ducked into a side road. Annan took the hint and angled the palfrey for the opening. The crowd parted before him, people alternately screaming and cheering.

The narrow side street—little more than an alley between buildings—provided a path free of people, save for Marek who raced ahead, light on his feet as any fallow deer. They ran, switchbacking thrice, before Marek finally stopped at the back of a tavern and wrenched open a door. Annan flung himself to the ground, pulling Gethin off beside him. Marek wrapped his jerkin hood round the palfrey's head, and together he and Annan pulled the lathered horse into the dark emptiness of the tavern's backroom.

Gethin hobbled in behind and shut the door. "Heladio will have plenty of townsmen to point out the direction we have gone."

"St. Jude," Marek said, "Why couldn't I have been indentured to a cloth merchant, tell me that?"

Annan tossed him the reins. "When I told you to leave, I rather assumed you'd have wits enough to drag the defenseless monk along with you!"

"I thought he was behind me. I'm hardly responsible if he prefers to gawk at the fighting!"

Annan turned, fingers still clenched around his sword hilt, and peered through the shadows. Silhouetted against the streaks of light that outlined a shuttered window in the back of the room, Gethin folded his arms into his sleeves. "Now what?"

"I've no intention of staying in Bari. Heladio seeks a fight he cannot finish."

The shadows began to fade, and Annan's eyes found tints of gray in the darkness. A mocking smile lit Gethin's lips. "Yes, go, Marcus Annan. Run away once again. You've been running ever since the day St. Dunstan's fell, have you not?"

"All men put their backs to the past, Baptist. We cannot turn about and live it again."

"Leave the responsibilities of yesterday unfulfilled, and the future will tumble into the past's abyss."

"Tell me, then. What was it we left unfulfilled?" He gripped the palfrey's saddlebow, and the dry wood prickled against his palm. "Is there any part of St. Dunstan's that is not better fading into dust?"

"Can you say this? You who know the truth of all that happened there? You knew of Roderic's sins, his *hypocrisies*." Gethin stepped forward, his left foot dragging in the straw. Again, the flash of energy possessed him, tightened his limbs, gave him a strength that all but eradicated his deformities. "You saw with your own eyes the bastard children he hid from the world even as he kissed the Holy Crucifix. You knew of his ambition. Ambition that killed a wife to gain a bishopric. You knew his contempt of us and of true holiness."

"What did we know of holiness?" Ice filled the emptiness in his stomach. It was an emptiness that had been his companion for longer than he wanted to remember. "What did any of us know?"

"Some of us knew. Some of us still know. *Matthias of Claidmore* would know."

The cold spread. His sweat froze upon his skin. "Enough. Tell me what you'd have me know, and tell me now."

"It is time we find Matthias."

Annan shook his head. "What he did that day at St. Dunstan's was a mistake."

"Nay, it was a battle. And I its first casualty." Beneath the rim of his cowl, his eyes glared, the pale orange-brown of the iris visible even in the shadows. "It was I who discovered Roderic's great sin, I who discovered the blood of his young wife still scarlet upon his hands twenty years after the deed. It was I who took the evidence to Matthias, because I knew him to be a man of vision and a man of action." Another uneven step propelled him forward. "When Matthias escaped the Abbey to inform the Earl of Keaton of Roderic's sins, do you know what Roderic did to me?"

"He killed you." The words echoed from the darkness of a thousand sleepless nights. How many years had Annan mourned the deaths of St. Dunstan's "battle"? How many countless times had he wondered about the manner in which his friend had died?

"*Yes*, he killed me. Even as I stand before you now, I tell you that he killed me. He and his minions whipped me with rods, flayed the skin from my body, broke my joints from their sockets, and poured the very wine of the Eucharist into my lungs to drown me. And, then, when I had nothing left but to die, he cast me into the wayside for the dogs to feed upon my flesh."

"But you didn't die."

"Heaven granted that I should live." Gethin drew a breath, his chest inflating. "And Matthias, at least, returned to wreak Heaven's justice upon St. Dunstan's. Dozens of the brethren flocked to him, dozens of them died in the clash against Roderic's followers."

Old gray memories staggered through Annan's brain. He had watched Matthias destroy St. Dunstan's. He had seen the twisted corpses strewn across the courtyard. He had smelled their stench, had breathed their terror.

Gethin lifted his chin, and the light from the window slats streaked his face. "Matthias gravely wounded Roderic that day. But Roderic did not die. And neither did I. Heaven granted me a second life, that I might orchestrate the finality of justice no one else has dared pursue. What began at St. Dunstan's must be played to the end. I must find Matthias, and he must kill Roderic for his sins."

Somewhere, abroad in the city, hoofbeats rattled. The count and his men were coming. They would find the hiding place before long.

As well as anyone, Annan knew what Matthias had done that day and why the young nobleman had afterwards disappeared. Since that day, sixteen years ago, no man had laid eyes upon Matthias of Claidmore. And that was as it should be.

Unlike Gethin, Annan had never been able to herald the would-be savior of St. Dunstan's as a hero. He had seen the man's raw temper, his anger, his hatred. Matthias had extracted a terrible price from the brethren of St. Dunstan's. Heralding his actions as the sword of justice would never change the stark reality.

On that fateful day, as he trudged away from St. Dunstan's, Annan had looked back at the black smoke on the wind, and he had known then, as he knew now, that the darkness in the abbot was no different from that of Matthias himself.

"Matthias of Claidmore is dead." The words scraped his throat.

Gethin didn't flinch. "Do you really believe that?"

"He is dead."

Gethin's lip curled. He took a step back. "Well, then know this. There is one other whose knowledge of the past may yet be able to shed light on Roderic's transgressions. William, Earl of Keaton."

The clatter of horses in the back alley sent Marek scudding toward the door, dragging the blindfolded palfrey behind him. But Annan barely heard.

Lord William.

How many years had it been since Lord William of Keaton had ridden through his thoughts? His nobleman mentor had stood by him all those years ago during St. Dunstan's hell. More importantly perhaps, he had been one of the last men to lay eyes on the bloody Matthias of Claidmore.

The approach of the horses grew louder, and Gethin edged forward half a step, the intensity of his shrouded gaze unquenched. "The Earl was under duress in the English court and has taken the vow of a Crusader. He, his wife, and his retinue left for the Holy Land several months ago." He folded his arms into his sleeves. "He cannot destroy Roderic, but Roderic may destroy him, if Matthias does not return to act as he must. Roderic is waiting for them."

"To kill them?"

"Does that matter to you, Marcus Annan? You cannot save them. Only Matthias of Claidmore can help the earl now." He limped across the room and shouldered past Annan to reach the door that would lead into the tavern. He cocked his head toward the sound of the oncoming riders. "The count will see you upon a gibbet if you do not make your escape before the day is out. It would seem you have no choice but to leave Bari. "

Annan's spine stiffened. "You mean I am *left* with no choice. Events today have played into your hands admirably. It occurs to me that Heladio learned of his nephew's death sooner than he possibly could under normal circumstances. You were the witness he spoke of, weren't you?"

Gethin pulled open the door. "Does not the pursuit of truth justify many means?" He lurched into the drunken gaiety of the main room, and the door bumped shut behind him.

"They're coming," Marek hissed.

Annan took one step after the Baptist, then turned to where Marek crouched against the back door, the palfrey's bridle clenched in his hand.

"Wait." He found his mouth had no moisture to swallow away the dryness in the back of his throat. "They're moving too quickly to be looking for hoofprints."

The hoofbeats approached. The sound swelled, and then traveled past and dissipated, like a bubble that had inflated and then popped into nothing.

Marek growled. "Ruddy lot of nerve that Baptist bloke's got. Little wonder every diocese in Christendom's got the habit of throwing him out. I wouldn't have owned to knowing him if'n I were you."

Annan opened his lips but found he had no words to speak. The Gethin he had known so long ago would never have betrayed a friend.

He sheathed his sword and crossed to the back door to take the reins from Marek. Easing the horse away from the door, he waited for Marek to open the passage to the alley. Once outside, he pulled the jerkin from the horse's eyes and handed both it and the reins to the lad. "Go back to the camp and pack up our trappings. It's unlikely you'll be recognized, and the gates won't stay closed long on the night of a tourney. The inns and taverns would lose too much business. When you've finished, meet me at the far end of the wharf."

"The wharf?" Marek threw the reins over the horse's neck and clambered into the saddle. "Why? Are we taking a boat?"

"Your prayers to join the Holy War appear to have fallen upon more willing ears than mine."

"I don't believe it." Marek grinned. "I knew I wasn't indentured to a tourneyer for no reason. The saints sent me to you to save your soul! I've heard the priests rattle on about it a hundred times. Raise our swords in a Crusade and we'll be absolved of all sins, from now until forever!" He crowed and laid his heels to the palfrey's side. "I should be sainted myself for this!"

Annan stood in the dust of the alley and watched the palfrey gallop around the corner. Marek faded into the clamor of the city, and Annan's arms fell to his sides.

Absolution.

The word clattered around inside his skull, but he could only stare into the distance with the weariness of a man who did not even hope that such might be true.

CHAPTER III

ANNAN BRACED HIS arms against the sway of the *Bonfilia*'s bow and stared across the dappled glare of the bay. An inert giant of tent-white camps stretched out upon the Holy Land's beaches, all the way to the city walls. Even from the middle of the bay, the great catapults, like two guardians of savage lore, were visible rising above the camp, swinging relentlessly amidst the heat of the day. He could hear the thunder of the stones against the walls; the crumbling of clay and rock; the distant, hollow ring of voices.

"We be at *infedele* blockade very soon." The gap-toothed Venetian captain jostled Annan's elbow as he strode past. "Go back to the quarterdeck with your *servo* now, *sì*?"

Annan nodded, took one last look at the shimmering hills of the besieged port city, and pushed away from the rail.

Slowly, he made his way to the forecastle, shouldering past the jostling sailors and their unintelligible speech. A long score of days had passed since he and Marek boarded ship in Bari, and he was ready to have the feel of sand once more beneath his feet and an enemy before him that could not run away as did the demons of his mind.

Marek, seasick since the beginning of the journey, sat cross-legged in a pile of hawser. As Annan approached, the lad made a rumbling noise that had no doubt been intended as a moan. "All this to be right with Heaven? I tell you, the priests are an unfair lot. This is all that Baptist's fault."

Annan leaned against the rail, his back to Marek, so he could watch the infidels skittering across their vessels, preparing for the skirmish that preceded every Christian ship's entry into the Acre port. "Last I heard, you were taking credit for this entire expedition yourself."

"That was before too many miles of rough seas. Anyway, we both know it wasn't my intentions, however noble, that got you here." He sniffed. "Tell me this. Why is it that when *I* argue for months to come on this pilgrimage, you act as if you can't even hear me? But as soon as that mad monk whispers one little word of it, here we are staring the infidels in their faces?"

"Your reasons weren't quite as good as his, laddie."

"I've been with you nigh on three years. You'd think you'd have the sense to listen to me before you do some raving heretic."

Annan watched the approaching galley. The infidel ship slid through the water on the strength of its oars alone, its sails of no use in the humid breathlessness of the Eastern climate. "If the Baptist is who I think he is, I've known him a long span past our three years."

"Aye, well, you might have been sharing whatever it is you *think* you ken about him with a faithful servant like meself, instead of stalking about the ship for the whole journey."

The *Bonfilia* gathered speed, and the air pushed against Annan's face. All around, the sailors tensed, their sun-darkened skin tightening across their faces. The captain, standing just behind the prow, murmured to them in their own language.

Marek began extricating himself from his seat of hawser. "Soon as I kill me one of these Mohammedans and get meself absolved, I'm going back to Glasgow and my Maid Dolly. *If*, of course, she isn't Goodwife Dolly by now." He pushed to his feet. "She, for one, would've been right pitying to me during the afflictions of the journey."

"You wish too much, boyo. Your Dolly'll have to wait another four years before your indentureship is over."

Marek grunted and stumbled over to stand at Annan's side. "Aye, and why couldn't you have just let that shopkeeper throw me into some dungeon three years ago for stealing his blinking bread? I'd have gotten out of there a lot sooner than it'll be before you're done with me." He squinted at the oncoming ship, now only a few lengths away. "We got to fight all those sailors?"

"Nay, we get to run from all those." Annan rubbed the tightness in his shoulder. Inaction agreed with neither his mental state nor his stiffening bones. A man's body at two score years was not the same as it was at half that.

"Probably our cursed luck to have gotten the slowest boat in Venetian waters," Marek said. "Blessed Saint— Ah, who's the saint of sailors anyway? I can't ever remember half of 'em."

"Best keep St. Jude then." The patron of the hopeless was Marek's oft-invoked guardian.

A moan grumbled in the lad's throat. "I hate water. And I hate ships. And I hate those Mohammedans or whatever they're called we're supposed to be fighting. T'awful hard way to get out of Hell, if you're asking me."

"Should have thought of that back in Bari."

The Moslem Saracens' battle cry floated up from behind:

Le ilah ile alah!

A volley of arrows spat overhead, overshooting most of the *Bonfilia* and smacking into the stern behind Annan and Marek.

Save for an occasional oath in their own language, the Venetians kept silent. The score of Crusading knights, along with their squires and serving men, stood with their swords bared, their bodies tight and expectant. To either side of the ship, the rhythmic creak and splash of the galley oars were the only signs of the straining muscles and pounding hearts striving from below decks to outrun the infidels.

Annan clenched his sword, his arm bulging. He had not come here to slay the followers of the Evil Prophet, but if they insisted on bringing the fight to him, he would cut them down with right good will.

The foremost Moslem ship drew almost prow to prow with the *Bonfilia*. Infidel sailors massed in the forecastle, swords in hand, grinning. Under the reign of the charismatic warlord Salah ed-in Yusef— dubbed Saladin by the Westerners—the followers of Mohammed had gathered from every region of the East. Moors, their skin the color of night, their faces painted white and red, howled their oaths alongside the Turks and Syrians in their billowy desert garments and their light chain-mail shirts.

These were the warriors who had wrested the nation of Jerusalem from Christendom and trampled the holy places underfoot. These were the men who believed the key to Paradise was Christian blood upon their swords. Did they know Christians pursued the same Paradise by means of Moslem blood?

Annan freed the tension in his sword arm and drew his blade. "Be ready. They'll board us."

Marek's eyes didn't leave the enemy.

The two hulls collided with a groan a hundred times as loud as a loose joint grating in its socket, and the whole deck lurched, nearly yanking itself from beneath Annan's feet. On the *Bonfilia*'s larboard side, oars clattered against oars, rowers groaned as they attempted to maintain the ship's pace, and the Moslems leapt across the open water to the Venetian deck.

Annan exhaled. This, at last, was a face of the enemy he could fight.

The deck hands at the rail took the brunt of the attack, two of them shrieking as they plunged into the sea. Annan lowered his shoulders, and he and the rest of the knights charged. Swinging his free arm wide, he hammered his forearm into a Moslem throat. The man's head snapped back, eyes bulging, and he fell to the deck to be trampled by his fellows.

Teeth bared, Annan pivoted on his heel and brought his sword into both his hands. His blade smashed against the lofted scimitars, cleaving flesh and bone, mowing through the Turks. At his side, Marek darted and plunged. His shorter blade flashed once and emerged dark with blood. The laddie fought like the peregrine falcon whose name he had taken: quick and darting. He would have made a decent enough soldier in a few years had he possessed the temperament and the inclination.

A hulking Moor, his mouth gaped to reveal a row of missing teeth, took a running leap at Annan, launching himself an arm's length above the deck. With a cry, he hurled his body forward, his pike aimed at Annan's throat. Annan swiped his own blade in front of his face, caught the Moor's pike just beneath the spearhead and smacked it aside, spinning his opponent half off his feet. He planted his foot in front of the Moor and hammered his fist into the back of the man's neck. With a gasped inhalation, the Moor fell and lay tremoring.

Grappling hooks clattered against the side of the ship, and more Moslems poured onto the quarterdeck. The *Bonfilia* tilted off course, dragged aside by the enemy's heavier ship. Half a dozen native tongues shrieked as one: Venetian and Frankish and Mohammedan words tangling in a guttural howl. The knights to either side of Annan fell, one of them toppling overboard and sinking beneath the weight of his armor.

Annan dragged a Moslem off a flailing squire and caught the youth's tabard before he could follow his master over the side. He snagged the squire's fallen sword from the deck and slapped it back into his hands. "Did you come to this land to fight or to die?"

The youth's white eyes stared up at him, and Annan spun him around to face the new onslaught.

Annan charged, his blood firing at the sound of his own wordless roar. He flung himself upon the enemy, scattering them before his blade, gaining ground step by step across the bloody deck. Marek darted to his side, and the rest of the men fell in behind him. He heard their shouts and felt the deck shudder beneath their blows and their fallen adversaries.

He emptied himself into the battle. For months, he had been pent up on this itinerant island, bereft of any outlet for his frustrations and his memories. The men around him, knights and squires and sailors alike, stared in wonder to see him flaying the infidels. No doubt they thought he did it to save his soul. But he fought today for the same reason he always fought: it was the only thing his life had left him fit for.

The Moslems' ranks waned, and at last the captain managed to get his men to the rails to hack the ship free of the grappling hooks.

The deck heaved beneath his feet, and Annan snarled in the faces of the few wild-eyed Moslems who remained. One of the infidels, sweat drenching his brow, retreated to the prow, and Annan stalked him one step after the other.

The *Bonfilia*'s oars finally scraped free, and the prow swung back to its proper trajectory. A parting volley of arrows rent the sails and clattered against the deck. Only half a dozen Moslems remained aboard, trapped by their fear of the water and their inability to swim. Shouting, the knights fell upon them.

Annan's Moslem fought blindly, wildly, his blows flashing with a speed Annan's heavier sword couldn't match. From Annan's right, Marek bounded into view, sword lofted, screaming.

The Moslem's attention broke between Marek and Annan. Annan took one step, stopped to brace his footing against the deck, and swung. The Moslem yelped and fell.

Marek skidded to a stop, just short of the man's death throes, and blew out his cheeks. "Why can't saving one's soul ever be a nice, clean operation? Tell me that, eh?"

Annan smacked the flat of his blade against Marek's backside.

"'Ey!" Marek whipped around, his sword darting back up. "What was that for?"

"When you kill an enemy, you don't stand over him philosophizing! They'll be throwing you over the side with a blade in your back."

"He was the last one!"

"This time. Doesn't mean it'll always be that way. If you plan on making it out of this place alive, you'd do well not to wait around on luck."

Scowling, Marek limped off, rubbing his rump. "Yeh, well, you smile on luck, and she'll smile on you, I always say."

"Keep your smiles to yourself, bucko."

"You can bet I won't be sharing them with the likes of you."

Annan bent to wipe his bloodied sword on the infidel's naked back. The oars still pounded beneath his feet, and to the rear the Moslems were turning their galley, preparing for one last attempt on the *Bonfilia* before any Christian ships could intervene. But they wouldn't get another opportunity. The *Bonfilia* was safe.

Dead and wounded strewed the decks, and already the sailors were pitching the Moslem corpses into the sea, lest they curse their ship. The captain shouted orders, sending his surgeon and the Knight Hospitaler passengers to tend the wounded. The surviving Christians knelt, hands propped on the crossguards of their swords, heads bowed. And then, one by one, their heads rose from their prayers, and their eyes flitted to the ship's prow and to Annan.

He turned away. If he had harbored any hope of hiding his identity, it was now lost. Most of Europe had heard tales, both true and false, of the giant tourneyer and his skill on the battlefield. As soon as the *Bonfilia* reached land, word of his arrival would gallop ahead of him, and all men—his enemies chief among them—would know he had arrived in the Holy Land.

He rested the point of his sword against the deck, a hand on either side of the hilt, and stared across the water. Spread on the shore in front of him were the finest armies of Christendom. They waited to crush beneath their feet these rebellious Turks who dared defile the sand that had borne the feet of the Christ—but only if they could first defeat their own squabbling and inertia.

Lurking in the hills beyond, harrying the besiegers, searching for the opportunity to scatter English and French alike with one well-aimed blow, was the mighty Saladin.

And somewhere, in the midst of it all, was the twisted path that had led Annan thus far, and would lead him on evermore, even to the very end of the horizon.

The Holy Land would not bring him redemption; neither did he ask for it. He had come here for one reason only: to still a flutter that had not been felt in his breast for many a long year.

He did not share the Baptist's need for vengeance on Bishop Roderic. He had already bought his vengeance, long years ago, and at a horrible price.

Nor did he care about saving Jerusalem from the tyranny of the infidels. False prophets would rise and fall without the aid of his sword.

And he was not even sure he desired to find Lord William, Earl of Keaton. The man who had been both father and brother to him for so many years was now just another shadow in his past.

Yet here he was, infidel blood red upon his sword, watching as Acre, gateway to Jerusalem, loomed ever nearer off the starboard bow. He filled his lungs with the heat-laden air, trying not to taste the fish and rot that permeated it.

He was here, he supposed, simply because he, who had seen the birth of this struggle in the gloomy corridors of St. Dunstan's, had the perverse urge to see if it would at last find its end here on holy ground amidst the greater struggle for dominion over Islam.

———————

"Nice place, this," Marek sniffed.

Annan kept silent and resisted the urge to close his knees around his horse. He and Marek and the other knights had disembarked from the *Bonfilia* in time for the sinking sun to illuminate the great siege engine in construction just outside of enemy range. The sight had sent the blood rushing through his veins in a way that even the skirmish at the blockade had been unable to do. A decisive battle—something that had been in sharp dearth before the English King Richard's arrival last month—was obviously imminent.

But beyond that one glorious sight and its equally glorious revelation, Annan saw little to brighten his mood.

The squalid camps were arranged with scant attempt at order, save to delineate the tents of one nobleman's entourage from another or from that of the commoners. The women's camp was isolated on the outskirts. Limp banners hung before each tent, and beneath them lounged Europe's greatest fighting force, some too ill to rise from their own filth, others too indolent or apathetic to stir themselves at all, save to cast an indifferent glance in the newcomers' direction.

Had his reason for coming here been to lift the heathen blight from God's Holy Land, he would have been appalled to the very core of his soul. But having accepted long ago that his soul was lost, he merely rode on.

They found an empty space of ground, barely large enough for themselves and their horses, in surprisingly prime area, though not without its price.

"Vacated just this morning," commented the sharp-faced lad who held out his hand for the price in silver. "Lots of folks woulda liked to keep this spot. But I find it a much more lucrative proposition to be in the settling and selling business, rather than the just plain settling kind. Know what I mean, Master Knight?"

Annan dug the price out of his pouch but kept the coin in his fingers as he nodded to the siege tower looming against the red sky. "How soon 'til an attack?"

The lad shrugged, hand still outstretched. "We expect to see some action on the morrow."

"Who's building it?"

"The English, though King Richard's sick in his bed last I heard. Him and the French King Philip both."

Marek snorted and tugged his girth strap loose. "Doesn't sound like a healthy environment, if you're asking me."

The lad grinned. "T'ain't. But if you're bound to die, at least you'll be skipping over Hell on the way out. My coin, if you please, good Sir."

Annan looked at the tents massed to his left, where England's scarlet and gold banner and the blue diamond of the royal Plantagenets fluttered above all the rest. "Is there a bishop named Roderic with the English king?"

"Aye, without doubt."

Annan flicked the coin at him, and the boy caught it in both hands. "Have you heard aught of the man called the Baptist?"

"Nay, not here. And if you're one of his followers, I'd mark a healthy distance from the bishop. His guards don't take kindly to threats on his Holiness. Good even, Sir Knight, and to you, young Master."

Marek grunted a reply that was mostly the result of hoisting the saddle from his palfrey's back.

The lad replaced his doffed cap and took two steps before Annan again raised his voice. "One thing more. Have you heard of an Englishman, the Earl of Keaton?"

"Nay. But this here's a war where most fall nameless, bondmen and earls alike. Good even, Master." The lad touched his cap and left.

"Aye." Annan jerked straight the flap of his coin pouch and turned to take his cloak from his cantle before Marek could pull the saddle off the destrier's back. He shook his head. "They all die nameless, but what's it matter if you're skipping Hell?"

Marek scowled. "Hell's no place to be jesting about."

Annan threw his cloak onto the ground near the pile of tent canvas and thrust his chin toward the English king's camp. "They can follow the likes of Father Roderic to the grave if they want, but what they find beyond won't be the arms of the saints, no matter how many pagan hearts they've bled dry."

"Eh. Well, pardon me if I keep tight hold on me own ideas. That Baptist fellow's a heretic, if you want my opinion, no matter who it is you think him. You can't go preaching against holy Fathers without calling horrible punishments down on your head."

"Roderic's no holy Father."

Marek's eyes narrowed. "Annan, you haven't— you didn't come here to kill this bishop? Did you? A mongrel dog with half a brain could see you haven't come here to save the Holy City."

Annan filled his lungs with the stink that permeated the camp. Through the labyrinth of tents, some hundred paces away, standing over the shoulder of a king, was a man who would one day burn in Hell, no matter how many times he had been granted absolution.

Another lifetime ago, hatred of that man would have smoldered in Annan's gut, seared his throat, overwhelmed even the flame of self-preservation.

He had not come here to kill the one-time father of St. Dunstan's. But that didn't stop the anger, cold as the hatred had been hot, from battering his innards. If he could condemn Roderic's soul to a Hell any deeper than that to which he was already destined, he would do it in an instant.

"I didn't come here to kill a bishop," he said. "But neither did I come to die a nameless death."

———————

Bishop Roderic of Devonshire stood within the relative cool of a crowded outer room in the king's tent, trying to ignore the blood-red sunlight that leaked through the canvas above his head. Visions of gore had been swimming in his sleeping mind for weeks now. He would be more than glad to leave behind this accursed land and its accursed way of making war.

Time is running out.

He felt it distinctly, with every passing moment.

The past is catching up.

He glared into the tanned face of the Norman knight who stood beside him, leather gauntlets clasped before him with both hands. "Is the king's health improving, or is it not?"

Hugh de Guerrant was the recent heir of considerable holdings in southern Normandy and a staunch supporter of Roderic's ambitions, if only because Roderic knew enough of his past to sentence him to Hell in a single sentence. "No improvement. But tomorrow's attack against the city proceeds."

Roderic fingered a handful of vellum. "And who is to lead?"

"I know not. The king is still in conference with his knights."

"The skin sloughing off his very body, and still he deems himself fit to direct a battle!"

"What would you have me do?" Hugh asked. "Insist he remain abed? The day King Richard allows any man to insist anything of him, is the day he *will* be abed—forever."

"What I would have you do is fall on your knees and entreat the saints to lift this accursed illness!"

"And smite the Baptist instead?"

"The Baptist? He has arrived?"

"And if he has? One insane monk cannot possibly do us harm." Hugh rested a hand on his sword hilt. His eyes were cold, hard—stubborn. "You chase sundogs again, Bishop."

"Be silent." Roderic darted a glance to the other courtiers gathered throughout the tent.

"Your fear makes you weak. You do not even know who he is, and yet you tremble within your robes at the sound of his name."

"Whoever he is, he knows too much of the past!"

"Then suppress him."

"I *will*." Roderic inhaled through his teeth, trying not to taste the stench. "But only after he has led us to Matthias of Claidmore."

Hugh regarded him, his mouth working beneath his dark beard. "You do not even know if this Matthias lives, much less if he is a follower of the Baptist."

"If he is, I cannot risk them finding me."

The canvas above his head shuddered as someone thrust past the crowded entry. Roderic glanced across the tent into the somber face of a Knight Templar—Brother Warin by name and, in most respects, a much more trustworthy, if rather visionless, subordinate than was Hugh. Judging from the expression beneath the tawny brown of his close-cropped hair, he brought some long-awaited announcement.

Roderic's heart beat faster. Matthias? The Baptist? Or was it merely tactical information?

Brother Warin elbowed through the crowd until the white of his blouse brushed against Roderic's and Hugh's shoulders. He inclined his head, pressing his hands together in front of the red cross on his chest. "Your Grace. Lord Hugh."

Roderic extended his hand for him to kiss. "You've news?"

"Yes, my lord. I've received another message."

"Message? From *him*?" Roderic cast a glance around the crowded tent, suddenly aware of how many might be able to overhear their conversation.

"Aye."

His pulse pounded in his temples. Since before they had left England, Warin had been receiving messages advising them of the Baptist's actions and urging them to eliminate him and his English compatriot, Lord William of Keaton. The messages, written in a flawless Latin that could only indicate a man of the Church, were always accurate to the point of clairvoyance. They were signed simply *Veritas*, meaning truth.

Who wrote the communications, none of them could tell. But he appeared to be an ally, and that was all Roderic cared.

Warin withdrew the slip of soiled parchment from his blouse and handed it to Roderic. "He says the Earl of Keaton has arrived."

Hugh's back went straight. "And the countess?"

Warin's lip curled, but he nodded. Despite their messenger's encouragement of Hugh's obsession with the woman—who had eluded him only through a hasty marriage to the earl—Brother Warin continued in his disapproval.

Roderic knit his brows as he read the short note. "He says they have been captured by the blockade. I wonder…"

Hugh shifted impatiently, his sword rattling at his side, but Roderic stilled him with a glance. "Reign in your ardor, Lord Hugh. Mayhap the game will play into our hands yet."

"What do you mean?" Warin asked.

"Lord William has been a thorn in my side since the beginning. In the arms of the Saracens, he is at least safely out of the way. And perhaps he will even cause Matthias to follow him there."

Hugh growled in the back of his throat. "And what if Matthias does not follow? You put too much stock in this unknown messenger. I still say you should kill them all."

"I have not the patience to hire petty bunglers. And you cannot be spared."

Hugh glowered. No doubt that had been his intent, though not due to any desire to rid Roderic of Matthias and the Baptist. Hugh's quarrel had always been with the Earl and Countess of Keaton.

"Your Grace," Warin said, "I have learned that a man of some renown has arrived in the English camp."

Roderic's chest constricted. "The Baptist?"

"Nay. But I believe he could prove the answer to removing that particular vermin from under your skin, as well as all the others."

"Who?" Hugh demanded, leaning his weight on the foot nearest the Templar.

Roderic lifted a hand high enough for Hugh to see it. He knew full well that his lieutenants did not appreciate each other's value. So long as he remained in command, however, they must tolerate one another.

Warin smiled, almost showing teeth. "What if I were to tell you I could supply you with a man who is no petty bungler? Who is renowned for his fighting skill and expertise?"

"I would say it is still not worth the risk," Hugh said.

Roderic glanced at him, then back at Warin. "And how do you guarantee this?"

Warin's smile revealed the cleft in his chin. "You've no doubt heard of the tourneyer Marcus Annan?"

The muscles in Hugh's cheek bunched near the base of his jaw. "He is here?"

"He is."

Roderic glanced at the Norman. "You know him?"

"All who fight in the tourneys know of him. But, yes, I have met him—in battle."

"And if one is to judge from your tone," Warin said, "he won?"

"We will meet again." Hugh looked at Roderic and angled a shoulder so that he had effectively turned his back on the Knight Templar. "I disapprove. This Marcus Annan is a dangerous man."

"We seek a dangerous man, do we not?"

"I have heard he is honorable," Warin said. "And he *is* skilled.

"How skilled?"

"Enough to rival our king in strength and your holy self in cunning."

Roderic lifted an eyebrow. "If you have that high an opinion of him, then I think prudence demands I at least give him an audience."

Hugh snorted. "You belittle your vaunted cunning if you court assassins before the eyes of all Christendom."

"You forget your place, Lord Hugh." Roderic gathered his robes and stepped forward. "I have no such intentions. But I think our sovereign lord King Richard would enjoy the momentary distraction of meeting such a famed fighter. Do you not agree?"

CHAPTER IV

NNAN WAITED BEFORE the closed entrance of a huge tent. Above his left shoulder, the flowers upon the blue pennant of the royal English family shone in the light of the rising moon.

At his side, Marek fidgeted. "What would an English king want with us?"

"Not you—me." Marek had already been informed he was to stay outside and keep his flapping mouth shut. Annan grunted. Even had he been in the habit of believing in miracles, the hope of Marek's mouth ever staying shut was too preposterous to inspire faith.

"You might need a second sword in there, you know."

"I doubt a king would be stirring himself from his sickbed just to have a wandering tourneyer's head removed from his body."

"Soothe your own concerns, but I still want to know what he called you for. Or how he even knew we was here."

"It's one of the unfortunate consequences of having a reputation."

"You don't have a reputation here. Not yet."

Annan shifted his weight to lean against a banner pole. "Not yet." His chest lifted in a sigh. Sometimes regret weighed as heavily upon him as did the oppressive heat of this sultry land. If new beginnings were possible, he would have started over long ago. But the past was written in blood. It could be neither forgotten nor remade, and the future always followed in its tracks, unwavering.

"Master Annan?" A man, dressed in colors so jaunty they were visible even in the moonlight, thrust aside the tent flap. "His Majesty bids you enter."

Annan pushed away from the pole, one hand landing reflexively on his sword handle. He batted Marek's arm as he passed. "Keep your eyes open for anything I need to know about. Like that shadow over there." He gestured at the dark-robed figure lurking some two tents down. He didn't pause to see the lad's reaction.

The courtier—probably a minstrel—held the tent flap for him and then led him through the empty outer partition of the huge tent. The curtains at the far end were pulled back and tied with cords of scarlet, and through the opening Annan could see the foot of a bed and several men gathered around it.

Some five paces from the opening, the minstrel stopped and turned to address him. He frowned, probably realizing how far he would have to look up to speak into Annan's face. "His Majesty is ill, and you are not to rouse him. You will bow as you enter and wait for him to bid you rise."

The minstrel beckoned with his hand and led Annan into the second partition. A score of knights crowded near the walls, their collective gaze focused on Annan as he entered, though he could detect little in their interest beyond curiosity. The far wall, shrouded in netting to deter vermin, was flung open to the night.

In the midst of a bed that must have filled an entire ship's cabin on its journey across the sea, the English king lay propped on silken pillows. Perspiration glinted beneath the red-gold ringlets on his forehead, and his blotched face bore the gauntness of pain. His eyes, however, were alight with interest, command, poise.

"The infamous Marcus Annan."

Annan halted near the foot of the bed and inclined his head.

Richard's eyebrows lifted, and the group behind Annan fell silent.

"You do not bow before our sovereign lord?" said the sharp accent of a Norman.

Annan glanced to his right, into the dark, handsome face of Hugh de Guerrant. The man's lip curled, and his hand clenched his sword. Annan's encounter with Hugh at a melee tourney in Paris more than a year ago was memorable only in the deep scar Annan still bore on his left hip—a result of the other's frustrated attempt to revenge his losses after the competition.

Hugh drifted to the foot of the bed. "Arrogance may perhaps be acceptable on the field of a melee, but not here, among your betters."

"I do not bow before foreign kings."

Surprised voices murmured behind him, and the king's chin lifted as he recognized the accent. "Scot."

"Aye."

"I have heard much about you." Richard pursed his lips. "Coming from another man, perhaps your words would find cause for offense. But if the rumors speak the truth, you are an equal to us all in arms if not in rank. Even still, there are those who whisper in my ear that you shouldn't be drawing a sword in the battle tomorrow." His eyes flicked to his left, and a colorless man, clad in the red and gold robes of a bishop, stepped from the shadows near the canvas wall.

The bishop's gray eyes had a cold glint, like the driving winds of a Highland winter. Annan met his gaze unflinching, but in the back of his mind something burned, like the touch of a spark on a bare finger.

And then the bishop spoke, and Annan, shocked despite himself, was driven back sixteen years, the force of the memory like a blow to his chest.

"You, a tourneyer, dare to think yourself worthy of this Holy War?"

Father Roderic... Annan stared, the name rising to the tip of his tongue. He bit down hard. The bishop's eyes held no recognition—and to change that would be to risk the life Annan had built for himself in those sixteen years.

As if it was worth the saving.

He had promised Marek he had not come to kill. But, at his side, his sword hand trembled, and in the back of his brain, the heat of battle kindled.

Rising from the haze of his mind was St. Dunstan's and all its dead brethren... Gethin, pale and unconscious, bleeding from wounds too numerous to count... Matthias with that unquenchable conviction blazing in his eyes...

Annan clenched his hand into a fist.

St. Dunstan's was over, finished—a part of the unredeemable past. He would not resurrect it. He would *not*. Neither Roderic nor the Baptist nor any other face from that past could force him to do so.

"You do not answer, Master Annan?"

He glanced back at the king. "I did not hear the question."

"The question," said Father Roderic, taking another step toward Annan, "is why an unworthy such as yourself dares to take the holy oath of a Crusader?"

Annan filled his lungs and looked the man in the eyes. "I have taken no oath."

A murmur passed through the knights gathered behind him.

Roderic's eyebrows lifted, widening the dark sockets of his eyes. A puzzled expression flickered through his stony gaze and then passed.

"You have not taken the oath?" Richard said. "And yet you dare to fight here upon the holy soil of our Lord?"

"I am not here to Crusade against the Evil Prophet."

"Then why?" Hugh demanded. "There are no tourneys here for you to bare your teeth in."

"I go where I please, Norman." The divot made by Hugh's sword in his hipbone ached with the rising of every morning's sun, but if Hugh believed that blow had subdued him in any way, he was so much the fool.

Richard lifted a hand from the purple coverlet and waved it in a conciliatory gesture. "Spoken like a man of the sword. And as for the tourneys, I enjoy them greatly myself." He leaned forward. "I should very much have liked to engage an arm as stout as Master Annan's." The torchlight flickered in his eyes. "Mayhap when I am well and the infidels are crushed beneath my destrier's feet, we shall have such a contest, eh, Sir Knight?"

"Your Majesty." Father Roderic's lips drew tight, as though with a purse string. "A vehement Scot, apathetic to our holy mission, may use such an opportunity to do you harm." He straightened his shoulders, his hands sliding into their opposite sleeves. He glanced at Annan, eyebrows cocked.

Beneath his pointed beard, Richard's mouth hardened. "Do not seek to control my actions, Bishop."

"Of course not, Majesty." Roderic's gaze did not leave Annan's face. "But perhaps we are mistaken in thinking this knight has any interest in plying his sword for a living?"

Annan met his gaze and held it. Something in the way Roderic was asking the question… so unstudied as to be pointed… as if he were here tonight just to ask it.

If Roderic hoped to recruit him for his Holy War, he miscalculated.

"Indeed, I have an interest, Bishop." He looked back at Richard. "The holy Father speaks the truth, Sire. Any contest between us could end no better than my meetings with Norman jongleurs posing as tourneymen." He flicked his gaze in Hugh's direction.

Hugh straightened, and his right hand darted across his body for his sword. His dark eyes flashed, surpassing in venom even the oath upon his lips.

"Have a care, Scot." Richard's own eyes narrowed in his wan face. "I would rather have my feet on Normandy soil than on any of your little isles."

"Then perhaps you should have remained there."

"By St. George! Is this your accustomed manner of dealing with kings?

Annan held his ground, though he could feel several of the knights behind him take a step forward. He knew Richard would not place him under guard. In affairs of honor, the English king was famous both for his rages and his need for personal retribution.

"Marcus Annan, if you remain in Acre when I have regained my bodily strength, I shall cleave you from skull to foot!"

Hugh's hand tightened on his sword. "Perhaps I shall save His Majesty the trouble."

"Or perhaps Heaven shall exact its own penance," Roderic said. "Perhaps the Saracens will find him first." The intense questioning look had not left his face. "Those who have not taken the holy oath have no place in a Crusade—especially if they bear the sins of an *assassin*."

The probing tone in his voice was unmistakable. But if Roderic sought to convict Annan as a tourneyer, he was going to be disappointed. Annan answered to no man.

"God's will be done." His eyelid twitched. He turned back to the king and bowed from the waist as one knight might bow to another. "I have your leave to go?"

Richard, blue eyes snapping, lay back on his cushions, the white-ness of his skin visible beneath his beard. He said nothing, only waved at the tent flap. The minstrel stepped into the opening to escort Annan back outside.

As they walked into the cool darkness of the antechamber, voices erupted behind them. He had provided enough of a scandal to amuse them for tonight at least, though he would make certain he and Richard never met in the lists. Killing a king or being killed by one—both begot the same outcome. He hadn't stayed alive this long by throwing himself against opponents who would win no matter how well he fought.

The minstrel stopped at the exit, one hand on the tent flap's cord. "You are either a brave man, Sir, or a very foolhardy one."

Annan ducked through the opening. "There is so much difference between them?"

The minstrel snorted and turned back.

High above the horizon, the moon drifted in a clear sky, its rays illuminating the hundreds of canvas tents, like so many white-bellied fish in a black sea. A breeze, cold compared to the afternoon's stagnant air, tingled through the damp roots of Annan's hair. Marek—and the shadow he was supposed to have been watching—was nowhere to be seen. Whatever precious amount of good sense knocked around in that lad's brain was too often outweighed by his insatiable curiosity. And Marek wasn't often curious of that which was harmless.

In the distance, the glow of firelight and the murmur of laughter and song wafted across the camp. But round the king's tent, there was nothing—only the breeze slapping against loose canvas.

Annan's frown deepened. That clumsy varlet would prove more trouble than he was worth yet. The thought of leaving Marek to find his own way home from whatever woe he'd got himself into sputtered long enough to give him pause. But Marek's was a good sword to have guard-ing one's back, if not quite good enough to keep himself out of trouble.

He sighed and started down the narrow, twisting alley between tents.

Perhaps he had made a mistake in coming here. It was always pos-sible that the Baptist had whispered his hints about Roderic's treachery with no other motive than forcing a battle with the bishop. It was a battle Annan had no desire to consummate.

Self-mockery rose again within him. Here he was, hands red with the blood of innocents, forswearing to kill perhaps the one man who deserved to fall beneath his blade. He forced himself to keep an even stride.

Ahead, a silhouette crouched against a wall of canvas, leaning forward in a hesitant manner that could only have belonged to Marek. Annan cast a glance ahead, trying to spot whomever, or whatever, Marek was trying so diligently to stay hidden from.

Most likely, it had been their watcher from earlier in the evening. Annan wasn't exactly surprised that Marek had managed to frighten him off. At least they wouldn't have to deal with whatever the shadowy individual wanted. And Marek, apparently, had managed to keep himself out of trouble. That almost—*almost*—brought a smile to Annan's face.

He stepped behind Marek and laid a hand on his shoulder.

Marek jumped and spun around. "Don't do that to me! You know I have a nervous stomach."

"If yours is nervous, the rest of Christendom's must be terrified."

"Chortle all you like, but you've no doubt gone and scared him off now."

"Him?" Annan peered down the dark alley, lit only by moonlight and a distant campfire's dull orange. "Who?"

"*Him.* You know, the bloke you told me to keep a watch on."

Nothing out of the ordinary appeared to Annan's eye. He turned back, intent on a shortcut to their own tent. "Quite a few shadows out tonight. Certain you had the right one?"

"How many shadows do you know who skulk around in long dark robes? An infidel spy's probably what it was."

Annan canted his shoulders to squeeze through a narrow opening between tents. "I rather think the holy Crusaders have more reason to spy among themselves than do the Saracens."

"Aye, well, you just wait 'til you get a better look at him. Then you'll be thanking me for me quick eye."

"The only thing I'll be thanking you for, young Marek, is to give your clacking jaws a rest."

"How'd your meeting wi' His Royalty go?"

"Two invitations for battle in the lists."

"Wha, only two?"

"Watch the mouth, laddie."

"You didn't accept, I hope? Do you have any idea what the penance would be for fighting in the lists here in the Holy Land?"

They came around the edge of a tent, almost in view of their own camp, and Annan drew to a sharp halt.

"Mark me," Marek said, "if you kill a Christian here, you can bid farewell to your absolution— Oh—" That last sound meant that he had seen him too: a helmed knight standing in front of them, one hand propped on his sword.

The man was easily a hand's breadth shorter than Annan, but his build was broad and deep. Here was someone who had hefted a heavy weapon for the majority of his life. And he was obviously waiting for someone—*them* from all appearances.

Without turning his head, Annan shot a quick glance to both the left and the right. If it became necessary, they could make an escape in either direction. He stood as he was, Marek behind him, waiting.

The stranger stepped forward, and a shaft of moonlight illuminated the red cross on his white blouse. Annan's chin lifted in recognition of the uniform. *A Knight Templar.* The sworn protectors of Jerusalem's Temple had a murky fame, sometimes hailed for their fatalistic bravery, sometimes shunned for their intractable defiance to any authority save their own.

"I seek Marcus Annan. You are he, are you not?"

"Mayhap."

Behind Annan's shoulder, Marek blew out a noisy breath. The irony was not lost on Annan either. The last time someone had asked that question, they'd barely escaped groveling in the damp murk of an Italian prison.

The Templar lifted his chin, as if to see Annan better through the helmet's eye slits. "My master bids me ask for your services. If that piques your interest, meet me before the night begins to wane on the shore near the women's camp."

Annan's gaze flicked to the knight's sword and then back to the dull gleam of the brass cross on the helm's front. The Templars, more than most, would have reason to destroy rebellious soldiers who refused to take the Crusading oath.

At the edge of Annan's vision, Marek gave his head a small shake. Annan brought his hand up to rest on his sword. "And your master is?"

"Someone who admires your skills." The knight bowed his head. "And that is all I am allowed to say."

Annan lifted an eyebrow. A Templar who lauded the talents of a tourneyer?

He tilted his head in a brief nod, but the flicker of a shadow between the tents to the Templar's right caught his eye. He froze, only for a second, and managed to make the glance he cast in the shadow's direction as casual as possible. If this was an ambush, he didn't want his attackers to know he was aware. And if it wasn't—if he and Marek had merely reacquired their follower from earlier in the evening—he didn't want the Templar to know that either.

The newcomer was already withdrawing, slipping back to where the deep shadows mingled with even deeper night. Annan's gaze narrowed.

He glanced back at the Templar, who waited patiently, not even tilting his head in the shadow's direction. "Have it as you will," Annan said. "If I choose to be there, I will be there."

The Templar inclined his upper body in a bow, and the chin plate of his helm clinked against the mail shirt beneath his blouse. "It will be worth your while, Master Knight."

Annan grunted, already using the brief moment when the knight's eyes were averted to check the shadows once more. Nothing. He and Marek stayed their ground, unmoving, and waited as the Templar retreated toward the English camp. Annan watched 'til he was out of earshot, then motioned Marek up to his side. "Did you see him?"

"Who?"

"Your shadow, laddie buck." He strode forward, reaching for the dagger sheathed in the small of his back. He entered the opening between the tents and quickened his pace.

If this shadow and the Templar were in collusion, he and Marek were probably walking into a trap. But he didn't think so. Before the dark-robed stranger had disappeared, Annan had seen the strength of his chest, the almost imperceptible slouch of his shoulders, the flash of his eyes.

The Baptist had arrived in Acre.

He gripped the hilt of his long dagger, grimacing at the glint of the blade in the moonlight. Had he known he was going to spend the night trysting with less-than-orthodox Knights Templars and heretic monks, he would have blacked the blade with ash.

They followed the ragged alley some five hundred paces to a dead end where two tents were placed back to back. Annan growled through his teeth and turned back.

Marek dodged out of the way. "Now what?"

Annan started to run. "Split up at the first opening. Yell like fury if you find him, but don't attack unless he has a sword."

"Who is it?"

"The Baptist."

"Eh." The sound was more a fully formed word than it was a grunt, and Annan could imagine the wrinkled nose that accompanied it. "If you don't want me to attack the blinking thing, then why go after him at all?"

Annan didn't slow. The Baptist would not escape him so easily this time. Too many questions begged an answer.

They reached the first opening in the wall of tents, and Annan sent Marek racing down the new lane. The lad had hardly the time to reach the end when his call staggered through the groggy night. "Annan!"

Annan jerked to a stop and spun around, abandoning caution and lengthening his stride. Ahead of him, Marek broke into the opening, and his short sword flashed through the darkness as he ran. Annan's legs pumped, the heavy eastern air clogging in his lungs.

They entered the open space near the edge of the Christian camp, and some two hundred paces in front of Marek, the Baptist hauled himself onto a gray horse, his dark robes gusting in the wind. Annan nodded in satisfaction. They had him.

But five hundred paces later, as Annan reached the boundaries that separated the Christian lines from Saladin's barricades, they did not have him.

Marek skidded to a stop near the last of the Christian fortifications and sheathed his blade in a gesture of finality. Annan caught up with him and stopped, managing to make his panting sound as disgusted as he felt. All that lay in the darkness far beyond them was a Moslem prison camp.

"I told ye he was an infidel spy," Marek said.

Annan grunted. "It was the Baptist."

"Mayhap the Baptist's a spy."

"Mayhap." But Annan didn't think so. The monk had led him here deliberately. He had been trying to tell him something. An answer? Or another question?

"Come on." He burned one last look into the darkness of the Moslem lines and turned back to the camp. If the Baptist had indeed been dictating another question, the answer just might be found in his meeting with the Templar.

CHAPTER V

CLOUDS DRIFTED ACROSS the moon, besmearing peerless gold with sodden gray. Annan dismounted some two hundred paces down the shore from the women's camp and handed his reins to Marek. "Use those sharp eyes of yours to some purpose, eh, bucko?"

"To live is to serve, Master Knight."

"If you don't swallow that wagging tongue you may *not* live."

"A silent existence doesn't strike me as worth the effort of keeping."

Annan straightened his tunic and loosened the dagger at his back. "A lot of questions could be answered tonight."

"Or else we'll never get the chance to be asking anymore. I still say this Templar is dangerous. Holy Orders don't go around wanting people stabbed in the back."

"We'll see."

Marek started to rein the horses back. "When you get into trouble, see if you can't give a try to getting out of it on your own, huh?"

Annan trudged through the damp sand. Waiting, feet almost in the foam of the surf, stood a man, the shrouded moon flickering against the red Templar cross on his chest. Annan filled his lungs and stopped five paces from the knight.

"I'm almost surprised to see you," the Templar said. He stepped closer and removed his great helm from his head. In the darkness of the clouds, only the vague outline of his movements were visible, but Annan perceived that he was a young man, younger than himself at least.

"I've never met a Templar's master who approved of my sort," Annan said. "Does he have a name?"

"As I said, I cannot tell you that. Only that he wishes to hire your services."

Annan stared, trying to make sense of the shadows. His ears buzzed with the strain of listening. "I am a man of varied talents. Which services does he seek?" The young Templar stood at ease, one knee bent, the line of his shoulders supple. But still the back of Annan's neck prickled.

"My master wishes you to secure the elimination of four persons."

"What four persons?" The question was more habit than actual curiosity. He was occasionally a mercenary, but never an assassin, if the two terms could indeed be disassociated.

"For the first two, my master offers seven pounds, in Turkish gold— apiece."

Annan lifted an eyebrow. Whomever this Templar answered to, he must have his hand in the purse of a king. "Not many men warrant such a price on their heads."

"You have heard of the heretic called the Baptist?"

Annan's diaphragm tightened. So that was it. Father Roderic *had* been baiting him tonight during his interview with Richard.

"I've heard of him."

"He is the first target. He is expected to arrive in Acre at any time. And with him, or shortly after him, my master expects a companion, a man named Matthias of Claidmore."

"Matthias of Claidmore?" His throat tightened.

"You've heard of him?"

"I have heard of many Matthiases in my time. The price is the same for him?"

"Aye. As for the other two, they may not yet have arrived. And if they have, it is possible they are in Saracen hands. The price is seven pounds for both together. The man's name is William, Earl of Keaton.

But my master expects your assistance only if they are not already infidel prisoners."

Annan willed his jaw muscles to relax, but only succeeded in transferring the tension to the back of his neck. He had suspected no less. The Baptist had warned him of the same. And perhaps—if he were to judge from the thud of his heart against his ribs—this was his true reason for coming here, despite all his denials.

The Templar hesitated and stepped a bit closer. "The fourth will be found in Lord William's company. A woman."

"I don't kill women, Templar."

"She's wanted alive." The words tumbled from the Templar's tongue, as though he were glad to be rid of them. "Further instructions on how to contact me will be left at your tent, if you wish to accept the task."

Annan gnawed his lower lip, and his gaze flicked to where the distant horizon was visible only as a darker line in a dark sky. *My master wishes the elimination of four persons…* How many persons had he eliminated over the last sixteen years? Far fewer than men wanted to give him credit for, but still too many. Every time his hand shed the blood of another, he swore it would be the last. And, every time, he found reason to raise his blade once more.

Why? Why was it so?

To feel the swell of his arms beneath the dead weight of a mail coat, to know the heft of his great sword in his hands, to smell the ripe sweat of battle on the dawn air—these were the things that had ignited his blood since his youth.

And yet he could easily have foresworn the anathema of the tourneyer and the mercenary. He could have joined the army—joined the Crusade—and battled on with the blessing of kings and Church alike. But he hadn't. And never would.

He would continue on this downward spiral, always downward, until finally he could no longer lift his sword before his face to protect his life. He would die in the heat of his own blood, writhing in the mud, as had so many who had gone before him.

All because, long ago, he had been forced down this path by the dictates of his conscience. A conscience that was killed by its own steadfastness. And by Father Roderic. Aye, it had been Father Roderic who had pushed him down this path just as surely as he had thrust himself.

Was it not ironic that he should stand here now, only a word away from cutting down the head of one more innocent, at the behest of that same father?

His gaze returned to the Templar. "I accept your master's offer."

The Templar lowered his head in a bow. "The fee will be delivered to you—"

"Bring only the fee for Matthias of Claidmore." The spiral was deep, but not so deep that he would kill the unprotected. Matthias, and only Matthias, deserved the death for which Father Roderic called. And he was already dead, no matter what Gethin or Roderic or anyone else might like to believe.

The Templar straightened, and Annan could hear the frown in his voice. "It is all four or none, Master Annan—save if the Lord of Keaton and the woman are in infidel hands."

He shook his head. "I guarantee the death of Matthias of Claidmore. But I will not spy on the Moslem camps, nor will I lay hands on a holy monk."

"His holiness is disputable, at best. My master will not be pleased to hear of your refusal."

"Tell him my armor clanks with trepidation."

Through the racing clouds, the moonlight showed flashes of the Templar's scowl. "Perhaps a greater fee could be arranged. If that would tempt you?"

"Tell your master what you will." Annan turned to go. "Fare well, Knight—I'm told this is a dangerous land."

"So it is, Master Annan."

With the Templar's words ringing in his ears, he turned his face to the wind and trudged through the darkness to where Marek waited with the horses.

Bishop Roderic stood behind the netting in his tent's entry and watched the clouds scudding across the sky, masking but never obliterating the huge moon. He stood with one arm round his waist, the other toying with the heavy crucifix that hung against the folds of his robe.

He should be asleep by now, lying among his pillows and coverlets, shielded from the cold breezes of a desert night. But he could not sleep. A strange disquiet had fallen over him after the king's interview with the assassin Marcus Annan.

Roderic had never before seen the man, and yet there was an unmistakable air of familiarity about him. When he had stood defiantly straight in the presence of King Richard, Roderic had felt the danger radiating from him like the heat of a great hearth fire. And it was not the danger of his tremendous build, his well-honed weapons. This was the danger that lurked behind the cold blue eyes.

Roderic had mentioned it to no one, but he could feel in the marrow of his bones that something was amiss. *Something.* Exhaling, he dropped the crucifix and raised his hand to rub the point of his chin.

Outside the doorway, a mail-clad figure emerged from the gloom of the camp, and Roderic detected the red cross on the man's chest. *Brother Warin.* Roderic had requested that he return with word of his meeting with the tourneyer.

Silently, Roderic lifted the netting and stepped aside to allow the Templar's entrance.

"Your Grace." Warin's tone was soft. Unlike Lord Hugh, he understood the advantages of circumspection.

Roderic replaced the netting and dropped the heavy canvas flap behind it. When he turned around, Warin was already lighting a candle. In the flare of light, Roderic tried to read his subordinate's features. But Warin's expression remained passive.

"Well?"

Warin settled the candle on Roderic's writing table and straightened. "He would agree to only part of the assignment."

"Only part?"

"He refused the money for the Earl of Keaton and the woman. And the Baptist."

Roderic's chest constricted, then expanded. "Matthias? He agreed to kill Matthias?"

"Aye. Though he might be convinced to pursue the others should you offer him a greater sum." Warin studied him. "You don't seem displeased."

The flame fluttered in its bed of wax. "If he will kill Matthias, that is all that matters." Roderic took a deep breath, filling him with relief such as he had not known since the beginning of the Crusade. "The Baptist and the others may keep their lives. For now at least."

"What if Matthias eludes this Scot?"

"If Marcus Annan is as dangerous and skilled as you and Lord Hugh claim, Matthias will not elude him." His fingers found the crucifix once more. "He will not elude him." He nodded to the door. "You may go, Brother."

Warin bowed, the folds of his mail shirt clinking. "Good night, your Grace."

Roderic rubbed the crucifix harder, his finger digging into the jeweled etching. He did not speak until Warin had reached the door and lifted the canvas flap. "Brother."

"Bishop?"

"I would ask your opinion." He stared at the candle's flicker. "Of our master tourneyer."

"Your Grace already knows my humble opinion."

"And have you nothing further to add after this night's encounters?"

Warin hesitated, then let the canvas fall back into place. "He is not the straightforward man I perceived him to be. He would not be a desirable enemy."

Roderic grunted. "That is all? You did not notice anything… peculiar?"

Again, Warin hesitated. Roderic swiveled his upper body to look at him.

"He… came very near to defending the Baptist. And he seemed to recognize Matthias's name."

"What?"

"May I say that perhaps that will be advantageous?"

"You may *not*." Roderic spun to face the younger man. "You know I will not tolerate complications!" Anyone—*anyone*—connected to Matthias was too much of a danger.

"I'm sorry—" Warin's stance did not falter, but his tone held the proper contrition.

"Do you think your sincerest apologies will alter the course we've taken this night? I will not have complications! Do you hear me?" He dropped the crucifix and turned around to begin pacing. The sudden nervous energy—energy that had been building in his innards all evening—demanded he do *something*. "Get rid of him. His assistance will not be required after all."

Warin stood a little straighter. "He will not be easy to kill. And mayhap his use—"

"Between yourself and Lord Hugh, if you cannot save the world from a ragged tourneyer, you hardly deserve to call yourselves soldiers of the living God!"

"Your Grace." Warin's voice held the slightest hint of a reprimand. "Perhaps he is still of use to us."

"If he knows the name of Matthias of Claidmore, he knows too much."

"Why not eliminate him *after* he has performed his task? If he knows of Matthias, so much the better. He will have the less difficulty in finding him."

"And if he chooses to betray us instead?" Roderic stopped his pacing and pierced Warin with a glance. What would Veritas, their mysterious messenger, think of these alarming new developments?

The Knight Templar inclined his head. "I believe he is a man of honor. He will keep his word, and he will kill Matthias of Claidmore. What you do with him then will still be yours to decide."

Roderic bit down hard on his cheek. He stared at Warin. Perhaps the Templar was right. Roderic did not fear this Marcus Annan. He could be eliminated at any time, no matter how strong his arm. But Matthias—the cursed Matthias, who tormented him beyond even the heinous wounds he had inflicted on his person all those years ago—still plunged Roderic's heart into the cold darkness of fear. *He* could not be eliminated so easily.

Mayhap that made Annan yet the best tool to accomplish the desired end.

"If you err, Brother Warin, in your estimation, I will not easily forgive." Roderic straightened, and some of the strain ebbed from his body. "I will give this assassin an opportunity. He is your responsibility. Watch him. And when he has accomplished his task, see to it that he will not become an irritant to us."

Warin bowed again. "Yes, your Grace."

"Go then." He gestured to the door and watched as Warin slipped from the tent. The door flap fell into place behind him, but not before a puff of wind extinguished the candle.

Roderic stood in the darkness, unmoving. What did it matter if one wandering knight knew Matthias's name? Indeed, it mattered naught.

But what he found strangely discomfiting was that in all those sixteen years since he had left the Abbey of St. Dunstan, he had never met a man who knew Matthias of Claidmore and yet was willing to see him die, much less kill him.

Perhaps Roderic and this Marcus Annan had more in common than mere cunning. He turned to his bed, swishing his robes out behind him, his fingers once again seeking the crucifix.

The morning had dawned hazy, the carmine sun borne skyward on a bed of dirty gray. With the dawn had come the knowledge that King Richard's words of a great battle had been no empty boast.

Annan sat his destrier near the front of the English lines and watched the work of the catapults as they prepared the way for the siege tower. Not far to his left, the English catapult, christened Evil Neighbor, had been spewing forth devastation since early morning, and now the target wall swayed amidst the dust. Far to his other side, the Knights Templars' catapult, God's Own Sling, wreaked its own destruction. Between them loomed the great tower, waiting the moment when it would be shoved up next to the walls of Acre, providing the necessary bridge for scores of eager foot soldiers.

The clouds above, turgid with the smoke of burning ordnance and the dust of crumbling stone, formed an eerie veil against the red sunlight. Save for the wind blowing in from the sea, the camps waited in uncanny silence. Annan rested his arm atop the great helm that sat against his saddlebow. Omens were rife this day—whether for good or bad, the number of the dead would soon show.

At his elbow, Marek scowled. "I don't like this. Looks twice as dirty as a tourney melee, and three times as bloody."

"'Tis." Annan glanced the lad's way. "But all you need to concern yourself with is staying alive."

"Would appear I've a very long day ahead of me."

Evil Neighbor's long black arm snapped forward, its frame bucking with the released tension. Far ahead, the volley smashed into the center of the wall. Stones crumbled and fell, and satisfied murmurs whispered through the men crowded about Annan. His back tightened around his spine, and the hair on his arms prickled. Anticipation rose in the depths of his mind.

It had been years since he had fought shoulder to shoulder with other knights in a legitimate battle. Some part of him sang with joy in expectation, even while another part, somewhere deep within him, was louder yet with its grim silence. This battle would not be a pleasant one. The Mohammedans would fight and die with a fierce vengeance despite the inevitable weakening of a two-year siege.

"You know," Marek said, "now would be a good time to be changing your mind about taking that Crusading oath."

Annan shook his head. Marek had been told all there was to say on the subject. Long before the war could reach an end, he and the lad would be gone from here. Even were absolution possible through this Holy War, breaking the oath would do little to increase their chances of receiving it.

God's Own Sling rebounded in the distance, and the crash that followed thundered louder than all that had come before. Stones tumbled to the ground, opening great spaces in the wall. On the ramparts, dark specks of men dashed to steadier footing, shouting to one another in their heathen tongue.

"They're almost through," someone said.

Annan straightened up, pushing his shoulders back to their full breadth, feeling the links of mail smoothing into place over his chest. The silence in the camp, save for the clatter and crash of the catapults, droned in his ears. He lifted his tongue to the roof of his mouth, allowing saliva to well in the dry crevices.

He had battled so many times in his life. And yet his sword arm still quivered with expectancy, his nostrils flared in impatience, his shoulders ached with restrained eagerness.

As the catapults hammered on, he lifted his helm and settled it onto his head, narrowing his vision to slits of light. His breath echoed against the iron faceplate and came back warm against his mouth.

At the behest of a last gift from Evil Neighbor, the wall tottered and fell, crumbling into a cloud of dust and disintegrating into nothing. For one long moment, there was silence. No one moved, no one breathed.

Somewhere in the rear, a horse jangled its bit.

And then, as if that were a signal, all of Christendom bellowed the call to battle.

"St. George! St. Denis! For the Holy Sepulcher! *Dieu veut ça!*"

As one, they surged forward, men-at-arms at the fore, footmen following, and, somewhere in the rear, the siege tower trundling after them all.

From the breach in the wall, the men of Acre poured forth, blades lofted above their gaunt bodies. The pounding of hooves and running feet destroyed the mere length of a bowshot that had separated the ragged defenders from the might of the West. The two lines smashed into each other, faltered, then continued on, mingling beyond any distinction save livery and accent.

Annan lost all sense of time and place. In the mad joy of it all, he forgot Marek, struggling somewhere behind him. He forgot he did not belong here among the holy armies. He forgot the clank of the Templar's gold, delivered only that morning and rattling in his purse even now.

All that had happened last night vanished amid the storm. What did it matter now? Perhaps this would be his final battle. And then there would be no more question of Father Roderic or the Baptist or St. Dunstan's.

He rode straight in his saddle, the strength of his arm pounding onto the upraised swords of his opponents. They fought with ferocity, with courage, but they could not match the strength of the mounted knights. Ahead, through the dust of the fallen wall, he could already see the hazy outline of the opening. The Crusaders would be through shortly, and the slaughter would begin.

Then, from behind, came a sound he should not have heard: the renewed clangor of arms against arms, the confused cries of French and English soldiers, and the cheers of the Moslems.

With one swing of his arm, he struck the sword from the hand of his nearest adversary and spun his destrier around. To the far west of the engagement, a dark mass of enemy cavalry converged on the hapless ranks of French footmen. Saladin, still entrenched beyond the Christian lines, had sent reinforcements. It looked to be a mere skirmishing party, but its mounted archers swept through the startled Christian ranks.

Annan gritted his teeth within the confining heat of his helm and laid his spurs into his horse's sides. With a grunt, the animal lunged, galloping through the tangled conflict, headed for the infidel horsemen.

"Annan!" Marek's voice, choked with dust and muffled by exertion, barely floated above the tumult. But Annan recognized its urgency.

He yanked his horse back around, toppling two bloodied Moslems and impaling a third. Arrows spattered into the ground all around him and clanked against the horses' mail-draped haunches. He gritted his teeth and shifted his head back and forth, trying to see enough through his narrowed line of vision to decipher the swirling patterns amidst the dust and struggling bodies.

Some dozen paces nearer the city, the faceted edges of Marek's mace flashed against the swords of the Moslems surrounding his palfrey. One of the Mohammedans rolled under Marek's horse, knife in hand, and raised it to the animal's belly.

Another volley of arrows hit the ground, sounding like giant raindrops against a sod roof, and Annan's destrier shuddered, its hind end nearly dropping out from under him. Annan spurred it again. He could waste no time to check for the arrow that had no doubt found its mark in the horse's hindquarters.

Stumbling forward next to Marek, he laid out two of the attackers with one sweep of his sword and thrust the blade into the man on the ground before he could disembowel the horse.

"I thought I told you to follow me!" Without waiting for an answer, he twisted around to jerk the arrow, imbedded some six inches, from his destrier's croup.

"They're cutting through the French like barley at harvest!"

"I know it!" He cast aside the arrow and spun around, searching through the dust for the dark ranks of Moslem horsemen. What had, only moments before, been the last blows before victory was quickly degenerating into a desperate brawl. The western ranks would be lucky to escape with their lives.

Saladin's forces galloped through the faltering troops, clinging to the backs of their war mares, guiding them with their knees alone, and wielding their blades with a dexterity unknown among the heavier Western fighters. Behind them, riding in a fluid line, came the archers. They had found the range.

Just ahead of Annan, a knot of English footmen, locked in battle with the defenders of Acre, fell beneath the rain of wood and iron.

Annan lifted his buckler to shield his left breast and sent his mount lunging into their midst. He threw himself into the fray, knowing from the way his destrier stumbled that he would have little time to reach safety before he was left dangerously afoot.

An arrow struck him, piercing through his mail shirt as only an awl-tipped bodkin could, grinding past flesh and bone. His left shoulder exploded in white-hot pain, and he choked as his breath caught deep in his chest. He squinted against the black fog that threatened to blind him, and his fingers instinctively sought the arrow.

The clash of battle faded in his ears, the thrashing bodies of the footmen grew dim. He rasped, and bile grated in the back of his throat. Pain washed over him again, turning his vision to white light and burning him with the heat of his own wet blood.

"Annan!"

From the corner of his helmet's eye slit, he saw the approach of a dark enemy shadow, and he raised his sword to meet its blade.

"Annan, beneath you!"

Too late, he realized the intent of Marek's cry. As a Moslem blade found its mark in the destrier's bowels, Annan was thrown free of the thrashing animal. He smashed onto his wounded shoulder, and the back of his helm hammered into the ground. He tried to reach his sword, to quell the wave of Moslems breaking past him, but he found he could not lift his arm.

The world began to fade. He blew out a long, aching breath... and accepted the cool nothingness of darkness.

CHAPTER VI

LL DAY SHE had stood near the boundary of the prisoner camp, watching the dust of the distant battle beneath Acre's walls, listening to the muted cries of the combatants.

But now it was growing too dark to see, and as Lady Mairead drifted back toward the tent that had been set apart for her husband, William of Keaton, she watched the Mohammedans usher their latest prisoners through the cordon of guards.

They had brought back only a few today. In the long, sultry weeks since the capture of Lord William's ship by the infidel blockade, Mairead had watched countless prisoners dragged or shoved into the camp. Thousands of people were confined here already: men, women, and children—mostly Frankish Syrians, the European natives of Jerusalem. By the count of one of Lord William's servants, Saladin had 2,500 prisoners in this camp alone.

Holding the folds of her shawl to her breast with one hand, she crossed the dust of the camp to where the Moslems had dumped their score of prisoners in the midst of the growing crowd.

A Frank stepped aside and allowed her to stand at his shoulder. "If that is the extent of their prisoners, God be praised. The Christians will take Acre."

"It is already taken," said another. "You can hear that the battle is over."

She scanned the bloodied faces. Most were French, most were wounded. The Turks threw the last of them into the group, then shouldered their way back through the crowd, shouting to one another in their own tongue. Immediately, the prisoners began their call for water.

Mairead sighed. It was always thus.

Pulling her linen shawl free, she went forward to bind the arm of a man—an archer by his livery—who held his hand to a shoulder wound. His arm was red down to his fingertips, and he swayed where he stood. His face had the blanched look of one who was slowly bleeding to death.

He stared ahead, unseeing, as she knotted the shawl over the wound. "God be with you." She placed a hand on his grimy cheek, then moved aside to allow a Knight Hospitaler to take over.

She stood still, one hand trying to hold her long dark hair from her face, watching as the prisoners ministered to the wounded among the new captives. So many wounded, so many dying. The priests decreed that a Crusader's death was only the unhindered passage of a redeemed soul into blessed Paradise and should be cause for rejoicing. But all she could see were the falling tears of faraway loved ones and the contorting pains of those who had not yet made it quite across Death's threshold.

She did not often come to this part of the camp. Lord William, grievously wounded during their capture, preferred her to remain with him, sequestered from the heat and the throngs of strangers. Whenever the infidels brought forth their prisoners, she always watched from afar as other women tended their wounds.

But she had ached to be here, to staunch the endless flow of blood, to hold in her lap the head of a soldier whose wounds she might heal, unlike those of Lord William, who the monks whispered would never recover.

She drew in a deep breath, biting her lip to forestall the tears, and turned away. She had come to the Holy Land to escape her fears. But she should have known better. They had followed her here. They would always follow her.

She started forward, but trudged only a few paces before the sight of another knight arrested her. He lay on his back in the trampled sand, while two brethren of the Hospital struggled to remove his blood-crusted armor.

He was a giant of a man, easily head and shoulders above most in the camp, and the breadth and depth of his chest and arms bespoke a terrible strength. He had a strong, square chin, barely cleft, and a set to his mouth, even in sleep, that revealed an iron will. A white scar rived his right cheekbone and disappeared into the fair hair above his ear.

The blood-blackened hole in the mail above his left breast showed what it had taken to bring him down. The bodkin that had inflicted the wound was gone, pulled from his flesh by his Moslem captor or perhaps by his own hand. His face was pale, his breathing shallow, his body still.

She drew nearer and stopped at his feet. "He lives?"

The Knights Hospitalers turned to look at her. The one on the left inclined his head. "He lives, Lady." His accent was unfamiliar, possibly from the southern regions of France.

The other, undoubtedly English, laid a knife to the knight's tunic and slit it up the middle. "For now, he lives. He's lost much blood."

"That is why he sleeps?"

"Aye."

"He is English?"

"I know not. His surcoat bears no symbol, not even a cross."

She watched their ministrations in silence, feeling once more the bitter cold of anguish rise in the pit of her stomach. They tended so many! Why could they not save Lord William?

As the moon rose full and bright against the murky sky, she knelt and reached out her arms to the Hospitalers. "Please—let me help."

In the days following the rout of Acre, Roderic slept but little. Between his own gnawing fears and King Richard's growing impatience with Saladin's lack of haste in acquiring the ransom money demanded for the prisoners of Acre, Roderic's hours of rest were precious few.

He stood in the anteroom of the king's tent and glowered at his lieutenants. "If Richard wants to slaughter the prisoners, that is his affair. I care not, so long as it gains us Jerusalem the faster."

"My lord bishop," Brother Warin ground out, eyes sparking, "the king is under oath to deliver the prisoners in clear exchange for those of

Saladin. Whether this delay in the gold payment is a deliberate tactic on the part of the Saracens or not, we are still Christian knights. How can we support this in good faith?"

Lord Hugh spat. "You argue that infidels deserve to live?"

"I argue only that we do not condemn our souls by breaking the treaty!"

Roderic waved an impatient hand. "We shall all be absolved."

"*If* we take Jerusalem," Warin said. "The armies are weak, the leaders are feuding. King Philip is returning to France."

"We do not need him. We have Richard."

"Even Richard cannot work miracles. I say we will never take Jerusalem. Richard may return to Normandy a hero, but he will not return victorious."

Roderic shot him a sharp look. "Watch yourself, Brother. You doubt the armies of Christ?"

The muscle in Warin's cheek churned, but his gaze faltered. He took a step back.

Roderic returned his attention to Hugh and the concerns that had brought them to this meeting in the first place. "As for you, I will have no more of these protests you've been hurling at me regarding the Earl of Keaton. If he and the countess are dead, God be praised. You must find yourself a new obsession, preferably one more in line with our holy mission."

Hugh's nostril twitched. "Do not think to reprimand me. My wish to claim the reward you have promised me detracts from Christendom's success no less than your dabbling with useless assassins." He thrust his chin at Warin. "Tell his Grace what you saw on the day of the battle."

Warin's frown deepened, and he exhaled. "The assassin Marcus Annan is no longer in the camp."

For the first time since the beginning of this useless dispute, Roderic gave his lieutenants the full measure of his attention. "What? He has escaped?"

"Whether dead or captured or fled, I know not, but he is gone. Neither he nor his servant remain in camp."

"*Gone.*" Roderic stared at the open tent flap, and the sunlight stung his bloodshot eyes. Fear again bared its fangs, ready to puncture his heart. "He's left us to join Matthias?"

"No doubt." Hugh planted a hand on either side of his sword belt. "I warned you he was dangerous."

"We don't know he betrayed us," Warin said. "It may be he is among the dead—or in the prison camp. But we shall never discover the truth if Richard continues with this mad plan to prevent us from exchanging the prisoners."

His words were a mere buzz in Roderic's ears. All he could see—all he could think about—was what would happen if this Marcus Annan had indeed survived and was even now on his way to find and warn Matthias. If he did, not only would Roderic never gain the chance of destroying Matthias once and for all, but very likely it would bring Matthias down upon him with vigor and resolve redoubled.

That could not happen. *Must* not happen.

"Find him." Roderic had to fight to keep himself still, had to concentrate on making his breathing even. "Kill him."

Warin dropped his head in a bow, almost in time to mask the compression of his lips. "You wish us to see to it personally, your Grace?"

"Yes." The sunlight burned in Roderic's eyes, drawing moisture from the corners. "First make certain he is not a prisoner. If he is and Saladin decides to slaughter them all in retaliation, we will have no need to worry."

Beneath his pointed beard, an expression of satisfaction tugged at Hugh's mouth. "Perhaps we shall also find the Earl of Keaton and his retinue."

Roderic snapped his gaze to the Norman's face. "I care not about the Earl of Keaton! And I care not about Richard's prisoners." He glared at Warin. "My very life may be in danger! All I care is that you find him and kill him. By all that is holy, can you not understand that?"

Both men, whatever their personal disagreements, could not but recognize the force behind his words. They nodded in unison, and, by their eyes, Roderic knew they would obey whether they understood or not.

All of Annan's dreams were battles.

The clash of iron against iron; the stampede of hooves pounding sod and rock alike; the wordless roar of men pitted one against another. Sometimes he dreamt of St. Dunstan's Abbey, sometimes he dreamt of the tourneys. And now he dreamt of the Crusade.

He jerked awake and knew immediately that he had been shot. His heart beat with a ferocity that left him winded, a lingering effect of the phantom battles in his head. He lay still for a moment, slowing his breathing the better to hear and casting from his mind the broken images of his dream.

He waited, listening to the moans and rasped mutterings of the other wounded in the tent and to the wind rattling across taut canvas. It was dark, save for distant firelight gleaming from the other side of the tent wall. Had he been rescued, after all?

Carefully, quietly, he thrust an elbow against the ground and levered himself up. The movement woke dormant pains all through his chest; the back of his head throbbed with a heaviness born in part of his long unconsciousness.

He sucked air past his teeth and waited until all the little pains resolved into a single great one, concentrated high in his left breast, just beneath the collarbone. Gingerly, he exhaled. He remembered now—everything up to the point when he had fallen from his horse. How long ago had that been? How many hours, days, weeks had passed since then? And where was he now?

Outside, voices murmured meaningless words. Foreign words, he realized. Turkish words.

His heart turned cold. *He was a prisoner.*

The voices stopped, then grew nearer, accompanied by the sound of footfalls. Ignoring the ache of his bones, he swiveled on his hip and fumbled onto his knees. His hand reached instinctively for his weapons, but both his sword and the dagger he wore at his back were gone, as were his mail and helm. He wore a loose white tunic, the sleeves rolled above his elbows, and, beneath that, a swathe of cotton across his injured shoulder.

The voices ceased as half a dozen shadows stopped before the tent flap. The canvas was thrust aside, and a scarred Moslem entered with a torch. Two Knights Hospitalers followed, supporting a semiconscious Christian.

Annan quelled the coiled intensity in his body. The Moslem merely glanced at him, gestured to a pallet at the other end of the tent, and muttered something in his own language. The Hospitalers lowered their burden to the indicated ground and set about straightening the man's fevered limbs.

Casting the light of his torch across the unconscious and semiconscious denizens of the hospital tent, the Moslem grunted and handed the torch to one of the Hospitalers. For the first time, the light fell on a dark-haired woman. She stood just inside the entrance, one hand lowering the tent flap behind her, the other clutching a bundle to her chest.

Her large eyes—the color of freshly turned soil—shifted to meet Annan's, and she started toward him, lithe and straight, like a reed in the wind. Her bearing spoke of nobility, but she bore it with a composure that was charming, even alluring. The hair hanging in confusion to her waist was thick and straight and not quite black.

She stopped before him, and a smile touched her mouth. "Master Knight."

"Lady."

The smile deepened slightly, and she knelt beside him. Her free hand pressed against his uninjured shoulder. "Are you not aware that you are yet an invalid? Lie down, please."

He yielded, ignoring the grumbling pains in his chest.

She helped him straighten himself, then leaned over him to lift the dressing from his wound. Her hair fell past her shoulder and brushed against his bare arm. "I'm glad you've woken. The Hospitalers thought you might not." She glanced at him, then back to the dressing. "The wound is healing well. If you were wondering."

"Who are you?"

"My name is Mairead. I am the Countess of Keaton."

"Keaton?" He breathed deeply, fighting back an overwhelming weariness of brain and bone. His eyes drifted from her face and focused on the shadows in the canvas above his head. "You were the woman with the Earl of Keaton. His... wife?"

"Aye." Her voice snagged on the word, and he shifted his gaze back to meet hers.

"Where—" He could feel the catch in his own voice even before he heard it. "He is here?"

"Aye. He was wounded." She replaced the dressing and tugged the collar of his tunic to cover it. She didn't look at him. "Do you know him?"

He lifted an unsteady right hand to rub his chin. "I did. A long time ago."

Her hands came to rest in her lap, clasping themselves with an utter calmness that bespoke inner pain all too well. "What is your name, Sir?"

"Marcus Annan." He exhaled, and an unrealized shudder filled the breath. Here, before him, was the woman Father Roderic had been willing to pay him to kidnap. They were all within his grasp—this woman, Lord William, even the Baptist. He had not accepted the commission, but did not the mere fact that his reputation had given men cause to think he *would*, make it fitting that he lay here now, in their presence, an arrow hole in his body?

Her face gave no sign that she recognized his name. "You fought in the siege of Acre?"

"Aye."

"I can tell from your voice that you are Scottish. But you wore no cross on your surcoat?"

"I'm not a Crusader."

"Then why come to the Holy Land?"

"A pilgrimage."

"To visit the shrines of the saints?"

"Nay."

The look in her eyes was one of further questions, but he gave no further explanation. She was young, perhaps a score and five years, and there was still much of the girl in her. The contours of her face were narrower than they would have been as a child, the lines harder. But he could still see the girl she must once have been—in the soft formation of her words, in the way she held her lower lip between her teeth, in the striking contrast between pale skin and dark unruly hair. "How did an English countess come to be in this sty?"

"I came with my lord." Her hair fell across her cheek, shielding her.

Annan stared at her. There was more than this to her story, including no doubt the bounty in Turkish gold placed upon her head by Father Roderic. The Baptist had been more right about Lord William's danger than he knew.

She stirred and turned her head to find her bundle, still without lifting her eyes. "I should go. Lord William is waiting—"

"What's the status of the prisoners?"

She hesitated. "There are rumors that we are to be released. The Christians have taken Acre. They took it the day you were brought here. King Richard's terms call for 200,000 pieces of gold, the return of our True Cross, and an exchange of prisoners."

"When?"

"I know not. Soon though, I think."

She began to rise, and he reached out to grasp her wrist. She looked down at him, and her lips parted in surprise.

Lifting himself onto his good elbow, he looked her in the eye. "Lady, I wish to see the Earl of Keaton."

"That's impossible. He is wounded, he is dying. He can see no one." She started to pull away, but he held fast, his eyes boring into hers.

"I must see him before he dies. Tell him—" He filled his lungs with the stench of sweat and filth and rotting flesh. "Tell him that someone who saw St. Dunstan's fall wishes to see him."

She stared at him, and her dark eyes grew wider yet. It was clear she knew at least part of the story behind the name. Did she know it was knowledge of the Abbey that had driven the earl to this place?

"You know Matthias?" Trembling, she drew away, her eyes still on his face. "Aye. I will tell him."

And then she left, tearing her gaze from his face and slipping from the tent in silence.

———————

She did not return until after the moon passed its zenith, hours later.

The night's coolness had done little to quell the heat of the sick tent or the fevered moans and thrashings of its occupants. If Annan had slept at all, it was only fitfully. Mostly, he had sat with his head in his hands and wished he might pray, though he did not know what he would ask. For redemption? For the chance to revoke the gory past? For peace?

He snorted; he would not waste his time in futility.

He thought of Lord William and of the Baptist and of the Lady Mairead. And of Matthias. Matthias who had destroyed Annan's life, who had left him this empty, desecrated shell of a man. Matthias who was responsible for the path that had led William and Mairead to this place, whose only legacy could be their deaths.

Gethin still thought Matthias the hero he had been lauded as so many years ago, when he had destroyed the Abbey of St. Dunstan's. But he was wrong, so very wrong. Gethin did not know the truth of what Matthias had been. Annan did. Hatred churned in his heart as he had not allowed it to in years.

It was then that the whisper of footsteps and the gentle kiss of cloth against cloth brought him from the darkness of his thoughts. A hand thrust aside the tent flap, and Mairead stood, silhouetted against a cloudy sky.

He took his head from his hands and watched her creep through the maze of pallets. She stooped before him, her features obscured in the shadows. "Word has come that Richard slaughtered his prisoners yestermorning."

His spine went stiff. He knew the implications of such an act. "Why?"

"Saladin delayed in collecting the ransom money." She leaned nearer. "Lord William fears retribution against us. I have told him what you said, and he bids you come to him if you are able."

"My legs will bear me."

"Then come."

She led him outside, into a night that was cold beneath its wind-blown sky. He could see no stars, and he could only surmise that the time was somewhere between midnight and matins. Campfires burned in the distance, flickering, dancing to the windsong. But there were no voices, no shadows of mankind. All the night was still, save the snapping of the lady's cloak and the crunch of his own footsteps.

His legs did indeed bear him, though he could feel the weakness that dragged at his muscles. The back of his head was still heavy from his long unconsciousness, and his shoulder throbbed in time with his heartbeat. But he could sense that full strength was not so distant as it might have been. He would be well enough to run—and fight—when the time came. If what the lady said about the English king slaughtering his prisoners were true, that time was near at hand.

She led him to a soiled gray tent languishing beneath two twisted cedars. Firelight gleamed inside the canvas walls, swaying in time with the shadows of at least two men.

Mairead stopped at the door flap and turned to look up at him. "He is not well, Master Annan. I pray your news is good."

On a raised pallet at the far end of the tent lay a man much older than Annan's memories of the earl. He was stretched prone beneath a thin coverlet, arms limp at his sides. Skin ashen, breath harsh, this man was not the stalwart, laughing knight who had once been both a mentor and a friend.

Slowly, head bowed to keep from brushing the low ceiling, Annan came forward, Mairead trailing him. The other men in the tent, a priest and a servant, drew back to let him pass.

At the bedside, he stopped. A splotch of brown showed against the muslin bandage that covered the shallow rise and fall of William's chest. Annan's mouth twisted. Gethin had been right. Father Roderic had wreaked his havoc once more.

If Annan had listened to Gethin... if he had believed... would this still have happened?

No. When Gethin had come to him in Italy, he said William had already embarked for the Holy Land.

For once, Annan could not blame himself.

Mairead drew near, glanced at him, then dropped to her knees beside the bed and laid a hand on William's. "My lord."

His eyelids fluttered open.

"He has come," she said.

His eyes flicked past her face. Annan stayed as he was, lips pressed together, and waited to see his reaction. When Lord William's breath rasped deep in his chest and his lips silently formed a name, Annan knew that here, at least, was one who had not forgotten him.

"Lord William." His own voice was low.

The earl raised his hand from Mairead's, and Annan stepped forward to clasp it. "I feared you dead," William rasped.

He referred to St. Dunstan's, Annan knew. That was the last they had seen each other, the last either knew of the other. But Annan brushed over it. "The lady says you seek Matthias of Claidmore."

William's eyebrow lifted just slightly. He darted a glance at Mairead and then nodded. "Aye—" The word was a hacking cough. He patted his wife's hand. "Leave us, child."

Lady Mairead lifted her skirt and rose to her feet, her eyes seeking Annan's in an expression that was as much a plea of hope as it was an admission of despair.

Lord William turned his head to look at the priest and the serving boy. "Leave us, all of you."

When they had gone, dropping the tent flap back across the cold expanse of night, the earl's eyes found Annan's, and he beckoned with his fingers, his arm not rising from the pallet. "Come to me."

Annan drew a step nearer and knelt.

"I prayed we would meet again." A smile carved its way through the slack skin of the earl's face.

Annan said nothing. He had thought never to see Lord William again. And now to have found him like this... dying.

"You've seen the Baptist?" William asked.

Annan forced a nod. "In Italy."

"Then you know?"

"That Father Roderic wishes to eradicate all memories of St. Dunstan's? Aye."

William sighed, and phlegm rattled in his throat. "He has hunted us like dogs." Still not raising his hand from the coverlet, he gestured with his fingers to the wound in his breast. "And now here I lie. The bishop fears the repercussions of what happened there more than you can know."

"So the Baptist told me."

Behind Annan, the fire hissed and snapped.

"And what—" The earl caught a cough before it could tear his throat, then paused to swallow. "And what is the news you bring me?"

"What news do you wish?"

"I've heard whispers that Matthias is dead." Life burned a little harder behind the brown eyes. "Is that true?"

"It's true." He met the earl's gaze.

"The Baptist insists that cannot be." The words had a hard, raspy edge. William stopped another cough from forming, but Annan could see the quiver in his chest, the specks of saliva gathering in the corners of his mouth.

"And if he did live? What could he do?" Annan said.

"He is perhaps the only man the bishop truly fears."

"What about the Baptist?"

William gave his head a shake. "Roderic fears the Baptist only by proxy. The Baptist will bring Matthias. *That* is what Roderic fears."

Annan shook his head. "The Baptist wants vengeance for what was done to him sixteen years ago."

"Did you know I took him into my home after Roderic finished torturing him? He is not the same man he was before his injuries. His mind and his soul were touched just as his body was."

Annan waited.

"But if vengeance were his only motive, surely his revival would not have borne such fruits as it has? Rousing the people? Mass repentance? Conversions and pilgrimages by the score?"

"I've yet to see these fruits. All I've seen is that this drive for vengeance is all that's kept him alive. He has eaten it, breathed it, lapped it up until he is drunk with it."

"Then why wait sixteen years? What need has he to bring all that remains of St. Dunstan's to this place?"

"He's seeking to recreate what happened that day. He believes Matthias should have killed Roderic, so now he will do anything to at last make it happen. So he can witness it."

William looked at him askance, but another cough seized his innards. His body shuddered with the force of his hacking, and flecks of red appeared in the bubbles of saliva at the corners of his lips. "Hold me— *Hold me up!*"

Annan slid his arm beneath the earl's shoulders and held him until he could breathe once more.

When finally William opened his eyes, he lay in Annan's arms, panting. His eyes found Annan's face, and he groped until he could touch Annan's hand where it crossed over his chest in support. "I am dying," he said.

Annan nodded.

"There is—" He wheezed and barely managed to quell another cough. "I must beg a boon of you." He swallowed, eyes drifting shut. "Mairead— Roderic and Lord Hugh will continue to pursue her after my death. I fear my marriage to her only increased her danger."

Annan's brows came together. "Hugh de Guerrant?"

"He— a Norman— the bishop's lieutenant." William sucked a full breath between his cracked lips. "He forced undue attentions on her— I believe with Roderic's blessing. I married her to save her shame. But now Roderic has placed a price on our heads. All of our heads."

Annan grunted.

The earl's eyes opened and behind them burned more energy than could possibly be left in his tired body. "Roderic will find her and give her to Hugh if she is unmarried, if only to punish me further." His grip on Annan's hand tightened; the cords of his wrist bulged. "Perhaps the Baptist would have you join his battle to wreak vengeance on the bishop. But I am a man dying a hopeless death, and I must ask for something else." He wheezed, groaning with the effort to keep air in his lungs. More blood spotted his lips. "You owe me—nothing, lad. Except friend-ship, perhaps."

Annan's mouth tightened. If there were one man on earth to whom he owed anything, it was the Earl of Keaton. "I will keep her safe. I swear it."

Lord William closed his eyes and bobbed his head in a nod. "There is a convent in Orleans—St. Catherine's. The entrance fee has already been paid. I feared—that this would happen." He relaxed against Annan's arm and slumped back on the pallet. "I would ask that you cover her with your name for the journey. She wishes to live in the convent… you need not take her to wife. But give her the protection of your name." He squinted. "*Your* name."

Annan stared down at him. He could turn and walk away, he could leave it at the promise to keep her safe. The earl asked too much, just as had the Baptist—and Matthias before them.

But he didn't walk away. He nodded his head just once, and Lord William's eyes closed again. "Thank you. Now—send her to me. And the priest. She will tell you— when I have died. We have arrangements for the escape."

Annan said nothing. He slid his arm from beneath the earl's shoulders and settled him back onto the pallet. William did not open his eyes, but before Annan let go of his shoulder, the man gripped his hand once more. It was both thanks and farewell.

Chapter VII

THE EARL OF Keaton's serving lad came to Annan as the gray of dawn began to seep into the eastern sky.

"The countess bids me tell you that Lord William is dead."

Without a word, Annan lifted himself from his damp pallet and once more crossed the camp to the earl's tent. No one stirred as he threaded his way through the maze of litters, but afar off, infidel tongues began to murmur and hooves began to clatter.

His hand clenched the air above his left hip where his sword should have been. So it was true. The Christians had slaughtered their hostages. And now, Saladin was coming.

This Norman King Richard had the honor of a pig. Annan quickened his stride. If he was to escape, it must be now, else his own head would be rolling in the sand ere noon. The Moslem sultan, renowned though he was for the verity of his word, would never allow such an offense as Richard's to go by without reprisal.

The hoofbeats grew louder.

Shoving aside the door flap, he entered the tent. The fire was only a mewing glow of embers now, but he did not need its light to see that the arms of the knight on the pallet had been crossed over a chest that no longer contained the breath of life.

Lady Mairead and the priest stood before the body, waiting.

"Saladin approaches," Annan said.

The lady turned to face him. She wore a dark cloak, the cowl falling back over her shoulders. In the flickering light, tear tracks glistened against her cheeks. Her eyes were bright and afraid.

"How near, Master Knight?" asked the priest in the accent of a Frankish Syrian.

"I can hear their horses. We don't have long to escape." He glanced at Mairead.

She bowed her head, the gesture as much one of exhaustion as it was a nod. "My lord has asked you to grant me safe passage to Orleans." She wet her lips, and when she looked back up, he could see the hesitation in her eyes, as though she were about to tell him a great secret and she feared his reaction.

"There are those who seek me, Master Annan. They are the reason I am here, the reason I stand at your mercy. And they will pursue me hence. It was not my wish to endanger you, but my lord asked that you grant me your name." Her chin lifted. It was a proud tilt. "You are a wandering tourneyer, Sir, I know, and I ask nothing of you but a safe journey. I will live in the Convent of St. Catherine. You shall be paid your dowry."

"I honor the earl's memory as do you, lady. I will fulfill my promise." He turned to the priest. "Hurry, Father."

The holy man nodded and drew nearer. "May the Lord grant pardon that you are unable to celebrate your vigils."

Mairead crossed herself.

The priest closed his eyes and lifted a hand, intoning the marriage blessings. Annan did not listen. With head canted toward the tent flap, he listened for the clatter of arms, the cries of pain that would herald the Moslem avengers. In his mind, he tried to plan. Any escape would be more difficult with a woman to protect—and he with no sword.

The thought of Marek flashed through his head. *Marek!* What had become of him during the battle? If he were still alive, he had probably been fool enough to take the Crusading oath just in time to participate in the English king's treachery—and jeopardize his master's life. Annan grimaced.

In the distance, dogs started barking. He returned his gaze to the priest.

"*In nomine Patris, et Filii, et Spiritus Sancti.* Amen."

Priest and lady crossed themselves. Annan's own hand had covered himself in no such protection of the Holy Ghost for many years, and he could not raise it to do so now.

"You haven't a sword, have you, Father?" he asked.

The priest raised an eyebrow. "Nay, my son."

At Annan's elbow, Mairead drew in a deep breath. "There will be one, Master Annan. A courser waits for us at the northern edge of the camp."

"Will you come with us, Father?" Without waiting for the answer, he started for the tent flap, trusting the lady would follow.

"Nay. I know from whom the courser came, and I will not burden my conscience by accepting the aid of a heretic."

Annan stopped and looked back over his shoulder. "The Baptist?"

"Aye."

Mairead confirmed it with a nod.

He grunted and turned again to leave.

The priest sighed. "So be it, then. God help you."

Annan shouldered through the tent flap. The sky was lightening, the stars fading. To the east, sounds of frightened life murmured. Fear clogged the air. Whether it was the fear of all the camp, or merely the apprehension of his own unarmed hand and that of the lady next to him, he knew not.

"Where's the courser?"

Before she could answer, the animal whinnied. Annan cursed. This doomed camp held nigh on 2,500 souls, and every one of them would willingly hand over a pound of flesh in exchange for that horse. "Come." He forced his legs into a run, his hand again reaching for the empty spot above his hip.

Shouts of alarm pitched higher, spreading through the camp like a plague. The attack would be soon—very soon. Saladin, ever efficient, would complete his retaliation by the time the sun rose.

"This way." The countess veered to the right, one hand beckoning from beneath her cloak.

Ahead, silhouetted against the brightening sky, stood a horse, its head high, ears forward. It whinnied as they neared. Growling, Annan seized Mairead's shoulder and jerked her into a crouch next to him. "Where are the guards?"

"The Baptist said all would be taken care of."

No man's word was shield enough for his back—and certainly not the Baptist's. "Stay here—"

The infidels struck, screaming their wordless battle cry. Everything around them turned to pain and death. Annan didn't wait to check for the guards. He clamped one hand round the lady's arm and lunged forward. The sounds of the slaughter surged after them with an intensity and a speed that bespoke all too well of the attackers' vigor.

He kept low, not daring to look behind him, knowing the Moslems were much closer than he wanted them to be.

He and the lady crossed the corpse of a guard, and Annan paused long enough to lift the infidel saber from the still-warm hand. It was a masterful stroke that had felled the warrior—silently, deftly, instantly. His nostrils flared in a momentary flash of admiration. Whatever else he was or had been, the Baptist was a man of many skills.

The courser, a muscled gray, snorted through distended nostrils, but he could not veer fast enough to escape Annan's hand on the tie-line.

"Master Knight!"

At her cry, he spun to see the approach of the horsemen, dark against the ruddy sky. With one stroke of the saber, he severed the tie line and vaulted into the saddle, narrowly clearing the high cantle.

The Moslems swept through the camp, shouting their curses of vengeance, and Mairead turned to look up at Annan, eyes dark with the sudden horror that he was abandoning her already.

He shifted sword and reins all into one hand, fighting to keep the snorting courser from charging away. He reached out with his left hand and caught the countess's outstretched arm. His wounded shoulder burned, and the tightness of the bandage nearly forestalled the necessary strength to swing her onto the pillion behind him.

She landed with a soft thump and let go of his wrist. Her arms came around his waist, her face against his shoulders. *"Go."*

He laid his heels to the gray courser's sides, and the horse lunged forward, dark mane unfurling against his rein hand. But this was a Western horse, bred for muscle and endurance. He had not the dexterity and fleetness of the Mohammedan war mares.

Behind them, the tattoo of hoofbeats grew louder yet, and Annan dared a look over his shoulder, past Mairead's blowing hair. Only paces separated them from two infidel pursuers.

He spurred the courser again. The horse was fresh and responded with another lengthening of stride. But Annan knew they would never outpace their followers. He could only be thankful that these infidels were not that brand of Moslem archer famed for their accuracy on horseback, else the countess's exposed back would already have become an easy target.

Not that it mattered. Once they drew near enough, the infidels would cut them apart at their leisure anyway.

He could not run. So he must fight.

Transferring the reins to his left hand, the sword to his right, he choked his eager horse to a halt and spun him around.

Mairead gasped and raised her face to look over his shoulder. "What are you doing?"

"Get off."

"What—"

"Get off."

With a breath, half of fear, half of resolve, she released her hold on his waist and slid to the ground.

Annan turned back to the Moslems and tightened his fingers round the strange grip of the infidel saber. Grinning savagely, he leapt forward to meet them. Caught off guard by the swiftness of his charge, they reined back momentarily. That was all the time he needed.

Leaning to the right as he neared the first, he dropped the reins and reached across his courser's neck to seize the Moslem's sword arm. The infidel blade hissed past him, tearing through the side of his loose tunic. He could feel its threatening chill against his skin as he dragged the infidel to meet him and drove his saber to its hilt in the war mare's milk-white chest.

The horse staggered and toppled, tearing the saber from his grip, leaving its rider hanging across Annan's saddlebow, sword arm still anchored in Annan's right hand.

With his free hand, the Moslem scrabbled for Annan's eyes. Annan pulled him closer still and twice hammered his elbow into a bare temple. The infidel's eyes lolled in his sockets, his body went limp, and Annan cast him aside, pausing only long enough to catch the man's saber from his limp fingers.

With a wordless yell, the second pursuer was on him, arm raised high above his head, ready to strike. Annan spun the courser and swung hard enough to catch the blade on his own and nearly knock the infidel from his horse. That brief moment as the enemy scrambled to regain his balance was the only moment Annan needed to switch the sword to his right hand and pick up his reins. Before the Moslem could look back up to meet his gaze, Annan plunged the blade beneath his armpit.

Muscles still humming with the tension of battle, he reined his dancing courser away and urged him into a trot. They passed the war mare, writhing in the dune where she had fallen alongside her unconscious master.

Lady Mairead rose to her feet. Deep lines creased her forehead, the angle of her narrow jaw tight. Her hand trembled as it thrust back her hair.

He stopped the courser next to her and held out a hand. Silently, she released her hair to the wind and slipped her fingers into his palm. He looked her in the eyes just once before pulling her up behind him, but it was a long enough look to know they held a new fear.

A fear of him?

As she took hold of his waist with one arm, he dismissed it. It mattered not what she thought of him. Their journey would encompass a few months at most. He would not harm her during that time; he would value her as the widow of perhaps the only man who had still called him friend.

Before setting his face toward freedom, he turned the courser around to check the distant camp. The sounds of death were only echoing wails now, and none rode in pursuit of the fugitives. He could see nothing— only desolation and the blowing robes of a man who stood at the edge of the camp, in the place where the courser had been tethered.

Annan laid the rein against the horse's neck, his heel against its side, and the courser sprang into a canter once more, carrying them far away from Acre, its desecration, and its destruction.

Brother Warin rode bareheaded beneath the heat of the summer sun, his tabard snapping in the wind that blasted across Saladin's corpse-strewn prison camp. From his position behind Bishop Roderic and Lord Hugh, he watched as the Christian leaders surveyed the remnants of the sultan's swift retribution.

All echelons of Christendom were screaming that Saladin's act was base treachery, that Richard had had every right to slaughter his prisoners.

And Warin did not argue. They were infidels; they had deserved to die. But his stomach, even hardened as it was by countless battles, had roiled as he had watched the Moslem prisoners fall. Men, women, children—all had died, not because of their ignoble religion, but because a Christian king refused to keep his word.

To that toll of death must now be added some 2,500 Christians. Warin blamed Richard and his counselors for those deaths more than he would ever blame Saladin.

Bishop Roderic's dainty bay palfrey stepped away from the other knights to allow its rider a better glimpse at some point of interest amid the bloated bodies.

Warin compressed his sunburned lips. The bishop's anger over the assassin Marcus Annan's disappearance had not abated. Saints help him and Hugh if they could not find the man ere they reached Jerusalem.

Warin had seen the raw fear in Roderic's eyes. It would not surprise him if the bishop abandoned the Crusade for the safety of some fortified European city. Crusades were all fine and well, but the holy cause paled next to fear for one's own life.

Before they had departed Acre, Warin had tried in vain to contact the messenger Veritas, in hopes that he would have information about

Annan. The man had seemed omniscient in the past, with his predictions of the Baptist's whereabouts and his suggestions of subterfuge. But for the time being, that source remained silent.

He sighed and rolled his shoulders, the movement trickling a bead of sweat past his shoulder blade. His honor, and possibly even his life, depended on his finding Annan. And, before God, those were two things he had no intention of losing.

Something warm rested on his leg, and he glanced down at a cowled monk who stumbled along at his stirrup, his scarred face upturned, his eyes flashing like a hawk's in the sunlight.

Warin's brows came together in a frown. Something very disconcerting shone in that gaze. "What is it, Brother?"

"You think to find the assassin Marcus Annan among the dead?"

Warin's throat constricted. "What?"

"Aye, I know of him," the monk said. "I know that your master seeks him, and that is why I am telling you your assassin is not dead."

"How do you know this?" Warin leaned over and gripped the man's shoulder. "Tell me, how do you know?" Mayhap Roderic had been right all along, mayhap Annan had agreed to the wage of a murderer only to pass his knowledge on.

"I saw him escape." The monk's glance shifted just enough to include Hugh riding a length ahead. "With a woman. Tell your master."

And then he slipped out from under Warin's hand and melted back into the crowd.

"You there! Monk! Come back here!" Warin reined his horse around, but the crowd pushed him onward.

He craned his neck to search the jostling, faceless masses that surrounded him. But the monk was gone, taking with him any further secrets to which he laid claim. Warin whirled his horse back into line, his spurs pricking its sides, urging it forward, apace with the bishop's palfrey.

How this strange monk knew these things, he could not tell. But no matter the messenger by whom it had come, it was an answer to prayer. He would tell Roderic of this discovery, and Roderic would send him and Hugh in search of this wayward assassin.

And Marcus Annan would be once more drawn into the battle, whether he chose to be or not.

Chapter VIII

ALL DAY MAIREAD and the tourneyer Marcus Annan had ridden in silence, the last words to have passed between them being his terse order for her to dismount that morning. She had obeyed him numbly, pushing away from his body and landing in the sand, one hand outstretched to catch her balance. He had whirled the charger around and ridden away from her without a backward glance, and her heart had stopped beating.

Every fiber in her body shouted that this man—this tacit, unyielding warrior whose blood she had staunched, whose lips she had moistened with red drops of vinegary wine, whose life she had saved—had abandoned her. He had left her to her fate, there in the desert, with the screams gusting on the morning breeze and searing her ears. He had sacrificed whatever honor Lord William had thought him capable of possessing.

No doubt had clouded the blinding light of her certainty that there she would stay and die, while he made his way westward, alone, to collect the dowry she had promised him.

But he had not left her.

He had battled their infidel pursuers with a skill that spoke too well of his occupation, and then, instead of laying his heels to the gray courser's dappled sides and galloping far away, he had returned to her and, without a word, held out his broad callused hand.

Now, as they rode together, the shadows of purple dusk settling all around them and the Orontes River whispering its secrets somewhere to their left, she almost wished she hadn't taken the hand he had offered and allowed him to swing her onto the pillion behind him.

She was afraid of him, this huge man with his cold eyes and his impenetrable strength. She had not feared him when he had lain asleep beneath her ministering hands. And she had not feared him when first he woke and spoke to her, his voice deep and hoarse from his long unconsciousness.

But when he had come to her after Lord William's death—when first she knew that here was the man who now held her life and her soul in his hands—she had seen the fierceness in his eyes. And she had feared him, her heart clenching in her breast, her skin tightening over her bones.

As the edge of the moon punctured the darkness of the eastern skyline, he at last drew their tired mount to a halt. "We'll pass the night here."

She nodded, though he couldn't see it, and tried to stop the shudder that sliced through her body despite the heavy cloak she had tugged once more around her shoulders. *Oh, William! My lord— why did you leave me!* And why *this* man, this tourneyer—why leave her to his care? The night, dark and endless, loomed before her, and the cold ache of fear rooted itself behind her breastbone.

Annan sat straight in the saddle, his weariness visible only in his uninjured arm braced against the saddlebow. He was surveying the landscape, looking, listening. Though they had seen no one since he had killed the two Turks outside the prison camp, she had felt his caution radiating off his tense shoulders all day.

But there was no one here for him to see now. Only a man, a woman, and a gray courser.

An old familiar fear clawed at her innards, twisting so hard her stomach lanced with pain. Without waiting for his permission, she took hold of the cantle and slid down the horse's sweat-roughened hindquarters. When the tips of her bare toes touched the ground, she dropped.

He glanced at her. But before he could speak, she turned away and started toward the bank of the river. Her throat burned with thirst, but she would not risk disease by drinking the water until she had no choice. She would have to wait for him to untie the wineskin the Baptist had hung across the saddlebow.

At the Orontes' edge, she knelt in the damp pebbly sand and played her fingers across the brown surface of the water. Behind her, Annan dismounted with a painful exhale. They had gotten off the courser's back only four times to give the animal a chance to rest, and no doubt the man ached as much as did she.

She bit her lower lip. Perhaps that alone would be enough to keep him away from her this night... She closed her eyes. She was his wife now; she had spoken the vows. In the sight of God and man, he could do what he would with her.

Her body tremored, and she clamped her eyes shut, willing herself to forget the night that had birthed all these fears and created the small, dark mound of earth she had been forced to leave behind somewhere in northern Italy.

Something smashed onto the ground behind her, and her heart bounced into her ribs. She turned just enough to see that it had been the saddle landing in the sand where Annan had dropped it. He rubbed the courser's sweaty back with his sleeve, his eyes on the horse's, the heel of his palm digging into the animal's muscles.

She might indeed be his wife, and all of Christendom might see nothing painful or wrong in her hasty taking of his name, but that did not mean she would surrender herself to him. She would resist, just as she had almost a year before. And this time, she would fight until she died.

Annan gave the horse's back one last slap, then flicked his eyes to the horizon. It was too dark to discern details, but the rising moon gave light enough to see movement. Only the swaying of trees and shrubs shadowed the riverbank, and for that every weary bone in his body was thankful. Before turning to gather the saddle from the ground, he rubbed his tender shoulder, feeling the burn of blood coursing through the new flesh that was filling the arrow hole.

His body ached as it had not ached in years. He could only imagine the lady's exhaustion. He turned for the saddle. Until they reached her safe convent in Orleans, she would have to bear the trek the same as he.

She didn't rise from the riverbank as he approached. He dropped the saddle and forced his stiff joints to bend until he could grasp the wineskin tethered to the saddlebow next to a hefty, flat-bladed sword that would have been more than helpful had he noticed it before his skirmish that morning.

"Drink." He uncorked the skin and held it out to her.

Her shoulders jerked in an exhale. Then she rose to her feet and turned. He watched her approach, her gait soft and liquid, as though he saw not her, but her reflection in the river's water.

An arm's length away, she stopped and accepted the wineskin. She did not sit across from him, and her dark eyes stayed wide open as she drank.

"That's enough," he said. "When that's gone, we'll have to drink water."

She hesitated, took one more drink, then held it out to him. He would have to lean forward to take it, but she did not step toward him. Her eyes, large like those of a frightened gazelle, did not leave his face. He could almost taste the sharp, acrid fear that filled the air between them.

Was it pursuit from the Moslems, or from Hugh de Guerrant, that she feared? Or was it him?

"We'll be safer here than in the open or near a city," he said. "I'll keep a watch tonight."

She lifted her chin, and he could see the tendons in her neck give a little quiver.

It was him, then. He lifted the wineskin to his lips. Eyes closed, he took a long draught—though not as long as he would have liked—and tried to push the flash of irritation to the back of his mind.

He had come to the Holy Land on an impulse, a mad desire to reconcile with the past. But he had only succeeded in reigniting old angers and reopening scabbed-over wounds. Not to mention receiving a few new ones. Rolling his injured shoulder, he corked the wineskin.

He looked back to where the lady stood, skirt and cloak spread to the breeze, arms clamped across her chest, lip between her teeth.

Now, due to Lord William's dying wish, he had to escort a skittish noblewoman halfway across the world, hoping all the while that her enemies had no knowledge of her survival.

"We'll follow the river as far as we can," he said, more because they couldn't just go on staring at one another than because she actually needed to know. "I've no idea what cities are in Saladin's hands, so we'll have to stay away from them until we reach Byzantium." And even then, he preferred to stay as far from people as he could. Constantinople had been ransacked by too many marauding Crusaders for the Byzantines to bear Westerners any great love.

"Once we've reached their border, we'll take a ship to Venice or whatever port we can get." He reached for the purse tied to the saddle and unknotted the drawstring. It was too dark to see the contents, so he just shook out a handful of what felt like crusty bread and a few chunks of hard cheese. "Here." He offered the purse, holding it so that she would have to take a step to reach it.

Again, a long moment grated past before he heard the whisper of her skirts as she leaned to take the purse. "What is it?" she asked.

"Bread and cheese. Your friend the Baptist planned well, though I doubt he intended for me to be participating in those plans."

"He didn't." She retreated a step before lowering herself to the ground, and he could hear her fingers searching through the purse.

To their left, the courser stamped a foot and nickered. Annan glanced at him. The animal was a stout one. Not many would have withstood so well the rigors of such a journey.

"The Baptist learned horseflesh since I last knew him, that's certain." Among other things. A memory of the artful blow that had felled the Moslem sentry that morning flitted through his brain. The Gethin of sixteen years ago could never have lifted his hand to shed blood with such a masterful stroke.

"You know him?" she asked.

"The Baptist?" He tore his bread. "Apparently not. The man I knew would fain have died rather than let the Church charge him with heresy."

"Heresy." A soft thump, as of the purse landing in the sand near her knees, punctuated the word. "Who are you, a tourneyer, of all people, to speak against heresy?"

His gaze narrowed, and he arrested the hand that held his bread halfway to his mouth. How much had William told this woman about him? "Only those who know it can speak of it. How else can the Popes be so free with their exclamations of excommunication?"

He could hear a puff of breath before she spoke. "*That* is heresy—to speak against the Holy Father."

"And that's not what the Baptist does?"

"His only crime is speaking against sins made blacker because their owner wears the robes of a bishop! If you had ever met Bishop Roderic, you could never say the Baptist is a heretic!"

"I didn't say *I* thought him a heretic, lady. And I *have* met Father Roderic." He bit into the bread and chewed.

"And how did he impress you?"

"As a man who has not virtue enough to warrant his breathing the air of the Holy Land, much less counseling the king who would save it."

Moonlight glinted off her dark hair as she lifted her head to peer at him. "Then you do support the Baptist?"

"Nay. I may share his opinion of Father Roderic, but I do not support him. He is consumed with hatred and blood lust." His lip twisted at the irony. Gethin had chosen a far different path from his own, and yet he had been unable to avoid arriving at the same end.

"It is not vengeance he seeks," Mairead said, "it is justice."

Annan swallowed and brushed his hands across the front of his tunic. "That is what he has deceived himself into believing." He stood, and he could sense more than see the tension that swept over her. She was suddenly like a hare, tensed, ready to run if the hound came but one step nearer.

"Lady Mairead."

"What?" She spoke breathlessly, and he could almost hear the heavy beat of her heart.

"You're afraid of me."

Mairead's breath caught so hard that pricks of light studded her vision. So here it was. She had hoped that if she kept him in the conversation, if she made him think of other things, that perhaps the night would pass.

But no. He was only a tourneyer, a man with the blood of countless knights upon his hands. What was one defenseless woman to him? He could crush her backbone in his arms without trying, and the deed would never darken his thoughts.

"You're afraid of me." He towered above her not more than five strides distant.

"Am I?" The words squeezed past her throat. Her fingers sought the drawstrings of the food purse. It wasn't heavy, but it would be her only chance of a weapon. The sword the Baptist had given them was still strapped to the saddle, and Annan had kept the infidel saber at his side.

"Aye," he said, but did not approach. "Why?"

Why? The word bounced inside her skull. Why, indeed? What had she left to be afraid of—save death? And even that was not so dark as before. Why not step into the maelstrom with arms stretched wide?

She rose to her feet. The hard leather of the purse strings dug into her fingers. She swayed a moment. *Oh, God—oh, blessed Savior—* Fists clenched at her sides, chin lifted, she stepped forward. "I'm not afraid."

"Yes, you are." Something akin to amusement colored his tone. "Why?"

She lifted her chin higher still. Would he allow her no dignity? "If I fear, it is between me and Heaven."

"Then keep it there. We've a long journey before us, and I've no desire to be tripping over your fears at every turn." He stepped forward, and she clenched her eyes shut. Broken, scattered images smashed through her brain... images of *before*. Cold sweat rose on her limbs. Her hands clenched tighter, driving her fingernails into her skin. *Let it be over quickly...*

But he did not come to her.

She opened her eyes. He had lifted the saddle to his hip and was unstrapping the sword. He turned away, toward the courser, then glanced back at her. His voice was still gruff, but the tone was frank. "You've nothing to fear from me, Countess. As far as I'm concerned you are Lord William's wife yet. I am with you only to give you safe escort to Orleans."

She stared at him, sinews still tight. In the starlight, she could see the glint of his gaze and feel the pressure of it against her own. The tightness in her throat eased. Tourneyer or no, the savagery she had seen and feared in others was not present now.

Lord William would not have given her to a knave. Lord William had trusted this man with his life and his honor.

She wished her assurances had strength enough to still the trembling that skittered across her clammy skin. "Thank you," she said and tried to ignore the cold sliver in her heart that whispered he was only trying to catch her off guard.

He looked for a moment more, then turned back to the courser.

She exhaled, the air clouding in front of her face and her body slackening. Lowering herself back to a crouch, she bowed her face into her hand. Think. She had to think, had to plan. Whether Marcus Annan meant what he said or not, she would not—could not—trust him.

If he planned to watch through the night, so would she. And if death came, so be it. She would welcome it. But she would not be caught off guard. She would not submit to him.

Annan dozed once during the night and woke, his back stiff and his brain buzzing with a sudden rush of energy. He froze, senses straining, his hand clenched round the hilt of the infidel saber. Carefully, he pushed away from the tree trunk against which he had been sitting and rolled onto his knees. His stiff body groaned as he forced his joints to bend and crack. The repairing flesh of his left shoulder throbbed. He counted the beats, trying to steady himself—regain focus—remember what had woken him.

A few paces ahead, the dark huddle that was the Lady Mairead blotted the sand. He cursed himself for not forcing her nearer to him and the horse, where he would have been able to better protect her. But her fear had been thick enough to taste, and he had not wished to do anything to further discourage her trust in him.

Not that trust would matter if his carelessness cost her life.

He stayed where he was, sword held just off the ground. He could tell by her tight, shallow breathing that she was awake, and the lines in his forehead deepened. Either she had been awakened by the same thing that had roused him, or she had so many misgivings that she hadn't dared sleep in his presence.

He shifted his gaze to scan the brush of the riverbank. Darkness still filled the sky, but the stars had started to disappear. Dawn was probably only a few hours away. He listened, straining his hearing until his ears filled with the hoarse whisper of the wind, the rustling leaves overhead, and, farther in the distance, the soughing brown water of the Orontes.

And then… a splash, a clatter against stone. His muscles jerked tighter. Behind him, the courser snorted, and he recognized it as the sound that had woken him.

The splashing stopped, and the air hung suspended. His skin burned as he debated a charge into the open. But the distance to the river was too great. Whoever was there would see him long before he could use his advantage.

He dug his fingernails into the polished wood of the saber hilt. The lady stirred, lifted her head from the cushion of her arm, and he bit back the impulse to tell her to be still. Any word now would bring the intruder down upon them, be he foe or friend.

And then, a voice, almost soft enough to be the wind or the river, murmured, and the splashing resumed. This time, Annan could discern that it was an animal of burden, probably a horse or donkey, crossing the river.

Abruptly, the lady sat up, her cloak sliding from her shoulders, and he could hear her intake of breath.

He hissed as loud as he dared, hoping that to the ears of the person crossing the river, it would be just another whistle in the wind.

She jerked around to find him in the darkness, and he growled. Afraid or not, if she fainted, he was going to bind and gag her for the rest of the journey. But her head dipped in a nod of acknowledgment, and then she was still.

The splash and clatter of hooves in the river ended in a flurry of falling pebbles as the animal bounded up the far bank. The hoofbeats paused, then resumed. Carefully, Annan unbent his legs, wincing as a cramp seized his calf. Motioning Mairead to stay as she was, he made his way through the brush until he could see the other side of the river.

Highlighted against the starless sky was the figure of a man on a donkey. Annan's eyebrows knit in a hard line as man and donkey bobbed their way out of sight behind a knoll.

The stranger was probably a pilgrim or perhaps a farmer or a wandering priest, if the Moslems had such a thing. And yet Annan's instincts tingled. He didn't believe in coincidences. Why had this place in the river, where there was no ford, no reason to encourage crossing, be the place this stranger on the donkey had chosen to make his way across?

By the time he returned to their camp Mairead was on her feet, her cloak held tightly around her body to keep it from blowing. "What was it?"

"A man on a donkey."

"Who?"

"I don't know." He thrust the saber into his belt and went over to the saddle.

"We're leaving?"

"Aye. It's cooler now, and suddenly I don't feel as safe here as I did." He caught the courser's bridle with one hand and threw the saddle onto its back with the other. As best he could in the shadows, he checked the animal over, noting with satisfaction that at least its ears weren't lolling with exhaustion. The Baptist had chosen a good animal indeed.

"Do you…" Mairead took a step. "Do you think it was one of Roderic's men?"

"Nay." He tightened the girth strap, then turned to look over his shoulder. "Roderic has no reason to think we're alive."

He ran a hand over the saddle, checking the Baptist's flat-bladed sword where it lay snug in its fastenings on the near side. "Fetch the food purse." She had kept it near her during the night, and he hadn't asked for it. What he had told her about having nothing to fear from him would sink in better if he stayed away from her.

He gave the cinch a final check and tossed another glance at the sky. With blessings from both the weather and the saints, he and the lady could be in Orleans within the month—if the horse held out that long. He patted the courser's shoulder. The horse blew through his nostrils and tossed his head. He was a far cry from the bay destrier Annan had lost outside Acre, but then the bay's stamina probably wouldn't compare with the courser's on a trek of this sort.

Without looking at him, Mairead handed him the heavy leather purse. "The horse should have a name." It was the first offhand comment she had offered since he had met her two nights ago.

"I don't name my animals."

"Why not?"

He tightened the knot that would hold the purse to the saddlebow, then turned to where she stood fondling the courser's dark head. Why indeed? The last animal he had named was the charger Lord William had gifted him with a few years before St. Dunstan's. He had called the big stallion Caird. Since then, he had owned and lost countless beasts, some through the tourneys, some to pay his debts. Marek named them all, but Annan never paid him heed.

Mairead looked at him, and he straightened. "Animals without names are easier to watch die." It was as good a reason as any.

"Oh." Her mouth set in a firm line once more. "I see."

She didn't see, but he hadn't expected her to. She had known the shelter of her father's and then Lord William's castles for too long; she couldn't realize that the pain and the death that filled a man's life were bearable only when kept at arm's length.

She didn't look at him until he had lifted her onto the pillion, and then her eyes met his only for a moment. But it was an unguarded moment. And in it, he sensed again a flash of pain—raw and burning—and he was reminded that perhaps Lady Mairead of Keaton was a woman who knew pain all too well.

He could guess at the cause. He could piece together the import of her fear and of Lord William's words and of everything left unsaid in her own statements.

But, that too, like all the horses he had seen fall beneath him in battle or forfeited for melee ransom, was something he needed to leave unnamed, lest he open himself to the realization of what had been done to her. Were he ever to allow a crack to open in the mental barrier of sixteen years, that would be all the gateway his own pain and fear and anger would ever need.

He mounted, wincing at the groan of his old hip wound. Reining the horse around, he headed for the riverbank where the going would be smooth. Mairead did not brace herself with her arms around him as she had yestermorn during their escape from the prison camp.

He urged the horse into a trot to loosen its muscles. The courser stumbled, then righted itself, ears pointed ahead, hooves crunching in the pebbles.

Annan glanced to his left. By now, the stranger on the donkey should be too far away to hear them. He rubbed the horse's rough mane with his knuckles. *Let the horse hold out.* It was as close to a prayer as he had come in a long time.

The lady didn't speak until the campsite had almost disappeared around the river's bend. "He deserves a name," she said.

The breeze, cool and still heavy with the damp of night, slid across the thickening stubble of his cheek, whispered secrets in his ear, then blew past him to caress the countess's long hair.

Lines knit themselves deep in his forehead. He touched the horse's belly with his heel, and the animal leaned into a canter. "Then name him."

CHAPTER IX

"WHERE ARE WE going?"

It was the first thing Mairead had said since Annan had passed her the limp wineskin some hours ago. It had been midday then; now it was waning afternoon.

Beyond the shade of mushrooming yew trees, the mountains loomed green against the sky, save where the silver heat shimmered. Mairead had spread her linen shawl above their heads to shade them from the unrelenting ball of fire that filled the pale blue sky. But even through it, Annan could feel his lips drying and cracking. He licked them before speaking, and they began to burn.

"Orleans," he said.

"I meant today. Where will we stop?"

He shifted, ignoring the dull ache in his seat bones. "I don't know. I didn't come here by land, so I'm not familiar with the precise location of cities. Probably somewhere between Tripoli and Marqab."

The courser plodded onward, hide roughened with sweat but not dripping. Annan reached down to pinch a fold of shoulder skin. It stood for only a moment after he let it go, then flattened. The horse seemed to be maintaining a steady level of moisture. He straightened, drawing his hand back under the shade of the shawl. He would stop in another half-hour or so, and let the animal drink again.

"How long until we reach Constantinople?"

"A week, or a fortnight maybe." He shrugged. "I don't know." If his long years of traveling from tourney to tourney and battle to battle had taught him anything, it had been that any number of things could happen to lengthen a journey such as this—including pursuit by a variety of assailants. With one hand, he held the shawl aside and swiveled to look over his shoulder. Roderic, Hugh de Guerrant, Gethin, Saladin's cavalry… any one of them might appear over the nearest hill before the gray courser could carry them to a Byzantine port. And he wouldn't be happy to see any one of them.

He flipped the edge of the shawl up onto the sagging portion that rode between his head and Mairead's like the drop between a camel's humps.

He wouldn't be happy, but he would be a long way from surprised.

"Excuse me…"

He swiveled to look her in the face. "Countess, the heat hasn't got to me so much that I'm engaging in anything nearing an interesting conversation with the courser. Don't excuse yourself."

She blushed, a dusky rose blooming on either cheek. He almost smiled. His first assessment of her, as he had laid on his back letting her bandage his shoulder, had been correct: much of the child still remained in this widowed noblewoman.

She looked away, and he turned back to the horse's bobbing ears and the path before them. "I apologize, lady. The years have made my tongue blunter than it ought to be."

"No… you were right. I… wasn't sure how to address you."

"What's wrong with Master Knight?"

"It seemed formal. I mean—" The breathlessness began to creep back into her voice.

He let the silence linger a moment. "What did you call William?"

"I called him my lord."

If her tone were any indication, she must have loved the old man more than even most marriage alliances warranted. Had William returned the affection with the same fervor? The earl had called her my child, not my wife or my beloved, his tone more that of a father to a daughter than a man to his bride.

The countess and her unfounded fears irritated Annan, even vexed him at moments. But they also stirred the compassion he strove so often—usually with too little success—to bury deep within his heart. He had the urge to break through her walls of fear and grief, and know the truth of her pain.

Weep with those who weep... The whisper of Scripture, one from the long-ago days of St. Dunstan's before the storm, wafted through his mind. He grimaced and shoved the thought back deep into the dark pocket of his soul, where he kept all his secrets, all the emotions and ideas that would be dangerous to a man of the sword... a man of the damned.

"When did he marry you?" he asked.

"I don't know... I don't know the days that have passed. Eight months—nine, I don't know. Not long enough." The breath she exhaled was pregnant with all the meaning the words could not convey. Desolation permeated that breath with an intensity that turned the back of his neck cold.

They were silent for a long time. Finally, he reined the courser in nearer to the riverbank and drew to a halt. Mairead slid to the ground without awaiting his help. He hesitated only a moment before unlocking his own stiff limbs and swinging to the ground.

As the horse drank, Annan knelt upstream and diluted the meager remains of their wine with the river water. He stood and approached Mairead, where she stood a few feet off, having splashed her face and arms and soaked the shawl. She met his eyes without flinching and stood her ground until he was near enough to hand her the wineskin.

"I have been called by the name Marcus Annan for a long time now, Countess. My lord doesn't seem appropriate somehow."

The smile she gave him was fleeting, tinged with sadness, but she held his gaze for its entirety.

He did not watch her drink. To watch the gentle bob of her white throat, to watch the way her hair left her neck as she tilted her head back—somehow it seemed too intimate, as if to watch her in these mundane tasks of life would be to see past the vulnerability and into the realness of her being.

He went back to the horse, and his smile turned mocking. It was not like him to be concerned with the vulnerability of a woman—any woman. The priests avowed that they were the souls of evil, better left to the lechers and whoremongers. He glanced back. She had corked the skin and turned to where the distant hills burned like green fire from between the twisted shelter of the cedars and the upright oaks.

Of course, it had never been his practice to believe what the priests avowed.

It was the *Church* who sinned in its demand for celibacy. If St. Dunstan's had proved nothing else, it had proved that. The bastards of the Church—Father Roderic's among them—screamed their defiance in the face of every sanctimonious decree issued by the holy Fathers.

He turned back to the courser, pulled his girth tight, and led him to Mairead. Before he reached her, she spun around, a sudden urgency in the rigid lines of her body. "May I ask you something, Marcus Annan?"

"You may." He stopped the horse and held out a hand for the wineskin.

She handed it over and even took a step toward him. A small bare foot, the white nails lined with dirt, flashed once before withdrawing again beneath the hem of her gown. He flicked his eyes back to her face. He hadn't realized she was without shoes. Here was yet another reason they couldn't afford to have the courser give out on them.

"You said you knew a man named Matthias of Claidmore?"

Her bare feet forgotten, he narrowed his gaze. "Aye. I did."

"I have heard the Baptist tell Lord William that this Matthias will come to Acre to mete justice to Bishop Roderic and… his followers."

"I told you before, it is not justice the Baptist seeks."

"What does Matthias seek?"

"Matthias is dead."

She stopped, and two little lines pursed the skin between her eyebrows. "The Baptist said he was in Acre."

Gethin's delusions were more dangerous than he had guessed. "The Baptist was mistaken."

"I don't believe you. You know Matthias, you told me so."

"I said I *knew* him, lady." He knelt at the water's edge to refill the wineskin, then tied it fast to the saddlebow. When he turned back to her, she was watching him, a strange intensity in her face. His eyes grew a little harder. "Why should it matter to you? You've never even met the man."

"The Baptist said he would kill our enemies." Her eyes were liquid brown, her voice the tremble of a highland stream.

So that was it. She believed Matthias was coming to slay Roderic— and Hugh de Guerrant along with him.

"The Baptist said he would bring justice onto the heads of the guilty," she said.

Annan snorted. "You speak of the Baptist as though he were a prophet. But, mark me, if that is what he prophesies, then he is false. Matthias of Claidmore is dead."

"How do you know?"

He took the wet shawl from her and slung it across the courser's withers. "Matthias couldn't have brought you justice. He was misguided, fanatical." He looked her in the eye, wanting to drill this knowledge into her brain so that she would never ask these questions again. "His hands bore the blood of innocence."

A flash of irritation, even anger, sparked in her eyes. Her shoulders squared. "Like you?"

He didn't flinch. "Aye, like me." He held out a hand to help her onto the pillion. "Come."

She didn't move. "How do you know?"

Inwardly, he cursed Gethin and his cryptic messages for churning these questions up from the dead past where they belonged. Gethin had known, better even than Annan himself, that the wounds of St. Dunstan's were yet unhealed.

Yes, he cursed Gethin. He cursed Father Roderic and the Norman Hugh de Guerrant. And he cursed his own stupidity for accepting Gethin's bait.

"I know, lady, because I killed him." His gaze did not soften at the horror that seeped into her eyes, the return of the fear that had abated for a little while. She had asked, and he had told her the truth.

"Come."

She balled her hands at her sides. Her nostrils flared. "The Baptist said he lived. He vowed he would come."

"The Baptist was mistaken. Mount the courser, Countess."

She recognized the iron in his voice; there was no way she could have ignored it. She put her hand in his, and he lifted her onto the courser yet again. And yet again her eyes would not meet his.

He bit back the growl that rumbled in his throat. Were all women so difficult? Or was it only his bad fortune that Lord William had married an inscrutable wench? He had told her she had nothing to fear from him. He had sworn to protect her with his life. Why should she care if he had killed a penitent she had never met, never even heard of, save in Gethin's twisted stories?

Were she Marek, he would have left her in silence to sulk all she pleased—and were she Marek, she would no doubt sulk aplenty.

Why shouldn't he treat her like Marek? They were not so very different after all. They had both been endangered, friendless children, and he had rescued them both through the misguided sense of compassion that was forever entangling him with the dregs of mankind.

"Countess." He stood at the horse's hindquarters and did not move until she looked down at him. "I did nothing that did not have to be done. If the Baptist told you Matthias was a good man, he did not speak the truth."

She shook her head. Some of the tightness seemed to ebb from her shoulders, but not enough to make his effort worth the trouble. "I believe you that you did not murder him." She lowered her eyes, until her eyelashes brushed her cheek. "But if indeed you silenced this man of Claidmore, you made a terrible mistake."

Dusk had closed upon them by the time Annan spotted a dark shape amid the brush fifty paces ahead.

He reined to a stop, one hand raised to keep Mairead silent.

"What is it," she whispered.

He shook his head. All he could see was a shadow that could easily have been a boulder—but wasn't. His free hand settled on the hilt of the Baptist's sword.

Ahead, the object shifted, and a horse's tail flicked through the air.

Annan nodded, his lungs hardening. It was as he had thought.

He had no way of knowing if the horse's owner was an old enemy or someone about to become a new one. Either way, he and Mairead had stumbled too close to leave without being seen. And that left only one option: attack now, while he yet had the element of surprise.

"Stay here." He withdrew the sword from its sheath on the saddlebow and dismounted, swinging his leg over the courser's neck and dropping to the ground with a soft thump. Neither the dark horse nor its owner seemed to notice.

He held the courser long enough for Mairead to ease forward into the saddle and take the reins. "If I shout for you to leave, go and don't look back. Follow the river until you reach the sea. I'll come after you if I can."

Her head dipped in a short nod, her bottom lip clamped between her teeth.

He drew the infidel saber from his belt. Keeping low, he crept through the sand. When he was near enough to discern the slight figure of a man crouching on the other side of the horse, he filled his lungs and charged, uttering the battle cry of the Moslems. *"Le ilah ile alah!"*

With a gust of breath, the horse shied hard to the side. The animal's owner spun on the balls of his feet to see his attacker, then turned and lunged for a weapon that lay about a pace to his right. With a quickness Annan could only envy, the stranger whirled, a short sword lifted before his face.

Annan was on him with a wordless bellow, even as the back of his mind grabbed at the realization that the uplifted sword was of Western design. He brought his saber down in a hammering blow that tore the sword from his opponent's hand.

"St. Jude—"

From beneath unruly hair, a pair of hazel eyes glared up at him, and Annan stopped his second blow at its apex. He whipped the saber around to touch the soft flesh under the jaw and lifted the other's head until he could see through the shadows' distortion into his prisoner's face.

With a growl, he cast the saber aside. "Peregrine Marek! I thought you on your way to Jerusalem by now."

Marek scrambled to his feet, slapping sand from his breeches. "And I thought you bloody well cold in the ground! What's the meaning of sneaking up on me like you was your own ghost and scaring me near to death!"

"If you'd been paying attention, no one could have sneaked up on you." Annan slid his sword beneath Marek's fallen blade and flipped it into the air so he could catch it. He thrust the hilt against Marek's chest. "How many times have I told you to always keep this at your side? Had I been a Saracen or a marauder, not even St. Jude would have kept you from having your guts thrown into the river."

Marek frowned as he sheathed his sword. "Having a sword didn't much protect you from that Turk's arrow." His gaze traveled to Annan's shoulder. "Speaking of which, why hasn't Saladin dragged you back to Jerusalem behind his favorite donkey?"

Annan ignored the question. He cast a glance round Marek's slip-shod preparations for passing the night. "You make a terrible camp, laddie." He drove his sword deep enough into the sand that it stood on its own, then bent to pick up the saber. "Bring your palfrey farther into the brush, and if you haven't already done it, fill your wineskin. I'll be back. If you've got any viands, now'd be a good time to break them out."

"Yes, dear ol' Master."

Annan shot him a glare.

Marek blinked. "I don't suppose now would be a good time to mention that the strain of watching one's master fall in battle should diminish one's time of servitude by at least half?"

"No, it would not."

"Then I also suppose this isn't a good time to mention that, since you were dead and everything, I was rather expecting to be in my Maid Dolly's arms before Christmastide?"

Something cracked in the brush behind, and Marek's palfrey snorted. Annan spun, saber whipping in front of his face.

From the deep shadows of the brush emerged the gray head of the courser. Mairead sat his back like a queen, her eyes wide open and her mouth rigid. She took in the scene at a glance, her gaze flitting over Marek, then coming back to Annan.

Lowering the sword, he stepped forward to take the courser's bit. His brows tightened into a glower despite himself. "I told you to stay where you were."

"Everything went quiet. I didn't know what to think." Her eyes flicked back to Marek, and her lip slid between her teeth.

Annan let out a sigh that sounded more like a growl. "It's all right." He looked back to Marek. "He's a friend."

"St. Jude." Marek stood stock-still, sword halfway out of its sheath, a tilt to his mouth that hinted at both laughter and bewilderment. Annan hoped the lad would show a little sense and choose to express the latter. The last thing he needed was for Marek to laugh his head off at the idea of his master escorting a countess through hostile territory.

But Marek showed more aplomb than Annan would have given him credit for. He drew his sword with a flourish, slammed its hilt against his heart, and plunged to one knee. "Peregrine Marek, gracious lady— forever in your service."

Mairead's mouth opened slightly, but a lady of high blood didn't gape when people pledged their allegiance. She dropped her head in a bow. "Thank you, Peregrine Marek." Then she glanced at Annan.

Marek looked up expectantly, and Annan raised an arm in a futile gesture, knowing he would never be able to explain the lad's quirks before Marek had a chance to demonstrate any more of them.

"He is indentured," he said at last. "Apparently, I wasn't the only one to escape the siege." He bit back a weary breath. "Marek, this is the Lady Mairead, Countess of Keaton."

Annan could sense her quick glance in his direction, her question— and probably relief—that he had not said *former* Countess of Keaton. But he had done it for his own sake as well as hers. Marek's charm, along with any tact he possessed, would die an instant death should Annan announce that this striking noblewoman—with her wide eyes and tousled hair—was his wife.

Marek's eyebrows lifted. "*The* Keaton?"

As Annan led the courser forward into the open slot of space between the trees, he fixed the lad with a warning look. Having to deal with Mairead's tears would be one trial too many for the day. And Marek certainly wasn't entitled to know the whole story. "The earl requested I escort her to a convent in Orleans," he said, and left it at that.

"Then I, too, pledge myself to your safety, lady." Marek bowed his head, then rose to his feet, sheathing the sword. "Welcome to my humble camp."

"Thank you." For the first time in the days he had known her, Annan heard a smile in her voice. He glanced at her, and in the last rays of light, he could see that the smile was fixed on Marek.

Was it any wonder she found Marek less intimidating than him? Even when Marek tried, his nature hardly lent itself to destruction. Marek was the one who had argued to come on this Crusade, not because he had old bodies from the past to bury, but because he desired absolution for his wayward master. Marek, superstitious wretch that he was, was the one who regularly invoked the saints and covered himself with the blessing of the Cross. Marek was the one who named the horses.

Annan stood back, one hand on the bridle, the other on the courser's damp neck, and watched Marek help the countess down. She did not shy from Marek's touch, nor look away from him, though she had known him only a handful of moments. Had she accepted him so quickly because she now had someone to buffer her from Annan?

He turned to lead the courser aside. Why should he care? It was not his duty to win the countess's trust. He was to take her to Orleans, nothing more; and for that, he did not need her trust.

This feeling wasn't the jealousy of a husband for his bride. Had it been that, Marek would have been set in place the moment his mouth had fallen open at the sight of her.

Annan was not jealous. How could he be, when there was nothing to be jealous of? She was William's wife even now, and would die William's wife, as far as he was concerned.

But this fear she had of him gored something deep inside. As Marek led her to a clump of brush he had gathered for his own bed—no doubt heedless of the thought that such would be clear evidence to anyone wishing to track him—Annan stopped the tired courser at a nearby tree and tossed the reins over a low-hanging branch.

When a man became such that a woman feared him, not because of who he was, but because of what he had done, he had probably crossed that irrevocable line of eternity Marek was always haranguing about.

Annan rubbed his palm across the horse's hard shoulder and summoned the bitter smile that had been his shield against these truths for such a long time. It didn't matter. Within two score days, the lady would be ensconced in the walls of St. Catherine's. And then, perhaps, it would at last be time for him to seek in earnest an opponent with an arm stronger than his own.

CHAPTER X

B Y THE TIME Annan finished unsaddling the courser and tethering him in the brush, out of kicking range of the bay palfrey, Marek had remembered to fill his wineskin from the river and haul out his sack of food. His supply was more than ample, which was hardly surprising. The lad had an appetite to rival any dozen bloated noblemen.

Annan lugged the saddle through the gathering darkness and dropped it next to Marek's crouched form. He could just make out the dark shadow that was Mairead, still poised upon the leafy couch to which Marek had led her. He could see the subtle movement of her head, the white glitter of her eyes as she looked at him.

"Just a moment, lady," Marek said, and Annan glanced down in time to see the skip of an orange spark and hear the scratch of flint against steel.

"Marek. No fire."

The lad looked up at him. "You can't very well let her shiver all night."

"I said no." He bunched up the linen shawl, now dry, and tossed it at Mairead's feet. One didn't build fires when facing possible pursuit. Keeping the countess safe was far more important than keeping her warm.

"But we can't see a blithering thing!"

Ah, so that was it. The laddie wanted to admire his new companion. "I said no." He turned toward the river, then stopped. He could hear Mairead shifting in her bed of boughs, no doubt believing this was the way he treated his servants all the time.

He forced an exhale past his clenched teeth. It didn't matter. He didn't need her to trust his decisions.

Didn't need it, perhaps, but despite himself he *wanted* her to—wanted her not to look at him with wide-eyed fear because all she could see was the bloodstained tourneyer.

He stayed where he was, arms at his sides, still facing the river, but made himself speak softly—slowly—with only a trace of the growl that had become his long-ingrained habit. "If we can see by firelight, then we can also be seen. We can fight the cold better than we can marauders."

Marek let out a little snort that wasn't half as impertinent as Annan expected. The boughs shifted again beneath Mairead's weight, but she said nothing.

Annan left it at that and started back down to the river.

Mairead watched Annan's dark shape retreat down the hill to the riverbank and found herself blowing out a sigh of relief. She shouldn't fear him. He had done nothing to her—*would* do nothing to her.

But he was so volatile, so abrupt. And if what he said this afternoon was true, then he was a black mark in the sight of God and saints alike.

Across from her, Marek clucked his tongue. "Well." He turned to her. "It's my personal opinion that my master has spent rather too much time avoiding humankind."

"Indeed." She picked up the shawl from where Annan had tossed it and drew it across her lap. Her eyes sought his silhouette against the river.

"Well, before he rescued me anyway. I've done me best to cure him, but he still behaves like a troll most of the time."

"Rescued you?"

Marek pushed to his feet. "This old shopkeeper back in Glasgow wasn't being all that generous about the sharing of vittles with a starving laddie like meself. He was going to heave me into the dungeon since I couldn't pay him." Marek stepped over to his food purse and began rummaging through its contents. "Annan saw him chasing after me, and he paid the bloke his money."

"Why?"

"It is my suspicion that he was in search of a top-rate servant and bodyguard."

She raised her brow. "Bodyguard?" That Marcus Annan would need a bodyguard was absurd in itself, but this lad didn't even have the width to stand in front of his master and act a shield.

"Well." The word wasn't quite a concession. Marek came away from the sack with a handful of food and brought it back to her. "Cheese, my lady? I've some fish and crusts as well."

She accepted the pieces and laid them on the shawl. Marek backed off to what he apparently deemed a respectful distance and sat down cross-legged in front of her. He seemed a good lad, even if he was hewn from a rough log.

They chewed in silence, and she could feel his eyes on her as they ate. She was almost glad Annan hadn't let him build a fire. The darkness gave her an anonymity she would probably never again have once the lad saw her by daylight. She rather doubted this Glasgow wretch had ever seen a noblewoman in such an intimate setting.

He smacked his lips with finality and slapped crumbs from his legs. "So I see Annan finally found this Earl of Keaton he's been looking for?"

She lifted her head. A queer flutter, half fear, half something else, prickled in the back of her brain. "He was looking for us?"

"Aye. He wanted to warn the earl about something that Baptist fellow had told him. Ever met the Baptist? Ask me and I'll tell you there's a loose rock clattering round in *his* skull."

"I—" Her mouth opened, but she found she had no words. Annan had been looking for Lord William? Was it possible his very presence at Acre's siege, wounds and all, was because he had come to extricate William from the straits into which Mairead had plunged him?

Aye, it was possible. He did rather seem to have a knack for hauling less fortunate people out of harm's way, herself among them. But the idea was a far cry from the gold-seeking tourneyer he proclaimed himself to be.

"So—" Marek leaned forward, an elbow propped on either knee. "Where is the earl?"

"He's—" The last thing she needed was to give this wide-jawed servant news of her plight. "He's still in Acre."

"Ah…" The lad let the word linger long enough to indicate he was rather hoping for a bit more of the details. When she didn't speak, he started a new tack. "Um. And how was it then that you came to be with Master Annan?"

She smiled. The lad's manners were rough, yes, and he was decidedly incorrigible. But at least she would hear no muttered platitudes from this boy. Not that she'd had to deal with any from Annan over the last few days anyway.

"Apparently," she said, brushing the last of the crumbs from the shawl and rising to her feet, "my lord trusted your master."

"Well, that's something."

She gave him a sharp look. "You don't trust him?"

"Of course, lady." He stood. "He saved me life, remember? I'd be dead or in the mud of the streets weren't for him."

"Then why say that like you did?"

"Because, I told you, he's a troll. He minds his own business, and I've yet to meet the man who knew him well enough to trust him. 'Cept maybe that Baptist person."

The lines in her forehead cleared. "The Baptist trusts Annan?" The same Baptist who Annan swore was a deluded fool?

"Well, *maybe* he trusts him." Marek shrugged and turned half away, as though he'd spoken too much. "Trusted him enough to tell Annan your earl was in trouble anyhow."

She pressed her lips together and took a step forward. "Did Annan come here because he knew Lord William was in trouble?"

"He didn't come to gain absolution."

Mairead bit her lip. Annan had all but said he wished the Baptist dead, and yet the Baptist trusted him enough to inform him of his plans and his concerns?

"How do you know the Baptist?" she asked.

"I don't. Never knew he was more'n a name 'fore we ran afoul of this rather disagreeable count person in Bari."

"But your master knows him. How?" She took another step.

He turned back to face her. The night sky was just bright enough that she could see wrinkles of thought between his brows. He couldn't possibly be able to understand her intensity. He wouldn't be able to understand how the Baptist and everything he did was entwined so inextricably with her life, with her every breath.

"He wouldn't tell me," Marek said. "I don't think he even hears half my questions, and I was ailing on the voyage over anyway."

"You must know something."

"All I ken is that neither of them like that bishop too much. I sweated myself half dead the whole time we was in Acre, thinking Annan was going to kill him."

Mairead's nostrils flared, filling all her senses with the damp night. "But he didn't kill him."

"He'd've gone straight to Hell for sure. He hasn't taken the Crusading oath, you know."

"The Baptist trusts him…" She shook her head and looked down to the shawl dragging in the sand at her feet. If the Baptist trusted Annan, then perhaps she had misjudged him. Never had she known the Baptist's judgment to be wrong, and Lord William had lived by his faith in the man 'til the day he died.

Marek tilted his head to look her in the face. "You know, lady, *you* could ask the master about this Baptist bloke."

She gave half a smile. "He'd bite my head off."

"Oh, he'd bite *my* head off. Wouldn't think twice about it. But not yours."

She flicked her gaze up to his face and let the smile reach both corners of her mouth. "Is that so?"

The flash of white through the darkness told her he was grinning. "Well, you have rather a better chance than I do at least. And anyway he barks harder than he bites."

The smile faded. "I've seen his bite."

Marek chuckled and leaned a little closer. "But—and on this I stake my meager life—he doesn't bite ladies."

————————

On the other side of the river, across from the shoddy camp where Marcus Annan brooded on the outskirts and Lady Mairead and the lad murmured together, Gethin the Baptist lay on his stomach. Fist-sized stones pressed into the flesh of his belly and grated against his bones. The night burned cold on the bare skin of his legs and the back of his tonsured head; he could feel the gooseflesh pricking his chapped skin into tiny ridges.

For hours, he had lain here, cold and alone, the wind drowning even the whispers of the rodents in the brush. He had been watching them—all of them—from the moment Annan and the countess had appeared, and his heart had throbbed with the knowledge of his successful hunt.

Had he so desired, he could have slipped silently into the waters of the Orontes and crossed over, unknown to them, in but a few moments. The sharp cold in his bones would have been more than worth the shock, maybe even fear, he would find on their faces.

But it was not yet time. He would wait a while longer, until he could discover Annan's plans. Why did Marcus Annan run from Acre, choosing instead to escort the widow of the dead earl to sanctuary?

He pursed his lips, his heavy brows pinching over his eyes. If Annan had been swayed by the countess's beauty, it was a step from the well-beaten path of solitude that had trailed him for the last sixteen years. And if he shielded her out of some sense of honor...

Gethin's exhale rasped. If that were the reason, it would be ironic indeed—that Annan would run from God-given duty in pursuit of some pale mockery of his own construction.

Another gust of wind brushed the nape of his neck and slithered down his back. He drew a careful breath, trying to calm the angry energy that had burned in him for so long.

All was silent now across the river, save the vague munching of the horses in the shrubbery. The lady and the lad had bedded down. Annan still stood, arms crossed over his chest, his silhouette black against the deep blue of the night sky. Perhaps he was contemplating the even darker blackness of his soul.

Soon, very soon, Gethin would find the means to force Marcus Annan—that blaspheming façade of a man—to face his duty, to forsake his lies, to join his quest for justice…

Soon.

CHAPTER XI

TWO DAYS AFTER finding Marek, Annan guided the gray courser away from the dwindling waters of the Orontes River. The port where the river debouched into the sea lay too far into Saracen territory to risk searching for a ship. Their best chance of gaining passage to Venice would still be found in Constantinople, which was yet a week's ride to the northwest.

They had been riding in the shadows of dusk for some twenty minutes, looking for a place to rest, when first he caught sight of the shadow on the horizon behind them.

His chest seized, his arm jerking a few inches closer to the sword strapped against the pommel.

Mairead, the tired lines in her face only inches from his, frowned and turned to look for herself. "What?"

He let his breath out carefully. "Nothing."

It probably *was* nothing, an overreaction caused by a lingering sunspot in his vision. But he didn't like it. Too many days had passed without anyone crossing their path. Sooner or later, someone was going to ride over the horizon. And then there would be trouble.

"It was nothing," he repeated.

"What was it? You saw something?"

"I saw a spot, lady."

He caught her frown out of the corner of his eye as he turned back, but it wasn't mingled with fear—and for that he was grateful. Over the past few days her mistrust of him seemed to have abated. Whether due to Marek's jovial influence or merely some inner strength of her own, he didn't know.

He twisted in his saddle to look at Marek riding some half-dozen paces behind the courser. "We'll stop in this dell to the right here."

Marek stood in his stirrups to look, then scowled. "T'ain't no boughs to make her ladyship a couch."

"She'll sleep on the ground—"

"I'll sleep on the ground," Mairead said.

Annan twisted to look at her. Marek had made her a bed every night since he had met her. Annan had thought she would resent his refusal to accommodate that courtesy, unavoidable though it was.

A smile lurked at the corners of her mouth. "Were it not unwise, I believe you'd provide me both boughs for a bed *and* a fire."

He squinted at her. "You believe that, do you?" Inwardly, he cursed the reflex that turned the question into a challenge.

But again she surprised him. The smile ripened on her lips. "I've heard tell that you have rather more respect for the weaker vessel than you'd like to show." Her expression was almost teasing, but he sensed the hesitation hidden in her gaze. She was testing him, taking a chance, making an effort to reach past the shields they had both erected.

He swallowed and made himself speak softly, almost a whisper, to keep the growl from his voice. "Is that so?"

"Aye."

"Well—" He glanced over to where Marek was leading his horse into the dell, talking his usual gibberish to the animal. "Marek never did learn mouths were made on hinges so they could be shut every now and then."

"Did no one ever tell you mouths were made on hinges so they might be *opened* every now and then?"

"Marek's mentioned it once or twice."

A few paces away from Marek's palfrey, Annan drew the courser to a halt and dismounted. For the first time, Mairead kept her place on the pillion and waited for him to help her down. He lifted her carefully—not wanting to jar this sudden burst of good humor. If he could keep her fear at arm's length for the rest of their journey, he would ask nothing more.

He set her on the ground. "What else did Marek tell you?"

"That you're a troll."

"Ah." He shot another glance to where Marek was whistling one of his troubadour songs as he unsaddled his mount. "Well, if the lad possesses no other virtue, at least he's truthful."

Mairead sobered, and he wondered if the admission had been a mistake.

"He also told me you came to Acre to help Lord William."

Annan's back stiffened. "Is that what he thinks?"

Her eyes looked huge in the gathering darkness, and he could see the tears misting on their surfaces. "Didn't you?" Something in her voice—some note of pleading hope—tore at him.

He couldn't very well tell her that he didn't know *why* he had come to Acre—that it had been a mere impulse. That he had found Lord William only by some strange twist of fate. That he could hardly have helped him even had he found him earlier. What *could* he tell her?

"Had I been able, I would have saved him for you."

A tear broke free of her lashes and slid down her cheek. She forced a smile. "If that is true, then I have misjudged you." Another tear dropped down the other cheek, sliding all the way past her chin.

He knew he should turn and go, should leave. He could do nothing for his own grief... how could he heal hers? Better to leave her to cry her silent tears alone.

But he stayed, his eyes on the tear track shining against her pale cheek. "He deserved to be mourned. He was a man deserving of a love that would remember him."

She wiped the tear aside and looked away. "It is not love that remembers him. It is just a woman." She walked a few paces behind the horse and wrapped her arms round her body.

Annan went to the courser and laid a hand on the animal's neck. The horse, already half asleep, cocked a hip and grunted.

"What did you name him?" He managed to keep his voice low, but the growl surfaced anyway.

She turned halfway around, one hand reaching to smooth aside another tear. "What?"

"The courser—what did you name him?"

Her eyebrow arched despite the tremble in her lip. "You're certain you want to know?"

When he didn't respond, she turned all the way around. "I named him Airn."

"Airn." He tugged the girth loose and let it drop.

"Aye. You approve?"

"Better than what Marek would have come up with."

Marek, squatting next to his palfrey with a hoof in his lap, peered beneath the horse's belly. "What's that?"

"I said the lady names horses better than do you."

Marek snorted. "And how would you ken?"

Annan pulled the saddle from the courser's back and set it on end. A cool wind whispered past, blowing the sun-warmed homespun of his loose tunic against his back. He tossed another glance at the horizon, but it was too dark now to see anything out of place.

Mairead drifted to the horse's head and pulled his forehead against her chest. "You think someone is following us, don't you?"

"Just being careful." If indeed someone were back there, they would find out in time enough.

For a moment, everything was silent, even the horses. Annan rubbed the courser's back with the heel of his hand and listened to the insistent whisperings of the wind. A shiver danced across his shoulder blades, and he leaned closer to the horse, reaching one arm over its back to rub the other side.

"He married me to save me, you know." Mairead's voice, almost a whisper, broke the stillness. She had lowered her face to the courser's forelock, the fingers of either hand resting beneath the bridle's cheek-pieces. "To save me from Hugh de Guerrant. He knew what would happen to us once he married me, but he did it anyway because he thought it was the right thing. He died for me." She breathed deeply. "For what he did for me, I would have carried his sons and I would have stood beside him until he was too old to carry himself. I would have made him happy. You're right—" she looked at Annan, "he did deserve to be remembered—and by so many more than just me."

He stared at her. "I remember him."

The earnestness of the little girl surfaced as she raised her face to see into his expression. "What do you remember?"

What did he remember? He remembered the earl's face—instead of his own father's—smiling on his successes, on his growing prowess with sword and lance. He remembered William laughing every time Annan took a spill from an unruly horse. He remembered the older man's pride when he had earned his spurs on the field of battle, fighting against the English King Henry II.

The lines in his forehead tightened.

He remembered the grief, the pain that had darkened his mentor's brow when first he had learned of the burst of temper that had led to the blows exchanged between Annan and his older brother. It had been an accident when his brother's wife had been struck in her attempt to intervene; it had been an accident that she and both the children she had carried within her had died. But Annan had borne the guilt of it none-theless. The fight with his brother had been his first step down his dark path. The second had been choosing St. Dunstan's as the monastery in which to pay his penance.

He had no memory of his master's reactions to the deeds of St. Dunstan's; after that black day, he had not seen the face of his mentor Lord William of Keaton 'til the night of his death in the prison camp.

"I remember," he said at last, "that he was a good man. If wisdom ever shone its light on me, it was through him."

Her cheek bent once more to the courser's forehead. "He was a good man because he was a righteous man."

Annan shifted, clamping down on a defensive flash. Her words, after all, were not a comparison of William's life and his own; condem-nation had not risen to clog the air between them. Had it been so, he would have told her she had no idea what had shaped his own life, what had led him down a road so disparate from the earl's.

He held the words in check. William *had* been a righteous man, and he well remembered it. He had respected the earl's righteousness, and he had tried to emulate it.

But he had not had the faith to hold his own bellicosity in check—a bellicosity that had been born, in part, of his hatred for the unrighteous. And so it was, were he to tell her what had led him here today, he would also have to tell her that, in its own ironic way, it had been William's righteousness that had sent him hurtling, unprepared, to the early holocaust that had so marked his life.

Mairead laid her cheek flat against the courser's forehead so that she could see Annan. "Would that all men could be even as he was."

Annan pushed away from the horse's side. "Some men are called of God, and some are not."

She raised her head, both eyebrows lifting. "Aye. But it is also true that there are those who are called and do not come."

She held his gaze with a steadiness he had never seen from her. Behind them, Marek began to sing the song he had been whistling. His high, clear voice resonated in the night air. *"I trained myself a falcon. He was as I wanted, gentled to my care."*

Mairead turned away, and her soft tone joined his. *"I bound his feathers proudly, gold the winding shone. Then he took the high road, and flew to parts unknown."*

Annan watched her go. He would not say that she was not right. A long time ago—a lifetime ago—he *had* been one of the chosen. He had been willing to give everything, even his very life, to the cause of Christ. But that time was long dead.

———————

Annan did not see the silhouette on the horizon until the eastern sky began to color with the blush of dawn.

They had traveled throughout the latter part of the night, mostly in silence, the whir of the wind providing the only barrier necessary for them to keep their thoughts to themselves. Even Marek seemed to have nothing to say beyond an infrequent muttering to his horse.

Mairead had descended into sleep slowly, her muscles softening and softening until at last she leaned against his back, her cheek between his shoulder blades. But as the courser plodded through the sand, its hipbones rocking in time with the bob of its head, Annan found that he had no need to fight the urge of sleep. His mind was too active, too aware of the woman who slept behind him.

Through the coarse warmth of the jerkin Marek had dug from his saddlebags, Annan could feel her arms folded against her chest, drawing her cloak tightly around her. He could feel her gentle breathing, the tickle of her hair at the nape of his neck. He rode straight, shoulders back to keep her from slipping.

Had she been awake, he doubted she would have allowed herself so near him. For that matter, she had never before fallen asleep behind him. He entwined the fingers of his rein hand in the courser's thick mane and wondered if she had allowed herself to fall asleep because the exertions of the trek had finally overtaken her. Or had their conversation—the first conversation they had held without one of them leaving either in doubt or anger—finally convinced her she had nothing to fear from him?

"Annan—" Marek's voice, hardly louder than a whisper, seemed to echo in the pre-dawn silence.

"What?"

"Someone's behind us. Can't see him now— he dropped down out of sight behind that hill."

Annan twisted his neck as far as he could without jostling Mairead and cursed himself for not keeping a better watch during the night. He had allowed his own weariness to overweigh his instincts. He *had* seen someone last night, but he had foregone keeping a watch behind them in exchange for letting Mairead sleep undisturbed.

"A Turk?" he said.

"It looked to be a donkey."

He brought the courser to an abrupt halt and reined him around just as the stranger topped the hill. Adjusting his course slightly, the man kept the donkey's bobbing head in line with Annan and Marek.

In a rush, Annan's instincts told him this was the donkey he had seen in silhouette the first night out of the prison camp, when he had questioned the coincidence that had led someone to ford the river exactly where he and Mairead had camped for the night.

Now he knew it was no coincidence.

As purple light streaked the sky behind him, the man on the donkey continued his leisurely journey. His cowl was thrown back across his shoulders, revealing the sunburnt sheen of a monk's tonsure. And from the midst of dark robes fluttering in the morning breeze, the glint of a crucifix shone.

Annan clenched his teeth, one hand seeking the hilt of his sword.

Mairead roused and tilted her chin to see over his shoulder. "What's wrong?" Her inhalation whistled past his ear as she caught sight of the approaching traveler. One hand darted from beneath her cloak to clench the jerkin at Annan's side. "Who is it?"

"The Baptist." Why did he feel only dread, when he should be welcoming this man gladly, if only because of who he wasn't?

"Thanks to Heaven." She straightened away from him, and the cold breeze immediately replaced the warmth of her body.

"Indeed." He hunched his shoulders, fingernails digging into the leather binding of his sword hilt.

Marek gave a little snort. "Well, I can think of a few people I'd rather see. Trouble hovers round him like flies at a charnel house."

Annan threw some slack into his reins and reached to rub his sore hip. "I suppose he's better than most of the other options."

"He saved our lives," Mairead pointed out.

Annan didn't remind her that Gethin had meant to save the lives of Mairead and *William*—not Mairead and Marcus Annan. He had no doubts the Baptist was about to be as surprised to see him as he was to see the Baptist.

But when Gethin at last drew near enough for the sun to cast its light upon his warped face, no expression of shock or confusion blurred the furor of his eyes.

Annan didn't move so much as an eyebrow. He owed Gethin nothing, not even an explanation.

"Baptist," he said.

Gethin drew rein with only a pace of sand between his donkey's head and that of Annan's and Marek's horses. "Marcus Annan." His features lay flat, but contempt burned in the back of those fearsome eyes. His gaze flicked to Mairead, and he inclined his head. "Countess, where is your husband?"

She hesitated, and Annan could sense more than see that she shifted her glance to him. "He is… in Acre."

Gethin grunted, then settled his gaze back on Annan. "And, pray tell, Brother Annan, what are you doing with his wife?"

On Annan's far side, out of Gethin's sight, Mairead's fingers slid tentatively against his ribs. A silent message burned in her touch, and he knew she was giving him permission to explain the provision Lord William had issued to allow her the protection of a husband's name. Gethin could neither condemn nor censure if he knew she was Annan's wife.

But Annan's eyes only hardened. Explaining himself to others had never been reason enough to bare secrets, especially to those he did not trust. And his old friend Gethin was no longer a man he trusted.

"Do you add to your sins, Marcus Annan?" Gethin's voice dropped lower.

"Perhaps."

Mairead's fingers tightened, and he straightened his shoulders. "And perhaps not. You impugn the lady with your accusations."

One heavy brow lifted. "On the contrary." The donkey moved forward a step until Gethin was able to look directly into Mairead's face. Her hand dropped from Annan's side, and out of the corner of his eye Annan could see her shoulders draw back.

Gethin pulled the donkey to a stop and leaned over to take her hand. "Are you well, Countess?"

She didn't flinch, but Annan's reflexes burned with the urge to strike Gethin's hand away. He brushed the courser's ribs with his heel, and the animal's hindquarters swerved to the side. Gethin didn't release Mairead's hand, and she had to catch hold of Annan's arm to keep from being pulled off. "I'm fine," she said. "Master Annan sees me safely to Orleans at Lord William's request."

"Orleans." Gethin let her go. "You travel all the way to Orleans alone—with this man?"

Annan narrowed his gaze. What game was being played here? This was a face of Gethin he had never seen before. He was not the generous, zealous brother postulant he had been at St. Dunstan's, nor was he the cold, dictating mendicant who had confronted him in Bari.

Now he was slippery, manipulating, backhanded. And he was angry. Annan could sense the anger rising from him like the sweat that beaded his brow.

Angry because Annan had left Acre?

Annan nudged the courser's side once more, swiveling the horse's hindquarters until he faced Gethin. "What is it you want?"

The mask dropped without a moment's hesitation, and Gethin glared at him. "I want you to go back. I want you to join the quest for justice. The armies are marching to Jerusalem as we speak."

"Hah!" Marek had an elbow propped on his saddlebow, his chin and one side of his face mashed against his hand. "Fighting in another one of them battles when we haven't taken the oath isn't going to do us much good."

Gethin didn't even glance at him. Marek sniffed and rolled his eyes.

Annan looked at the monk levelly. "Why should I go?"

"Because murdered blood cries for vengeance. It is a responsibility that all those who survived St. Dunstan's must bear. Bishop Roderic cannot be allowed to live."

"And who was it he murdered?" He clenched a fist in his lap, trying to keep the fire of his temper under control. "I had thought *you* dead at his hands once. But if not you, then who?"

"Many died."

"You said yourself that was war. Warfare is not murder. Roderic will pay for his sins, but his judgment is not my responsibility."

For a long moment, Gethin stared at him, unblinking. "I see. And when is it that you pay for *your* sins—*Marcus Annan*?"

A chill lifted the hairs on the back of Annan's sword hand, and a warning, small and cold, shivered in the depth of his thoughts. "You've changed."

A smile crept across the Baptist's face, skewing his mutilated lips, damping the animal gleam in his eyes. "Aye," said he, "we both have." He closed his eyes and sighed with a weariness that, for the briefest moment, made Annan wonder if this delusional anger, this lust to bring pain upon his enemies, was yet another face hiding the real Gethin—the Gethin he had called brother—from his sight.

Then the Baptist's eyes opened once again, dropping into place a mask of tacit determination.

He nodded his head to Mairead. "It will be my honor, Countess, to escort you to Orleans. In the company of a priest, your safety will be ensured."

"I—" She sounded breathless, confused. "Thank you." Her voice calmed, and she fell back into the role of a noblewoman. "You are most welcome to join us. Were it not for your aid, we should have been killed at the prison in Tyre."

Annan did not look back, but by the sound of her voice, he could sense she had glanced at him, as though seeking confirmation.

It was a confirmation he would not give. Years ago, when he had thought Gethin dead, he had lain awake in the cold of night and mourned his friend with a ferocity that had made even his bones ache. He would have given anything, most especially his own wretched life, to bring Gethin back.

Now he wondered if perhaps it would have been better had Gethin truly died that day at the Abbey.

CHAPTER XII

OR FOUR DAYS, Brother Warin and Hugh de Guerrant, with a small body of men-at-arms, had pursued the escaped assassin Marcus Annan. They had searched every city between Acre and Tarsus, and amongst the lot of them had broken the wind of six horses. Annan and the woman riding with him were nowhere. No one had seen them, heard them, nothing.

Until now.

Warin's chest constricted at the sight of two horses and a donkey trotting toward a cypress-ringed oasis. "We've found them." The words were hoarse from between his burned lips. He crossed himself. "God be praised."

Hugh, who had galloped up from behind at Warin's signal, reined his snorting bay to a halt. He took one look at the riders below and uttered a sound that was more growl than laugh. "That's him. And the woman…"

Warin knew what he was thinking. The woman's long black hair—her only identifiable feature at this distance—had drawn his attention as well. For the entirety of their search, Warin had suffered all too patiently through Hugh's examination of every dark-haired woman whose misfortune it was to cross his path.

Warin had never approved of Hugh's fixation with the Earl of Keaton's wife—even now that both she and her husband were undoubtedly dead at the hands of Saladin's butchers. He had never understood why Veritas, their anonymous informant, had wished to encourage Hugh's amoral pursuits. His lip curled. Especially *that* amoral pursuit.

Hugh flipped his lance up under his arm with a flourish. "Do we have a plan, Master Templar?" His dark eyes gleamed.

Warin's frown tightened. "They'll dismount once they reach the trees, and we'll be able to ride them down easily."

"Good. Tell the men. And tell them the tourneyer is to be mine." Hugh flexed his sword arm, shaking straight the links of his loose mail sleeve.

Warin loosed his sword from its sheath and shot Hugh a look of warning. "*Only* the tourneyer. The bishop has no quarrel with the others."

"If they ride with Marcus Annan, then I have a quarrel with them."

Mairead watched Annan and Marek water their horses, the reins looped over their elbows as they knelt beside the animals' heads and drank. The Baptist had moved away from them, leading his donkey along the brim of the water to a spot clear of rocks. But she stayed behind to straighten the ache from her bones and wait until Annan or Marek brought her the wineskin.

She watched Annan's broad shoulders as he shrugged out of his ruddy jerkin before again dipping his hands into the water. The animosity that had clogged the air between him and the Baptist had been suffocating—so thick she could have reached out a hand and squeezed it with her fingers.

Marek had said the Baptist trusted Annan. But it was not trust that flashed in the man's eyes. It was closer to hatred.

Gooseflesh prickled her arms, and she rubbed her sleeves. For as long as she had been Lord William's wife, months before she had even known the name of Marcus Annan, she had trusted the Baptist.

How was it then, that in the short time she had known this tourneyer, he had gained the power to make her doubt the brave devotion of the monk in whom she had so long put her faith? She bit her lip, her gaze shifting to where the Baptist urged his donkey to the edge of a clean shallow.

Thunder pounded somewhere in the back of her head, and she turned to look. Rolling down from the edge of the valley, already close enough for her to see the flash of the crosses on their tabards, charged a dozen knights on horseback.

Her breath caught so hard it felt like someone had tried to tear her breastbone from her chest. "Annan—!"

"Annan!" Marek repeated her shout, and Mairead spun around, heart hurtling against her ribs.

"It's him—" Her fingers clenched in her skirt. "It's Hugh—"

Annan, his jerkin a forgotten splash of red on the ground behind him and the cold fire of his eyes raging to life, pulled his sword from its sheath on the saddle. "Get behind me." Not once did he look at her. All his focus was on the approaching riders. "Marek! Give me that misericorde, and get the countess on her horse."

Marek hesitated. "What about y—"

"*Now!*"

With a snap of his wrist, Marek pulled loose the small dagger hidden in his boot and tossed it to Annan. Then he ran to take the horses' reins.

The men-at-arms were close enough now that Mairead could see the tabards of the two knights at their fore—the white and red blouse of the Knight Templar and the black griffin in a field of blue that was Hugh de Guerrant. He had found her. She had known he would. How could she have ever dared to hope he would not? She knew his persistence, knew his pride, knew the lengths he was willing to go to gain what he wanted.

Annan's eyes bored into hers. "Go with Marek. Tell him I'll meet you at the home of Lord Stephen. He knows how to find it."

She shook her head, wanting desperately to draw strength from his solidness, from the absolute lack of fear in his eyes.

He turned back. Hugh and the Templar were almost to the trees. "Gethin!" he barked.

"I have no sword." The monk stood beside his donkey's head, his arms folded into his sleeves, a strangely placid expression diluting the intensity of his eyes.

Without a look in his direction, Annan tossed him the Mohammedan saber.

Marek, leading both Airn and his bay palfrey, trotted over to Mairead. "Hurry, lady." He stood at Airn's side, hands cupped for her to step into.

She whirled back to Annan. "You'll have no horse! They'll kill you!"

"Nay, lady."

She caught his sleeve. She knew the disadvantage of a man on foot against a mounted, charging knight. She knew that to unhorse a soldier was a death sentence. And yet he had every intention of just standing there, sword held before him with both hands, eyes unswerving, the quiver in his taut muscles testifying to something that could only be anticipation.

And she knew, with a certainty that surprised her, that this man would die for her today. He had *never* been a threat to her. She had doubted him from the beginning, had feared him despite Lord William's avowal of his honor. And now... now, he was going to throw his life away on the point of Hugh de Guerrant's lance—because of her.

"Don't do this. I don't want you to do this!"

He didn't look at her. Hugh crashed through the trees, only paces from crossing the stretch of sand that separated him from Annan.

"There's no reason you should all die! Let them kill me! What have I left to live for?"

He ignored her. "Marek!"

Marek clutched her arm. "Lady, please! He knows what he's doing! All of us *will* die if you don't come now!"

She exhaled through clenched teeth, took one last look at the foaming charger that bore Hugh de Guerrant, and let Marek boost her into the saddle.

They galloped away, the horses churning through the shallows. When they emerged from the shade of the cypresses into engulfing sunlight, she looked back, her lip between her teeth, to where Annan stood, waiting.

Annan could see the triumph in Hugh's face, the exclamation of victory on his lips. He was only a step away from winning—and Annan knew it.

He waited, hearing the seconds slip past with each echo of his own breath. He had to wait; he would have only one chance to gain the upper hand.

Hugh's charger closed to within a mere length, and Annan lunged. Shouting, Hugh drove his spurs into his horse's already bloody sides. But Annan was too close for Hugh to strike. Trapping Hugh's lance under his arm, Annan ran forward and levered the shaft against the knight's body, forcing him against the high pommel.

As the rest of the men-at-arms entered the clearing, Marek's misericorde flashed in Annan's hand. Hugh saw it and kicked back hard with his near foot, driving his spur into Annan's side. Annan jerked away, the lance snapping under the pressure, and the dagger buried itself in the wood of the saddle tree.

"You're going to die here like a dog—you know that?" Hugh whipped his sword from its sheath.

Annan's time was running out. The others would be upon him in moments. He would be surrounded and he *would* die.

Hugh slashed once with the sword, and Annan caught it on his own blade. As the shadows of the men-at-arms surrounded him, he slammed the splintered end of the lance shaft into Hugh's unprotected throat. The Norman reeled, and Annan leapt halfway onto the horse, his foot catching the stirrup Hugh had left empty after his attack with the spur. He drove his elbow into the bridge of the man's nose, toppling him from the saddle.

Fire coursing through his veins, Annan yanked the misericorde from the seat behind his leg and turned to meet the onslaught of three out of the five remaining knights. From the corner of his vision, he caught sight of Gethin standing down the charge of the Knight Templar.

One of the men reined in behind the bay charger, and Annan lost sight of Gethin. He buried Marek's dagger in someone's chest, took a glancing blow to his sword arm, and spun the charger in time to see one of the men-at-arms dismount to lift an unconscious Hugh.

To his left, Gethin gave an involuntary cry as the infidel saber flew from his outstretched hand. The other remaining man-at-arms shouted at the monk and spurred his charger forward, sword arm stretched tight above his head in readiness for the final blow.

Annan's whole body gave a little jerk. His sword swung up before his face. How many times had he seen variations of this very scene repeat themselves over and over again in his brain? He had blamed himself for Gethin's death, had wished himself dead in his place so many times that the words had become a mantra. Now, after so long, was he to watch it all happen for real?

But the man-at-arms's sword never fell. The Templar's arm shot out and, in the same voice Annan had heard on Acre's beach, shouted, "Leave him!"

The man-at-arms obeyed, hauling his horse aside to gallop between Gethin and the Templar.

Annan gritted his teeth and lifted his spur to prick his charger's side. This Templar's sudden fixation with Gethin would be his downfall.

"Drop your hood," the Templar ordered.

Gethin lifted both hands to push back his cowl. Even with the distance separating them, Annan could see the irritation in his gaze, hidden behind the sardonic twist of his lips. "Greetings, Master Templar."

"You— You stopped me as we were leaving Acre." The Templar wore no helm, and his ruddy face, veined with sweat, contorted. "Who are you?"

"A messenger of God."

The Templar stared. Annan drove his heel into the bay's side, and the horse charged.

Behind him, the knight with Hugh, shouted something in a Frankish-Syrian dialect, and the Templar jerked around to face Annan. "Kill him!" he shouted as the other man-at-arms wheeled to meet Annan's attack. "But spare the monk! I want him alive!"

Annan dropped the reins and swung two-handed, his blade crashing into the man-at-arms's sword and wrenching the knight from his saddle. He heard the man thud into the sand, even as he twisted to face the Templar. "Still passing out bounties?"

The man raised his sword. "This time the bounty is on your head."

Annan sat back, slowing the charger's pace, his gaze on the Templar. Sooner or later, every man's eyes revealed his intentions. This man was no different.

The Templar's gaze flicked to the side for just a moment, focusing on something behind Annan. And in that moment, Annan heard the click of a crossbow quarrel locking into place. He shoved his leg into the charger's side, and the horse leapt forward, snorting foam all along his reins. A jolt slammed the horse forward, and Annan snarled, more at himself than at the enemy who had fired the shot.

"Close in!" the Templar said.

Annan didn't wheel to face the attack. Behind him, he could hear the crank of the crossbow reloading. It would be yet half a minute before another quarrel could be fired, but he knew better than to hope the next one would miss.

Without a backward glance, he brought the flat of his blade down hard on the frenzied charger's haunch. "Hyah!"

The horse was long-legged and half-mad, whether through pain or by temperament. Whatever injury it had sustained wasn't enough to slow its furious pace. As soon as they were clear of the trees, it stretched into a gallop, its strong, hard legs flying through the golden sand.

Annan leaned over its neck, both hands buried in its dark mane. Three-hundred paces out, his two pursuers were already losing ground. Flecks of blood flew from the charger's haunch with every stride, but no quarrel protruded from the muscle and the animal favored the leg only slightly, if at all.

"Come on, bucko," Annan whispered. "Get me out of this, and I'll name you myself."

The Templar and his man-at-arms were no longer in sight by the time the charger at last began to falter. High overhead, the sun was the only smudge in a sky of clearest blue. Its rays were dazzling and distorting but powerless to disguise the fact that only the line of hoofprints behind broke the endless stretch of sand.

The horse slowed to a choppy trot, then stopped, its breath rasping. The froth on the reins had turned the sickly pink of raw capon meat. Annan blew out a long sigh and leaned back, flipping the reins onto the animal's withers. The tremor in the horse's hindquarters told of its inevitable collapse.

"It's all right." He dismounted. "We tried." With a cough, the charger fell to its knees. Annan dropped his sword into the sand and stepped away as the animal struggled once to rise, then lay down on its side, belly heaving. The wound in the haunch, and an exit hole near the flank, still oozed onto its blood-blackened hide.

Annan dropped to one knee beside his sword and winced as his joints cracked. The sun beat down on his bare head, unrelenting. He would have to wait until dark before trying to move on, else the heat would kill him. He snorted. Not that it mattered. Unless he found another mount, or unless Marek used his penchant for disobeying orders to some use and came back for him, he wasn't likely to come through the desert in very good shape.

As soon as the first wisps of dusk's cooling veil cast themselves between the sun and the heat of the ground, Annan rolled out from beneath the dead charger's scant shadow. He walked until the bones of his feet felt as though they were grinding through his skin, and then he walked still more.

He *had* to walk.

Now that Hugh had seen Lady Mairead, he would not let her escape again, and Annan doubted the wounds he had inflicted upon the Norman would be enough to keep Hugh flat on his back very long. Hugh would find her, and Marek would never be able to defend her.

Marek would try, Annan gave him that much. He was an honorable youth despite his gringing. But he hadn't the nature of a warrior. Hugh would cut him down where he stood, and then there would be no one to stand between him and the countess. No one—unless this desert decided to spit Annan out whole again.

If it did spit him out, *he* would stand between them. Aye, he would stand and he would fight. Grimly, he hoisted the crude baldric he had fashioned from the saddle girth higher onto his shoulder and lengthened his stride.

When he had promised Lord William to deliver his wife safely to Orleans, it had been nothing more than a favor long overdue to an old friend. Now it was personal, whether he wanted it that way or not. William had been wise to make him cover her with his name. He would not let Hugh find Mairead. He would deliver her safely to Orleans if he had to storm Hell itself; and he would tear asunder anyone—man or devil— who dared threaten her.

And so he walked on.

It was not until the moon reached its zenith that a new sound interrupted the hum of the wind. He rocked to a stop, shoulders tensed. Again, he heard the shuffling of feet in the sand, the tired grunt of a horse.

Drawing his sword, he pivoted to face the newcomer. Someone was about to either have his destination slightly altered or his mount appropriated. The silhouette surfaced above the dune at his right hand and continued for a moment before the horse's head shot up and it snorted.

Annan took a step forward, lowering his sword to his side. He spoke, his tone the growl it inevitably became when he dropped his voice. "It's urgent that I reach Constantinople. Can—"

"Annan?" The voice was unmistakably Mairead's.

He halted, his intended words stopping up his throat for a moment. "My lady?" *She was safe. She had gotten away.* Something fiercely, surprisingly exultant hammered against his breastbone.

She flung herself from the saddle and then just stood there with her bare feet in the sand. "I feared you dead."

"Not yet." He took a step toward her, then stopped. "Where's Marek?"

"I don't know. Some of the men-at-arms followed us, and he tried to lead them away."

The pit of Annan's stomach hardened. "Is he dead?"

"I don't know. He was better mounted than the soldiers."

He grunted and lifted the baldric enough to sheathe his sword. "He's surprised me before, mayhap he'll surprise me again. Did you tell him about meeting at Stephen's?"

"Aye."

"And did he not point you in the right direction before he took off on this mad chase of his?"

"Aye, he did, but..."

"But what?"

"I came back for you." Moonlight flashed in the hollow of her throat as she raised her chin. "And since you're without a horse and in such urgent need of reaching Constantinople, it is well that I did."

"Wouldn't have been so well for you had you found Hugh de Guerrant instead."

Her chin lifted a little more. "Would it have made such a great difference if I met him here or on my way to this Lord Stephen's? It would have made no difference at all, so stop arguing."

"You wouldn't have been likely to meet him were you so far away as Lord Stephen's. They'll be too busy burying their dead tonight."

She stopped. "Their dead... How many?"

"Only two. But Lord Hugh is incapacitated, for the moment at least."

"And the Baptist?"

He came forward to take the courser's rein. The horse sniffed the loose collar of his tunic, then snorted, apparently satisfied that his bugbear was an old friend after all. "The Baptist," Annan spoke slowly, "seems to have more worthy protectors than that saber I gave him. The Templar took great care that he be unharmed."

"Why?"

"Mayhap because he is the one who led them to us? Why else should they know we had escaped the camp?"

She drew her cloak tighter round her shoulders. "Why say such things? The Baptist would not betray us."

He shrugged and stepped past her to the horse's haunch. "He's done it before—in Bari, the day before I journeyed here."

She spun to face him. "He wouldn't do that." But her tone wasn't one of denial, only incredulity.

Annan glanced at her. Perhaps meeting Gethin face to face had done more to convince her of his flaws than any of his own arguments. "Not to you, perhaps." He pushed the pillion straight and turned to offer his hand. "There may be a good man still buried within the Baptist, but he *is* buried. Trust me."

Her hand slid into his, and even through the darkness he could tell she was looking him in the eye. "I do trust you. Forgive me if I have been less than grateful."

He smiled, an expression he had cause to use far too seldom. "Best seek a higher court at which to beg your forgiveness, lady, for you never had cause to ask mine."

Through the shadows, a crooked smile blossomed on her face. "Thank you."

He pulled her closer and lifted her to the pillion. As he turned away, she stopped him with her hand on his shoulder. "Annan." She leaned over, her hair falling past her shoulder. His eyes followed its sway, and he fought the sudden urge to reach up and rub it between his fingers.

And why should he not? She was his wife.

The thought arose from the blank depths of his mind with an intensity that stunned him. He did not want a wife, did not need a wife. He was a condemned tourneyer, a wretch who despised himself worse with every passing day. He could not ask a woman—any woman—to share that with him, even had that been his intent in marrying Lord William's widow.

He dragged his eyes from the swinging shadow of her black hair, back up to her expectant face. He was taking her to Orleans, that was all. She would be safe there, and that would mark the end of his promise.

And then they could both return to their miserable, solitary existences. "What is it?" he said.

"What if this Templar recognized the Baptist?"

"He did."

"Then Roderic will kill him."

"Oh." He took a step toward the horse's shoulder, sliding out from beneath the light pressure of her hand. "You mean if he was recognized *as* the Baptist." The thought hadn't occurred to him during the heat of the battle.

He stepped into the stirrup and mounted, swinging his leg over the courser's withers. He dropped into the seat, and she put a hand on his arm. "Even if he is untrustworthy, as you say, we can hardly leave him to Roderic's wrath. His revival *has* borne good fruits."

He touched his heel to the courser's side and reined it northward.

"But I can hardly leave you either." He blew out a gusty breath, trying to ignore the whisper in the back of his mind that asked him why he would even consider going back for Gethin. The man had brought nothing but black omens since the day he had reappeared from the dead. Why the Baptist would collude with the lieutenants of a man he so desperately wanted killed made little sense. But Gethin was weaving a tangled web these days.

Mairead leaned closer, her chin just above his shoulder. "He saved our lives."

"More than once." The words passed his lips almost before they were a thought. Mairead referred to the infidel prison camp; but it was St. Dunstan's that Annan saw once again.

Once again.

How many more times would he have to be reminded, only to close his eyes and wait until the clattering skeletons of the past had faded from before his vision? He inhaled through clenched teeth. He was tired of remembering, tired of fighting to forget.

It was a cruel God that would not let him end this life. Few men could survive sixteen years on the fields of a tourney; most would have been cut down by now, torn free of the cords that bound them to painful life. But not Marcus Annan.

He grunted, and somehow even that pained him, deep down in the core of his body.

No, Marcus Annan hadn't died. He had survived, he had become a legend. He had become an unconquerable.

Was this the price he paid because he had withdrawn from before the face of a God he was no longer worthy to serve? A God who could no longer love him? The knot behind his breastbone hardened. Perhaps it was a God who had never loved him.

"Annan—"

He exhaled and reached up to rub the lines from his forehead. The dried blood of the flesh wound on his upper arm cracked and flaked, and he could feel the warm oozing as the cut reopened.

"What's wrong?" Her voice was soft, like the whisper of silk.

"Nothing. Only memories that won't be forgotten."

For a long while they rode in silence, the steady footfalls of the courser the only cadence in the wind's song. He thought Mairead asleep, and he was nearly so himself. The exhaustion of the last five days had finally penetrated every fiber of his muscles, every particle of his bones. He ached in every old wound, in every scar and divot, and his head felt too heavy to bear up.

I'm getting old, he realized, without any of the wry humor Marek would have injected in such a jab. He was getting old, and he was ready to die. His lip twisted. God grant it be so.

Behind him, Mairead stirred, and again her chin lifted above his shoulder. "Master Annan?"

"Aye."

"You said last night that some are called of God and some are not."

"And you said there are those who are called who do not come."

"Yes." She fell silent and drew back a little.

He looked back at her. "Were you referring to me with that statement, Lady Mairead?"

"Mayhap. I do not know your heart. And I do not know what memories you wish to forget, but—" She leaned forward again. "I have been cruel in some of my accusations, and I am sorry. I do not know your past, and I do not know what crosses you bear."

"No, you've said nothing wrong." He lowered his chin to his chest. "My past is a dark path better not trod by any."

"The past is over."

"The past, the future—it's all the same."

"That isn't true. With the dawn of every new day there is a new bend in the path, a new chance to turn aside from the past, if only we will take it. Are we not promised that by the blood of the Christ?"

"Some are promised. But not me."

"Why?"

In that single question was a depth that sounded and resounded against the hollowness he felt inside. "Because not everyone deserves the mercy of that blood."

They spoke no more after that. They rode into the night, weary step after weary step, until at last the eastern horizon began to bleed with the color of yet one more dawn that would bring no new bend in his path and no chance to alter the course of the future.

CHAPTER XIII

MAIREAD WOKE AS Annan drew rein at the gate of the estate belonging to Lord Stephen of Essex. Only a rim of red marred the smoky gray sky. The road, which would lead them to Constantinople when came the time, passed before the Englishman's walls and carried on, a mere flaw etched in the rippling hills.

The road lay empty. Marek, on his bay palfrey, was not to be seen. But that coin had two sides: Lord Hugh and the Templar weren't awaiting them either. And for that, Mairead was profoundly grateful.

A servant admitted them to the courtyard, gave the reins of the tired courser to a groomsman, and escorted them to the Great Hall. Mairead hugged her cloak round herself and stayed close at Annan's shoulder, almost brushing against him, as the servant inclined his head and asked them to be seated.

Annan made no motion to sit, and she stayed beside him.

"Did a Scottish lad come through here yesterday?" Annan asked.

The servant shook his head, the gray hair of his eyebrows flitting with the motion. "Your pardon, Master Knight, but I do not know. I think not."

Annan grunted, and the servant bowed once more before leaving. "Wretch."

Mairead didn't ask if the comment referred to the servant or to Marek. Annan had said nothing all morning; but she could sense the deep, knotting tension within him.

"Do you think they killed him?" she asked.

"Either that or he's on his way back to Maid Dolly in Glasgow." He moved to a narrow window between two tapestries.

She shivered. The heat of the day had yet to rise from the ground, and gooseflesh prickled her skin. "Can you trust this Lord Stephen to tell you if Marek did come?"

"I trust him. I saved his life once, a few years past. He had debts he couldn't pay back in Essex, and I helped him and his wife gain passage here." He turned to look her in the eye. "You'll be safe with them, until I can find Gethin."

The small oaken door in the corner near the hearth slammed open against the inside wall, and a stocky gentleman with the shading of wisdom in the hair above his ears stepped into the room. "Marcus Annan. By St. George, I never thought you'd come Crusading."

"Better me than moneylenders. Hello, Stephen."

The Englishman burst out laughing and came forward to offer his hand. "I'll toast that. You will, of course, indulge our hospitality?"

"Until the morrow. I have some unfinished business to tend back Jerusalem way."

Stephen lifted both eyebrows. "Ah?"

Annan ignored the implied question and turned back to where Mairead still stood, wrapped in the protective sheath of her cloak. "I would beg a boon, though. Until I return, will you and your wife grant sanctuary to this lady?"

Stephen looked her up and down, then withdrew his hand from Annan's that he might bow to her. "But of course. At your service, lady."

She inclined her head in return but didn't offer a hand for him to kiss. "I am in your debt, Sir."

"Not a'tall." He rose from the bow, clicked his heels in salute, and returned to the doorway. "Ducard!" The bushy-browed servant trotted into view. "Inform Lady Eloise I would like for her to join us." Stephen turned back to Mairead. "My wife will see to all the necessary arrangements."

"Thank you." She glanced to where Annan still stood in the same soiled tunic he had worn since the prison camp. A ribbon of blood marked a tear in the right sleeve, probably from the battle yesterday. His sword was girded at his side, and his right hand rode the hilt.

He had promised she would be safe with these people. She had nothing to fear with them.

Except losing him...

With a sigh, she reached to rub the stiffness in her shoulder. It was a strange thing to have no one in the world save a gruff, battered tourneyer... A tourneyer who had done everything in his power to protect her and had been more than willing to give his life for her.

He was a far cry from the man she had thought him. And now, just as she was discovering that, he was leaving, perhaps to be mangled on enemy swords and never to see her again. Suddenly, she wished she had never asked him to return for the Baptist. God would save the monk if he were innocent. And, if he were not, as Annan claimed, then wasn't it much better that Annan stay with her, his broad shoulders a buffer between her and the winds of a cruel world?

"I don't suppose you've seen my lad Marek out this way?" Annan asked Stephen.

"That fidgety runt? Nay, I thought you'd have let him go years past—indentured or not."

"He comes in handy on occasion."

"But now he's missing?"

"We were separated yesterday. He was supposed to meet me here."

Stephen shook his head. "Sympathies, but he has yet to arrive. Likely he got it in the back, eh?"

Annan's jaw tightened: again the swirl of emotions in his eyes. Mairead caught another glimpse of the hard painful knot buried somewhere inside, and her chest ached.

To wake each morning, as he did, with no hope of better things to come, no knowledge of acceptance by a higher love, would leave even a better man in a mire of darkness. She longed to lay her hands on those knots that bound him so tightly and to smooth them into nothingness.

She had the inexplicably ridiculous desire to hold this battered warrior in her arms, as she would a child, and sing away his pain.

But Marcus Annan would not be held, and his was not a pain that could be sung away.

She let her arms fall to her sides, feeling suddenly as if she had no more strength left in her at all.

The door banged open again, and a silver-headed woman marched into the room. Quick gray eyes took in the two visitors and brightened when they landed on Mairead. She bowed to the room at large and turned back to Annan. "Master Annan—delighted to see you, of course. I rather expected you to be dead by now."

He smiled, but no flash of good humor lit his eyes. "You and I both, Lady Eloise." He turned to Mairead and held out a hand. "May I present the Lady Mairead."

"Indeed you may." The flush of Lady Eloise's cheeks glowed even beneath the lead base she had obviously used to lighten her complexion. "And I hope you continue presenting her for a long bit yet." She looked at Mairead. "You'll forgive me, my dear, but this heathen land hardly produces feminine companionship in great droves."

"Lord Stephen has granted that she remain with you while I pursue a personal matter," Annan said.

Eloise fluttered a hand in his direction. "Get on with you, laddie, and good riddance. You can leave her to me as long as you like." She returned her attention to Mairead. "How long a journey has it been?"

Mairead bowed slightly. "Since Tyre, madam."

"Tyre! And here I stand gossiping, with you exhausted on your feet. Come with me, and let these knaves bore themselves with tales of their inept war." She cast a glance at Annan's unshaven face and torn and bloody tunic. "Though if Lord Stephen has any civility, he'll give Master Annan into a servant's hands ere long as well."

With Mairead's elbow clamped between two ring-adorned hands, Eloise shepherded her to the door.

Mairead wasn't quite out of the room when Lord Stephen spoke. "An admirable woman. You surprise me again, Annan. I'd no thought of your taking a wife."

BEHOLD THE DAWN – 161

She stopped. Would he tell Stephen the truth? He had not told Marek.

By unspoken agreement, they had yet to disclose their marriage. Lord William had placed her under Annan's name to protect her from *her* enemies—certainly not to draw skeptical glances from those who knew him.

And yet…

His gaze shifted past Lord Stephen's face to meet hers, and for that moment she wondered what it would be like were they to drop the charade and tell the world she was his to do with as he liked.

Her lower lip crept between her teeth. *And he liked only to protect and honor me.*

"No," he said. His gaze pulled from hers, and the connection snapped and shattered, falling to the floor between them like so much broken glass. "I am entrusted to grant her safe passage to Orleans. She is the wife of William of Keaton."

Mairead turned away, the muscles in her back clutching with renewed intensity.

Lady Eloise waited outside the doorway, her hands folded into the wide sleeves of her kirtle. "Hmph. I thought you too nice a maid to be lying in Marcus Annan's arms. Come, dear heart, no frowns while you're under my roof. By the saints, life will be beautiful again come the time we've finished our fun and I must send you back to your Lord William."

Mairead followed in Lady Eloise's wake, trying to absorb the Englishwoman's chatter. But somehow, as she was ushered through the hallways and up the twisting stairs to a bedchamber that was huge and cold in all its English splendor, she heard not a word—only the dull beating of her heart beneath her cloak.

———————

The late meal was served in the afternoon's fourth hour. Annan, too restless to sleep, had spent the day pacing the upper ramparts, watching for a rider on a bay palfrey. With every passing hour that brought no sign of Marek, the frown lines in his brow deepened.

Now, as he stood in the noise of the Great Hall, behind the seat Stephen had indicated, he gritted his teeth in frustration. It was Marek he should be searching for. Not Gethin.

But Marek would have to wait. Mairead—and now Gethin—took precedence. Annan gritted harder, his back teeth stabbing pain down his jaw. If that lad was out dawdling somewhere, Annan would yank every hair from his loitering head.

From where he stood behind the seat of honor in the middle of the high table, Stephen leaned in Annan's direction. "My wife would doubtless have done worse than call me a knave had I disturbed your rest this afternoon, but I would like the opportunity to discuss these plans of yours sometime this even."

Annan nodded.

"An English courier rode in an hour ago." Stephen pointed to the tables on the cavernous floor below, where some two score servants waited to seat themselves. The courier was distinguishable from the others only by the flowered blue livery of King Richard, which bore considerable evidence of a long journey. He seemed to be having trouble communicating with his Syrian neighbors and was gesturing with his hands to explain some point of confusion. To Annan, it looked as though he were recounting the storied proficiency of Saladin's mounted archers.

"He's brought some rather interesting news from the Crusade," Stephen said.

"So I see."

The double doors at the room's far end ground open, pulled by two lads, and the crowd below quieted.

Stephen straightened away from Annan. "Ah, the ladies. At last."

Annan followed his gaze to where Lady Eloise, garbed in scarlet, her wimple embroidered in gold, promenaded between the lower tables. Her keen eyes sparkled like a child's.

Mairead walked behind her.

In silence, Annan watched. The reason for Eloise's glee was evident: Mairead had been transformed. Blue the color of midnight illuminated her fair skin better than the sun's rays could ever do. With her skirt trailing her like the last whispers of night, she walked like a queen.

His eyes drifted to her dark hair. No longer the long, unruly veil that had blown in the hot winds, it was now a crown of braids piled on the back of her head. An absurd resentment for Lady Eloise seized in his chest.

Mairead's eyes found his, and for a moment the queen disappeared and she was again the frightened girl who had ridden through the long nights with her head against his shoulder. Her lip found its place between her teeth, and he knew she was trying to read his expression, trying to understand the flash of anger that had burned there for a moment.

He knew she wanted a smile, the encouragement of a friend among strangers. But he could not. If he said anything to her now, it would surely surface in the growl that had caused her to distance herself from him so many times.

He turned to Lady Eloise as she mounted the steps to the high table. At the trumpet flourish, played by the lips of a servant lad no higher than Annan's hip, she took the seat at Annan's right, placing herself between him and Lord Stephen. Mairead sat at Stephen's other side.

After a visiting monk had invoked the blessing and as the servers began bearing in the platters of capon and wood pigeon that would be their first course, Eloise leaned over to speak to him. "You may know, Master Annan, that my opinion of you has never been very high. But this is twice now you've done me good service. Lady Mairead is delightful. I should have died for want of companionship before winter had you not brought her when you did."

"How fortunate."

"Indeed. And now I should like to offer you a proposal." She tipped back for a moment, until the server had finished heaping their trenchers with the fragrant meat. "I should like," she said, "to relieve you of your responsibility to this girl."

Annan reached for his wooden drinking bowl, which another servant had filled with a mulled wine.

"She has told me enough of her story for me to know she will be safest from her enemies if she is delivered to this St. Catherine's with all haste."

"Indeed."

"And since you can hardly deliver her anywhere with any haste while you are pursuing your business back in the Holy Land, I should like to offer our services in seeing her safely into Christian hands. Stephen already plans a journey to Constantinople within a few days."

"And what of my promise to Lord William of Keaton?"

"Explain it to him. I'm sure he'll agree it is the best thing for her. I heard of him often when we were yet in England, and I know him to be as sensible a man as can be made."

Annan stared at the cloves drowning in his wine. "And what does the Lady Mairead say of this?"

"She seemed content to leave the matter in your hands, but undoubtedly she wants to be returned to her husband as soon as possible."

His lip twitched. Returned to which husband? The one that was already in the grave—or the one that was walking dead? "Yes, of course."

Eloise flipped her long sleeves off the table and dipped her fingers into her trencher's mound of oily meat. For a moment, Annan didn't stir. He smiled a sardonic little smile that meant nothing to anyone but himself and tossed back the contents of his bowl. He set it back on the table and turned his head just enough to see Mairead, two seats down. Her eyes, larger in her face now that her hair was caught back, darted away from Lord Stephen. Her lip crept between her teeth, and Annan saw the tiny bead of blood where she had punctured the skin.

"Yours is a strange kind of honor," Lord Stephen said from his fur-piled seat behind Annan. The smile in his voice dimmed what might otherwise have been an affront.

Annan, arms crossed against his chest, stared into the flames that snarled within the hearth of the now empty Great Hall. They were flames that mirrored those within himself. Telling Stephen his reasons for returning for Gethin hardly made them sound any more satisfactory. "The Baptist was once a friend. I can't leave him to his fate, even if he is guilty of falling into his own trap. Besides, where I find Gethin, I may also find Marek."

Stephen's chair creaked as he pushed himself to his feet and walked up to stand beside Annan. "Well then, I wish you Godspeed, and I don't doubt that you'll need it. Any idea where you'll begin this search of yours?"

"In Acre, I suppose, or wherever the Crusaders are camped."

"May I suggest Arsuf?"

Annan glanced at him.

"That courier I was telling you about—he's brought word of a great battle near there, in the plains between Acre and Jerusalem."

"Did he say who won?"

"The Christians, led brilliantly by King Richard. Though the courier may perhaps have been a bit prejudiced."

"The king's left his sickbed then." He rubbed absently at his sore shoulder.

"Yes. And the French king has returned home. His own illness and a number of petty quarrels with Richard overwhelmed his spirit of piety, apparently. He did leave the majority of his force behind, however."

Annan sighed, calculating the days it would take him to ride to Arsuf and back, even without delays. "I'll leave at daybreak tomorrow." He pressed his middle finger in the corner of his eye and held it there, trying to relieve the pull of weariness. "I'll have to borrow a horse."

"I'll have to give you a horse, you mean." Stephen's smile grew a little crooked. "This saving one's life business is rather profitable, isn't it?"

"On occasion."

Stephen chuckled and laid a hand on his arm. "Indeed. And what about Lady Mairead? My wife beleives she would be better off if we provided her an escort for the rest of her journey. Business takes me to Constantinople in a few days' time. Eloise feels it would be wise for me to take Mairead with me."

"So she told me."

"You disagree?"

Annan let his hand slide from his eyes down over his mouth. He stared harder into the fire, watching the blackened logs flake beneath the heat. "I don't know." He met Stephen's gaze. "You don't think she'd be safe here until I return?"

"You insult me, Master Knight. She's safer within these walls than she was in the hills with half a score of men-at-arms trailing her."

"They're trailing her still, Stephen."

He waved a dismissive hand. "You have my pledge that she will be safe until you return or until you send word that she is to go on without you." He lowered his hand to grasp Annan's. "That much I owe you. Trust me."

"I do." He turned from the fire. "And if Marek happens to arrive at your gates, make him sleep in the cold a few nights for his tardiness."

Stephen's smile deepened. "Decidedly."

Mairead stood at her narrow slit of a window, watching as rosy dawn dispelled the dark clouds of night, waiting for the gates below to open and for a knight on a borrowed horse to ride away from her. The chamber's heavy door grated open, and she turned to see Annan ducking his head to pass through the doorway.

"I've come to take my leave, lady. Lord Stephen has lent me a horse."

Suddenly cold, she folded her arms over her chest, one hand reaching to finger the crucifix that hung from her neck. She had been watching for the last hour, aching at the thought that he was leaving her here. But now she almost wished he had just gone. She didn't want to say goodbye.

The silence hung between them. She refused to look at him.

"You'll be safe here," he said at last. "Lord Stephen has promised he will guard you as though you were his own daughter."

She bit down hard on her lip. And now had come the time when she was to curtsy low and thank him kindly for his services—and then release him from his promise.

In the pressing blackness of the night, buried deep within the bed of muslin-covered straw, she had lain awake, fighting desperate battles with herself over what she was now about to do.

When they had parted the night before at the door of Mairead's chamber, Lady Eloise had whispered that, if Mairead would but say the word, Annan would not be returning for her after his search for the Baptist. Lord Stephen and Lady Eloise would see her delivered safely to Orleans; Master Annan's services were required no more.

If Mairead's heart had turned to stone at the thought of Annan's leaving for the few weeks needed to free the Baptist, it had died a cold death upon Lady Eloise's calm utterance. She should release him from his promise. She knew she should. He was no longer needed. She would be just as safe under the protection of Lord Stephen. She had no reason to cling to him.

No reason except the black fear that welled in the depth of her stomach at the thought of his leaving her.

"Master Annan—"

His face was unreadable. "Lady?"

She made herself hold her eyes to his. "Lady Eloise has proposed that it be Lord Stephen who provides for the next leg of my journey. She suggests I release you from your vow. You need not come back for me." A dangerous tremble filled her throat. "Thank you, Master Annan."

The scar on his cheek twitched, then stilled. His shoulders straightened. "Farewell, lady." He kissed her hand, and when he rose again, something in the iron set of his eyes had softened just slightly.

For a moment, she didn't breathe. He could ride away from her so very easily; he could leave with his mind clear of any debt he thought he owed William; he could forget about the blood and the sweat and the pain she had brought upon him here in the land of the Holy One; he could forget even to wonder if she lived or died.

He straightened to his full height, until her head could barely top his shoulder. "Lady Mairead, the vow belongs to me—not Stephen. I will come back for you."

The sun and the moon and all the stars exploded inside her chest. Slowly, she let her breath out. "Thank you." The words refused to rise above a whisper.

He turned to go. His expression was grim once again, and a new line creased his forehead. "Look for me within the month."

"I will pray for you."

He stopped at the door and looked back at her, almost as if he wanted to tell her not to trouble. But he said nothing, only nodded.

And then he was gone. She stared after him, her arms clamped across her chest, her lips pressed together. She would not weep; not a tear would she shed. Not over this tourneyer.

This bloody, bloody tourneyer...

A tear slid down her cheek and fell, warm, against her hand. She turned to the window and pressed her shoulder against the wall. Her tears fell unchecked as the gates creaked open and Annan galloped away.

The chamber door swung inward, and Lady Eloise came to stand at her shoulder. "Away he rides, I see. And why this wet face, Lady Mairead?"

She didn't look at the other woman. With chin lifted, she faced the wind that chilled every tear where it glistened on her face. "Is it not right for a woman to mourn in the absence of her husband?"

CHAPTER XIV

HE DAY AFTER Annan left, the servant Ducard pre-
sented himself at the door of the living chamber where
Mairead sat plucking the strings of a long-necked lute.
"A Master Peregrine Marek wishes your attendance,
m'lady."

She dropped the lute beneath her stool and sprang to her feet.
"Marek—"

With a resigned lift of his heavy brows, Ducard stepped back, and
Marek sauntered into the room. "Greetings, lady."

"Marek, you blessed lad! We feared you dead."

He kissed her offered hand, eyes sparkling in his ruddy face. "Not
I, fair one."

She pulled her hand free. "You're a rogue, Peregrine Marek."

"Of course." He tugged off his cap and scratched his fingers
through his tousled hair. "But a lucky one, I must say."

"Indeed. How is it you're not dead—or marching back to Acre in
chains?"

"Quick wit will ever conquer brute strength. And a fast horse is
also rather useful."

"Not fast enough to get you here before Annan and I."

He shrugged and walked over to the bench in the inglenook. No
fire burned at the moment, only sleepy embers, buried in the covering

of ash left over from the night. "I had to stay out of sight for a while." He plopped into the middle of the bench and spread his arms on either side of the seat's back. "Where's Annan?"

Mairead sat across from him. "He's not here."

"Not out looking for me, is he?"

"The Baptist was captured during the battle. Annan's gone back for him."

"Go on with you, lassie. Master Annan's not going to risk his head for that raving mooncalf."

"But he has." She rubbed her hand along her leg, her fingers tingling against the softness of the blue silk gown. She wondered how much of his reason for going had been her prompting and how much had been this innate desire he seemed to have for rescuing the helpless.

Marek huffed. "Why is it he can't keep himself clear of trouble for a few days without me? It's beyond me ken, I tell you. I suppose this means I'm off again to save his hide, and me without sleep and vittles for two days."

She lifted a shoulder. "He thought you dead."

"Far from it, dear lady, far from it—so why this long face?" He leaned forward to chuck her under the chin.

The lad's insolence knew no bounds, but the gesture was so flippant and brotherly as to draw a smile instead of the rebuke it deserved.

He grinned. "You're much more beautiful with a smile."

"You're not only a rogue, you're a knave."

"You wound me to the quick, lady. Please tell me you don't also think me as much a troll as you do my master?"

The smile disappeared. "Hardly." She returned her gaze to her lap and smoothed the wrinkles she had created in her skirt. Tears gathered in the back of her eyes, and she was surprised to find she no longer despised herself for it. "I fear for him."

Marek leaned back again, the spread of his arms just long enough to touch the edges of the bench's back. "Takes a mighty hefty blade to put that life in any danger. Tourneymen can't dent him, the Saracens couldn't do more than poke a hole in his arm, and he fought off all those blokes t'other day and still managed to get you back here before I could. That should be evidence enough to lay your fears at rest."

She didn't look up. "He's only a man. All men must die."

"You fret yourself too much, lady. I'll be off at first light no doubt, and I'll have him cleared out of this mess in a flash, eh?"

"Nay, you're to stay with me until he returns." And he *would* return. *Holy Father, may he return to me!* She did not know what future she might face if he did not. She did not know if she wanted to face the future if he did not.

Marek sat up a little straighter. "Ah, well that's more as it should be. I say, it's about time he gave the devoted slave a little ease and repose."

The door opened, and Lady Eloise entered, her rust-brown skirts billowing like a sail. Mairead rose, and Marek leaned to peer around the corner of the inglenook. Eloise stopped and frowned. "Who's this?"

He stood and bowed with a flourish of his cap. "Your ladyship, may I introduce myself as Peregrine Mar—"

"Marek." Her frown deepened. "Aye, I remember. Well, get along with you, boy, and don't trouble the lady any longer."

"Trouble her, gracious one? I assure—"

"Oh, get out with you. One would think you believed yourself a troubadour, 'stead of a sharp-faced swindler."

That, apparently, brought him back to his senses. Living with a man like Annan, who made up his own rules as he went along, hadn't likely been a very good lesson in gentle manners. He shut his mouth, bowed once more—this time without the flourish—and ambled to the door, tugging his cap back over his ears. Before he left the room, he turned to glance at Mairead, such a look of long-suffering on his face that she couldn't help but smile.

Lady Eloise shook out her skirts and glided over to where Mairead had dropped the lute. "That rogue Annan did a good turn in pulling that lad from the streets, but, merciful Heaven, what a villain." She picked up the instrument and ran the backs of her fingers down the strings.

Mairead sat back down in the inglenook. "Annan's done many good turns."

Eloise sniffed. "Aye, and he's also created his share of villains. Men like Marcus Annan are more trouble than they're worth."

Mairead spun back to her feet, ducking out of the inglenook. "You say that so smugly. But you and your husband would not be here today were it not for him."

Eloise clucked. "My dear girl, he's only another tourneyer, no better or worse than the lot of them."

"Then you do not know him." Mairead snapped the words without thinking. No, Eloise did not know him. But did she? What if he knew the extent of her shame, of the scars in her past that had brought her and Lord William to this heathen land? Would he still have been so willing to close the door she had opened to release him from his promise?

With her eyebrows lifted, Eloise looked rather too feline. "Child, you place too much trust in the man. The Church has condemned the tourneys for three score years. The Devil's mark is on men like him. I'm not even sure the Crusade could absolve him."

Mairead looked at her levelly. Her breath came in quick tugs, but it did not clutter the calm of her voice. She had never thought herself capable of such calmness. "There is always redemption."

Eloise laid the lute on the stool where Mairead had been sitting before Marek came in. The movement was deliberate, final. "Not for the likes of him. Even God Himself is not always merciful."

"He is when one seeks His mercy."

"That man doesn't seek mercy. He's more interested in the blood on his sword and the gold in his purse." Eloise tugged her bodice, the movement seeming to yank straight all the lines in her face. "What would your husband think were he to hear these things you say?"

Mairead's breath slipped past her lips. "I hope he would agree with me."

For three days Annan rode a hard course due south. He entered the fertile Orontes valley as purple dusk began to burn the horizon's edge, and immediately, he knew something was different. In the trampled sand only paces to the east were horses' hoofprints. Not camels, not donkeys, not oxen. Horses. And in this time of war, only soldiers rode horses.

Filling his lungs with the cool of evening, he nodded to himself and turned his bay charger's head aside. Under the shelter of darkness, he would discover whether the horses' riders wore the white of

Mohammedan muslin over their chain mail or if they labored under the gay caparisons of the Knights Templars and the House de Guerrant.

He tracked them until it was too dark to see, and then he lifted his head to see the orange glow of fire against the moonless sky. He smiled. Leaving the tired charger secured in the darkness of a juniper's shade, he checked his weapons and started forward, all but invisible in the darkness, his footfalls silent beneath the mutterings of the wind.

He almost missed a sentry posted some fifty paces from the fire, but the murmured voices of one Frank to another as they changed the watch stopped him in his tracks. He kept an eye on the retreating shadow until the man had seated himself by the fire. Then, rising from his crouch, his dagger slipping from its sheath, he crept near enough to hear the shuffling of the man's feet.

With a speed born only in battle, he caught the man's shoulder and spun him up against his own chest. The Frank's grunt was cut off by the dagger against his neck. Annan shoved his jaw alongside the man's ear. "You'll be silent if you value your life."

The Frank's panting told well enough that he had no desire for his blood to be let by the blade of an unknown assassin.

They were five paces from the fire when the seated men-at-arms caught sight of their approach. Annan kept his blade tight against his prisoner's neck and waited until the two knights had completed a general scramble to find their weapons. "Hold your blades, laddie bucks. I'd have a word with your leader before you get yourselves killed."

The Templar straightened from his defensive posture. "Marcus Annan. We meet again."

"Indeed. My heart sings with the pleasure." He cast a quick glance around the camp. Only two men-at-arms accompanied the Templar. Hugh and those who had given chase to Marek were not to be seen. Gethin stood at the edge of the firelight, having also risen in the moment of alarm. His face was passive, his arms folded into his sleeves. But the dancing firelight could not hide the twist of his eyebrow.

The Templar came forward a step but did not lower his sword. "Be assured, the feeling is reciprocated, Master Knight. But perhaps you haven't been informed: we were to follow you, not you us."

"He that diggeth a pit shall fall into it, Templar."

Gethin's brow lifted a bit more.

The Templar shrugged. "As you will. You only make the task easier for us."

The other man-at-arms began inching forward.

Annan held his ground. "If you've not learned your lesson from our last encounter, I'll be more than happy to teach it again." He looked at the approaching man-at-arms. "Hold fast, laddie." The man took another step before stopping uncertainly.

The Templar frowned, then lowered his sword. "All right. Have your say."

"I've come for the monk."

Gethin remained passive, but Annan thought he saw a flicker of confusion tighten his brow.

"The monk?"

"Aye, grant the monk's freedom, and we shall all be spared the trouble of killing each other at this late hour."

"Why should you want him? He told me he was a passing acquaintance, merely a fellow traveler."

The Frank in his arms twisted his head, and Annan pressed harder with the blade. "What the bishop does with his prisoners is not something I'd wish upon even the most passing of acquaintances."

The Templar's head tilted back warily. "The bishop?"

"Aye, I know you answer to Bishop Roderic. If stupidity was a requirement when you hired me that night in Acre, you should have looked elsewhere."

"I should have looked elsewhere anyway. I had been told you were a man of honor, but apparently I was misinformed. Men of honor do not decamp with their hire jingling in their purses unfulfilled."

"I promised you only Matthias of Claidmore. The others were not part of my agreement."

Gethin's expression froze. He limped forward, his hands dropping from his sleeves and revealing the thick rope that bound his wrists. "With every new discovery, I find you sinking a bit lower."

"Do I indeed?" Annan didn't take his eyes from the Templar. "Well, Master Knight, do I regain my fellow traveler, or does the dying begin with this unfortunate fellow?" He bumped the blade against the corner of the man-at-arms's jawbone.

The Templar's expression hardened. "I was sent to kill you."

"So be it." Annan's hand tightened on the dagger's hilt. The Frank stiffened in his arms.

"Wait." Gethin slid forward between the Templar and the other man-at-arms. "Ask him *why* he was sent to kill you."

Annan flicked his gaze in the Templar's direction.

The man shifted, the shadows of the fire catching against his rigid jaw. "Because you betrayed Roderic."

To that, Annan could only laugh. "Forgive me if I save my surprise for a more worthy occasion."

Gethin took another step. "Roderic fears you've betrayed him to Matthias."

He glanced at the Templar. "Is that true?"

The knight nodded.

"Why?"

"I don't know."

Annan narrowed his eyes.

"I tell you the truth," the Templar insisted. "He fears him, but why I don't know. Matthias knows something about his past."

"How much does he fear Matthias?" Gethin's question was for the Templar, but his eyes burned into Annan's.

"More than any man—save the Baptist."

"And the Baptist he fears *because* of Matthias." Triumph gleamed in Gethin's face. "Now what do you say, Marcus Annan?"

For a moment, he wondered how much more self-respect it would cost him to leave Gethin with the Templar. Between Gethin and the money Roderic had offered for him, the gold would certainly be the more agreeable.

He released his hold on the man-at-arms. Keeping one hand choked down on the Frank's collar, he allowed him to step away to the end of the blade. "I say what I have said from the beginning. Free the monk, and I'll let you return alive to your unholy master. Else let us end this now."

Firelight flickered in the Templar's eyes. "First, I would ask a question of you." He lowered his sword still more, until its point almost touched the ground. "Do you know why my master fears this Matthias?"

Annan said nothing for a long moment. Gethin stared at him, a silent, mocking challenge burning in his eyes.

"If Father Roderic fears Matthias of Claidmore, it is because he fears judgment upon a soul that is worthy of all the fires of Hell."

"You are a follower of the Baptist?"

Annan glanced at Gethin. "Nay. But if he is a heretic for such beliefs, then his heresy is also mine."

A smile flashed across Gethin's face, but Annan ignored him. "You do not know the man you serve, Templar. You will never win God's battles so long as your lords are murderers and whoremongers."

The Templar shook his head. "Bishop Roderic will be beatified when he dies."

"And that makes him less a murderer or a whoremonger?"

"Perhaps he has repented."

"Then why does he fear judgment?"

The Templar lifted his face, a look of caution in his eyes.

"If you don't know the answer, ask him. Ask him why such a man as he should wear the holy robes of God's appointed." Annan took a step, pushing the man-at-arms along with the point of the dagger. "And ask yourself why you pledge your allegiance to this man when he calls for you to destroy the blood of innocents simply because such are his enemies."

They stared at each other a long time, until at last a log in the fire crumpled into a sparking, snapping mass of embers. The Templar sighed. "All this from a tourneyer?"

Some of the tautness ebbed from Annan's shoulders. "Aye. All this from a tourneyer." He had not spoken convictions such as these for many a long year. Some part of him had forgotten he even believed them.

The Templar turned to the other man-at-arms. "Fetch the monk's donkey." He turned back to Annan. "You may have your traveling companion, Master Annan." He sheathed his sword. "If you turn out to be a messenger of the Most High, I will thank you. If not, then I suspect we will be meeting again."

Annan shoved his man-at-arms forward. Gethin, his hands freed by the Templar, met him with donkey in tow; they left the camp without a backward glance.

Nothing was said until they returned to Annan's horse and both had reined their mounts northward.

"Have you changed your mind then, Marcus Annan?" For the first time since they had met in Bari, Gethin's voice did not bear its hard edge.

Annan rubbed the back of his neck. He wearied of rebuffing the man's persistence. "The years have not changed me so much as to make me fickle in my decisions."

Gethin reined his donkey close enough that his knee pressed against Annan's. "You said he deserved God's judgment."

"*God*'s judgment, Gethin! You are mistaken in this belief of yours that there is vengeance yet to be paid out for what happened sixteen years ago. What happened then was wrong. Reconstructing what happened at St. Dunstan's will not make it right."

"Won't it?" His voice was cold, heavy, like the fall of a stone from a battlement. "Sin begets sin. Haven't you of all men learned that?"

"Aye, and I have paid the price for my sins every day of my life. Who's to say Father Roderic does not the same?"

"You believe that?"

"Nay." He sighed from the depths of his soul. "I do not. He is hungry for blood even still."

"He is hungrier. People die everyday now because Matthias did not exact the full price from him sixteen years ago. No longer is he a mere abbot, able only to squeeze in his fist the lives of monks and penitents and villagers. Now he is a bishop." Gethin's voice dropped to a hiss. "Now he holds armies, lords, *kings* in his hand. That kind of corrupt power can be protected against only one way."

"No." For sixteen years, Annan had striven to put the distance that only time can bring between himself and the crimes of St. Dunstan's. He would not be drawn back into them now. "I will not. Besides, you forget—Matthias is dead. He will not be your tool to find vengeance."

Gethin laughed. "You delude yourself, Marcus Annan. Matthias is not dead. And I *will* find him." He exhaled, the breath barking in the back of his throat. "Grieve you though it may."

Annan rode with his back stiff, his fingers so tight on his sword hilt that they trembled from lack of blood.

Gethin reined the donkey aside. "When that day comes, perhaps we shall find that we are once again on the same side. Farewell."

The donkey lumbered some dozen paces before Annan again forced his tongue to speak. "Gethin."

The Baptist did not stop.

"What happened to Marek?"

"I know not. The men-at-arms returned empty-handed."

"What about Lord Hugh?"

"He lives—unhappily for you. He took the other knights and has gone on a mission of his own." Off to Annan's right, the shadow of the donkey stopped. "Be wary. Bishop Roderic is most dangerous through his pawns. You may have cooled the Templar's zeal tonight, but Hugh de Guerrant is a blade of another metal. Perhaps he will yet teach you the truth of my words about the bishop's ravaging."

For a moment there was only the silence of night. Then the donkey's jostling steps resumed, and Annan was left to sit in the dark, alone, until even the hoofbeats were only a memory in the darkness.

CHAPTER XV

IN THE BLACK depths of midnight Mairead woke with her sweat cold upon her scalp. She had heard his voice. Hugh de Guerrant's voice. She was certain of it.

She rolled onto her back and lay still, her breath trapped in her chest as she listened. Only the scampering footsteps of a mouse and the night wind purring outside her window marred the silence. She lay back against the pillow, her blankets rolled down to her waist. Had she imagined it? Could it have been only a dream?

Outside, the stamp of a horse's foot made her heart catch. Carefully, shooting a quick glance at her bedchamber's closed door, she rolled to the bed's edge and slid from beneath the blankets. The cold stone of the floor sent an immediate chill up her spine, but she hardly noticed. At the window, she peered around the corner. No moon lit the clouds, but she could see the silhouettes of horses in the yard below. One tossed its head, bit clanking.

"No…" The word was soft, a reflex. She twisted her neck to see the sky, forgetting there was no moon, no stars, no light on the horizon to tell her the hour. But she knew it was too early. The hard, cold knot in the deepest part of her stomach told her it was too early for vassals to be about or for the lord himself to have returned from his trip to Constantinople.

It could be Annan.

The thought seized her, then fled. It was not Annan; it could not be Annan. She would not have confused his voice with Lord Hugh's.

Muffled footsteps slapped the hall outside her door, and she froze. She should have thought of finding a weapon before this, should have located a poniard that could now have been within easy reach. She would not be taken without a struggle, not this time. The price for her soul would be a high one.

But the footsteps did not stop at her door. Farther down the hall, she could hear the rap of a bony hand against a door. Lady Eloise's door, she guessed.

"Lady—" The voice was that of the servant Ducard.

Again, a horse stirred outside, and she turned her head in time to hear the clank of mail armor and the low voices of men. The coiled tension in her muscles shot loose. She shoved away from the window, her bare feet silent against the floor that lay between her and the chair across which the maidservant had cast her clothes.

She did not know these men or their purpose. Perhaps she had only dreamed Hugh's voice. But she would not stay here until she knew. She was not safe here. The honor of the nobleman could not protect her so well as the arm of the tourneyer. If she were to die, it would not be defenseless in the silence of night.

With hands as cold as the stone beneath her feet, she dressed herself in the blue gown from the day before and found her cloak folded atop the wooden coffer at the foot of the bed. Clutching its rough bulk to her chest, she crept to the door and listened at the crack.

Lady Eloise's door opened and her footsteps clacked down the hall. "Did you inform him that gentlemen do not rouse ladies from their sleep? Not even in this heathen land is such accepted! Did you tell him that?"

"Yes, mistress. But he said it was urgent."

Mairead lowered her face to the warm pile of cloak in her arms. It smelled of horse and wind and sun.

"Urgent, my eye." They passed Mairead's chamber door.

"I thought it might be about his lordship. The Norman did not say."

Mairead closed her eyes. Then it *was* him! *Oh God, why?* Was this fate to be her destiny?

The footsteps faded once more into stillness. She inhaled, swelling her lungs, then yanked open the door.

The hall before her loomed silent and blind. Casting her cloak over her shoulders, she threw one searching glance behind her in the direction taken by Lady Eloise and her servant, then fled to the narrow stairwell that would lead her to the cool freedom of the night.

She ran round the back of the keep, the silk and wool of her clothing whispering as she ran. At the west wall, she stopped. The horses were still in the yard, heads low, their riders either inside with their master or slouching in the shadows. She wrapped herself in her cloak and forced herself to creep across the empty ground that separated her from the stables. Neither the horses nor the men-at-arms stirred.

The stable was dark and warm with the heavy smell of animals. "Marek?" she whispered too softly for him to hear, knowing that at least half a dozen others might sleep here during the warm months. Breathing between her teeth, she crept down the row of stalls. Airn lifted his dark head over his door and blew through his nostrils. In the stall beside him, Marek's palfrey, Duncan, shifted in the straw.

She leaned over the door. "Marek?"

The dark shape at the bay's hind feet did not move, but she could hear him snoring softly. "Marek."

Outside, one of the men-at-arms' voices drifted across the yard. Footsteps sounded against the flagstones, drawing near to the stable.

She eased open the stall door and pushed past Duncan to crouch at Marek's shoulder. "Wake up."

Her hand on his arm jerked him out of his sleep. He reared up on an elbow, his eyes squinted, one hand scrabbling through the straw for his sword. "Eh— what?"

"We must leave here now. He's come— Lord Hugh has come—"

He blinked and coughed. "He's what?"

"He's *come*." She could have slapped him right across his rosy cheek.

The footsteps were almost to the door. A sword clattered free of its sheath.

Someone called from back in the yard: "Where is it you're off to?"

The other, so near that Mairead started, replied, "Thought I saw someone come in here."

Marek pushed himself up higher, and his short blade flashed in his hand. "What do you want me to do?" he whispered.

She *wanted* him to find Annan, to make him ride back to her as he had promised and place himself between her and her foes once more. But that was hardly an option. She clenched her teeth and listened. The man stopped just outside the roof that covered the open front of the stalls. If he would just stay there...

But he didn't. He took another step, then another, his strides falling with the soft regularity of a man who did not wish to be heard. Mairead pushed Marek back down and leaned so near that her lips brushed his ear. "If he discovers me, stay here. Saddle the horses. If I don't find my way back to you—" She stopped, trying to swallow the thump of her heart in her throat.

The man-at-arms paused at one of the stalls and said something in French. From the tone of his murmur, she could tell he spoke to a horse.

"If I don't come back, find Annan."

She pulled away, until she could see the glint of Marek's wide-open eyes. He wouldn't like running away from her, and Annan would be furious with him. But by himself Marek didn't stand a chance against these men. Hugh would tear him limb from limb without a pause of conscience, and then she would be truly lost.

Better to die with the hope that someone was coming for her.

Airn snorted, and again the man-at-arms spoke in a hushed tone. He was one stall away. One stall.

She shifted in the straw so that she was almost under the palfrey's mud-flecked belly. *Blessed Father, let him pass me by...*

A hand, framed in a mail sleeve, reached through the darkness above the stall door and Duncan shifted his head to avoid it. "*Calme-toi, poney.*"

She closed her eyes and tried not to breathe. The beat of her heart thundered in her ears.

The man-at-arms paused for a moment—a long, long moment—then withdrew his arm.

Mairead opened her eyes, daring to hope he would go on and that would be the end of it. Behind her, Marek shifted in the straw, and both she and the man-at-arms froze.

Again, the straw rustled and something hard bumped against her ankle.

The man-at-arms drew near again, his sword lifted. *"Qui vive?"*

She shifted her head just enough to see that the object Marek had pushed at her was his short sword. The knight shot a glance back down the row of stalls, then reached for the door latch. If he entered the stall, he would see them both, and then all hope of rescue would be lost indeed. He could not see Marek.

The door swung out and open, and Mairead reached for the sword's hilt. Duncan snorted, his eyes gleaming white at the corners. Praying the horse wouldn't trample Marek, she shot to her feet and lunged at the man with a cry.

An oath on his lips, he snapped his sword up to meet hers. The ringing force of the blades connecting sent tremors of pain dancing through the bones of her arms. She took a step back, sword raised, ready for the next blow. God help her, she would not die here tonight!

But though he kept his sword before his face, the man-at-arms did not attack. "Maurice!" he shouted. "Esmé! *Elle est là!*"

Footsteps clattered against the ground outside, and she tightened her grip on the sword until the leather binding of the hilt squeaked beneath her clammy fingers. "Who is it you seek?" Perhaps she could convince him she was not the prize his master pursued.

The wind blew through the stable, plastering her hair against her hot cheek, and she could see the knight's eyes tracing it.

"You, my lady." He lowered the sword a bit. "Just you."

He wasn't going to be convinced. Serving maids and common wenches did not speak the language of the noble English and have hair to their waists.

She clenched her chattering teeth. "I will not be sought."

The summoned men-at-arms, Maurice and Esmé, clanked into the stable, and she drew back against a closed stall door.

"Bertrand?" one of them called.

"Here," said the knight.

Straw rustled in Duncan's stall, and she prayed again that Marek would stay where he was.

"Well," said one of the men-at-arms, "on the run already, she is."

The one called Bertrand took a step toward her, his free arm raised enough that the mail sleeve slid to his elbow. "Put down the sword, lady. His lordship's ridden long and hard for a word with you."

"More than a word, I've little doubt." She didn't release her grip on the sword. These men could take it from her in an instant, she knew that. Could and would. She hesitated. To give it to them now would be the surrender of her only defense. But perhaps it was better to save her strength for later battles in which she could actually grasp a chance of victory.

Bertrand took another step. "Give here the sword."

Marek shifted in the straw once again. If she stayed any longer, he would be lunging from his hiding place to die at her feet.

Her arms dropped to her sides. The sword fell with a dull clatter to the hard-packed dust at her feet.

Bertrand said nothing, only grunted. He took her by the arm, manhandling her as though she were a common charwoman, and nodded to one of his men. "Get the sword." Then, without another word, he led her from the stable and back across the yard.

She held her breath until she heard Maurice and Esmé follow. Marek, at least, was safe. She closed her eyes and breathed out. Thank God for that.

He would saddle the horses before he did anything else. And when he came for her, she *had* to be ready to leave with him. Annan would come for her if Marek summoned him, she did not doubt that. But by then it would be too late—much, much too late. Her stomach cramped. This time she would have to save herself.

Bertrand led her to the front entrance. The doors stood open, torches lighting the chambers. Their footsteps sounded huge in the empty foyer. They neared the Great Hall, and voices shrilled, Lady Eloise's most strident among them.

"I don't care what you say, Sir! That girl is in the charge of my husband—"

Hugh's voice rumbled, "And, as I've told you, it was *her* husband who sent me."

"Why should he?"

Mairead and Bertrand came around the corner. From either side of the hearth, Hugh and Eloise faced each other. Ducard knelt between them, feeding the fire, his head low, as though ducking the verbal match that raged above.

Lord Hugh, begrimed with the dust and sweat of a ride that had probably lasted since his battle with Annan five days ago, twisted his gauntlets in sun-darkened fingers. His stance was wide, the cords in his neck taut, his nostrils flared. The skin of his throat bore the mottled purple of a swelling that was just beginning to subside. A badge of shame, administered by Annan's unforgiving hand? "I have come for the Lady Mairead, madam, and that's the end of it."

Mairead pulled her shoulders back. Chin raised high, she allowed Bertrand to press her into the room. The conversation ceased. Every eye, even Ducard's, turned to rest on her, and suddenly a determination blazed in her that she had not known she still possessed. Perhaps Lord Hugh had not yet robbed her of everything.

Bertrand nodded at her. "She was in the stables."

"Clever girl." Hugh's eyes burned. For a moment, all was still, save the snap of the flames, and in that moment Mairead held his gaze without flinching. This man, who had taken so much from her—everything save life itself—would never have the satisfaction of knowing that he had broken her so utterly.

Ducard, eyes averted beneath his shaggy brows, rose and dusted his rumpled tunic. The sound of his hand against the rough cloth broke the spell of silence.

Hugh let go of his gloves with one hand and dropped his arms to his sides. Slowly, with the grinding precision that had always so marked him, he sidestepped a chair and shortened the distance between him and Mairead to a pace. Bertrand released her arm and stepped away; Mairead stood fast.

Hugh panted, whether with anger or with the satisfaction of finding at last the prize for which he had hunted so long, she didn't know. "Lady Mairead, have you no word for an old friend?"

"Aye."

His white teeth glittered.

"But you are no friend of mine, Lord Hugh." Mairead looked to where Lady Eloise stood with creased brow, her intense eyes following the exchange. "And he is no friend of my husband's. Whatever he has told you, it is not true."

Eloise grunted and lifted a jewel-adorned hand in a shooing gesture. "You have heard it, Sir Knight—the lady wants nothing to do with you. Now get out, all of you."

Hugh glared at Mairead, but his words were for Eloise. "And do you put your faith so strongly in the lady, even over myself?"

"Indeed I do."

"She has never mentioned me to you?"

"Nay, and I've no wish to hear any further mention."

Hugh took another step, pushing a fur-covered chair aside. "You mean to say she has not told you her secret?" He clucked his tongue.

Mairead's skin burned. Was it not enough to rob her and to shame her? Must he now proclaim it to the world? But no, he could not tell everything. Even he did not know all her secrets. He did not know of the small body moldering beneath French soil—the tiny body that cursed her dreams, waking and sleeping, the body that was half *his*.

Lady Eloise's sharp gaze shifted to Mairead. "What secret?"

Hugh stopped a mere step away and smiled. "That she was once mine, in all but name." With a forefinger glorified by a great ruby, he traced the sharp definition of her jaw.

If there truly was a Hell as the priests preached it, it blazed now in Mairead's vision with a white-hot vehemence. She slapped him across the face—that arrogant, handsome, Norman face—so hard the bones of her hand shuddered.

He reeled, shocked no doubt that someone dared strike out at him. He would be shocked indeed when Heaven finally meted out its justice.

She stepped away, her aching hand clenched to her breast. "Why the hand of God does not slay you, I know not!"

He swore and took one long step toward her. His hands clamped round her upper arms, squeezing flesh against bone. "I made you mine when still in London, and you will be mine yet again!" He drew her close to him, the air from between his lips hot against her face. "And then perhaps I shall kill you."

She shoved a palm against his chest, putting almost an arm's length between them. "Then kill me! I cannot leave this world any poorer than you have already made me!"

He did not laugh, but the smile on his face spoke to laughter nonetheless. "Oh, yes, you can, my lady. So I'll ask you again. Become my wife?"

She threw her head back. "I cannot. I am married."

"The Earl of Keaton died in the Holy Land."

Eloise sucked in a breath, its angry whistling seeming to indicate she blamed Lord Hugh himself for the deed.

Mairead didn't flinch. "Aye, Lord William is dead."

"So you see…" He stroked her arms with his thumbs but didn't relax his grip. "You are as free as the sun."

"No." She looked him in the eye. Perhaps Annan did not want it known at all, perhaps that was why he refrained from speaking the truth. But *this* was the reason he had given her his name, and if it could not save her now, then little else could. "I have married again."

Hugh's brows came together with a ferocity that made her breath catch. "To whom?"

"Marcus Annan."

Lady Eloise uttered a strangled sound, her mouth flopping open, then snapping shut again, her jowls a-quiver.

Hugh's grip tightened until Mairead could feel her blood pulsing beneath his hands. "That accursed assassin? *That* is the sort of man you prefer to me?"

"*Yes!*" She hurled the word at him. "The sort of man I prefer is one who knows how to fulfill honor, instead of defiling it!"

"Then you should not have taken Marcus Annan to husband! Honor will leave him in all too great a haste when I find him. I *will* find him, and he will die at my hands. Slowly and painfully, he will die. And you will live long enough to watch it!"

Hatred bit down hard within her. The man could do what he would to her, and she could not stop him. But she would kill him herself did his blade ever find its way past Annan's defenses. With all the fury that had been building, building, building for month after month, she spat at him. "No, I will not!"

He roared, his oath blackening the air between them, and he struck her with the back of his hand, felling her to her knees.

"Enough!" The red heat of Eloise's skirt billowed as she thundered across the room. "Not under any roof of mine, Sir! Nay!"

"Silence, bellwether!"

Eloise's head reared up. "What! You dare say this to me?" She spun. "Ducard!"

But Hugh seized her arm and dragged her back. "If you value your life, you will be silent! My men and myself shall be gone before your husband returns. And the lady with us."

Mairead, one hand pressed to the throb that had come of Lord Hugh's red gem against her cheekbone, lifted herself to her feet by the arm of a chair. She was near enough the slit of window that she could hear the men-at-arms talking in the yard below. The hollow sound of hoofbeats plodded against the hard-packed dirt.

A voice rose above the others, loud enough for her to make out the words. "'Ey, there—where is it you're off to?"

"I have to be in Constantinople today. I thought an early start—"

Marek.

She stayed where she was, leaning against the chair, hoping Hugh would think her still stunned.

"And is it usually that you leave for your journeys in the middle of the night?" asked the man-at-arms.

"My good man, haven't you noticed? 'Tis only a few hours from dawn!"

The soldier grunted.

Mairead inched closer to the window, still clutching her cheek, her head bowed so that her hair fell past her shoulder and shielded her face. Marek looked up at the window and seemed to see her. He lifted his voice just a notch. "So can I be on me way, sirrah, or have you any more complaints about the unholiness of the hour?"

The man-at-arms waved toward the gate. "Get on with you."

"Thankee." Marek glanced again at the window. "And since I seem to be such a bother to you, I'll just wait 'til I'm outside the gate to be checking me girth, eh?"

"Move along, *garçon.*"

Mairead blew out softly. He would wait for her. He would be waiting for her outside the gate.

"Lady Mairead cannot leave until my husband returns," Eloise insisted. Mairead turned to see the restraining hand Eloise had clamped on Hugh's sleeve. "Do you hear me, you great oaf? If she's married to that ruffian Marcus Annan and you lay a hand on her, he'll kill you! Are you aware of that?"

Mairead cast a quick glance round the hall. Only three knights, including the one called Bertrand, attended their master.

Ducard stood near the half-opened door, one hand upon the latch, looking rather lost amidst these knights' intrusion. He caught her gaze, and his huge eyebrows lifted enough for her to see into his eyes. His head bobbed, and he stepped farther into the room, pulling the door with him until it stood all the way open.

She understood. He was giving her the opportunity to run away and leave before his poor mistress worked herself into any greater a fettle. She tensed, her hand falling from her cheek.

"Lady Mairead."

She jerked around. Hugh had shaken off Eloise and now stood a mere step away, his hand outstretched, his eyes as dark and fearsome as she had ever seen them. "I offer this hand just once, my vixen. Come of your own will, or come of mine."

She did not move. She fought the urge to look again at the door, and looked instead at Eloise. Her hostess's face was splotched red, her gray eyes blazing. She shook her head vehemently. Her hands dropped to her sides, and she gestured with her fingers to the open door.

"I'll ask just once," Hugh rasped.

She looked back at him, and her whole body ached with the hammer of her heart. "No." She ran, lunging forward, landing on the balls of her feet with each step, every sinew, every muscle strained to bursting.

Hugh swore. "Stop her!"

From the corner of her eye, she saw Eloise swinging a fire iron. "Go!"

Hugh caught the iron in an upraised hand and wrenched it away, but it gave Mairead a few precious seconds. She was already through the door by the time a crash of mail armor against the floor indicated that perhaps Ducard had been able to stop one of the men-at-arms. The others pounded after her down the hall.

Her cloak swelling behind her, she ran as she had never run in her life, through the great doors Bertrand had left open upon their entry and into the yard. The waiting men-at-arms looked up only when their horses started, and by then she was halfway to the gates.

One of her pursuers shouted, "Stop her!"

Behind her, voices clamored and more footsteps ran. "Marek!" A heavy hand grabbed her shoulder, nearly knocking her to the ground, but she twisted loose and kept running.

She was only paces away, and still the gates remained shut. *Marek!* Her breath came too hard for her to cry aloud. If she had to stop to open the gates, she would be caught, and that would be the end.

Then, slowly—so very slowly—the gates ground open to the length of her arm. One last burst of energy surged in her veins. Ignoring the searing of her lungs, the stiffening of her calves, she threw her body forward.

And then she was through, and the gate was dragging shut. Airn's gray flank shone in the darkness before her.

"Get on!" Marek's voice strained as he struggled to keep the gate closed.

She mounted the too-long stirrups and waited until Marek had vaulted into his own saddle. Then she leaned against the courser's dark mane and released him into the night.

The gate crashed open behind them, but the men did not pursue.

They would have to find their own horses, and even then they must wait until morning to locate any tracks. By then she would be halfway to safety. Halfway to Annan.

CHAPTER XVI

FTER PARTING WAYS with Gethin in the middle of the night, Annan had ridden until dawn, then ridden yet farther, his bones stiff and shot full of dull, familiar pains. His mind would not rest, would not allow his body to rest. He rode through the day, stopping only to allow the charger to drink at the river. Now, as he reined to a stop in a village on the far side of Shaizar, the depths of night once more surrounded him.

He did not utter a sound as he dismounted in front of the only inn to be found this side of Stephen's castle, but his heart groaned inside him. His body ached with an intensity he had not forced upon it in many a year. He should have halted long before this, but he had kept riding, hoping that when at last he stopped to rest, his weary muscles would forestall the insistent whisperings of his mind.

The charger blew through its nostrils, flecking his arm with moisture as he lifted the reins over its head. He had pushed the horse too far, something that was fast becoming a habit. He rubbed the back of a weary hand against the animal's jowl. Was this to be another casualty he had failed to name?

What would the Lady Mairead say to that?

His shoulders were too heavy to lift in a shrug, so he left the thought unanswered and lumbered to the entrance of the inn.

His dogged knocking upon the rough-hewn door roused the innkeeper from his bed. The slump-shouldered Syrian stood in the doorway, one hand holding the waist of his breeches. He hooked a thumb over his shoulder to indicate a stable behind the house and spoke in heavily accented French: "When you've done with your mount, there are two rooms in back of the house. Take your choice." Then, grunting, he shut the door, to presumably return to the warmth of his own coverlet.

Annan left the charger with an armful of provender and, with his saddle over his shoulder, made his way through the darkness to a back door. The inn was drafty and dirty, and he had to nearly double over to pass through the doorways. But the musty straw on the floor would be thick enough to keep his joints from grinding into the ground. Tonight that was all he cared about.

He dropped the saddle in the corner where an uncovered window revealed the diamond glintings of stars. For a long moment, he stood at the window, arms at his sides, and let the night breeze cool his face. He felt a hand shorter tonight, as though the weariness that weighted his bones was dragging him down to the grave.

His lip twitched. That was what he had wanted, wasn't it? For the hand of God to bring an end to the pointless existence he had been leading since—when? When *had* it started? When had he become less than meaningless? Was it all the years he had spent hiding behind his sword? Was it the choices he had made at St. Dunstan's?

Or was it before?

He dropped his head, his chin coming to rest on the collar drawstrings of the linen tunic Lord Stephen had given him. The breeze ruffled his hair. He had always been turbulent, violent, hot-tempered. War and blood and the fire of battle had been his sirens since boyhood. If his sister-in-law's death after his brawl with his brother, and later the destruction of St. Dunstan's, had not been the defining point in his life, then was it not inevitable that sooner or later he should have been shaped by another travesty just as violent?

Yes. The answer was yes.

"Then why did Heaven not stamp me out while I was yet in my mother's belly?" He lifted his head and stared into the wide infinitude of night.

Gethin had wanted him to help correct the past. But that was something he could not do. *Would* not do. Even if he was convinced it was the right thing to do, his history was a book he refused to open. Heaven would bring its own avenger to deliver justice to Father Roderic. Annan was not party to it.

But if his quarrel with Father Roderic had ended long ago, it yet remained with some of the man's followers. He reached down to unbuckle his sword. Hugh de Guerrant, for one, would find his blade ever sharp.

He cast the sword and belt against the wall, next to the pile of straw on which he would sleep, and was unapologetic for the muffled clank. Loosing the dagger at his back, he tossed down his cloak for a pillow and dropped onto the floor. The smell of decay and the prick of the straw against the side of his neck would not be enough to rouse his weary body this night.

But even behind his closed lids, sleep did not come. Within the next few days, he would be once again within sight of Lord Stephen's home. Mairead would be there—safe. She *would* be safe in his absence. Stephen had pledged his life on it, and Annan could not allow himself to doubt it.

He pressed his lips in a firm line. If she were not safe, his enemies would find a battle fire rising inside of him, terrible to behold.

He rolled onto his back. How was it that this woman—this insubstantial, wide-eyed countess—could rouse that fire in him as nothing and no one had ever been able to? That all-consuming urge to protect, to defend?

It was a possessiveness that was rash, at best. She was his wife only in that she claimed his name. His only take on the bargain was a dowry in gold that he didn't want and could only spend in folly. What he wanted—

He stopped himself and let his breath out in a long, slow murmur. What he *wanted* was to catch her hair in the roughness of his fingers, to crush her against him and let her feel in the beat of his heart that she was safe, to breathe in the scent of her until it drowned out the stench of blood and smoke and death that had filled his nostrils for so long.

When he had left her in her chambers at Stephen's castle, he had kissed her hand. And when he had straightened, he had seen a look in her eyes that perhaps he would have understood were he better versed in the ways of women. He had thought he had seen more than mere regret at the departure of the one best suited to protect her.

And when he had promised that he would return for her—as if there could have been any doubt—and she had lifted her face, her lips parted in an unutterably guileless expression, he had seen hope. Hope for the life he could never give her? Or were his own unjustified longings to keep her by his side coloring his perceptions?

The scampering of a rodent made an empty scratching sound in the street. He exhaled and rolled onto his side, his eyes coming open to stare at the square of gray light on the floor beneath the window.

He knew it was impossible. Even could he offer home and hearth to a woman such as her, he could hardly turn his back on the black past. It would invade even the sanctuary of her arms, and it would destroy him yet again.

"But am I not destroyed already?" He spoke aloud to the darkness, the words hissing past his teeth.

With her, he could almost—almost—forget Roderic and Gethin and St. Dunstan's. With her, at least there was the potential of happiness, was there not? With her, he was almost able to believe his inability to reconcile with Heaven did not matter. And that was worth something, maybe everything.

The wind droning among the rafters was his only reply. He lay for a long time, listening to its whispers—whispers that only seemed to confirm those in his own mind. After a time, he closed his eyes.

———————

He did not know how many hours had passed when he was roused by the sound of horses outside his window. Habit led his hand to where his dagger lay at his side, and he listened in the darkness to the steady clop of two horses passing. Someone with a Scottish accent murmured to them, "'Ey there, watch me toe."

He raised his head from the warmth of his cloak. *Marek?* But the speaker said nothing more, and a moment later the horses halted near the stable.

Brushing sleep from his eyes with the back of his hand, Annan propped himself on an elbow and listened harder. Could it have been Marek? If he had survived, he was supposed to have gone to Lord Stephen's.

No. He shook his head and lay back down, this time on his back the better to hear. Marek couldn't be here. If the rascal were yet alive, he would know better than to leave Mairead by herself against instructions.

Still, he waited, until at last the grate of the front door opening and the heavy Syrian accent of the innkeeper interrupted the wind. The Scot's voice spoke again, too low to discern words, but loud enough to know that its texture could well enough be Marek's.

As the voices continued their hushed discussion, footsteps started down the hall. Annan rolled onto his elbow, watching the door, listening. Those footsteps—too light to be that of any man—were the rhythm to a song that could only be made by the whisper of a woman's gown against her legs.

At his door they stopped, and the bar bumped open as the drawstring was pulled in from outside. The door swung inward, creaking on worn hinges, and in its place stood a woman, her arms at her sides, her hair long over her shoulders.

She entered and eased the door shut behind her, muting the murmur of the voices in the front room.

It was Mairead. He didn't need to see her face to know it was her. He just knew. He could hear it in the way she breathed, could smell it in the scent of her hair even from across the room.

For a moment, they didn't move, they didn't say anything. Then, slowly, he rolled to his feet, the straw crackling beneath him. With the dagger still loose in his hand, he started toward her.

"Annan—" Her voice was muffled, afraid.

Hard lines etched themselves in his forehead. If she knew it was him, she should hardly be afraid. Not anymore.

His throat bobbed. "Lady."

Still, she did not move, except to clench her hands in front of her. "We— we saw the charger in the stable. I recognized it... I—"

"Why are you here?" The words were gravel in his throat. Why should Heaven send her to him now, when he was most vulnerable? When he needed her most?

"Lord Hugh… found me."

His innards turned to iron within him, but he didn't stop.

"We—Marek and I—we escaped."

He couldn't see her face, but he didn't need to. He could feel her presence filling the room, filling him with every breath. *Dangerous ground,* his mind whispered. But he didn't care; it didn't matter anymore. All that mattered was that she had found him. And he would not leave her again to face Hugh de Guerrant's ravaging by herself.

Face to face with her, not even a pace between them, he stopped. She stared up at him, the whiteness of her throat glimmering even in the darkness. He could hear by her breathing that she was still afraid, almost near tears. "Are you angry?" A tremble marred her voice. "Because I came after you?"

Something like joy—incredulous, wonderful joy—shot through him. She was afraid! But not of Hugh, not of him. It was his rejection she feared. And even if he wanted to, he could not reject her now.

His head bowed, tired shoulders hunching, and he kissed her. He could feel her surprise, her shock, the flash of uncertainty. But she didn't resist, she didn't pull away.

He kissed her again—and again. If they were moving he didn't know it until the thump of her shoulders colliding with the door stopped them. He pulled away, his breath heavy, and he stood looking down at her, his head bowed so that wisps of her hair touched against his forehead.

"Annan—" Her voice was soft, almost inaudible. But he could hear the tears in it. "Annan, you don't know what you're doing—"

"Aye, I do."

"No—you don't. I have been defiled—"

"I know it. It doesn't matter." He bowed his head still farther.

"There was a child—Hugh's child. A child of sin. Does not that matter to you?" Her voice cracked.

"The sin was not yours."

"But—"

"No." He held her face in his hand, tracing the line of her cheekbone with his thumb. His words rumbled. "You are my wife. That is all that matters."

She caught a sob in her throat, and her fists clenched in the tunic over his chest. "Annan—"

He didn't let her get any further. He kissed her again, feeling the warmth of her tears against his face, the hammer of her heart against his.

CHAPTER XVII

BENEATH THE SHADE of a ruined wall, Brother Warin waited for the bishop to summon him. A trickle of sweat leaked down the line of his scalp, and he fidgeted, pulling the collar of his tunic away from his body, trying to stir the heavy seaside air.

A gull shrieked overhead, diving low across the broken walls of Jaffa. After his victory on the plains of Arsuf, King Richard had moved his army here until the Jaffa port could be repaired enough to act as a supply base. Then he planned to move, at last, on Jerusalem.

The gull swooped back into sight, its black-tipped wings slapping the air high above. Warin emptied his lungs and let his tunic cling once more to his sweat-dampened skin. He had been in the camp not even an entire day, and already he had heard the murmurings of the soldiers. Most of them didn't think Jerusalem could be taken. After so recent a victory as Arsuf, that was a bad omen indeed.

The door flap of Roderic's tent was pushed aside, and a pock-faced youth stepped out. "His Grace wishes your presence now, Master Templar."

Warin set his teeth and forced his shoulders back. He hoped the bishop did indeed wish his presence. He had, after all, returned without their quarry, without Lord Hugh, and without Roderic's summons. And he did not come bringing excuses or peace offerings. He was here to ask questions.

The questions of a tourneyer.

He entered the shade of the tent and stood at the door, waiting until the sunspots dispersed before his eyes.

"Brother Warin." Roderic's voice held neither severity nor clemency.

"Your Grace." He bowed in the direction of the sound, and when he rose, his eyes had cleared enough for him to see the bishop where he sat in the rear of the tent in a high-backed chair, his hands draped on the scrolled armrests. Both chair and posture were all too suggestive of a throne.

Warin swallowed a putrid taste in his mouth. A hired assassin's insinuations were hardly grounds to doubt the bishop's sincerity and piety. Why did he have to keep reminding himself of that?

"You haven't brought me Marcus Annan." Roderic's expression remained impassive.

The corners of Warin's mouth deepened. "No, your Grace." He wasn't surprised the bishop already knew. Roderic had an impressive collection of informants—Warin among them.

"Why not?"

"I was… compromised."

"Compromised?" Roderic lifted a hand to the etched crucifix on his chest. His wide, elegant sleeve slid across the smooth wood of the armrest and dropped into his lap.

Warin fought to keep from shifting his weight. He hated that the bishop felt the need to examine him like this, to look at him as though he were a maggot wriggling in a breaded air pocket.

Roderic's eyes were like the wind in winter—sharp, biting, impenetrable. "Why were you compromised?"

"I lost too many men." Another line of sweat rolled past the vertebra at the top of his spine and gathered speed down his back until it hit the waist of his breeches. It was true. Counting the men Hugh had taken with him, Warin had lost almost all his command. But that wasn't why he had come back. He straightened and clasped his hands behind him. "It was my faith in the mission that was compromised."

"Oh?" Roderic arched an eyebrow. No hint of surprise colored his tone.

"I spoke with the assassin."

"You were sent to kill him, not speak with him."

"He talked as if he knew you."

For an instant, Roderic's long fingers stopped their motion upon the crucifix; then they resumed. "He lied."

"Bishop, I can only pray the things he said about you were lies indeed. *That* is why I have come back. To know the truth."

A wary look, like film upon the surface of standing water, entered Roderic's eyes. He sat a little straighter. "What truth?"

Warin took a step forward, unbidden. "He said you bore innocent blood upon your hands. He said you were a murderer and an adulterer, unrepentant before God."

Roderic's fingers dropped from his crucifix. "That is the heresy of the Baptist."

"Marcus Annan does not follow the Baptist."

"He speaks the Baptist's very words. He refuses my generous compensation for killing the man. Of course, he is in league with him!" Roderic shoved against the armrests and pushed himself to his feet. "Brother Warin, *why did you not kill him?*"

Warin swallowed. Roderic's wrath could be terrible. He had seen it meted upon others often enough to know. To continue now would be to risk that same wrath upon himself. But he had to know... "He said we would never be able to take Jerusalem if you continue to advise King Richard. Your Grace, I have seen for myself the apathy of our soldiers. We could have taken Jerusalem by storm long ago, crushing Saladin under our horses' feet. Yet here the armies sit, frightened and shriveling!" He took another step. "If God wills it, as you and the other priests say, then how can this be?"

"Be silent." Roderic's voice grated in his throat. "Veritas was right."

"What?" Warin blinked. Veritas? Never had their anonymous messenger written to Roderic; the messages always came to Warin himself.

Roderic's eyes snapped back into focus. "Where is Lord Hugh? Dead?"

"No, he was... diverted." Warin wet his lips, trying to clear his thoughts. "We found the Countess of Keaton with Annan."

"You fool! Marcus Annan consorts with the wife of the Baptist's chief disciple—a man who personally knew Matthias—and you let him go! I was right from the beginning. This man Annan *is* a follower of Matthias!"

"I disagree—"

A sound like an angry cat scratched behind Roderic's pale lips. "You—" Spittle quivered at the corner of his mouth. For a moment, all he did was stare, his chest heaving beneath his finery.

Warin waited, watching as the bishop collected himself, seemingly with great effort. Roderic's gray eyes blazed with anger and frustration and—aye—desperation. His fear was greater than Warin had imagined.

Warin held out a tentative hand. "Your Grace—" The man had to calm himself before his heart seized within his chest.

What secret power did these men hold over him that could produce such terrible results? Or was it perhaps the bishop's own guilt, as Annan had suggested?

"Be still." Roderic raised himself up, straightening his hunched shoulders. "Veritas *was* right." He scrabbled through the folds of satin on his chest until he found the crease that hid a heavy piece of parchment bent twice upon itself. Warin's throat tightened. He recognized the parchment; it was the same upon which their allusive messenger always sent his warnings.

"Shall I read it to you, Brother?" Roderic unfolded the parchment, but his red-rimmed eyes never left Warin's face. "He says, *Fidere* Templar *nullus. Vir cernere conspicere inimicus; vir fluctuare.* Need I translate?"

Warin's hand fell to his side. Nay, he need not translate.

Trust the Templar no longer. He has seen the enemy, and he has faltered.

How? How had Veritas known? How could he know these things? His knowledge had always been uncanny, always unerring. But this... even had Veritas somehow planted a spy among the men-at-arms, how could he know what was in Warin's heart? How could anyone have known unless he had stood face to face with him, eye to eye?

And, suddenly—like a fist in the softness of his belly—Warin knew who their messenger was. And the knowledge of it chilled him to the bone. "Bishop—"

Roderic lowered the parchment to his side. His chin lifted, his eyes hard as ice. "If you argue with Veritas, you waste your breath."

The moment froze around them, their eyes locked. Warin knew not what Roderic saw in his own eyes; but in the depths of the bishop's gaze he saw the truth for which he had come searching.

Annan was right, and Warin could no longer serve this man. He would no longer be his eyes and ears. And he would surely not tell him that it was the great Veritas—not Warin, as the bishop might like to think—who was going to stab him in the back.

Step by step, he backed toward the doorway, until he stood again in the glow of sunlight that pooled on the floor. He dropped his chin to his chest in the abject humiliation Roderic expected from his servants. "Have I your leave to go, Father?"

For a moment the only sounds that competed with the murmur of the camp were those of Roderic's robes rustling and the parchment scratching back into its nest against his shallow chest.

The bishop came forward.

Warin stayed as he was, knowing that Roderic might kill him where he stood—though in light of having to execute the deed himself, in Lord Hugh's absence, it hardly seemed likely.

"Brother Warin."

"Your Grace?"

"I have taught you by my own mouth, guided you with my own hand. But you have betrayed me—"

"Your Grace—"

"Veritas has never been in error. You admit yourself that you were compromised. Nevertheless, I will be merciful. I will give you one more chance."

Warin darted his head up. This was not what he expected. Nor what he wanted. "What?"

"I am leaving. Our messenger tells me I am no longer safe here. My presence is needed in Antioch, so I serve two purposes in going there."

"What about Richard?"

"Richard can manage his own army. You—" His eyes narrowed, the brows lowering over them like furry white worms. His signet-bearing forefinger stabbed the air between them. "You are to remain here. And if you see aught to substantiate Veritas's warnings, I wish to hear. Otherwise… I know you no longer, Brother. Never enter my presence again. Do you understand?"

Warin dropped his head once more. "Indeed, your Grace." *Indeed. And thank God for it.* God—and the heretics of the world, Marcus Annan and the Baptist among them.

After Warin left his tent, Roderic slumped in his chair, one elbow propped on the armrest, his fingers tracing the line of his chin. Once more he had come so close, only to be pushed back farther yet.

He did not think Warin had purposely betrayed him. The man was too honorable for that. But he had exchanged words with the enemy, and he had *agreed* with them. Henceforth, he would be useless. Utterly useless.

Darkness fell all around him. Sleep stung his strained eyes, and he pressed his lips together. Not yet. The blood-soaked nightmares would have their way with him later. But not yet. He had to plan, had to find a taste of sweetness in all this bitter gall.

It was a sweetness that could only come of his enemies' spilled blood. He pushed himself up from his seat and walked to the door flap. The careless lad who attended him had not drawn the netting across the opening, and flies, black as drops of spilt treacle, buzzed round his head. He dispersed them with a wave, and pushed the door aside to see into the starlit night.

Lord Hugh would have to continue the pursuit on his own now. Roderic grimaced. That was most unfortunate, especially now that William of Keaton's wife had reappeared. Hugh, hotheaded Norman that he was, needed the steadying influence of someone with Warin's scruples.

That was something Roderic was going to have to remedy. "Odo!" He pushed farther through the tent flap, instinctively tightening his nostrils against the unavoidable sourness of the camp. "Odo!"

His truant servant, perpetually red in the face, rolled onto his knees from behind a nearby tent. Roderic's frown deepened. Undoubtedly, the lad had been gossiping with the king's servants instead of thinking on his own work. What was it that today all his minions had decided to prove themselves unreliable?

"Odo! I wish for you to attend me!"

"Yes, your Grace." Still on his hands and knees, he turned to speak over his shoulder.

"Now!"

Roderic waited until the boy scrambled to his feet, then he returned to sit in the darkness. Odo stayed outside long enough to drop the netting, then entered.

"Light a candle." Roderic sat straighter in his chair, draping a hand over either armrest. "And bring me parchment to write on."

"Yes, m'lord." In the corner, flint struck against steel, sparks danced airborne for a moment, and then the expected flame burnt a golden hole in the darkness.

Roderic waited in silence for the parchment, ignoring the sting of his sleep-starved eyes. He would have no dreams tonight. Not of the past, not of the future, not of the blood that permeated both. Tonight he would write his instructions to Lord Hugh, and this time he would not err. He would defeat them all... he and the indomitable Veritas together.

He lifted a hand to his chest and felt the crinkle of the message against his sweat-pricked skin. These words—the first he had ever received personally from his faithful messenger—were all he needed to crush them all to a powder:

Debilitas cum vir: femina.

Under these words, they would all fall. And he would dream the dreams of death no longer.

Debilitas cum vir: femina. The weakness of man is woman.

CHAPTER XVIII

ANNAN WOKE TO the streaky gray sunshine that mottled the hard-packed floor beneath the window. He rolled onto his back, the prickles of straw yielding under his shoulders. Beside him, Mairead lay curled beneath his cloak, still breathing the steady breath of sleep. A single lock of hair, mussed just enough to catch the rainbow glints of the day's first light, had fallen across her cheek and into the hollow of her throat.

The urge was strong to slide the strand back across her cheekbone and behind her ear. But he didn't disturb her. When she woke, he had no idea what he would say to her. That it had been a mistake, a dream?

You are my wife.

Nay, it had hardly been a dream. And if it was indeed a mistake, he could never take it back. He blew out a deep breath and rubbed the sleep from the corners of his eyes. *If* it was a mistake? He bit the inside of his cheek to forestall a groan. How could it not have been a mistake?

She *was* his wife now. No one could deny it or circumvent it. Nor could he pretend he would leave no duties unfulfilled when he delivered her to the convent in Orleans. But did he want to pretend?

The moment—the mad, headstrong, willfully ignorant moment that had been last night—stretched a little farther into the morning. He sat halfway up and leaned on his elbow so that he could look at her. She stirred but didn't rouse. His brow knitted.

His wife she might be, but could he actually be a husband to her? This moment, golden even in the gray morning light, must eventually burst. She could not save him forever: he had been right last night when he had told himself she could not wipe out the past.

He had never been married before, had never wished to marry. The lines in his forehead deepened. If he wanted to be honest and objective—which he really didn't—he must remember that he had not wanted to marry *her*.

The life of a tourneyer was too short to be shared, even were there opportunities to do so. He made his home in filthy inns like this one, in ramshackle camps on melee fields, and a-horseback. He had no place to leave a wife while he traveled the roads that would call him 'til the day he died. He had no way to provide a home where she could stay and pray him safely through another battle, while she kept busy doing whatever it was women did.

He couldn't. But he wanted to.

He wanted it so deeply that it clenched like a fist deep inside his chest. He exhaled. If only thoughts could dissolve as easily as this breath upon his lips.

With the backs of his fingers, he brushed her hair from her face. What would it be like to have his first-born son handed to him from out of her arms? The fist in his chest clenched harder. It was yet another thought that had no place in his life.

She stirred, straightening her legs, rustling the straw. Her eyes opened and turned to find him looking down at her. No sleep marred them, no confusion, no wondering, as he did, if everything since the Saracen prisoner camp had been a dream. Eyes wide open and steady, she stared up at him.

She was afraid. He could see it deep in the back of her eyes, far behind the black circle of pupil, in the place where she tried to hide all her fears.

"You're afraid, Lady Mairead." He spoke softly with only the faintest rumble of the inevitable growl coming from deep in his throat.

Her eyes softened into liquid, and she pressed deeper into the straw, the tangles of her hair coming up to frame her face. "Yes, my lord." Her voice was still husky with sleep.

"Why?" But he didn't need to ask.

"Because it can't last forever."

The tightness in his chest twisted so hard it hurt. Why? Because she knew the truth? Because she felt it too and was not deceived? "Do you want it to?"

The curve in her throat bobbed. He didn't need the glimpse she gave, past the wide-open fear of her eyes and into her soul, to know she wanted it; he could feel it burning in the air between them.

"Yes," she said, "but it's impossible."

"I know." But, just now, he couldn't allow himself to understand.

After dropping a few coins into the innkeeper's hands, Annan left the house and entered a morning gray and blustery enough to match his mood. He hefted his saddle over his shoulder, ignoring the knock of the high cantle against his hipbone.

He had left Mairead in the musty backroom to make whatever preparations for the day women were in the habit of making. They had said no more about the inevitability of the future. He had to think first, had to clear his head and make himself know the folly of choosing any course save that of fulfilling his promise to Lord William.

He had to know his plans before he let himself speak truths that could only hurt them both.

As he rounded the corner of the inn, the wind struck him afresh. Marek sat on the ground in front of the stable, his arms propped on his bent knees, and a look beneath his upraised eyebrows that plainly said he considered himself less than well informed and only slightly more appreciated.

Annan stopped short and looked him in the eye. "Well?"

One eyebrow lifted a little higher than the other. "Now, that is the question, isn't it? But I daresay *you* seem well enough."

Annan swung the saddle down from his shoulder. He'd forgotten about Marek and what the boy might be thinking of all this—especially since as far as the laddie knew, Mairead was still the wife of Lord

William. He looked back up, squinting against the gusts. "Well enough, bucko. What about you?"

Both eyebrows shot up to an even height. "Since when are you in the habit of asking after my health? And that's not what I'm talking about anyhow."

"You're overstepping." Annan stalked past. He was in no mood to justify himself to this whelp.

"*I'm* overstepping, am I?" Marek scrambled to his feet and ran around in front, walking backwards when Annan didn't stop. "I brought her to you to keep her safe. I never thought you'd overstep the line like this. A line of honor, Annan!"

His old friend the gray courser raised its head from its hay and nickered at the sight of him. Marek backed into the stall door, and Annan pulled the courser's head between them, putting the soft black skin of the horse's nostrils against his cheek. "What happened at Stephen's?"

"Are you even listening to me? Would have been better for you if I'd left her there!"

The horse snorted against his neck and tried to lift its head away. But Annan held it fast, leaning forward a bit more so that the courser would have to hang its head over his shoulder. "No, it wouldn't have been better."

Marek barked in frustration. "St. Jude—"

Annan shoved the courser's head aside and faced his servant.

Marek's head went back a little farther on his neck, but he held his ground, his jaw set. "She's married."

"Yes, Marek, yes." He exhaled, long and deep. "To me."

Marek's mouth, opened for another reproach, froze. "What?"

Exhaustion hit Annan again, like a winter gale in the Cheviot foothills. He didn't repeat himself. Marek, bright lad that he was, would figure it all out, given a few days more or less. And between here and Orleans, they would have plenty of days. "Saddle the horses. We need to leave."

Marek stayed where he was. "You're— you're— mar... I don't understand."

"You don't have to." He picked up his saddle and carried it to the bay charger's stall. Lifting aside the rope that closed off the opening, he laid a hand on the horse's chest and stepped inside.

"But—" Marek lurched forward and stopped in front of the stall, a hand on either side of the entrance, "—how did this happen? And why didn't I happen to hear so much as a ruddy word about it? Eh?"

Annan swung the saddle onto the bay's back, and as he bent to pick up the girth, he gave Marek a hard stare. "Go saddle the courser."

"All right, all right." The lad threw up his hands and turned away.

"And, Marek. This isn't a matter that's open for your blathering, not with me and not with the lady. I hear one word of it, and I'll tie your feet beneath your palfrey's belly."

Marek shrugged and ducked under the rope into the gray's stall. "Oh, not a word, I vow. But—how's this all affect our plans? If you're going to stop this chasing around after melees in favor of making yourself a family, I can't see as you'll hardly be needing me anymore. Maybe I haven't told you, but my Maid Dolly's pining her heart out, waiting for me to do the same as you're planning—"

"No." Annan straightened, one hand rubbing the small of his back.

Marek's head bobbed into sight above the courser's withers. "Why?"

"Because the plans haven't changed. Weather and saints providing, we'll be in Orleans in twenty days."

"Orleans? I thought we was going to Orleans 'cause there was a convent or something there."

"We are."

"But men don't go around chucking their lawful wives into French convents. T'ain't right and t'ain't nice. I thought you said you was married to her?"

"So I am." He stepped forward to the charger's bridle and faced the slap of the wind. "For twenty days."

———

Mairead was waiting, Annan's cloak folded in her arms, when he returned for her. One hand cupped round the edge of the door, he stepped halfway into the room and cocked his head to avoid knocking it on the lintel.

"The horses are ready."

"Annan—" Her fingernails bit into the heavy gray wool of his cloak. She couldn't say the rest... that she was sorry. Because she wasn't sorry.

Even beyond the dread of the inevitable future, the warmth in her stomach whenever he was near could never be interpreted as sorrow. "Where do we go?"

"To Orleans."

She had known the answer, but still her heart felt like a stone. What right had she to think anything had really changed since the day he had taken leave of her in her chambers at Stephen's?

He sighed and took another step, straightening to his full height as the ceiling allowed. "Mairead, I can never give you a home." Bitterness chimed in his tone. "I have no home to give."

She looked to the ground between them, squeezing her lower lip between her teeth. "I'm sorry. Know that. Please, know that. I didn't mean for it to happen. It would have been better had we gone on as before—"

"Would it?"

She looked up. Beneath the lines of his brow, his eyes—those eyes that could be as cold and sharp as shards of stone—looked at her with all the force of his fierce nature.

He left the door and crossed to stand in front of her. "Don't believe me sorry." He lifted one of her hands from its grip on the cloak and held it in the calluses of his own. "I meant what I said."

Joy rose up inside and smashed against her breastbone. *You are my wife. That is all that matters.* He knew what Hugh had done to her, he knew of the child she had borne and buried—and it didn't matter. They had not been words yielded of the moment's impulse. He had spoken the truth.

If he had done nothing else to deserve her accolades, that alone was worth enough to raise him above any man she had ever known, even Lord William.

He raised her hand, his thumb resting on the backs of her fingers. "But where we go from here, I don't know. If you could ride behind my saddle for the rest of my days, I would not be unhappy." His eyes left her face in favor of her hand, and the bitter smile he wore so often hardened on the corners of his lips.

She said nothing. She would have ridden behind him to the end of the world if he would let her. But it was impossible. She knew it was impossible. And now was not the time for desperate foolishness.

"In twenty days' time, we'll have to find an answer." He looked up. "Twenty days for us to pretend there isn't an answer."

Her throat cramped, and she swallowed past the sudden burn of tears. "God's will be done."

"Aye." His face bowed once more to her hand, and the stubble of his cheek, just long enough to be soft, brushed against her skin. "Tell me why it is that God always seems to will for my heart and soul to be torn asunder?"

Again, she saw it—that raw, bleeding wound inside him that made her ache with the need to hold him in her arms and sing away the pain. She raised her other arm, cloak and all, to the back of his neck and held him.

Now that it was her right to do so, how many chances would she have?

———————

Hugh was in the little port town of Jebail when he received Bishop Roderic's message.

It was a message that said Veritas the Omniscient wanted him to find Lady Mairead and kill her. It was a message that Roderic and Veritas sought to justify with a single line about woman being the weakness of man.

Crumpling the parchment in his hand, he crossed the dingy upper room of Jebail's finest inn and stood at the window, bathed in the red and violet hues of the sunset. Whether he wanted to or not, he must agree with that single line.

The Lady Mairead was more than capable of creating weaknesses in many a man; he was himself chief among them. And mayhap, if her nonsense about being the wife of Marcus Annan were true—utterly mad as the thought might be—there truly was a weakness to be exploited.

But not in the way the bishop wanted.

No, indeed. When Hugh was through, even the great and mysterious Veritas himself would be groveling in admiration at the thoroughness of Hugh's skill. His lips straightened into a hard line. When it came to these sorts of things, no one was more thorough than himself.

He peered into the narrow street below and nodded when Bertrand looked up with a salute that said the men were ready to move. If the bishop's messenger was right, and they had discovered that this wench was Annan's weakness, then Hugh could do much better than kill her.

Indeed, if Veritas was right—and Hugh could not help but believe, in the pit of his stomach, that he *was* right—then he would wring a weakness from Annan that would scar far deeper than the lady's death.

His hand pressed tighter round the crumpled message, driving its creases into his palm, burning the truth of its message into his veins as surely as Lady Mairead's hand had burned his face.

"Bertrand." He spoke loud enough to be heard through the window. "Come up here. I wish to speak with you before we leave. There's going to be a new plan."

"M'lord." Bertrand nodded and ducked out of sight beneath the overhang of the first story.

Hugh stepped back from the window and turned to await his lieutenant. Heretofore, they had ridden as a single unit; but it no longer mattered if someone other than himself found the Earl of Keaton's widow.

There was a greater purpose now. And Hugh prided himself that even he could appreciate that.

CHAPTER XIX

OUR DAYS FROM Shaizar and the night that changed everything, Annan stopped somewhere in the verdant hill country between Turbessel and Edessa.

In front of them, carved in the face of a hill, was a square hole, perhaps as tall as his shoulder. Other holes, of varying sizes, stretched eastward along the side of the hill, each of them no lower than his waist. Larks perched in some of the holes, looking at the approaching threesome, black eyes shining in their cocked heads.

"What is that?" Mairead asked, as Annan dismounted his bay charger and came over to take her courser's bridle.

"Hermitage." He stopped at her side and reached for her.

"Aye, but where's the hermit?" Marek lifted his leg over his palfrey's shaggy neck and slid to the ground, catching his rein on the way down.

"Do you know there is one?" Mairead asked. The soft dirt puffed beneath her feet as she landed beside Annan.

"Aye. Stephen knew of him." He let go of her and reached for the courser's rein.

She stayed close to him, her shoulder against his side. "We'll be safe here?"

He shrugged. Safety was a matter of coincidence more than anything, and, when necessary, a fair amount of skill. "Brother Werinbert!" His left hand shifted, out of precaution, to his sword hilt. "*Pacatis*!"

As soon as the Latin greeting of peace had left his lips, he felt Mairead's quick glance on his face, sensed her astonishment that he, a wandering soldier, was able to speak the language of the Church.

It was so easy to forget she knew no more of him than what she could see with her eyes. He had forgotten that St. Dunstan's, that black hole of his being, meant nothing to her.

Perhaps, if he had been granted the rest of his life with her, he would have told her. He would need at least that long after speaking his tale to convince her not to shrink into the shadows every time he drew into sight.

From the gray-black depths of the largest hole came the scuffling of sandal-shod feet, and then a man appeared against the blackness. Perhaps Annan's own age, with a tonsure wormed with veins, and bones that jutted beneath the folds of his ragged sackcloth, he was bent with the rigors of his solitude, and his steps were the shuffles of an elder. Only his eyes, sparkling against the sun-speckled bags of his skin, were young.

Annan took a step forward, leading the horses. "Greetings, Brother. We are travelers, in need of a place for the night. Lord Stephen of Essex directed me to you. May we share your hospitality?"

Smiling, the hermit slapped his ear with the hand that was not supporting him against the doorframe.

Marek slacked a hip. "Maybe he's deaf."

Annan tried a Saxon dialect, and Werinbert's smile immediately widened to a snaggly grin. When Annan had finished speaking, the hermit crossed himself and bowed to them. "Greetings in the name of Christ and St. Beuno." His accent was heavy, probably from east of Normandy. "Please be welcome to rest with me for the night. You are English?"

"Scottish." Without looking around, Annan reached back for Mairead, and she folded both her hands into his palm.

"You are pilgrims to the Holy Land?"

"The Crusade brought us."

"Yes, yes." Werinbert blew out his cheeks in an expression that did nothing to soften the hard ridges of his cheekbones. "The defense of Christ's city is a mission most worthy."

Annan grunted.

"Soldiers traveled past only a few days ago. They bring word that peace negotiations are under way."

"If all the Christians wanted was peace, they shouldn't have come in the first place."

Marek shot him a glare.

"Come." The hermit lifted both hands and gestured over his shoulders. "I will prepare a repast for you. The horses you may leave near the water."

Annan followed the line of his pointing finger to where a stand of shrubs closed the gap in the hill. If he listened hard, he could hear the chimes of a waterfall. He pressed his hand against the small of Mairead's back. "Go with him."

She looked up into his face, hesitating. But she had nothing to fear from this man, and she knew it. She looked away, let go of his hand, and gathered her skirt. Ducking beneath the gray courser's reins, she came forward and met the hermit with the sign of the cross.

Marek started for the pool, but Annan tarried, watching as she bowed to Werinbert with the grace of nobility.

Werinbert's ragged sleeves weren't wide enough to hold both his wrists and the opposing hands, but he tried to fold himself into them nonetheless. "What is your name, mistress?"

"Mairead."

By itself, the name sounded naked. Annan frowned. He had no home for her to claim as her own, no title to gift her with. He had taken all that from her to save her life.

No, that wasn't true. She could have kept her title, the prestige of Lord William of Keaton's name, if she had wished. She had chosen differently.

His stomach, empty since midmorning, tightened. Aye, she had chosen—but poorly. She had chosen a man whose life was nothing but a long chain of mistakes. A man who, even with all the blood and sweat and strength of his body, could give her nothing come the end of the day, save his own life in exchange for hers. And he *would* give it without question. To die for a cause worth living for was far more than he deserved.

He turned to go, his tired bay charger falling into step behind him, and the gray courser trotting up to walk at his shoulder, ears perked forward, nostrils distended with the scent of water.

"Mairead." Werinbert rolled the name on his tongue as Annan walked away. "Meaning a pearl of great price. Like that in the most excellent proverb, for which a man sells all that he owns."

Annan reached a hand to the courser's bridle and brushed his fingertips against the soft short hair on the horse's jowl. How many men had sold everything for this particular pearl?

Lord William, who had given his life. Lord Hugh, who had sold his soul. And now himself. What had he given? Who was to say he had not given both body and soul?

He trudged to where the waterfall churned lacy bubbles into the silver-green pool at its base. Surrounded on three sides by the steep hills and deep enough to drown a lad of Marek's size, it was the clearest water he had seen since the plains of Lombardy in early spring.

Marek, flat on his stomach on the bank, flung his head back from its immersion in the pond, water droplets shimmering through the twilight. He blew through his lips like a horse and rose to his knees to give his streaming locks a good shake. "Whew. Right cold, I'd say."

"Better than drinking sour wine, that's sure." Annan stopped at the bank, a horse on either side, and tugged once on the courser's rein to keep him from nipping at the palfrey's neck.

"Tell me this—" Marek rocked back onto his haunches and pushed a hand against the bank to gain his feet. "Why's it the Church comes a-fighting its head off for hot, stinking places like Acre, and leaves a paradise like this to the heathen?"

"Tell me why any man goes a-fighting." Annan stripped halfway out of his sleeveless jerkin, keeping one armhole looped round his elbow as he knelt to wash his face.

"If you don't know the answer to that, probably nobody does."

He did know the answer—knew all too well. But right now there was a heaviness in his bones, and in his soul, that he wondered if even the hottest battle fire could melt. He bowed to the pond and splashed his face with both hands. As the water, cold and smelling of moss and mud, slid from his jaw down the front of his neck, he rubbed a hand across his eyes and pressed until white and yellow lights danced behind his lids.

"What do you think?" Marek asked. His saddle creaked as he loosened a strap. "Are we clear of trouble?"

"Are we ever clear of trouble?"

"There've been moments. But I gather you don't think this is one of them?"

"Maybe." Annan dropped his hand from his eyes and waited until the spots cleared and he could again see the red streaks of sunset reflected in the pool. "Depends what's happened to Hugh."

"Well, I didn't best him in a sword fight if that's what you were hoping."

Annan gave a little snort.

"If that's the best answer you can muster, I guess you *must* be expecting trouble."

"Trouble is what you make of it, laddie buck."

"And right now you're making it, is that it?"

Annan blinked and turned to look at him. Marek's ruddy face, framed by the water-darkened hair that clung to his forehead, was as wide-open and frank as Annan had ever seen it. For the first time since he had picked the lad out of the mud of that Glasgow street, he saw a man looking back at him from behind the wide-set eyes.

Annan leaned his chin against his propped-up hand. "What are you saying?"

"I'm saying nothing. Just that if there is trouble, it's 'cuz of her."

"So you'd have me leave her to her fate?"

"Course not." Marek's scowl flashed as he ducked to loosen his girth. "I'm just saying you shouldn't have married her. She's in enough trouble without adding ours to hers." The girth swung free and bumped against the palfrey's knee. Marek straightened back up and took a good hold of the saddle, front and back. "You know full well you're not exactly the most difficult person to find under the sun. If this Hugh fellow can't find her, he'll find you."

"That's hardly a deterrent."

"Well, surprise though it may be, one of these days you're gonna find out you're not as immortal and all powerful as ye think you are. He almost bested you the last time you two collided. Mark me, Annan."

"Is that so?" But the throb of his hip wasn't likely to let him forget.

Marek dropped the saddle to the ground and reached to catch his palfrey's rein before the horse could wander. "All I'm saying is you shouldn't've married her."

Annan rose to his feet, knees cracking. As his arm straightened, the jerkin fell, and he caught it in his hand. Shadows were descending over the pool, sharpening his hearing, even as they damped his ability to see. The waterfall plummeted with a rush and gurgle that spoke something different with every passing moment—and yet was always the same. For years it had fallen; for years it would fall.

As would mankind. As would Annan himself. His fall hadn't ended after St. Dunstan's. He was falling yet, adding more mistakes to his chain.

He looked over to where the lad had moved to unsaddle the courser. "When it comes to that, there's a lot of things I shouldn't have done."

By the time Annan and Marek trudged back into sight of the hermit's cell, the only remaining light was a thread of violet against the tapestry of black and, from within the hillside, a yellow glow of candlelight.

Annan entered first, hunching his shoulders to fit through the misshapen hole of a doorway. The smell of damp earth and broken herbs swelled his nostrils. He could sense more than see the opening that stretched out to his left; no doubt, it was the same passage marked on the outside by the line of window holes.

The hollowed-out room in which he now stood was just wide enough for a rough table and a low stool. A bowl of something brown and lumpy and an open book, both spread beneath the glow of an oil lamp in the center of the table, were the only other objects in the cell.

Neither Mairead nor the monk was in sight.

Marek peered round Annan's shoulder. "What happened to the hermit and his hospitality?"

Annan didn't answer. The wind whistled an eerie song through the window holes. He moved forward, past the table, until he could see down the passage. A glow of light, barely visible, softened the darkness some twenty paces down.

"Least he left us some scoff." Marek plopped onto the stool and reached for the wooden bowl. "Have some? Though I dare say I could bolt t'all myself."

"Help yourself. I'll be back." He sidestepped Marek's outstretched legs and ducked into the passage.

"Dinna hurry on my account. I'll holler if I find myself a problem."

Annan didn't respond. Likely, Marek's only problem would be running out of food. They might end up being more of an imposition on the holy hermit's hospitality than Annan had foreseen.

He followed the tunnel, cool with the chill of moist earth, down a blackness splotched only with the starlight blinking through the holes. Even before he reached the glow of firelight, he could hear the murmured incantation of Latin, spoken in Brother Werinbert's high singsong.

At the oblong opening that led to another room dug from the hillside, he stopped. Werinbert and Mairead knelt, side by side, both of them cloaked in the warmth of the torchlight. Before them, flickering in the shadows of a dozen candles, was a shrine—to St. Beuno no doubt, though it featured little more than a crude crucifix upon the wall.

Werinbert glanced once over his shoulder, and the quiver of the shadows made a ghoul's mask of his missing teeth and shriveled features. He crossed himself with the quiet leisure of piety—"*In nomine Patris, et Filii, et Spiritus Sancti.* Amen."—and struggled back to his feet.

In the doorway, he smiled and eased Annan backwards with the touch of his bony fingers. "She approaches Heaven's throne."

Annan nodded, his eyes still on where she knelt, praying so fervently. So innocently.

"She tells me you have a long road ahead of you."

"Aye."

"She is your wife?"

He glanced at the hermit. "Aye." Save Marek, this was the only person he had told.

Werinbert nodded, his smile closing over his teeth. "Then I will pray to St. Beuno that the Lord blesses you with many sons."

Annan's lips tightened, and his gaze returned to Mairead. "You waste your kindness, Brother. There can be no sons at the end of our road." Or, if there were a son, he would never know it.

For a moment the only sounds were of the wind outside, the night birds warbling, perhaps a wolf afar off, and the murmur of Mairead's prayers. What was it she beseeched Heaven for tonight? Were her prayers, like Werinbert's, for a son? Or did she entreat the mercy of death, as Annan had for so long? As he would once again when they separated for the final time.

"Do you wish to pray too, Master Knight?"

His mouth tried to quirk but could not. "I have no prayers Heaven would hear, Brother."

"You are so certain?"

He forced a smile. But it held no mirth. "Indeed."

Werinbert said nothing more, but the hand he laid on Annan's shoulder carried all the power of a blessing. Annan pulled out from beneath its pressure. He would not accept the blessings of this pious hermit. He couldn't accept them. They would only grind him deeper into the ashes. He stepped into the shrine to join Mairead, and he didn't wait to see if the hermit was offended.

Behind Mairead, he stopped, but she didn't look up. He could hear by her breathing that tears had been shed, but he did not kneel to comfort her. He would wait. She was Heaven's before she was his, and he would never begrudge her that.

His gaze found the rude carving of Christ upon the cross, head slumped against a slack chest. Werinbert had no doubt fashioned it himself, his careful handiwork evident in the wood's soft burnish.

Annan clenched his jaw, drawing tight the cords of his neck. Would that he could say of himself, as he did of Mairead, that he was Heaven's.

It was a thought that would have brought Marek's mouth gaping open in astonishment. It was a thought Annan had not released from the closed doors of his soul in many a long year. But standing here in the flickering shadows of this hermit's dreary shrine to some unknown saint, the emptiness of worthless life struck him as it had not since the years directly following St. Dunstan's and his great sin.

The carving of Christ had no eyes, but Annan stared into the empty wooden features and felt once more the call of Almighty God. Another lifetime ago that call had been his obsession, just as it had been Gethin's. His hand clenched involuntarily, the nails digging into his palm.

Neither of them had been strong enough to carry its burden.

Mairead, hands still pressed together before her chest, twisted her head until Annan could see the glisten of a tear track against her cheek. "My lord."

"What do you pray for tonight?"

"For you."

He shook his head. "Don't."

"I promised. You don't remember?"

Aye, he remembered. Slowly, he knelt behind her and closed her into his arms. He remembered leaving her at Stephen's, remembered being so close to telling her, as he had Brother Werinbert, that Heaven would not hear her prayers. "What have you prayed for me?"

She crossed her arms over his, her hands on his elbows, and let him hold her against his chest. "That Heaven will bless you as you deserve."

He laughed, but it caught in his throat. "Spare me that, lady."

She looked back at him, and the softness of her hair tickled against his neck. "And I prayed for peace and for happiness and for joy." She looked away, and he laid his chin on top of her head.

"Those are things I have never found—save with you," he said.

"What about when you were yet a child? What about before—" She chopped herself short.

He would have said *before St. Dunstan's*. But she had no knowledge of the ill-fated monastery. Her meaning was more along the lines of *before you became the monster you are now*. She did not think those words, of course. But they were there, nonetheless, lurking in the blank, unread depths of her.

"Yes. I was happy before." Even after the fight with his brother, and the deaths of his sister-in-law and her unborn children, he had found happiness. The fiercest, most spectacular joy he had ever known had been in the dark scriptoriums of the monastery, reading and learning from the sacred manuscripts as he copied them. He had drunk them in, making the words of Heaven so much a part of him that even now they sometimes echoed in his head.

But that time was long past. And the irony of it bit hard.

She shifted her head out from beneath his chin and leaned to the side to peer into his face. "Are you angry with God?"

He shook his head and freed one of his arms to rub a strand of her hair between his fingers. "It is right that He should allow no evil in His presence. I know that."

"You are not evil." The firelight flickered in her dark eyes.

"Yes, I am. Without forgiveness."

"Then seek forgiveness."

"Nay, lady. There are sins which even God does not forgive. I have struck Moses's rock; I will never see Canaan."

"And so you wander in the desert for the rest of your life?" She lifted her free hand to his face, and he leaned against its warmth. "Without me?"

"I will not drag you into darkness with me, Mairead."

Her stomach tightened beneath his arms. Some emotion deepened in her eyes. Not abhorrence, as he half expected, not even fear. Just... sadness. Her hand slipped from his cheek to the back of his neck. He dropped his head onto her shoulder and let her hold him, her other hand coming up to cradle his face. She whispered, the breath of her words close beside his ear, "All this because of Matthias."

He closed his eyes against the dancing shadows.

Nay, not because of Matthias.

Matthias's death had not been his great sin. It had been his greatest good.

Chapter XX

A HAZE MISTED the morning sky outside the window hole when Mairead woke. She lay still for a moment, curled in the warm nest of blankets and straw. The hermit had insisted they take his own pallet for the night and would not brook no for an answer. She stretched her legs out straight until one foot emerged from beneath the blankets, then she rolled onto her back.

One glance sufficed to tell her what she already knew: that Annan had left. He was never beside her when she woke; how he left without disturbing her she didn't know. A smile touched her lips. He must have the stealth of a cat. She stretched her arms above her head, pulling at all the muscles in her chest and stomach. The smile deepened. The image of Marcus Annan with the feet of a cat bordered on hilarity.

She laughed. It must be the morning air. Hilarity, after all, hadn't been the word to describe anything that had happened to her in the last year.

Kicking back the blankets, she rose to her feet and leaned her head out the window. The morning air, full of dew and the sharp scent of cypresses, cleared her head and filled her chest with their pungency. She smiled again. No, hilarity wasn't the right word; but in the midst of all this strain and sorrow, a thread of happiness had certainly been woven.

The insane happiness of a bride.

Right now, she could manage insanity. For the next twenty days, she could manage it.

A horse nickered, and she leaned farther out the window to catch a glimpse. But the animal was too far away. Only the unruly green of the hillsides, rising in all directions, filled her vision, and that only dimly through the fog.

As she started to withdraw, she caught sight of a horse's round, open-ended prints upon the ground beside the hill. The prints were too large to belong to Marek's palfrey. Had Annan gone scouting?

She bit her lip, but the sound of his voice farther down the passage, speaking in low tones with Brother Werinbert, forestalled the frown. A note of music vibrated her throat, and she turned to where her clothes were folded. She was happy today, happier than she deserved to be, happier than last night's talk of supplications and sins should have left her.

Annan's heavy stride approached and stopped on the other side of the crude wooden door that partitioned the tunnel. "Are you awake, lady?"

"Who can sleep on a morning like this?" Would that make him smile? She tugged tight the drawstring in the side of her gown. His smiles were as rare as desert ice, but she could find one if she tried hard enough.

"Marek's bringing up the horses. When you're ready, Brother Werinbert will give you something to break your fast." The words were as gruff and straightforward as everything else that proceeded from his mouth, but she could hear the little rumble that meant he was at least thinking with a smile.

And that, for some reason, made her want to laugh aloud as she had not done since before leaving England. "I will be only a moment, my lord. If you're smiling, save it for me at least that long." She had a right to laugh this morning. She would have plenty of time to shake her head at their folly after they reached St. Catherine's.

"I'll see what I can do." This time she could most definitely hear the smile tugging at his mouth. "Don't be long." He started back down the passage, and she twisted to draw the strings on the other side of her dress.

It was the work of only a moment to gather her cloak and Annan's few blankets and fold them into a neat pile. Her hair swung past her shoulder as she bent for the last blanket, and she shook it back. How long was it since she had been able to wear it on her head, beneath the wimple of a married woman, as it should be? Annan liked it long, she knew, liked to rub it in his fingers when his thoughts were far away. But the heat and wind of their journey had dulled it; it had lost the virgin luster of only a year ago.

She straightened and took a last look at the barren cell that was one more jewel on the silver chain of memories that would have to last her the rest of her life. As she turned to go, a footstep fell on the other side of the door that led deeper into the tunnel.

Frowning, she turned back to hear better. "Marek?" But Annan had said Marek was with the horses, and she had heard Annan and Werinbert through the opposite door.

A hand scuffled, groping in the dark, and the latchstring pulled in, raising the bar from its cup. The door grated open. Framed in the crude entry, a man-at-arms, sword in hand, hunched his shoulders to step through.

She cried out and started back.

The knight came forward, and the light fell on the battered features of Hugh's lieutenant.

Bertrand.

Mairead's scream ripped through the morning fog.

Halfway to the waterfall, Annan jerked to a stop just as surely as if someone had cut his feet from under him. He groped for his sword and spun around, his instincts chasing him back to the hermit's hillside shelter before his mind could even begin its frantic grasping for scenarios and reactions.

She screamed again, not so loud, and then all the world went still— all but the blood pulsing in his ears. He burst through the ragged entry and flew down the tunnel, shoving past the hermit, skidding to a halt at the closed door that barred the next section of the tunnel—Mairead's section.

Footsteps scrambled on the other side, and he slammed past the door in time to see a mail-clad knight climb through the window. The man glanced back once, flashing the features of a stranger, a Norman.

Fire surged beneath the surface of Annan's skin. He took a quick step forward, ready to pursue. But he went no farther. The fire turned to ice and froze solid within his veins.

Before him, limbs a-tangle, her hair strewn across her face, lay his wife. And the red stain creeping down her side, seeping into the blue of her gown as fast as the tide of any sea and dripping from the fingers of one hand, was the first sight of blood to bring the prickling sweat of fear to his skin.

He lurched to her side. "Mairead—" Long association with wounds led his hand to the tear in her gown just beneath and to the back of her armpit. He pressed his palm to the ruined flesh, and her blood squeezed up between his fingers. With the other hand, he cleared her hair from the sudden clamminess of her face. "God…" The word was both prayer and imprecation.

Her eyes, the pupils shriveled to mere specks, came wide open, and flickered 'til they found his face. A ragged whimper stumbled through the trembling of her lips, and she raised a hand, flailing, until he caught it in his own. "Mairead—"

Her breath came in fast gasps. "Help me…"

He clenched her hand, his own bones aching with the fury of his grip. He couldn't help her. *He couldn't help her.* Her life was seeping out beneath his fingers. "Be still, Mairead—be calm—"

She closed her eyes, the lines in her cheek rigid, and terror seized him such as he had never before known. Not even his anger was match enough for terror such as this.

"Live." The word was barely a whisper. *Don't die*—and that *was* a prayer, even though he knew he deserved that she should die. Even though he deserved that everything that had ever meant anything to him should be torn away.

He shoved his hand deeper into her wound. Why should he be surprised? Why hadn't he realized it before? The very fact that he cared for her had endangered her more than Hugh de Guerrant and Bishop Roderic and all the infidel host.

"Annan—" Her eyes opened, stared straight ahead, then slid to the left to find his face. She pulled the weight of her other arm from beneath her side and tried to raise it. It faltered, and he caught it, pressed it against his mouth.

"I—" each word was a breath "—love—you."

He stared into her eyes, feeling the finality of her words, and he could not reply. But he knew, in the deepest part of him, that if there were any love left in his body, it would have belonged to her until the end of time. That admission was a sword with the ability to plunge deeper even than that which had cut her down.

"I love you," she said. Her eyes closed; she drew one more breath. And then she left him, her body falling slack in his hands.

For a long, long instant he held her, still feeling the pulse of her blood against his hand. Behind him, Brother Werinbert's shuffling footsteps came to a stop, but Annan didn't turn to see the sign of the cross that no doubt accompanied the hermit's gasp. He lifted his gaze from the body of his wife—one more dead he must add to his tally—and the lines of his face hardened into crags of stone as his eyes found the daylight shining through the window.

Her murderer had escaped through that window, and even now, in the distance, he could hear the trampling of hoofbeats that marked his escape. Anger gusted through him, scattering his terror and his pain like ashes on the wind, leaving him once again with only the desperate heat of his rage.

With a precision that bound his trembling hands, he laid Mairead onto the earth, straightened her arms, and rose to his feet.

"Sir Knight—" Werinbert said.

Annan took two steps to the window and heaved himself through. His feet touched the ground, and he started running. Ahead of him, only halfway up the first hill, rode a knight on a red horse. He would kill that knight before this day was over.

In the corner of his vision, he saw Marek frozen on the path from the waterfall. The lad's mouth fell open at the sight of his master's bloody hands and sleeves. "Annan—"

But Annan didn't stop. He ran across the valley, blood pulsing behind his eyes with every beat of his heart. The rider looked back once, his hand against his cantle, then urged the horse, in leaping bounds, up the face of the hill. He merged with the sun and vanished in a wink of light.

Annan felt the strain of his own bulk the moment he reached the incline of the hill, and he wished, not for the first time, for Marek's nimble feet. He reached the ridge with his breath hot in his chest, his throat swollen, his muscles clenching in his calves. Far below, the man who had struck down his wife rode his chestnut with a speed that even the Moslems and their fleet-footed war mares would have admired.

Annan stopped. Never on foot would he be able to overtake the murderer. His sword dropped to the shale at his feet. Its bitter clang echoed once, then faded into the rustle of the trees.

He growled, the sound deepening in his throat, filling his body. Pain, as strong and as real as the ache in his hip and the cramps in his sides, exploded against his ribs. The growl turned to a roar. "*God!*"

He could bear up no longer. The punishment was just, yes! Hadn't he always borne it as just? Had he ever once complained that Heaven's wrath was any more than he deserved? Nay! He had thought it too little. He had always been ready to face the death that was his due.

But for others to pay for his crimes? He could bear it no longer. Gethin had nearly died because of his folly. His brother's unborn children had never known life because of him. And now—

He held his hands before him, the streaked red of his palms facing up. They trembled as they had not since his first battle as the Earl of Keaton's fifteen-year-old squire.

And now his hands bore the blood of the woman he had vowed to protect.

"*Why?*" The cords of his neck pulled tight. "Why punish me any longer? Why do You care! Why not let me die?" His life held no purpose anymore. Except...

He lifted his head to see the speck of dust and blue climbing the distant hill. The murderer had to have been sent by either Lord Hugh or Father Roderic. Annan would find him. If it took until he was a crippled old man, he would find him.

He bent to pick up his sword. Marek had been right. Hugh de Guerrant had won, after all.

But the Norman had best savor his victory while it was yet untainted.

———————

Wind had shredded the clouds by the time Annan reached the hermit's hillside home. He hunched his shoulders to enter the first cell. Only the angry lashings of the wind penetrated the thick sod walls. It whistled through the row of windows down the tunnel, mournful and eerie. A dirge.

The sound of it caught somewhere in his middle, pulling at his innards, tearing them apart. His eyes burned, and he threw his head back, breathing through his nostrils. So this was Marcus Annan, the famed tourneyer? Renowned for his strength, his unmovable power, his composure?

He closed his eyes. God had made him strong. Life had made him stronger. How was it, then, that he had been destroyed in a single blow—by a woman?

The wind screamed, rattling something in the tunnel, and human voices murmured. Opening his eyes, he made himself unclench his fists. He ducked through the second doorway and followed the tunnel until he found the glow of firelight that he knew would be Mairead's Requiem Mass.

In the doorway, he stopped, unsure how to brace himself against the blast of pain he would find around the corner. But when his eyes found her still, white form, it was not pain that swelled within him—it was shock and yet another burst of rage.

He swore and leapt at Marek, snatching him from where the boy knelt at Mairead's side, his bloodied little fingers ripping at her bodice. "What in the name of the faith do you think you're doing?"

He slammed him against the wall so hard the lad's teeth rattled, and then he slammed him again. Battle fire hummed inside his skull. His hands tightened on the front of Marek's tunic. "You filthy cur! She is yet my wife!"

"Annan—" Marek scrambled for air. The fingers of both hands clamped round Annan's forearm, and he tried to force him off.

Behind him, Werinbert struggled to his feet. "Master Knight! Please—"

234 – K.M. WEILAND

"No," Annan said. "Don't touch her."

"Annan!" Marek's eyes glittered. "Don't be a fool! She's not dead!"

He dropped the lad as though his hands were full of hornets and spun around. "What?"

Werinbert had taken Marek's place at Mairead's side. With one swift movement, his hands pulled away from each other, and he tore her blood-blackened bodice down the side, revealing the unnatural crimson beneath. At a glance, Annan saw that they had already bound a dressing into the wound. Werinbert glanced once over his shoulder, as if to assure himself that Annan hadn't killed Marek, then laid a length of muslin bandage to the dressing and stretched it across her chest. "Raise her up."

Annan's frozen limbs would not allow him to move. Marek darted past him to Mairead's other side and dropped to one knee. With a tenderness Annan had never really appreciated, he raised her shoulders so that Werinbert could pull the bandage beneath her and begin another wrap.

And it was then that Annan saw the shallow dip of her stomach, just beneath her breastbone. It rose and dipped again. Blood rushed back into his fingers; the hair of his scalp and his arms lifted; a chill raised gooseflesh. *She was alive.*

Alive.

The word was a desperate sweetness upon the back of his tongue.

Werinbert looked up at him again, the shadows catching in the bags beneath his eyes and making them pop even more than usual. "She lives, Master Knight." He spoke as if reassuring a young son.

Annan shifted his gaze back to the monk's face. "I am to blame for this."

Marek dared a quick look up from Mairead, but he kept still. No remonstrance, no crowing, no sage and knowing expressions.

Somehow that cut past Annan's defenses with a sharper blade than any of the lad's impertinence and disrespect had ever managed. Marek had been right. Annan had been wrong. That was the whole of it. And Mairead lay here now because he had been wrong. His lower legs suddenly felt like water, and he sank to his knees. Had he been wrong his entire life?

As Marek and the hermit bound Mairead's wound and finally laid her upon the floor and covered her cold limbs with a blanket, Annan knelt and watched, his hands hanging limp and useless upon his thighs. All he felt was the roaring hole of blackness in his middle.

She wasn't dead. That should have been enough to fill the hole. But it wasn't. If anything, the roaring screamed louder.

Werinbert leaned his head over her, invoking the sign of the cross in the air above her. "In the name of the Father, Son, and Holy Ghost. The wound was red, the cut deep, the flesh sore, but there will be no more blood or pain 'til the blessed Lord comes again."

He turned to look over his shoulder. His expression was passive, his eyes calm with a peace Annan had been questing after all his life. "I know not why you think yourself guilty of what another man has done to her," Werinbert said. "You have chosen to keep your sins to yourself, and I am not a confessor. But I would ask you something."

Annan made himself look into the hermit's face, made himself see the movement of the man's shrunken lips, the quiver of his protruding throat.

"Do you think Christ came only to forgive those whose sins are little? He did not, my son." Werinbert shook his head. "He died for the greatest of sins as well as the smallest."

Another chill lifted the hair on Annan's arms, and for a moment the howling of the black hole within him calmed. For a moment it was still. The blackness disappeared, and a pale, shivering light surfaced in its stead. He waited, feeling it tentatively enlarge to fill the empty space, feeling the kiss of its warmth.

Farther down the tunnel, the wind shrieked, its cold breath rattling in the hillside. It touched his skin, and he flinched. The light inside him flickered, rebounded… died.

He exhaled, and his eyes dropped back to the blood on his hands. "Nay, Brother." The light of a guttering candle could not hold back the darkness of a lifetime. He shook his head. His eyes drifted back to Mairead's cold, still form.

Werinbert laid a hand on his shoulder and used it to support his weight as he dragged himself to his feet. His hand lingered. "Pray for her, my son. Mayhap this time it shall be the pearl that shall buy the treasure."

He left, his sandals scuffing against the hard-packed floor, and Marek stole out after him.

For a long time Annan didn't move. Didn't move, didn't think, only felt. Finally, he rose up off his haunches and inched closer to her side. Only her lips moved, parting slightly with each breath. His heart ached at the sight. The pain of it was new and strange.

He had loved but little upon the long, winding road that had led him here. And now he thanked Heaven he had not. The pain of steel against his flesh, of broken bones, and shattered muscle—these things he could bear. But not this. Not this.

This had broken him inside. All that was left of his strength was his rage. And God.

And of the two, his rage was by far the weapon that fit better in his hand.

He lifted a strand of her hair and rubbed it against the roughness of his thumb. She did not move, did not respond, did not soften her eyes at his gesture—and he felt the need to cry out. Had he been able to, he would have thrown himself upon her and held her to the warmth of his body, breathing his own life into her, filling her veins with his own blood in place of that which she had lost.

But he could not. He was helpless. "God," he said, "there are no chances left for me. I know. But… save my wife."

That was all he could offer. He laid the strand of hair back onto her shoulder, straightening it atop the blanket, all the way down to her waist. Then he rose in search of Marek. Time was short, and they would have to move with all haste.

He could do nothing more to save her life. He had no choice but to admit she was in the hands of Heaven. But he *could* act where he was best suited.

His face hardened. His vengeance would be swift: within a fortnight new names would be etched in his tally of dead.

"Annan, this is madness." Marek stood a few paces off from where Annan was saddling the gray courser. His arms were clamped against his chest, as much from stubbornness, Annan suspected, as from the chill of the wind. "She could die, even on a journey as short as that."

"Just as she'll die if Hugh finds her here." He pulled tight the girth strap and dropped his stirrup to the courser's side. His hand stroked the horse's hard flank. Mairead had named him well, for indeed he was like iron. Even after his already long, twisting journey north from Acre, the courser was still the best suited of the three mounts for another trek. And only the saints knew how long this one would be.

He reached for the rein and turned to face Marek. "She's not safe here."

"She wasn't safe at Stephen's either."

"Stephen is the only man in this country I can trust. I am trusting her to him—and to you."

"Why? Why trust me with her? You've never trusted me before."

"Don't believe that."

Marek's arms unfolded. "Then you come with us. If something happens, you could protect her better than me."

"No." His gaze shifted to the horizon, to the darker storm clouds gathering there. "I have other things to do."

"You mean more blood to spill. Annan—" Marek shook his head, and again there was that look that made it hard to remember foolishness ever being this boy's playmate. "Don't. Don't do this. This time, let it go. For me." He took a step back. "And for yourself."

Werinbert appeared in the darkness of the hillside's entryway. Annan's gaze darted to him, searching for the solemnity, the tears, the sorrow that would mean Mairead was gone. But of the three, only solemnity darkened the crags of his face. The hermit laid one bony hand against the side of the doorframe, watching them, but saying nothing.

Marek turned to look at him. "Brother, tell him. Finding and killing this man cannot help him."

Werinbert pursed his lips. "Vengeance is mine, saith the Lord God."

"Sometimes vengeance is the only way to justice," Annan said.

"Annan—" Anger, darker than any of his exasperated fits had ever been, hardened Marek's voice. "I *know* you, and I know what this is all about."

Annan leveled his gaze at him. "Do you?"

"Aye, I do! You fell in love with her. How, I know not, because I never thought you capable of it, but you did. And now the only thing you know to do to kill the pain is to wash it away in a sea of blood." He stopped. "But that won't work."

"Finding this man and killing him cannot save your wife," Werinbert said. "And it will not save you."

"I'm past saving." He turned to mount the courser, holding his sheathed sword out of the way as he swung his leg over. He looked once more at the hermit and at the cell beyond him where Mairead slept. Perhaps he would never see her again. And perhaps it wouldn't matter, because he might never return.

Marek exhaled. "Annan." He came forward and stood at his stirrup. "You think this is that bishop's doing, don't you?"

Gethin's warning whispered in his ear: *Perhaps Hugh will even yet teach you the truth of my words about the bishop's ravaging.*

He steeled his jaw. "My fight is not with the bishop." Mairead's murderer he would find and kill. Hugh de Guerrant he would slay. But he *would not* repeat Matthias's mistake at St. Dunstan's. Roderic could wallow in his sins come the Apocalypse, but it was not Annan's concern.

He stared down at Marek. "I'm trusting you."

"St. Jude help us."

Annan forced a nod and wheeled the courser around. Iron-shod feet drummed a rhythm upon the sod beneath him, and he set his face to the gray-shrouded green of the mountains. He didn't look back; he would not turn back. But God knew they would need better than St. Jude's help.

CHAPTER XXI

UGH DE GUERRANT stood in the shadow-flooded cell of earth and cursed. His left hand clutched at the hilt of his sword. "Bertrand, you're a fool. This is the last time. The *last* time!" He spun to face his unfortunate lieutenant.

Bertrand didn't cower. As always, he would face whatever punishment Hugh meted out and accept it as his due. It took all the self-control Hugh possessed to keep from beating the man to a cringing, whining pulp right where he stood.

They had lost *again*. Bertrand vowed the Lady Mairead's wound had been the artful blow Hugh had demanded—not a killing stroke, but deep enough to put her life in doubt.

But, apparently, Bertrand's opinion of "art" was not up to Hugh's standards. The wound had either been light enough that Annan had risked moving her, or so deep that it mattered not. Whatever the case, Marcus Annan and his company had fled, leaving Hugh once more with nothing but shadows to clench in his fists.

He ground his teeth. So often had he ground them since their arrival at this bloody hermitage that his jaw ached as though it had been smashed in by a cudgel. He ground harder.

Bertrand winced. That one tiny display of weakness was enough to make Hugh relax his expression, if only slightly. Little did Bertrand know how much pain that one flinch had spared him.

Hugh opened his hand upon his hilt, stretched the fingers beneath his glove, and turned to the window. "Fetch the hermit."

"Yes, m'lord." Bertrand stepped to the door. "Bring him in."

Esmé, one of Hugh's personal retainers from Normandy, and one of the men-at-arms provided by Bishop Roderic entered with the gawky little monk suspended between them. They threw him on his face at Hugh's feet and left him there.

"Look at me." Hugh kicked the man's shoulder. Judging from the pained groan and the way the arm flopped, the joint was already separated. Hugh pressed his lips together. Perhaps now this foolish little Saxon would speak. "What's your name?"

"I am Brother Werinbert." The monk struggled to his knees and pulled both flopping arms into his lap. "You do wrong in persecuting me, my son."

"I am not your son, hermit. I serve a higher authority."

"But not the highest, I see." The monk looked absurdly like a bird, his bulging eyes fixed wide open, and his wispy hair mussed into tufts above both ears.

"As far as you're concerned, *I* am the highest."

Werinbert shook his head.

Hugh took a step forward, bile burning in his throat. This hermit had better be careful; Hugh could extract answers just as exquisitely as his men. "Do you wish to continue what was started in your tunnel?"

"No, Master Knight."

Hugh stopped and rested his hand once more upon his sword. "Good. Now tell me, how recently did your guests leave—a man, a woman, and a boy?"

"Are you so certain I had guests?"

Hugh shot a look at Esmé. The man-at-arms smashed his mail-clad hand into the back of the hermit's head and knocked him to the ground. Werinbert writhed, his useless arms unable to push himself aright. He made it halfway up, and Hugh shoved him back down with his foot. "You grovel well, monk." Slowly, he knelt close to Werinbert's shoulder until he could speak in his ear. "Tell me. I *know* they were here. You do them no disservice by admitting that."

Werinbert's breath rasped. He turned his head, still resting it upon the ground, to face Hugh. "If you know, then I hardly need say."

"Answer me but two things, Brother, and not only will I see that your wounds are given the greatest attention, but I will personally give you any price you wish."

A hacking sound that might have been a laugh quivered in Werinbert's jowls. "Do you really think there is anything I would want that you could give me?"

"I can give you your life." He leaned closer, his lips almost brushing the stubble in the hermit's ear. "*Tell me.*"

Werinbert laughed again. The sound degenerated into a groan as he forced his body upright. "That depends on what your questions may be."

"Just this. Was the Lady Mairead killed? And where have they gone?"

Werinbert closed his eyes, and a red-green worm of a vein in his temple quivered. "No, Lord Knight, I cannot tell you."

Hugh roared at him and backhanded him so hard he skittered across the floor. "Take him!"

Esmé and his companion dragged the hermit out by his disconnected arms, the monk hanging half-conscious between them, blood from his temple interfering with the Pater Noster on his lips.

Bertrand started after them, probably hoping to avoid a similar edict spoken on his behalf. Hugh stopped him with a chopping motion. "Stay."

"Lord?"

Hugh glowered. "Don't think this is over."

"Nay, my lord."

"There *will* be tracks, and I will find her." He would not fail Roderic and Veritas. And he would not fail himself. He filled his nostrils with the smell of the earth-laden air and rose to his feet. He came within a few steps of Bertrand and waited until the other man flinched beneath his hot gaze. "But this is the end for you."

Bertrand's lips parted, then sealed.

"You're to return to the bishop."

The man-at-arm's features relaxed just visibly.

"Be glad for what faithful service you have given me in the past. Deliver a good report to Roderic, and tell him what you like about your dismissal."

Bertrand saluted, his fist against his chest, and waited for the leave to go.

"Tell the men to tend the horses as soon as they have finished with the monk." Hugh turned back to the windy sky outside the window. "And then, we search for tracks."

Annan lost the murderer's trail even before the first day was out. He kept to a mostly southern route, determined that he should run across him sooner or later. Rumor placed the Crusading army at Jaffa, and he set his face in that direction, knowing that was where Father Roderic was most likely to be found.

Where Father Roderic was, Lord Hugh would eventually come; and where Lord Hugh was, there also would be his blood-filthy minion. Annan would stamp out two at once, and leave Roderic only to gape in horror.

He was three days from the hermitage and approaching Antioch when he saw the unmistakably gay colors and banners of a tourney. For the space of just a heartbeat, his stomach warmed. He reined Airn to a halt atop the hill and braced both hands against the pommel, watching the pennons of green and red and yellow snap in the wind.

The tournament was encamped on the outskirts of Antioch, looking for all the world like a little city of its own, differing from its greater sister only in the glory of its spectacle and the transience of its dwellings. He could hear the clatter of arms practice, the stamp of restless hooves, and he smelled the smoke that came as much from the fire suddenly kindled within his own blood as from the dry wood burning in front of the various tents.

Airn lifted his head, ears pricked, and blew through both nostrils. Without looking down, Annan patted the courser's shoulder. "Aye. The first sight is like that. One gets used to it."

But why any sight at all? His brow furrowed. Since his arrival in the Holy Land, he'd had it on good authority, more than once, that this sort of thing wasn't looked upon too highly by either man or God. Mayhap the Saracens were sponsoring it in an effort to lure a few more

Christians to Hell. The curl of his lip was as close as he came to laughing at his own joke.

He touched his spur to Airn's side, and after one more snort, the horse lowered its head and started down the hill.

Annan detoured through the tourney camp on his way into the city. He kept Airn to a walk, his own shoulders hunched, as much to prevent anyone from recognizing him as from weariness.

The storm from the mountains had followed him to the seaside, and the clouds sagged with the humidity. The rain would descend soon, probably before the day was out.

A freckled squire walked past with two gaily bedecked horses, and Annan turned his head, watching them until they were far down the muddy alley between the tents. A burly, sun-darkened servant raised an eyebrow at his curiosity, but Annan let the look pass without even a frown.

Right now he had the feeling—a feeling every bit as old as he was himself—that everything would be right with the world if only he could gallop across a melee field, sword in hand, his legendary prowess clearing the field before him like the wind against a pile of chaff.

But no. He filled his lungs with the wet air, making himself douse the fire. All *would* be right with the world—for a few hours. But those few hours would just add to the cache of hours he had been gathering all his life, the cache that had held his sins from the very beginning.

He turned away and rode on. There would be no tourney this time. For once in his life, he had a greater purpose upon which to spend his rage. He pricked Airn's side again, and the courser broke into a trot.

Even still, it beckoned.

———————

Annan found an inn on the edge of town, close to the tourney, where the competitors' gossip would be rifest. He left Airn bedded down in the stable and sought an empty table amid the shouted jests and dancing lantern shadows.

Sitting with his sword arm to the door, he nursed a pot of watered-down ale and waited until the innkeeper's wife slid a wooden trencher onto the table before him. "Eat hearty, luv."

He leaned back just enough to keep out of her way and grunted his reply. The simple fare of black bread and hard cheese was hardly the best he'd seen proffered during a festival week, but as he stared at it in the wavering light, it didn't really seem to matter. His teeth ached, and even the motion of swallowing his ale hardly seemed worth the effort.

He swirled the dregs, wondering absently how much sludge he would find in the bottom. Someone at a table behind him erupted in raucous laughter, but he afforded them not a glance. It was careless to ignore his surroundings, he knew. If he'd ever caught Marek doing the same, he'd have scalded the laddie's ears.

But he was tired. He was losing his edge. And if that was something to be worried about, he couldn't remember quite why.

He sighed and rubbed his face. Sleep. He needed sleep. Things would be clear—or at least as clear as they ever were—come morning. He drained the last of the ale, and as he reached to gather his meal into his purse, a rosy-faced little knight stepped up to one of the empty chairs. "Mind if I join ye, good master?" His eyes twinkled in the redness of his wind-slapped face.

Annan nodded. "Make yourself welcome."

"Thankee." The man set his beaker on the edge of the round table and pulled his chair in close. He propped both elbows on the table, took a long draught of his ale, then peered at Annan. "Here for the exhibition then, are ye?"

Annan shook his head and pulled the flap of his purse down over his supper. "I think not."

"Pity. You've the look of one who could be doing a fine job of exhibiting." The man laughed and sipped his beaker. "If you haven't an invitation I shouldn't think 'twould be too hard for a man of your sort to obtain one. They'd be glad to have ye, no doubt."

"No doubt." He pressed both hands against the edge of the table, ready to rise to his feet. But then he stopped and gave the knight another look. Here was as good an opportunity as any to seek a few answers. And this fellow was a good bit more talkative than the likes of the sullen innkeeper.

He settled back down and pulled his chair in closer. "Why's there a tourney here at all? In the Holy Land, during a Crusade?"

"Not a tourney. As I said, 'tis an exhibition."

Annan's brows came together. "Why? Is the army here?"

"Nay. Just some bishop or other."

The hair on his arm prickled. "What bishop?"

"Roderic, I think. An advisor to King Richard."

"Roderic." Annan slumped against the back of his chair.

"That's right. Not that I rightly care, you know. After all a bishop's as good an excuse for a tournament as any other, hey?" The knight smacked his lips. "A little bit of play between battles is just the thing, I say, wot?"

"What's he here for?" Was this the hand of God, then, that he should stumble upon Father Roderic and his nest of vipers, when his search was only yet begun?

The other man shrugged. "To oversee the defense and all that, I suppose. Though we were doing not so bad on our own, methinks."

"Did he come alone?"

"You mean is His Majesty with him? Nay. The king's more interested in Mohammedans than he is in fortifying dusty Antioch."

Annan leaned across the table, forcing his eyes to focus. "What about Roderic's lieutenants? A Norman and a Templar?"

"The Norman, Hugh de Guerrant?"

"Aye." Despite his effort to maintain a level tone, his voice rumbled.

The man gave him a long look. "I haven't seen aught of him here. And if you're thinking you'd like to engage him in a little test of strength, then it's well for you he isn't. They don't make many finer knights than he."

"Too bad he's not less of a knight and more of a Christian."

"Could be. But if you've a quarrel with the nobleman, then I'd warn you twice over not to challenge him." He sniffed and returned to his ale. "Anyway, I saw one of his men reporting to the bishop only this morning, saying the earl wouldn't be here."

Annan's skin burned. "One of Hugh's men?"

"Aye, though I've not heard if he's staying for the demonstration tomorrow. Probably will, I expect. I know *I* would, if'n I was in his saddle and had the opportunity. Right?" The knight gave a wink and nudged Annan's arm with his elbow.

"Aye." Annan pushed away from the table, seeing vaguely that the innkeeper's wife had stepped into his path, awaiting payment for the meal.

He had no way of knowing if this messenger of Hugh's was the same who had tried to kill Mairead. But the stutter of his heart told him that it was, that it must be. Whatever winds had blown the man here had blown him into Annan's waiting arms, and right now that was assurance enough.

His companion leaned his head back to see Annan's face. "And have you changed your mind about plying that brawny arm of yours after all, friend knight?"

"Aye." Annan started for the door. "I have."

———————

Mairead opened her eyes to a haze of gray. Her lips parted to release a breath, and the fist of pain that hovered relentlessly in her foggy dreams battered her left side. The air, rich with the taste of rain, caught in her throat and tangled with her whimper.

"Lady."

She hadn't realized her whole body had been jostling, rocking gently from front to back, until it stopped in concert with the voice. It was a familiar voice, friendly, despite the high pitch of its worry.

Above her head, sounds of movement, of creaking wood and the brief clang of metal, reached her. A horse snorted and stamped a foot.

"My lady?" Footsteps brought the voice alongside her head, and this time she recognized its tentative tone.

And then she remembered. Her side burned with pain, and she managed to slide a trembling hand across her stomach until she found the wrinkle of the bandage that swelled beneath her left armpit.

"Don't—don't." Marek's fingers slipped beneath the coverlet to catch her hand before she could press the wound. He moved her hand back to her stomach and pulled the blanket all the way up to her chin. "You're going to be just fine."

She made herself open her eyes, and this time she was fully aware of her eyelids' great weight and the scrape of grit against her eyes. "Annan—"

Marek's face shaded her gaze from the gray light of the clouded sky. "He's not here." He smoothed her hair back from her face, inviting the cold sting of the wind against her skin.

She blinked and turned her head enough to see mottled crags, striped here and there with the green of cypresses. They were somewhere in the hills, in a day that bespoke of rain, herself on a pallet rigged with a horse on either end. The drowsy face of the bay charger given to Annan by Lord Stephen blinked at her from above her feet.

But Annan did not ride its saddle.

"Where is he?" The question thrummed in her chest, the words thrusting past her lips. A painful blackness threatened for a moment to wash out her vision, and she clenched her eyes. "Marek—?"

"He's… gone to find the man who did this to you."

"Why?" But she knew why. Annan had gone because he was driven to go. Because by entering his life, she had perhaps brought greater pain to him than all the unspeakable horrors of the years gone past.

"I don't want him to go…" Tears, welling from the pain of her side and the pain of fears laid bare by her injury, bled at the corners of her raw eyes.

"I know." Marek's hand was warm on her shoulder, even through the thickness of the coverlet. "I told him. But he'll come back. He always does."

She shook her head, but she didn't have the strength to speak the thought that filled her head: He couldn't come back every time. And when the day came when he didn't come back… she would spend the rest of her life, however long it might be, knowing she had been unable to save him from the darkness. She had been unable to save him from himself.

The tears flooded from her eyelids, falling warm upon her cheeks and turning cold in the breeze.

"Don't cry, lady. Please—you'll hurt yourself."

But she had to cry. What else besides her tears did she have left to bring before Heaven's throne?

A knight clad in the blue livery of the earldom of Guerrant galloped toward his enemy, spear couched beneath his arm, shoulders hunched in readiness for the impact.

From where he sat his horse between two striped tents, Annan watched. His chest tightened and, inside the confines of his helm, his breath echoed with an intensity that burned deep within his nostrils.

Only minutes earlier, this man, this minion of the accursed Hugh de Guerrant, had raised his helm in respect to Bishop Roderic, and in that instant Annan had no more doubts that he had found Mairead's would-be murderer. Whether or not it was the hand of God that had led him here, he knew not. But one way or another, here they were, together in the same place, in the same time.

The knight, toes forced down in his stirrups and his whole body braced for the impact, spurred his horse's side. The animal's stride lengthened, and the two combatants crashed one into another, lances splintering.

The blunted end of the murderer's spear caught his opponent in the shoulder and flung him from his horse. The man landed hard, face-down, and lay there a moment, windless, while his conqueror waited until he was helped from the field. As a squire ran to catch the riderless horse, the victor trotted to the purple-shrouded dais that bore Father Roderic and his company.

Annan's fingers closed round the axe that lay across his saddlebow. Sweat stood out on his limbs, trickling its heat down his chest, infecting his blood.

It was time. And he was ready.

CHAPTER XXII

ORD HUGH'S LIEUTENANT—a Norman who had been with Hugh since childhood, as far as Roderic knew—had acquitted himself well. Better than well, in fact; he had swept the field before him. Not one knight had been able to challenge him.

Whatever Bertrand had done to displease Hugh must have been unpardonable for Hugh to have deprived himself of such an able soldier. Roderic rose from his cushioned seat of honor at the front of the dais and applauded against the back of his hand. Hugh's loss was about to become Roderic's gain.

In the absence of Brother Warin, Roderic's need of a new lieutenant was growing most inconvenient. Bertrand's crime against Hugh, whatever it may have been, was about to become the means to his promotion. Roderic's lip curled. What would Master Hugh think of that development?

For now though, plots and successions would have to wait. Roderic stepped to the front of the box and lifted his hands to still the crowd's excitement.

"Yeomen!" He raised his hands higher still. "Your silence, please. Come forward, Sir Bertrand!"

The knight's chest rose beneath the black griffin de Guerrant. He approached, lance raised before his face in a salute.

The crowd's murmuring swelled, changing from adulation to alarm. Across the meadow, a lone knight galloped, the raindrops dashing against his helm.

Roderic's limbs jerked taut, his speech freezing in his throat. He had walked among the greatest political leaders of the world for too long not to hear the silent scream of danger that flew before the strange knight. The hair on his arms prickled; gooseflesh rose and pinched his skin.

Almost before Bertrand could turn his head to see through the eye slits of his helmet, the knight was upon him. The knight's right arm rose behind his head, the blade of his axe glinting against the raindrops.

Time slowed. All Roderic could hear was the beat of his heart. His vision faltered. He watched, mouth still parted, wanting to believe this was just another specter raising itself from the red murk of the dreams that had haunted him since Acre. But it wasn't.

The knight cut Bertrand down without slowing and without looking back. As he galloped past, the silver of his blade dull with blood, he turned his head in Roderic's direction, and behind the faceless, expressionless mask, Roderic could feel the man's gaze burning into his.

The crowd broke, most of them rushing to Bertrand's headless body. As if they could help *him*. A few of the mounted knights gave chase to the unknown assassin. But they would not catch him. Roderic could not even begin to hope they might catch him.

Realizing his arms were still lofted, he cinched them around himself and tried to pretend his bones did not feel as though they were trying to melt into the tightness of his muscles.

"Your Grace?" The clipped Syrian accent of Sir Alard, the Antiochan noble who stood at his side, might have been a mace against a rock wall.

Roderic gritted his teeth. His eyes did not leave the swift trail of the knight's gray courser galloping into the anonymity of the city.

Sir Alard gripped Roderic's sleeve. "Who was he? Do you know who he was?"

Roderic could feel the pinch at the base of his skull that would clamp into a vise by the time he reached his quarters. "Marcus Annan."

"Who?" Alard darted a look after the group of horsemen who were giving chase.

Roderic caught up his robes. He should never have agreed to this barbaric exhibition. Alard released his arm and said no more, probably because he thought that was where the matter ended.

But what could he possibly understand? Nothing!

The heat of anger and the cold of fear clashed in Roderic's stomach, churning his innards into nausea. How could Hugh have erred to such a colossal extent? For all Roderic knew, Hugh might have stolen off with Mairead of Keaton and left Annan to seek revenge on whom he might. Or mayhap *this* was the mistake for which Bertrand had been dismissed?

His blood turned to sludge beneath his skin, and he stopped, halfway down the dais's hollow-sounding steps, and cursed them both.

"Your Grace?" Alard, close behind him, leaned forward.

"Be still, you fool!"

"Ah... Yes, your Grace."

Roderic stalked to where Odo held his bay mare in readiness. Earlier that morning, as he appeared before a cheering crowd, he had held his trailing robes up from the dew-wet grass. Now, he hardly cared if they were ruined forever.

Not waiting for his escort, he mounted the mare and whipped her forward. He was no longer safe in Antioch, that was clear. And he had no intention of ignoring Marcus Annan's all too clear warning. As soon as he could gather his entourage, he would be leaving.

His spur gouged the mare's side. He would return to Jaffa and to Richard. Perhaps, after all, he would be safest in the middle of a war.

After his parting with Bishop Roderic in Jaffa, and all the revelations their severance had entailed, Brother Warin had discovered he no longer believed in the cause of the Crusade. He had wanted to believe— had wanted to fight for it, even unto the shedding of his last drop of blood.

But he couldn't.

The tourneyer Annan had been right. Though God Himself must shudder at the infidel occupation of His blessed Holy Land, He could never want it rescued by men such as led this Great Crusade. This Kings' Crusade.

And so Warin had left behind Jaffa, his brother Templars, his King, and his dreams of winning back the Temple of the Holy City.

He had set his face toward the northern ports, in order that he might leave unnoticed. Tonight he had made it almost as far as Lattakieh.

Full darkness had fallen only minutes before, forcing him to dismount. His footfalls and those of the horse walking behind him were muted in the sandy bank of the Orontes River. He listened to them, hearing the sand sliding beneath his feet. The wind soughed through the leafy branches overhead, whispering to itself, *tsking* its displeasure at this stranger in its midst.

At that moment, Warin had never felt more alone.

———————

Footsteps, no more than three spans away from where Annan's head lay in the sand of his bedding place, yanked him up from the beginning fog of sleep. His reflexes wrenched him to his feet and his dagger into his hand before the intruder could take another step.

The man's horse reared and tore its reins free from its master's restraint. Before the intruder could turn, Annan's arm clamped across his chest, pinning his arms to his sides. He slammed his blade against the man's throat, hard enough to bruise but not break skin.

"In the name of God—" The man, a knight judging from the grate of mail armor against Annan's forearm, lunged forward. His words were strangled with frustration and surprise. But some halfway familiar note made Annan's sword arm freeze, his blade hovering over the knight's windpipe.

He blinked, trying to shake off his exhaustion long enough to think. All day, he had ridden, fleeing the posse of knights who had given chase after he had slain Hugh's lieutenant that morning. He tightened his grip across the man's chest. "Who are you?" His voice was hoarse. He hadn't spoken to anyone since the previous night in the inn.

"A soldier of the Temple." The knight eased his hand toward his sword. "A Crusader. Kill a Crusader, and you risk eternal damnation."

"Too late for that, Templar."

The man froze. "Marcus Annan?"

"You—" Annan leaned closer, the side of his chin pressed against the knight's cheekbone, and his knife bit deeper. "Roderic's Templar."

"Aye." The man straightened as much as he could, his hand no longer searching for his sword. "But if you think adding my death to your reputation will rid you of an enemy, you're wrong."

Annan shoved him away, nearly toppling the man to his knees. As the Templar regained his balance and turned to face him, Annan backed up until his feet were in the wet, crumbly sand of the waterline. He kept the dagger in plain view but lowered its point. "I've no reason to trust you."

Through the shadows, lit by the moon against the shifting clouds, the Templar gripped his sword, but made no motion to draw it. "Bishop Roderic and I have parted."

A heavy breath slid past Annan's nostrils, and he resisted the urge to rub at the grit of his eyes. Right about now would have been a good time to have the ever-suspicious Marek at his side—someone to remind him that this was likely nothing but an elaborate ruse to make him drop his guard.

"You don't believe me?" Warin said.

"Should I?"

"My word was good when you and the monk left my camp, wasn't it?"

"You didn't have a choice then." If they'd resisted his efforts to free Gethin, he would have strewn their bodies across the desert.

"I swear by the True Cross that I've left the bishop's service forever. If that isn't enough to satisfy you, and if it's a trial by battle you want, then let us have it."

"Perhaps we will." Annan stepped forward, and his dagger rose once more to point at the other man's heart. "Were you involved in the attack upon my wife?"

"Your—wife?" Moonlight flickered against the Templar's incredulous expression.

Annan took another step. His voice deepened until it was almost inarticulate. "The Lady Mairead."

The man looked as though he had been hit by a charging horse. "Lady Mairead—the countess? Hugh's attacked her?"

The weight of Annan's shoulders was suddenly too great to hold up. "She may be dead." He lowered his dagger to his side.

The Templar drew himself aright. "You have my word as a Knight of the Cross, a soldier of the Temple, and a Christian that I had no part in it. I swear it."

Against his every better judgment, Annan believed him. He was too tired not to believe him. Too tired to keep in mind that once he had gotten some sleep, he would probably remember he had reason to hate this man.

"Aye." It wasn't the right thing to say. It probably didn't even make sense. But it didn't matter.

A gust of wind churned through the riverbed, whipping the water into white breakers.

"I'm sorry," the Templar said.

Annan only nodded.

———

By the time they reached Stephen's home, a haze of red shrouded Mairead's vision. Marek brought her to the door and sent Ducard scrambling to find his master.

She exhaled and heard herself whimper before she could even remember making the sound. She needed to see Annan again, needed to tell him it wasn't his fault. She *needed* him to hold her against him as the pain avalanched through her body.

She clenched her teeth. Her throat felt clogged and sticky with phlegm and only half the size it was supposed to be.

"What is this?" Lord Stephen's voice boomed in her ears.

"It's Lady Mairead, Sir." Footsteps brought the voices nearer. "She's wounded."

A hand too large to be Marek's pressed her forehead. "Where's Annan?"

Marek didn't answer.

"Never mind," Stephen said. "I can guess. Who's done this?"

"I don't know. Annan's got a tolerable share of enemies."

"And the lady herself has at least one, or so I gather. Lady Mairead—" Stephen's hand lifted, and he leaned close enough that his words thundered inside her head. "Can you hear me?"

She made herself squint her eyes open, but all she could see was the occasional flash where the fire of a torch penetrated the night.

Stephen swore under his breath. "What have they done to her? Ducard!"

A moan seeped between her teeth. She could only wish for strength enough to pull her arms from beneath the warmth of the blanket and cover her ears with her hands.

Stephen, unaware, kept roaring. "Get her off this thing!"

No doubt they tried to unfasten her pallet gently, but every time they touched the frame, waves of pain hammered against her heart.

Somewhere between the courtyard and the bedchamber, she must have swooned, because the next thing to penetrate the red haze was the palette bumping to a stop.

Lady Eloise's voice raged somewhere not too far away. "Fiends! They're fiends, I tell you! What have they done to her?"

"Hush, woman." Lord Stephen scooped Mairead up, and her body crumpled between his arms. She bit her lip until she tasted blood, and the scream welling inside turned to another moan.

"'Tis all right," Stephen said. He laid her down and a straw tick rose up on either side to surround her. Blankets fell into place over her, but a shuddering wave of chills came anyway.

Stephen's voice again, farther away: "Get the priest."

"Nay—" She forced the word out. "I don't need the rites—"

"Nay, dear heart, not to read the rites." Eloise's hand was soft and warm against her cheek. "He'll pray over you."

She groped until she found Eloise's hand. "I need Annan."

"He's gone away to keep you safe."

"Then send Marek to me, please—"

"Ssh. The lad needs to sleep. As do you. Hush now, Father John will be here soon. Very soon."

Under the steady rhythm of Lady Eloise's hand upon her hair, her shivers began to dissolve. She released the clench of her jaw and let herself sink once more into the blur of red and black. Later, when she had more strength, she would insist they keep a man by her side... in case Annan *couldn't* make it safe for her...

———

By the time the Templar, Warin, caught his horse, Annan had built a small fire. If someone had tracked him this far, which he doubted, the fire might possibly be a death sentence. But he was fairly certain he had lost his pursuers before he had even left Antioch.

And as things stood now, if he were going to stay awake long enough to make certain this Templar wasn't going to stab him in his sleep and use his death as grounds to regain Roderic's favor, he needed a fire between them for at least a few hours longer.

Once the crackle of flames was bouncing knee high and their bellies were partially full of black bread and dried stockfish, Warin surprised him by being the first to speak. "Does the name Veritas mean anything to you?"

"It's the Latin word for truth."

"It's also the name of a man."

"What man?"

"Someone who has been acting as an anonymous informer to the bishop. His knowledge is uncanny, clairvoyant even. And most of it has been in regard to this monk they call the Baptist. You're familiar with him, I know."

Annan ignored the satire. "What about the Baptist?" The wind shifted, bringing the tang of wood smoke to his nostrils. Did Warin know the truth about Gethin after all?

"Veritas told us what the Baptist was preaching, what towns he traveled through, and how we could thwart him. His missives came to me, and I brought them to the bishop. We never knew where they came from, only that his words were never false."

Warin looked up from the piece of cheese he had been rolling back and forth in his fingers. "It was Veritas who encouraged Lord Hugh's attentions to the Countess of Keaton. He was keeping us informed of the Earl of Keaton's actions and the Baptist's and this Matthias of Claidmore's—so that we could kill them when the time came."

"And when the time came, you hired me."

"Aye."

"What's your point?"

Warin turned his head toward the river, staring without really seeming to see. He flicked the cheese onto the sand of the shore. "Maybe I don't have a point. Not one you would care about anyway."

"If it involves any man who encouraged what happened to the Lady Mairead—I care."

Warin turned back. "I know who he is."

"Veritas?"

He nodded. "I've seen him twice, but I didn't know it was him. I don't know his name or where to find him." His eyes, almost orange with the flickering reflection of the fire, grew as sharp as any of Annan's blades. "But you do."

Annan's brows came together. "What?"

"It's that man. Your traveling companion. The one you wouldn't let me take to Roderic."

What? Annan had to make himself blink. *Gethin* was informant to Roderic?

"I didn't know it was him at the time," Warin explained. "But he made me curious. When the army was leaving Acre, he stopped me and told me you hadn't died in the prison camp as we had thought. That you had escaped, with a woman."

The air mired in Annan's windpipe. Gethin was responsible for all this? Gethin, who had once been more to him than any brother? He had orchestrated all this—the mendicant charade, Lord William's death, the attacks upon Mairead—just to wreak his own twisted vengeance?

He barked out a laugh that wasn't a laugh at all.

Warin peered at him. "I would never have realized it myself except he wrote to the bishop about things that none could have known save those who were present that evening you came to rescue him."

"Does Father Roderic know?"

"Nay. I didn't tell him. He'll wake up some morning to find himself entangled in his own web."

Annan's limbs trembled, and he found he could stay still no longer. He rose to his feet, paced a few strides into the darkness, and stood with his hands on his hips, pulling the cold night air into his lungs.

Behind him, the Templar spoke on, more to himself than to Annan. "One thing I would know. Why should this man care about destroying Matthias and the Baptist? When he was with me, he talked as if he agreed with them."

Annan whirled. "You fool. He *is* the Baptist."

It was Warin's turn to look as if someone had slammed the end of a cudgel into his stomach. "What—" The firelight turned the hollows of his face to ghastly canyons. "That can't be true."

Breathing as though he had forgotten how, he rose to his feet. When his eyes lifted to meet Annan's, they held the light of full realization. "Then Roderic has been a pawn in the Baptist's hands since the beginning."

"We all have."

"But why?" Warin took a step to join him. "What does he want? Not for us to find him and kill him, obviously."

Annan swallowed the copper taste of bile. "He wants to reconstruct what happened at St. Dunstan's the day Roderic had him tortured. He wants to change it, so it ends the way he thinks it should have. He wants Matthias to kill Roderic."

"I thought you said you'd killed Matthias?"

"Gethin doesn't believe me." Gooseflesh pimpled the skin of his arms.

"Then…" The Templar took another step and stopped in the corner of Annan's vision. "He won't stop this madness. He's going to try to kill all of you. You know that. And probably the countess first of all."

"He's not going to get the chance." Forcing his exhaustion, his pain, his confusion down deep inside himself, Annan filled his lungs and turned to fetch his equipage. He hefted the saddle onto his shoulder and rose to find the weary gray courser. The courser that Gethin had given him. The courser that he would ride in pursuit of Gethin. All the way into the depths of Hell if he had to.

In the dark alley outside the inn where Hugh and his men had stopped for the night on their way to Antioch, Hugh was accosted by a shadow in a black cowl. Alone and half-drunk, he nearly pitched onto his face. But the stranger was too quick. He seized Hugh by the throat before he could fall and slammed him into the wall.

"Listen to me." The voice that hissed from within the cowl was English, with a strong Cheviot accent. "You're following the wrong trail. Marcus Annan goes to Antioch to kill your man Bertrand. If he finds you there, he will kill you too."

"Wha— Who are you?" Hugh fumbled for his sword, but the stranger, though a head shorter, slammed him against the wall once more, knocking the breath from his lungs.

"Go back to the home of Stephen of Essex."

"Stephen of Essex?" He squinted.

"Aye. The lady is there."

"She's still alive?" His brain was beginning to clear. Who was this man? How did he know these things? "Who in the name of St. Denis are you?"

"Roderic is returning to Jaffa. Take the lady to him. Annan will follow, and you must leave word for him that the only way he can save her is to bring Matthias of Claidmore. Tell him." The stranger relaxed his fingers, and the blood began to throb back into Hugh's throat. The stranger backed away from Hugh and reached with both hands to straighten his cowl.

"Who are you?" Hugh pushed up from the wall, remembering suddenly that he should probably be reaching for his sword. "Tell me now why I should believe any of this."

"Because—" the shadow turned his head until his face, warped with scars, gleamed in the moonlight— "I am *the truth*."

Hugh staggered away from the wall, but his assailant had disappeared into the night winds. Only an echo of him remained: *The Truth*.

Veritas.

CHAPTER XXIII

MAIREAD'S FEVER HAD cooled, and when she was awake, she could make her thoughts form straight lines. But pain still dominated her dreams. She dreamt she was in child labor again, her body tearing itself in half from the hips up, the hand of a foreign-speaking midwife crushed within her sweating palm. Lord William waited elsewhere, probably preparing the passage that would take them from Marseilles to Acre.

When first he saw her with her son lying in her arms, he was kind. He smiled and laid a hand on tiny David's head. He would have raised him as his own, she knew. But he never had the chance. The very next day, they buried the baby who was her shame and her joy.

The day after that, they sailed for the Holy Land and the darkness of the future.

She woke with a start, her brow cold with sweat. "Marek—"

A sleepy grunt from the chair at her bedside told her that he, at least, was still there. "Lady?"

"I heard something."

He leaned forward, the chair creaking, and he inhaled as he rubbed his face. "Probably just beasties."

She lay still, one hand covering the throb of the wound in her side, and listened with all her strength to the hum of the silence. Something had woken her, just as it had woken her the night she had escaped from Hugh.

Marek shifted again in the seat he had occupied almost constantly since their arrival at Stephen's castle. A bird flapped past the window. The rafters groaned in the night wind.

She heard it again: the clatter of arms, the stamp of horses' feet.

Her body went tight as the string of a lute. "*Marek.*"

This time he started fully awake. "What?"

"Listen."

Across the courtyard, a voice, ghostly in its solitude, called from atop the wall, "Who goes there?"

The answer was indistinct: no words, no voices. And yet, Mairead knew who had spoken as clearly as if he stood at the foot of her bed. "It's him— He's come for me." Her voice clawed her throat. Her aching body lurched to a sitting position.

"Who?" Marek got up and trudged to the window. His body blocked for a moment the shaft of moonlight that pooled across the bare floor.

"Hugh. It's Hugh."

"How do you know?"

Because I know. But she had no need to answer. The unmistakable twang of a crossbow preceded the elongated shriek of the sentry.

Marek jumped a full pace away from the window. "St. Jude!"

Metal clanged against stone; someone shouted below.

"Marek—" With one hand pressing the blankets against her side, she forced her spine straight. Her other hand clamped onto the bed frame, the blood throbbing beneath her fingernails.

"Grappling hook." He spun around, one hand on his sword. His eyes were wild, desperate. "He's sending someone over the walls to un- bolt the gates. I have to tell Stephen—"

"Don't leave me!" If Hugh found her here, she would never escape.

Marek's stride wavered for only a second. Then he pressed on to the door, dragging its weight into the room and drawing a gust of wind from the window. "I must. I'll return before they breach the castle, I promise." Darkness veiled his eyes as he looked back at her, but the quiver of his body declared that he was torn. The raw terror of her voice was only doubling his own fears.

But, somehow in the days since she had met him, Peregrine Marek had become a man. He would do what was right; he would do what Annan would have done. More lives than just her own were at stake.

"Go," she breathed, even as her heart screamed for him to stay. She knew he had to go. It was the only way to prevent Hugh and his men from storming through the castle's every room. She shuddered.

God of Heaven, help us!

———————

Hugh hadn't even time to wipe away the sweat beneath the edge of his mail hood before Esmé threw open the gates from within the courtyard. "The way's clear," Esmé said. "No alarm call yet."

"Let us keep it that way." Hugh filled his lungs, lifted his lance, and touched a spur to his horse's side.

Far away, somewhere near the mountains, a wolf cried, and Hugh raised his lance in a silent salute. Good hunting to them both.

"Who goes there?" A man's stentorian voice rang out through the night.

Hugh swiveled his head to find the speaker. There. A shadow flickered on a balcony two windows up, and a sword gleamed against the moonlight as it was fastened round a waist. His smile deepened. "Lord Stephen?"

"Who are you?" The man turned away and spoke to someone behind him, "Send Ducard for a guard."

Hugh stopped his horse in the middle of the courtyard. He would make a handsome target should anyone have brains enough to pull out a crossbow while they still had time. His smile deepened. "There's no need for that, I assure you, my lord. I come to you as a fellow Englishman, far from the warmth of a home fire!"

Stephen paused. "You have breached our walls, Sir."

"On the contrary—" He lowered a hand and motioned Maurice to take half the men forward and find entrance however they could. Since Lord Stephen was in such an agreeably garrulous mood, Hugh meant to make good use of it. "We found the gates open."

"Bah!" That was a woman's voice, shrill and tight. "He's lying. It's that Norman, I tell you."

Hugh's chest tightened. Lady Eloise was going to pay her own price before this day was over.

"Call for the sentry," she demanded.

Stephen hesitated. "Adam?" He stepped farther onto the balcony, his figure perfectly silhouetted against the darkness of the castle. "Adam?"

Hugh looked at Esmé. "Kill him."

His retainer broadened his stance, brought up his crossbow, and loosed a quarrel that struck Lord Stephen just beneath the breastbone. A beautiful shot.

Lady Eloise screamed as her husband grabbed for the arrow in his stomach and crumpled like an undermined mountainside. Hugh pressed his tongue against his lower lip, considering for a moment having Esmé put a swift end to her grief. Nay, the old hag deserved a better sendoff than that.

"Lord?" Esmé and his men looked up at him, bodies tensed.

From the stables, men were running, no doubt wakened by their mistress's screams. Hugh took them in at a glance and curled his lip. "Dispatch 'em."

"Yessir."

The first drizzle of arrowfire spattered from the window slits high overhead. He galloped to the doors. "Maurice?"

"We're through."

He could have laughed. These fools! They hadn't even had time to bolt their doors. He leapt from his horse and tossed the reins to one of Maurice's men. One glance over his shoulder was enough to satisfy him that Esmé had the group of would-be defenders well in hand. Good. He had no wish to end this night with a misericorde in his back.

"Come." He led the way, sword in hand, his heartbeat heavy with the joy of victory. Save for that heartbeat and the clanking footsteps of his men, the great cavernous halls stretched before them, empty and silent. "Split up. Whoever finds the countess is not to move her until I come. And be cautious, she's wounded." He lifted a hand above his shoulder and gestured for Maurice to accompany him.

Mairead had made Marek help her dress—she would not face Hugh de Guerrant in naught but a chemise—and now she sat in the shadows by the window, one hand against her side, the other pressed to her face as she prayed.

Outside the door, footsteps thumped at the end of the empty passage. She forced her eyes to open and lowered her hand so that it covered just her mouth. Marek, sword clenched at his side, stood before the door. Only the heave of his shoulders betrayed the strain of his nerves.

Hugh would probably kill him. The breath she had been holding came out as a sob. "Marek. Don't try to stop them. Let them come. I want you to be able to go back home, please—"

"Quiet."

Halfway between the stairwell and her chambers, a door crashed open. "Swine!" Eloise shrieked. "Touch her, and I'll kill you myself!"

"Go back to your husband, woman. Tell him that tonight his castle will burn down around his corpse."

Hugh's voice summoned a prickle of cold from the heat of Mairead's skin. Her hand slid down the taut cords of her neck and came to rest on her collarbone. Her pulse thrummed beneath her fingers.

Eloise uttered a strangled, wordless cry, and Mairead could almost see the woman hurling herself at Hugh. The scuffle lasted only minutes, Eloise screeching the whole time. "Lock her in," Hugh said. "We'll deal with her later."

A thump, as of Eloise being thrown bodily into her room, and the door slamming closed upon her screams, were punctuated with the resumed tread of Lord Hugh de Guerrant and his companion.

Marek stiffened, his body tilted forward, balanced on the balls of his feet, ready to spring. He crossed himself with his free hand, even as the door's lock clicked stubbornly against Hugh's hand on the latch.

Hugh tried it once more and then two mail-clad shoulders pounded into it. Once, twice—and on the third attempt, the lock snapped and the door flew inward. Marek didn't wait. He charged with a roar that all but swallowed up his lithe body.

Mairead could tell at a glance which of the two shadows in mail was Hugh de Guerrant. Were she anywhere in the world, she would recognize that tall, straight form. But Marek had not the benefit of her familiarity. Unable to see faces in the dark, he lunged at the stockier body of the man-at-arms.

Mairead's hand fell from her throat to the dagger in her lap. Marek had the chance for only one blow, one kill. And he had chosen the wrong man.

His blade connected below the shoulder joint while the man-at-arms was regaining his wits after his stumble through the doorway. A sickening crunch of bone and a rush of exhalation from the man-at-arms was all Marek's momentary advantage purchased them.

Hugh swore, obviously caught off guard, and swung with his own sword. The movement was pure reaction, with no art and no strength, but it caught Marek squarely in the side, clattering against his mail coat. He kept his feet, but the moment in which he was doubled over was all Hugh needed to pivot into a fighting stance and swing with both hands.

"Marek!" Mairead lurched from her chair and made it all of one step before her brain started spinning within her skull.

But it was enough. Marek's blade flashed up to protect his face. He parried two more strikes before Hugh struck his sword from his hands and sent it hurtling across the floor into the hall.

"Very noble of you, *garçon*." Hugh's breathing came in gusts. "But misguided. Maurice?"

The man-at-arms had his good shoulder against the wall and was easing himself back to his feet. "Broken arm... methinks."

Hugh grunted and turned his searching eyes toward the window. Mairead's swirling, panicked world tilted crazily. She heard a clank of metal—probably Maurice retrieving his sword—and Hugh telling him to watch Marek. Then he started toward her, and she made her stiff arms lift the dagger to point at his heart.

"Tut, tut, my dear. I hardly think you want to add to your wounds. I must say I'm glad to find you in such surprisingly good health."

Her breath tore at her lungs, more with fear than with pain. Hugh's hand closed round the dagger's handle, his fingers brushing hers, and he wrenched it from her grip. She dropped to her knees, and pain stabbed through her joints and her side.

"I find you in a much sweeter mood this time around." Hugh chuckled as he walked to the window, running his hand over the top of her head as he passed.

"She's wounded," Marek said.

"Shut up." Maurice shoved the point of his sword against Marek's ribs.

"Esmé!" Hugh shouted out the window. "Bring the pallet and half a dozen men!"

Down below, someone raised an assent, and Hugh turned back around. "What's your name?" he asked, his voice directed past Mairead.

"Marek."

"Marcus Annan's little manservant, I'd wager?"

Marek didn't answer; only glared.

"All the better." Hugh came forward again, swaggering, until only a pace separated him from Marek. "If you're still alive when I'm done with you, I want you to tell your master he can find his quean in Jaffa. Tell him if he's any wish of having her back, he'd best find this Matthias of Claidmore for an exchange." He leaned closer. "Tell him we're tired of waiting."

He hammered the flat of his blade into Marek's stomach, and the lad collapsed to his knees, air exploding from his mouth. Hugh laughed deep in his throat. "Good." He shoved Marek down and kicked him in the head.

Mairead squeezed her eyes shut. Would they beat him to death before her eyes? She clenched her teeth, begging for the mercy of unconsciousness.

More footsteps tramped down the hallway, and Maurice stepped away to call to them. They stopped at the doorway, but Mairead didn't open her eyes. Another blow, another of Marek's cries, and her chin fell to her breast.

"Well, well." Hugh was as cheerful as she had ever known him. "A profitable night. Danton, put the lady on the pallet. Esmé, come with me. This laddie, here—" Another kick. "—saw fit to break poor Maurice's arm. Let's see if we can't return the favor. We'll take him into the next room and bid him farewell over the balcony."

"No—" Mairead's head snapped up. "You can't."

Hugh barely glanced at her. Marek lay in a ball at his feet, his eyes squinted and his gritted teeth visible through parted lips.

"My Lord Hugh—" She planted a hand on the floor to either side of her knees and struggled to get up. Pain pounded in her side and flooded through her brain, ricocheting against her temples.

Someone pushed against her shoulders, holding her down.

Esmé dragged Marek, struggling and kicking, to his feet, and hauled him from the room. In the doorway, Hugh paused to watch his men heave her into the sag of a canvas pallet.

"Listen to him scream, my dear." He might have winked; through the shadows, she couldn't tell for certain. "And then I think I'd better see to the lady of the house. Danton, when you're done there, tell the men to fire the castle."

"Aye, lord."

Mairead closed her eyes and listened, too exhausted even to loose the tears that welled inside as they hurled Marek from the neighboring balcony to meet the hard stone of the courtyard.

CHAPTER XXIV

NNAN AND THE Templar weren't yet within sight of Stephen's castle when the realization of something amiss penetrated the shield of Annan's focus. He reined to a halt.

"What is it?" Warin asked.

"I don't know." He frowned. The hills were silent and dreary, but some intuition he couldn't yet describe told him something very wrong had happened here.

Beside him, Warin threw back his head and sniffed. "Smell that?"

Annan breathed deeply. Smoke tinged the morning air. It wasn't the smoke of a wood fire; it was the heavier, fouler smoke of devastation. And here, in the hills above the road to Constantinople, the only possible target for someone's devastation was Stephen of Essex.

His lungs, his heart, and whatever else made its home within his chest collapsed with the weight of the knowledge. Hugh had found her again… He slammed his spurs to Airn's sides, and the horse leapt into a headlong gallop. He pulled his sword as he rode, but he knew by the smell of the smoke that whoever had set the fire was long gone ere now.

At the brow of the hill, he reined to a stop. The move was reflex, a futile attempt to make good the hope that this was all a dream.

But it was not.

The walls of thick, square-cut stone stood as erect as ever, stolid and stalwart and stupid in their inability to know that a reason for them to stand no longer existed. Smoke trickled from the windows, from the arrow slits, from the tower crenellations, shadowing the courtyard under its film of gray and blurring from sight the possibility that Hugh de Guerrant—for who else could it be?—had left anyone living to tell the bleak tale. A groan built up inside, swelling his ribs, aching to be released. But he wouldn't let it go.

He would not find Mairead. If Hugh had not at last taken her as his prize, then he would undoubtedly have made certain she was dead this time.

Warin reined up beside him. "Blessed Mary…" His hand moved to cross himself, his eyes on the shell of Stephen's home. "These are the people you spoke of?"

Annan pricked Airn forward, his hand heavy on the reins, controlling the horse's jitters. He had come here to find Mairead, to see if she still lived. But Gethin and his minions—his deceived and twisted minions—had bested him yet again.

They trotted through the gates. Burnt down to hardly more than the blackened iron hinges, they hung wide open on the gateposts. As they entered the courtyard, dodging the bodies of fallen men, none of whom were enemies, the wind shifted, blowing eastward into the red of the rising sun. The courtyard cleared, but there was nothing to see, save more bodies.

He reined to a stop and swallowed past the dryness of his throat. His eyes lifted of their own accord to find the window from which, a lifetime ago, Mairead had bid him farewell. It was empty, as he had known it would be.

He started to turn away, but the sound of a cry—high, shrill and unearthly, but definitely that of a woman—chilled his flesh upon his bones.

Warin's horse spooked, half-rearing and running backward. "In the name of the saints—"

Another scream shivered in the morning air, but this time it was mostly inarticulate words. And this time, Annan could tell the voice was not Mairead's.

Lady Eloise, then?

Sword still in hand, he dismounted and handed the reins to Warin. "Wait for me."

He entered the foyer through gaping doors and stood for a moment, sword held before his left shoulder. The fire here had not burned as intensely as in the outbuildings. Perhaps someone had been able to put it out before it had properly started. Thin sunlight, choked with the smoke, trickled through the windows to either side of the door. The wooden furniture—chairs, tables, and coffers—bore the unmistakable black scars of the flames.

Relaxing his arms, he took a step forward. No one came to challenge his entry. No one seemed to know of it at all. Did that mean they were all dead? His stomach, empty since the repast of the night before, twisted.

The circular stairway at the far end of the passage had burned more thoroughly than much of the house. From what he could see around the curve of the wall, the steps had crumbled into cinders in as many as half a dozen places. Footprints not quite small enough to be a woman's showed where someone had climbed through the soot. He stared at them. Mairead's? His stomach cramped. It was a false hope. He knew it was a false hope.

The stairs groaned under his weight, the boards straining and cracking, but they held. He reached the top and turned the corner—right into the point of a blade.

"Stop!"

His left hand snapped up to thrust the blade away, even as his right hand brought his own sword swinging against his attacker's neck. Before the blade could connect, his eyes found the other's face, and he jerked both hands back as though they had been burnt. "Marek—"

"Annan—oh, God…" Marek swayed where he stood, and his free hand crept up to hold his shoulder. Blood, most of it dried deep red, stained his face, starting at a gash on his brow and streaking like angry fingers down across his cheek. Beneath the blood, his face was splotched purple, one cheek swollen and blackening with bruises.

"Mairead— What's happened to Mairead?" Annan came forward, his heart thumping loud enough to drown his own thoughts. He reached to grasp the lad by the shoulders, but Marek fended him off.

"Don't. My shoulder came out." Marek closed his eyes, and his brow creased as though he were an old man. "I got it back in."

"*Marek.*" Annan's voice rumbled. "*What's happened?*"

He just stood there, swaying. "They took her."

Annan's hands fell to his sides. Marek had allowed them to take her? He had stood here, alive, while Hugh de Guerrant committed God knew what atrocities against the woman whose life Annan had trusted to him? "You let them take her?"

Marek's eyes snapped open, his pupils tiny against the red veins of his eyes.

"I trusted you!" Annan said. "I trusted you to die for her!"

"I tried." He closed his eyes again, his voice hoarse.

Annan took a step closer, looming over the lad, the strength of his arms trembling. "Not hard enough." And then he pushed past, suddenly wishing with all his heart that he had left Peregrine Marek to rot in that Glasgow dungeon.

In her chambers, he found Lady Eloise sitting in a half-burnt wreck of a chair, wrapped to her chin in a dirty gray blanket. Her eyes were closed, her silver hair falling around her face like a veil. She was shaking with more than cold.

Annan came farther into the room, and his rage turned chill within him. What had they done to her? But he knew. Another step showed him the body of Lord Stephen, a black hole in his stomach, eyes staring at the ceiling.

"Lady." His voice cracked.

Her eyes flew open. They were glassy, unseeing. But she recognized him. "Master Annan."

He came closer and knelt on one knee at her side. "Lady, I'm sorry. I brought this on your house."

Her eyes focused with some difficulty, and she curled herself tighter into the blanket. "It was the will of God."

And that made it less his fault? He swallowed past the thickness of his throat, and his eyes shifted to Stephen's body. The man had been a friend. One of few. "We'll bury him."

She shook her head, and one arm emerged from the blanket and groped to find his shoulder. "Your boy... they dropped him over my balcony."

His neck muscles spasmed. They dropped Marek from the balcony? Marek—his son, his brother, his friend? Marek, who *had* given his life for Mairead. Was the lad to be blamed if Heaven hadn't been ready to take him?

Behind him, the frame of the door creaked, and he turned to see Marek leaning there, his swollen face damp. "Annan—"

"Never mind." The words came out in the reflexive growl that had for so long frightened Mairead. He rose to his feet. "What about your shoulder?"

The lad looked at the floor. "It'll be fine."

"We're leaving." He turned back to Lady Eloise. She stared at him, waiting. He couldn't very well abandon her here, no matter how desperate his need to pursue Mairead. "Where can I find you a haven?"

"Nowhere."

"Lady, I can't leave—"

She lifted her hand from her lap in a wave full of weariness. "Find Mairead. Ducard went for help. He'll be back before the night falls. And if he is not..." She shrugged.

The scar on Annan's cheek quivered. "Lady Eloise."

She dragged her eyes up to his face.

"I'll find them. Where, I don't know. But I *will* find them."

"I know where," Marek said.

Annan turned. "What?"

Marek tilted his head up, and his shaggy hair fell over his eyes. "They're taking her to Jaffa."

"Jaffa..."

Marek lifted his head a bit more. "They said, to get her back, you have to bring Matthias of Claidmore in exchange."

274 – K.M. WEILAND

Annan froze. So *this* was Gethin's master stroke.

"Annan!"

His senses jerked back into focus, and his hand scrambled for his sword, even as Marek leapt into the hallway to engage Warin.

"Stop!" Annan crossed the room and jerked the lad back by the hood of his jerkin. Marek grunted his pain, and Annan immediately regretted the act.

"It's all right," he said, as much to Warin as to Marek.

"But it's him! The Templar!"

"It's all right, lad." Warin lowered his sword. "I've no notion of fighting you any longer."

"And why's that?" The swelling of Marek's face stretched tight.

Annan didn't let him answer. "Hugh's taken her to Jaffa," he told Warin.

"How do you know?"

He nodded to Marek. "How many hours head start have they?"

Marek lowered his sword slightly. His eyes remained flinty with suspicion. "Maybe five."

"Five hours. If we take the time to bury Stephen and see Eloise to safety in the nearest Christian city, we could give pursuit in less than a day."

Warin shook his head. "If the countess is still alive, Hugh will have to protect her fragile condition, and since time is short that would mean traveling by sea."

Annan was silent, figuring in his mind. "Then they could already have reached port in St. Symeon."

"Aye. Which means we wouldn't be able to overtake them before they reach Jaffa itself—*if* Jaffa isn't under siege by then."

"Siege?" Marek's frown burrowed deeper. "I thought peace negotiations were under way."

Annan had heard rumors of the renewed siege while still in Antioch. It seemed the Turks couldn't resist one more strike upon the Christian army. They had attacked Jaffa once already, within the last week, and the city had been saved only by Richard's hasty intervention. "Sometimes the best peace is when there is no longer an enemy with whom to negotiate."

"If Richard's stuck in Jaffa, the Moslems could stamp out the whole Crusade in one more battle."

Warin shook his head. "Richard's summoned troops from Caesarea."

"The battle could be over and done with before they get there."

"They'll get there." Warin looked at Annan. "But if the Turks have the city surrounded how do you propose to get in?"

Annan rubbed the lines in his forehead. They were deeper than he remembered. "I don't know." His hand slid down his face. A prayer welled in his heart, and for the first time in sixteen years he didn't crush it into silence. *Christ in Heaven, I am unworthy... but show me. Show me the way.*

"If the Moslems don't capture you, the Christians probably will. You realize that?"

His hand dropped from his face. He cocked his head. "That's a bad thing?"

"It is if you're a marked man, and after what happened in Antioch you undoubtedly fall into that category."

Marek spoke, "Even after we gain entrance to the city, we'll still have to find a way past the bishop's personal defenses."

"Maybe—" Annan pressed his lips together, staring at the ash-streaked stone of the passage wall. Warin was right. Besieged cities lived and died on their alertness. Anyone trying to gain entrance to Jaffa would probably be put under arrest until his identity could be ascertained.

But once Annan's identity was known was it not likely he would be taken directly to Bishop Roderic as a prisoner?

"I'm going to let them capture me."

Marek's gaze sharpened. "What?"

"Once they've taken me to Father Roderic, I can escape." He turned back into Eloise's room. "Lady, I'm going to Jaffa. Marek and Brother Warin will stay here with you until I can return. Do you understand?"

Her shoulders lifted beneath the gray blanket, but her eyes stayed on the floor. "Go, Marcus Annan. If you can find the Lady Mairead, perhaps you deserve her after all."

None of Stephen's horses remained within the smoldering stable, so Annan tightened Airn's girth once more and accepted the wallet of food Warin had scraped together from somewhere. The Templar looked him in the face, his gaze frank. "Good luck, Master Knight. God help you."

"And you." Annan's gaze wandered to where Marek waited a pace off, his body rigid, his head down. Marek and his gentle heart. The guilt was killing him... guilt that Annan's unthinking condemnation had only strengthened. "Laddie?"

Marek whirled. His eyes flashed in their hollow sockets. "Let me come with you."

"Nay—"

"Annan, please. I need to come with you."

"I said nay. You'll stay with Brother Warin and Lady Eloise. They need you more than I do."

Marek's shoulders dropped.

"Marek." Annan stepped closer and grasped the boy's uninjured shoulder. "Listen to me."

The lad looked up. The knot of muscle at the corner of his cheek worked itself back and forth.

Annan stared him in the eye, wanting to bore this into his brain more deeply than any message about swordsmanship or wisdom or keeping his confounded mouth shut. "I'm not sorry."

"What?"

"That Hugh didn't kill you. Don't think I'm sorry you're still alive."

The smoke against the sun made shadows of Marek's unruly hair, and Annan couldn't see into his eyes enough to tell if that knowledge made any difference. The knot in the lad's jaw didn't relax.

At the other end of the courtyard, the shattered gates groaned in the wind.

"It wasn't your fault," Annan said. He gave Marek's shoulder a squeeze, then turned to accept his reins from Warin. He mounted and paused to look over at the lad who had been his only companion for nigh on three years. "If you get out of Palestine alive, you go back to Maid Dolly."

Marek's head came up, his mouth opening. That was all Annan had time to see before he reined his courser around and spurred him into a run. They galloped through the broken gates, past the crumbled walls, into the gray-green of the hills.

CHAPTER XXV

RODERIC STOOD AT the mouth of the dark cell and stared at the woman upon the pallet. His heart pounded so hard it pained him to breathe, much less speak the fury tumbling in his brain.

This was the Countess of Keaton. She lay curled beneath the blanket, her face hidden in the dark riot of her hair. Whether her sleep was real or feigned, he had been unable to decide. But the very fact that she was here turned the pit of his stomach cold.

Lord Hugh, standing with hands clasped behind his back, spoke over Roderic's shoulder, "She'll live, your Grace. She isn't hurt so badly as that, and she's convalescing nicely."

Roderic whirled past him and stalked into the dark hallway. He waited until Hugh joined him, closing the cell door behind him.

"You fool!" Roderic spat. "It was Veritas's plan that she die—not that you bring her here as bait in some absurd trap!"

In the flicker of the torchlight, Hugh's eyes hardened. "Veritas changed the plan."

"He had no right to change anything! And you had no right to take his advice without consulting me!" He clamped his arms across his chest and groped for the comforting weight of his crucifix. "You don't even know for certain that this cloaked messenger *was* Veritas. It could have been a drunken Turk for all we know!"

"A drunken Turk who knew of Matthias and Annan and where to find the Lady Mairead? I think not. Besides," Hugh came forward a step, "his plan is brilliant."

"Hah!" Roderic pinched the crucifix harder. How could he tell Hugh that the plan's brilliance was the very thing that left his insides shaking? "Jaffa is about to come under siege again—this time by a force three times our current strength—the Baptist has been seen preaching within these very walls, and now you have the audacity to lure my enemies into my bedchamber!"

Hugh arched an eyebrow. "The Baptist is here?"

"*Yes.*"

Hugh's lips drew back, parting just enough to show his teeth. It was as close to a smile as Roderic had seen since they had left Normandy. "Then it appears," he said, "that Veritas has maneuvered all your rats into one fire. Doesn't it?"

Roderic could only glare as a sudden wave of nausea swept over him, muting upon his tongue the conviction that this fire would burn more than just the rats.

From Stephen's castle to Jaffa was a ride of six days. Annan made it in little more than four and a half. When he stopped, at last, mere miles from the city, it was only to give way to the infidel hordes encamped in the plains roundabout.

He leaned an elbow against his saddlebow, squinting at the Turkish army. Then he straightened and inflated his chest with the first scent of the evening's cooler air.

This was the fortress city of Jaffa, its repaired walls dark against the sunset red of the sea, pinpricks of early firelight just beginning to show through the window slits in the wall. Somewhere within those walls was Mairead—and probably Gethin and Father Roderic. All that separated Annan from them was a defeat. And with Saladin's armies crawling just within sight, Jaffa's watches would be double. It should be easier than teaching a cod to swim for him to engineer just such a defeat. *His* defeat.

Emptying his lungs, he laid the rein against Airn's neck and clucked. "Come along then. I've it in my mind to reward the first deserving patrol I can find."

The moon, swollen just beyond half-full and glowing a frothy yellow, hung above its distorted reflection in the sea. Annan wet his lips and tried to keep his breathing even. It was a useless effort. His body didn't understand that the Frankish-Syrian patrol ambling on the beach below wasn't yet a target. His limbs quivered in anticipation.

The soldiers' equipage clanked, just loud enough to be heard above the sweep of the tide as it rose and fell and rose again. Annan touched a spur to Airn's side, and the horse started forward. *God help me.*

The fall of sand from the courser's sliding hindquarters caught the attention of the Franks before he was halfway down the hill.

"*Arrêtez!*" one of them called, his mail sleeve glinting as he pointed.

The excitement of battle blossomed in Annan's brain, but he kept his right hand away from his sword. The courser lunged the final steps to the ground and tore across the beach toward the city gates.

"*Arrêtez! Vous êtes en état d'arrestation!*" The knights scrambled to follow, the hoofbeats strangely muted against the wet sand. Annan could hear the kiss of battle-honed blades leaving their sheaths.

He clenched his teeth, his hand clamping down on the courser's mouth, forcing it to slow its pace. The walls loomed before him; he was almost within their shadow. Any nearer and he would be shot by the archers on the embattlements before the knights could arrest him.

Hoofbeats pounded behind him. He waited, feeling the strain in the cords of his neck. *Almost, almost—now!* He grabbed for his sword and whirled the courser.

The nearest knight, little more than a length behind, hauled at his horse's gaping mouth and slid to a stop in time to engage Annan.

If this had been a true battle, the young Frank's head would have been rolling in the sand a long eternity before his sword could have met Annan's. But, for just this once in his life, Annan wasn't fighting to the death. He parried the youngster's blow, feinted to the left where he knew his blade would be easily blocked, then spun his horse to face the arrival of the others.

"*Arrêtez là-bas! Se rendre!*"

"Sir Bartholomew, we have him!" cried another.

Annan disengaged his sword and swung it in front of him to guard his face. The dark-haired knight, probably their leader, judging from the way their ranks shimmied apart to let him through, laid the edge of his own sword against the tip of Annan's. "*Qui vive?*"

"My name is Annan."

The man's eyes narrowed. His sword inched nearer. "Marcus Annan? The tourneyer?"

"Mayhap." He let his lips smile. "If I say yes, does that mean you've caught a bigger fish than you've net for?"

Bartholomew's eyelid twitched. "You're under arrest."

"What for?"

The squire on Bartholomew's left tensed to grab Annan's sword.

"For conspiracy against a holy Father of the Church and for the murder of a sworn knight of the Crusade."

The squire's mail-sheathed fingers caught hold of Annan's blade and tore it from his grip. Neither Annan nor Bartholomew flinched.

Bartholomew kneed his horse forward and leaned the point of his blade against Annan's heart. He smiled, his eye still twitching. "Come along. I hear the bishop is rather interested in seeing you one more time."

Bartholomew and two of his knights escorted Annan through the city with exemplary haste. Save for the light from an occasional house of merriment, Jaffa lay in silence. The anticipation of battle and the inevitable fear of a city about to be laid under siege was a dank vapor upon the empty streets and the shadows that swayed like drunkards at every corner.

Finally, after weaving through street after narrow street, they dismounted before a building of three stories. Annan craned his head, trying to see if a light still burned in any of the windows, but the overhang of the second floor and, higher up, that of the third floor, precluded the sight of anything but a sliver of sky and its smattering of white-hot stars.

Bartholomew pounded a fist against the door, and Annan grounded his attention. The other two knights stood on either side of him. They each rested a hand on him, one on his right shoulder, the other on his upper left arm, probably hoping to remind him, by the mere pressure of their hands, that resistance was futile.

They hoped in vain.

He flexed his hand against the bite of the rope that bound his wrists in front of him, then clenched his fingers into a fist, feeling the swell of his upper arm against the rough homespun of his sleeve. They had taken his sword and dagger—as he had expected. And they had bound him tight enough to make his hands throb from lack of blood— something he *hadn't* planned.

But if they thought he had any intention of continuing this docile act of following them like someone's pet goat, they were mistaken. They did well to fear Marcus Annan's reputation. A few minutes more, and they would discover why they feared.

Bartholomew pounded again, and this time the door creaked open. A hunched servant stepped halfway out, lofting a candle with one hand and trying to jam the hem of his tunic into his trousers with the other. "Stop it! Stop your banging! This is the bishop's house. Ye can't be banging on his doors!"

Bartholomew hesitated, probably weighing Roderic's anger at being disturbed against his gratitude for the delivery of such a coveted captive. "I've brought him a prisoner."

The servant, a Londoner from the sound of his accent, shook his head. "What's his Grace want with prisoners? Take 'em to the king or the Duke of Burgundy or whoever 'tis ye answer to. We've no want of them."

"He'll want this one."

The servant huffed and lifted his candle the better to see Annan. "Ah, well... Bring him in, then. If ye haven't already woken his Grace up, we can at least keep your prisoner 'til morn. Come."

Bartholomew stepped aside, and the escort pushed Annan into the doorway. He tensed, ready to swing his arms against the servant's candle and douse them all in darkness.

A voice stabbed across the street. "Wait, wait! Stop a minute! I know that bloke!"

His concentration snapped. *Marek?* He spun, bumping into one of the knights and setting them both off balance. In the flicker of the servant's candle, he could see Peregrine Marek—in person and in direct defiance to orders—blundering into Bartholomew's arms.

His fist clamped. What was that scurvy idiot doing here? Was the lad stark, raving drunk?

Marek pushed away from Bartholomew far enough to thump himself on the chest and then wave in Annan's direction. "I knows him."

"Do you now?" The Frank's twitching eye looked him over. "And just how is it you know him?"

"I'm *with* him. Whatever he's doin' here—" another thump on the chest "—I'm doin' it with 'im."

Bartholomew frowned, then turned to nod at the knight Annan had bumped against. "Throw him in, just in case the bishop wants to see him too."

"That's right. The blinking old bishop wants to see me too." Marek smiled happily, and then before Bartholomew's reaching hand could close round his collar, he slammed the hilt of a narrow-bladed dagger into the knight's chin.

Bartholomew staggered back, and with a cry, the other two Franks lunged at Marek. Annan swung around and battered his bound hands into the stomach of the London servant. The man's breath rushed from him in a gasp, and he and his candle fell into the mud of the street.

Annan plowed into the scuffle. He found one of the knights' mail-clad fists and ran his hands down to the blade. The edges bit into the calluses of his palms, but he wrenched it away with a single sweep of his arms and clubbed its hilt against the knight's face.

The man reeled, leaving only a ghost of movement where he had been standing. Annan flipped the sword around, took one step forward, and swung. He connected with the soft tissue of the man's abdomen, and the knight fell with a groan.

Sword in front of his face, Annan pivoted toward the sounds of the continuing skirmish. "Marek!"

"I'm busy!"

That was more than enough to distinguish Marek's voice from his opponent's furious grunts. Annan tore into the fray, swinging wide to compensate for his blindness. This time the blade crashed against bone. The man stumbled, and Marek tackled him, finishing him with his dagger.

Annan turned in time to hear the old servant picking himself out of the mud. "Saints in Heaven—!"

Annan took one running step, met him before he could rise from his knees, and dealt him a solid blow with the flat of his blade on the back of the head. Behind him, a similar thud told him Marek had remembered to administer the same service to the groggy Bartholomew.

For a moment they listened to their own breath gusting in the sudden silence of the street.

"Think anybody heard us?" Marek asked.

"Would you like to tell me what in the name of the faith you're doing here?"

"I came to help you, you great troll. Are your hands still tied?"

"What do *you* think?"

They withdrew into the shelter of the doorway, and Marek felt along Annan's arms for the ropes.

"Where's Warin?" Annan demanded.

"With Lady Eloise." Marek inserted his blood-sticky blade between Annan's wrists and slit the ropes in two quick cuts. "Don't worry. They're fine together."

Rubbing his wrists, Annan growled. "I don't suppose it even occurred to whatever swims around inside your head in place of a brain that plans are decided upon for a reason?"

"This plan had a fault in it." Marek ducked his head out the doorway, shot a glance in either direction, then pulled himself back in and eased the door shut. "Most notably, that you'd be dead if I hadn't decided to come along as protection."

Annan's snort wasn't quite as emphatic as it should have been. Despite its inevitable crooked bent, Marek's logic wasn't entirely without truth.

"Besides," Marek peered up at him, arms slack at his sides, "I had to help make this right."

Annan sighed. Blood oozed from the cuts in his palms, and he pulled one hand away from the sword to wipe it against the front of his tunic. "Aye. I know you did."

Somewhere down the passage, footsteps, no doubt of some awakened servant sent to find the meaning of the commotion in the street, creaked against the floorboards.

Annan glanced at Marek and gestured with his chin for the lad to go ahead. "Sheathe the sword," he whispered.

Marek's head flashed up and down in a nod. This was a ploy they had used more than once. Annan withdrew to the side of the foyer's doorway where he would be hidden. The footsteps drew nearer, and Marek straightened the front of his tunic with a jerk before stepping into their path.

"Hallo! You there, is there a physician in the house?"

The glow of a candle fell across the threshold of the door, almost touching Annan's feet. "What's happened?" The servant's voice was that of a young Londoner.

"Nasty little brawl, looks like. I just happened to be walking by, of course. Appears as though some of those poor wretches is going to be in need of a holy man."

"I'll fetch the bishop…" The servant's voice started to fade, as he turned away.

"No—wait, wait! You have to help me carry them in first."

Annan pressed farther into the corner, shoulders hunched and head bowed to accommodate the ceiling. He could hear the servant's shifting feet following Marek into the entry chamber. Annan's fingers squeaked against the sharkskin leather of his sword's handgrip, and he again rubbed one of his bleeding hands across his tunic.

The candlelight drifted in through the door, was blocked momentarily by Marek's shadow as he entered first, and then sprang forth again as the servant stepped inside.

Marek turned to face the servant and laid a finger to his lips. "Ssh!"

With Annan's hand over his mouth and the sword's edge against his ribcage, the lad shushed nicely. Marek caught the wavering candle and snuffed it between his fingers.

The servant thrashed against Annan's grip, then came to rest with both hands clamped on the wrist of the hand against his mouth. Annan bent low, his jaw shoved up against his prisoner's. "If you want to still have a heart in your chest tomorrow, then you'll help us."

The serving boy's fingernails bit into Annan's wrist.

"Bishop Roderic is holding my wife here."

The squirming stopped for a moment. Then she *was* here, undoubtedly. And every jack of a servant knew of it. Annan pressed harder with the blade. "Where is she?"

The lad started to shake his head, but Annan clamped down on either cheekbone hard enough for this impudent underling to know how easy it would be for him to crush his face without even trying. The head shaking immediately became a nod.

"Do you swear by the Holy City that you will not cry out if I let you go?"

Another nod.

He released his hold on the boy's mouth and drew back enough to take him by one shoulder and spin him around to face the door. "Take me to her."

From the other side of the street that Marcus Annan and his servant had just strewn with the bodies of a Frankish-Syrian sentry group, Gethin the Baptist limped into a narrow glow of moonlight. He lifted his cowl over the gooseflesh of his tonsure. His nostrils flared, his eyes narrowing to a hawk's-eye glint.

Annan had come. Just as Gethin had known he would, he had come. He folded his hands into his sleeves and picked his way across the muck of the street, avoiding the still forms that lay upon the road—detritus of the late battle.

His eyelids quivered. The quest for justice was almost at an end. For sixteen years, he had played the game, had nursed his hopes that everything that had happened to him at the Abbey of St. Dunstan's would finally be made right. Roderic of Devonshire and Matthias of Claidmore—they were the ones who had caused him to be beaten like a rabid dog and then cast aside for dead. They were the reason he even still carried the deep, riving scars upon his person.

But they would finish what they had begun. Just as would Gethin himself. Justice would be had. *Truth* would conquer.

And Marcus Annan would become a prisoner with no other choice but to comply with Gethin's demands.

At the doorway, he stopped and listened to the silence. Then, with a smile, he slipped inside.

Chapter XXVI

R ODERIC'S SERVING LAD led Annan and Marek to a staircase at the end of the passage. At the bottom of the stairs lay a stone-encased dungeon. Packed with cells, and only a narrow path between them, it smelt of earth and rust and ash. Water dripped somewhere. Annan brushed his free hand against the wall and felt the stones' moisture and the moss within the crevices.

"Who's there?" a voice, heavy with sleep, called. "MacDonald, is that you?"

Prison guard. "Answer him." Annan prodded his guide's shoulder.

The lad spoke through locked teeth. "Douglass, it's Odo. From upstairs."

The guard grunted. He jangled as he moved at the far end of the passage. Annan stopped short, one shoulder against the wall, and reached out to touch the other side of the passage. He had no room to maneuver here, and no way to rush the guard with this Odo lad stumbling along in front of him like a soggy bag of flour.

"Wait there 'til I find a torch," the guard, Douglass, grumbled. "If this is about the lassie again, ye can tell the bishop I ain't no nursemaid. If'n he wanted to keep her alive, why in the name of Bethlehem's star did he have that fool Earl of Guerrant drag her all the way to ill-fated

Jaffa? Eh?" Flint sparked against steel, and half a dozen pinpricks of orange spiraled towards the floor before winking back into darkness.

Annan tightened his grip on his handful of Odo's tunic, his eyes fixated on the spot of darkness that disguised the body of the guard. "Marek."

The lad moved in closer, his breath hot against the back of Annan's neck. "What?"

"Keep a hold on him."

"A hold on who?"

Flint and steel kissed once more, and this time the torch burst to life, illuminating the hunched figure of a portly, balding Scotsman. Annan shoved both himself and Odo sideways in the narrow passage, giving himself just enough room to hurtle past. He released the servant's tunic, leaving him to Marek, and once again closed both hands round his sword.

Douglass whirled to face him, his flint and steel clanging to the stones at his feet. "Sweet Virgin Mother! Who the devil are you?"

Annan didn't slow, and the guard had not even time to withdraw his sword before Annan smashed into him, knocking him halfway down the passage with a blow from his forearm. The torch clattered to the floor, its guttering light splashing the dungeon with grotesque shadows. Annan stood over the fallen Douglass, sword at his throat. "Where's the Lady Mairead?"

Gasping, Douglass inched himself onto one elbow and groped for a quivering front tooth. "She's there—in the last cell—"

"Where are your keys?" He grabbed the man's shirtfront and hauled him to his feet.

"Yessir, here they be. Take her— I wish you would."

Annan dragged him to the end of the row. "Unlock it."

"Yessir."

"Mairead?" He leaned against the rusted iron of the door, praying in his heart that more than silence would answer his plea. She wasn't dead. She couldn't be dead. Gethin would not triumph in his twisted game to force Matthias back into the open. She would still be alive, and he would take her away from this place, and they would disappear forever. The past, as always, would have to fend for itself.

The key grated in the lock, and Douglass dragged the door across the stones. Annan shoved him aside and yanked the door all the way open. "Fetch the torch. Marek, keep an eye on him."

Marek grunted. "All right. But hurry. This laddie here's been eating too many raisin puddings of late, feels like."

Annan stood in the doorway, seeing nothing but the shifting shadows as Douglass raised the torch from the floor. He fancied he could hear the rustling of blankets, heavy breathing, maybe a whispered prayer—and his heart thundered against his ribs. "Lady?"

This time he had no doubt he heard a quick exhalation. "Annan!"

He didn't wait for Douglass and the torch; he stumbled into the cold darkness of the cell. His knees hit the frame of a raised couch, and Mairead's warm fingers clutched his arm. "Oh, Annan— God *is* merciful—"

"Hush." He buried his face in the hair that draped her neck and held her against him, this flesh and bone and blood that was his wife. He breathed her in—the scent of dust and damp upon her hair, the stink of fear and illness that clung to her body, the smell of life—indomitable and unbroken. She was alive, and he could feel her heart beating against the emptiness of his chest. For just right now that was all that mattered.

"Annan, I was so afraid—so afraid I'd die before you came—"

"We have to leave. Are you able?"

"Yes. I'm able. Take me away from here."

She closed her arms around his neck and held him as though he would disappear if she couldn't hang on tight enough.

"We *will* live through this," he whispered and started to raise her in his arms, blankets and all.

Behind them, Marek yelped. "Annan!"

And then all Hell came tumbling down around their ears.

From the stairwell, Hugh de Guerrant and a man-at-arms burst into the dungeon, swords at the ready. Laughter rumbled in Hugh's throat, deep and satisfied. "Well, Master Annan, you're becoming rather predictable, are you not?"

For the space of one long second, Annan stood as he was, staring across the flickering of the torchlight into the Norman's laughing eyes. Mairead's fingers tightened upon his neck, and even with all the blankets between them, he could feel her chest constrict. "Annan—"

He dropped her to her feet, praying her legs would support her long enough for him to dispatch this enemy once and for all.

With a snarl, Hugh lunged. Letting Odo go, Marek spun into Hugh's path, sword arced in front of him. Hugh caught it and parried without slowing. Marek's weak shoulder, unable to withstand the brunt of the Norman's strength, gave way, and his sword hurtled from his hand. The man-at-arms lunged for him, but Marek dove at his feet, rolling past him somehow and recapturing his blade.

Annan whipped his sword in front of him and stood before the door of Mairead's cell, teeth bared. Since the fall of Acre, he had been waiting for this day. The beat of his blood throbbed in his left hip. Nay—since that day at the melee tourney in Paris, he had waited. And now the time had come.

He took one giant step forward and met Hugh's unabated charge. Their swords tangled, the crash reverberating against the stone walls and against every bone of Annan's arms. For a moment, they held, their straining faces only a hand's breadth apart, before tearing away once more.

Annan kept nothing back. His strength thundered against Hugh's, raining blow after blow upon the other's sword. And Hugh gave way. Experienced though he might be, he was Annan's match in neither strength nor skill.

The look of iron in Hugh's eyes wavered, the long shadows beneath his cheekbones deepening. Annan grinned savagely. That expression was the only admission of the truth he would ever gain from Hugh de Guerrant: by himself, he would never be able to take Annan.

"Esmé!" Hugh roared.

From the other end of the cellblock, the man-at-arms risked a glance at his master's plight, then whirled back to Marek, vigor redoubled. He slashed the lad's blade back to the ground and kicked it away.

"Leave him!" Hugh shouted as he staggered beneath yet another of Annan's tremendous blows.

Somewhere on the edge of his senses, Annan saw Marek scramble after his blade only to be tackled by the jailer. Then Esmé joined Hugh, and Annan became too busy to notice anything beyond the extra blade added to his own battle.

The two Normans, neither of them possessing his own breadth of shoulder, wedged themselves side by side in the narrow passage and pressed the attack. It was evident they had fought together many times before. Their movements segued, one thrusting, then falling back to allow the other to push forward. The cramped space was all in their favor; it kept Annan from maneuvering. Nothing but a straight, head-on approach could be accomplished here.

He fell back, parrying, always parrying. Sooner or later, he was going to run into the back wall of Mairead's cell. And when they reached her, his choices would be restricted even further. Hugh and this hench-man of his would not scruple to use her to their advantage.

The shadows began to lengthen; their battle was almost outside the range of the torchlight. Annan gritted his teeth, his blade flying as he struggled to gain an offensive foothold.

He watched the faces of his opponents, waiting for them to shift their attention, even ever so slightly, as an indication that they noticed Mairead. But they didn't flinch. Perhaps she had retreated back inside. He couldn't be more than a few steps from the entrance to her cell, but he couldn't hear her, couldn't sense her.

His breath burned within his lungs. Sweat beaded the edges of his scalp. In the palms of both hands, he could feel the slippery heat of the blood that seeped from his wounds. Already, his sword was less than solid in his grip.

With a strong overhand blow, Hugh drove him back another step, and Annan's left shoulder collided with the doorframe. His concentration snapped. He stumbled, and the man-at-arms penetrated his defense with a lunge at his abdomen.

"No!" Mairead screamed from the darkness behind him. She hit his right side, both hands shoving against his shoulder, and instead of penetrating his innards, the sword glanced against bone.

He crashed against the cell wall so hard his vision turned to black. Before he could open his eyes, his head slammed the stones once more, and the chill of a blade pressed against his throat.

Cursing, Hugh knocked Annan's blade from his bloody hands. "Were the decision mine, I'd lay you open where you stand." His blade cut into Annan's wind. "You may be thankful—very thankful—that Bishop Roderic has other uses for you."

Annan strained a breath past his gritted teeth and twisted to find Mairead. She lay on the floor, propped up on one hand, the other pressed to her side.

"Put her back on the couch," Hugh commanded, and Esmé bent to lift her. "You may be interested to know, my dear Countess, that—unlike your husband—*you* have now served every purpose your wretched life was intended to fulfill. Except one." His eyes narrowed even as his teeth showed in a smile. "And that purpose, at long last, is my own."

Annan lurched around, heedless of the blade at his throat, and swung blindly at Hugh. The Norman whipped his sword down and caught Annan's blow before it had gone half its intended distance. The blade's edge pierced the thin flesh of his lower arm and grated against bone. Annan's other fist found Hugh's chin like a moneyer's hammer against his anvil. "Marek!"

"I can't get to you!" The reply struggled from the other end of the passage.

"Then leave! Leave *now*!"

Marek's eyes, wide and surprised, found Annan's through the doorway, and Annan had just enough time to see the lad slam Douglass's back against the door of a cell and break free of the jailer's bear grip. They both fell to the ground, Marek scrambling once again for his sword. Douglass rolled over and grabbed the lad by the ankles, his own sword coming up once and falling against Marek's head. The lad jerked stiff, then collapsed.

"Behind you!" Mairead shouted, and Annan turned in time for Hugh's lowered shoulder to crunch against his ribcage. Air exploded from his lungs. The shoulder he had injured in Acre struck the damp stone of the floor, and he felt something pop within the healing tissue.

Fighting for a breath that refused to come, he rolled onto his back, hands rising to protect his face.

"Hold him!" Hugh rasped.

One of Esmé's knees dropped onto Annan's chest. Fingers closed themselves in his throat. Mist the color of bruise and ash swam before his vision, filled his ears, clogged his senses.

Somewhere in the background, he could hear Mairead screaming for Marek to come, screaming they would kill him.

Then the pitch of her cries changed. And then they went silent.

His heart stopped beating. A crackle, like lightning against water, seemed to chase the blood from his veins.

"Turn him around!" Hugh demanded.

The weight of Esmé's knee lifted from his chest. His grip on Annan's throat released for a moment only to be replaced by the crook of his elbow as he hauled Annan onto his knees and shoved him around.

Mairead lay flat on the bed where Esmé had dropped her, her hands clutching the neckline of her bodice. Hugh stood over her, facing Annan, his hand clamped on her neck, holding her down. "Now," he panted, "witness."

Annan's eyes fell closed. Fire filled his body.

Esmé looked over his shoulder to check on the jailer behind them. And in that instance, Annan smashed his elbow into the knight's ribs, yanked himself free of the collaring elbow, and lunged for his sword. He spun to his feet, both hips thudding pain. He hefted the sword like a poleax and swung almost before Hugh realized he had gotten free. The blade's honed edge caught bone just beneath the shoulder joint and cleaved through. Hugh shouted and fell beside his severed arm, his torso divided in half, even unto his breastbone.

Annan left him choking on wet curses and writhing in the flow of his own blood like the filthy worm he was. He would be dead within moments.

Slowly, he lifted his eyes to Mairead's. She had sat up and was huddled against the cold of the wall. Her chin trembled.

He coughed against the ache of his throat and took one stuttering step toward her.

And then the rest of the noises he had been forcing into the back of his brain suddenly swelled into the clatter of weapons and booted feet. And voices: "Lord Hugh!" "Sir Esmé?" "They are in the Countess of Keaton's cell."

That voice he knew. He swung his aching body around to see armed men choking the passage. Four burst through the cell door and took in the scene at a glance. "Don't move!"

He lifted the sword in front of his face. His breath rasped its way out of his mouth as two of the knights charged.

"Let us return to St. Dunstan's, Marcus Annan," said the voice of Gethin the Baptist, and Annan looked at the hooded figure standing in the doorway, crucifix gleaming against his chest in the torchlight.

He had just enough time to see Gethin smile before the knights closed in. A rush of air heralded the crashing of something cold and hard against the back of his skull.

Mairead gasped as Annan staggered forward and fell to one knee. In the moment when his attention had been distracted by the voice from outside the cell, one of the knights had struck him with the flat of his blade. The guards fell upon him, tearing his sword from his grip, twisting his arms behind his back. He rumbled in pain, like a wounded lion, but he didn't fight. His head nodded, his chin brushing the collar of his tunic.

She pushed away from the wall and flung herself at him. "No! Don't kill him! God, my God—don't let them kill him!"

The nearest man-at-arms, a lanky Syrian with a wind-chapped face, caught her before she could reach him. Her fingers tore at him frantically. Had Hugh been right after all? Would they cut Annan down before her very eyes?

The man-at-arms muttered a curse in French and clamped both of her hands inside his larger one.

"Annan—!"

He tried to bob his head up and turn in her direction, the muscles of his arms straining. Someone hit him across the face, but that only seemed to clear the grog from his head. His face came up, blue eyes glaring death. The man-at-arms hit him again, and this time he sagged. "Scottish filth."

Beneath its tentative covering of congealing flesh, Mairead's wounded side pulsed.

"Fear not, Countess. They only take the precautions his reputation requires."

She flinched. It was the Baptist. The same Baptist whom Annan had risked his life to save? He had let these soldiers do this? He had betrayed them? She strained against the Syrian who held her, and at a motion from the monk, the man released her hands.

She stared at the Baptist. "I don't understand."

"You will."

Two knights hooked their hands under Annan's arms and dragged him from the cell.

Her heart hurled itself against her ribs. "Where are they going?"

"I will show you." The Baptist stepped forward, hand outstretched, then stopped, seeing for the first time Hugh's body where it lay behind her.

She didn't follow his gaze. She didn't want to see. He was dead. That was all that mattered. Never again could he touch her.

"Well," said the monk. "Perhaps he knows a thing about justice after all." Falcon-sharp eyes lifted to meet hers, and he smiled. "That is most encouraging."

A cold worm wriggled down the back of her bodice. "What do you mean?"

He came one step closer, scooped her up in arms that were shockingly solid, and carried her from the cell, his broken gait jostling her with every step. They passed through the cellblock, crowded as it was with soldiers. Marek, still unconscious, had been dragged into a cell.

The Baptist did not pause. They reached the stairs, and he started climbing, dragging himself up one step after the other. They kept going until they reached the main level, found another set of steps and climbed again. And again.

At every level, at every open window, she heard the restless sounds of an army gathering for battle. They passed an unshuttered eastern window, and she shivered at the rim of evanescent gray against the black horizon. Jaffa would be under siege ere dawn.

They reached the third floor, and Bishop Roderic's voice broke through the increasing buzz from beyond the city walls.

"What is the meaning of this? How did he get within these walls? How? Tell me *how*!"

"We meet again, Father." Annan's voice was throaty, hoarse. By the sound of it, Esmé had come near to crushing his windpipe.

"Aye, we meet again, tourneyer. Though I doubt circumstances such as these were in your plans."

"Not my plans, Bishop. Veritas's."

The bishop paused fully long enough for the Baptist to complete two steps down the hallway. "What?"

Another voice offered, "A monk by that name came to our quarters. He told us a man had forced his way into the dungeon."

"Monk? What monk?"

The Baptist rounded the corner of the doorframe and stopped, feet spread. Bishop Roderic, clad in cassock and yellow shawl, stood beside a huge central chair of scarlet and oak. Annan was on his knees between the men-at-arms who had borne him hither.

"This monk, Bishop," said the Baptist.

All four men snapped around to look. Annan started up at the sight of Mairead in the Baptist's arms, but he was forced back down. He quivered under the pressure of the men-at-arm's hands.

"Who are you?" Roderic demanded. One hand darted for the jeweled crucifix upon his breast; he rubbed it as if he thought it some kind of charm.

The Baptist shrugged, his broad chest shifting against Mairead's side. "I am called many things." He nodded to the soldiers. "*They* know me as Veritas."

Roderic panted. "Is this true?"

The Baptist continued, uninterrupted, with a gesture to Annan. "He would know me as something else. And she—" He hefted Mairead a little in his arms. "Ask the Countess of Keaton who she knows me as."

Roderic's pale eyes darted to her. A hunger filled them—a desperate, fearful hunger. She faltered. This man was an enemy, and the Baptist... she had thought the Baptist was a friend. Her eyes crept to where Annan knelt, his eyes closed. Nay, the Baptist was no friend.

"Speak!" Roderic thundered.

She raised her chin and stared into the bishop's face. "He is the Baptist."

His Grace jerked as if he had been shot. "That cannot be."

"Can't it?" The Baptist laughed. "Do not fear me, Bishop. Everything I have done has been to bring to you the one man in all the earth who knows where to find Matthias of Claidmore."

Roderic stirred. His fingers dropped from the crucifix and gestured to the soldiers. "Leave us." The hand remained aloft. "But first, give me a sword."

The indicated man-at-arms hesitated, then gave him the hilt of his one-handed sword. The Baptist stepped out of the doorway to let them pass and kept walking until he reached one of the long windows flanking Roderic's throne. He dropped Mairead to her feet and turned away without a second glance.

She buried her hand in the ruddy folds of the curtain and braced against the windowframe.

Outside, red burned into the wispy gray of the skyline. An armored horse galloped through the street beneath, and in the plains beyond the walls, the bedlam of a thousand instruments—conch horn and shawm, nakers and cymbal—began their rhythm. And below, as if the whole city had suddenly ignited with the same spark, the Christians began to fidget, to call, to worry.

She turned away. Her hand trembled as she lifted it to cross herself. *Heaven preserve us—from the wicked that oppress us, from our deadly enemies, from those who compass us about...*

Annan knelt on aching hips, his eyes closed, head bowed, listening to Gethin's laughter. How far they all had fallen. He had known this moment was coming. He had waited for it, tried to brace himself against the base treachery of it. But it still felt like a mace shattering his bones.

"I have baited your trap for you, Bishop," Gethin said.

Annan opened his eyes to find the Baptist extending a hand in his direction, as if introducing nobility. "Gethin—"

In front of them both, Roderic stood, sword hanging at his side, chest heaving. Behind him, the howl of war—the clangor of iron, the thunder of war mares' feet, the screams and the drums of the Moslem hordes—rose with the sun.

Roderic stared at Annan, his face twisting. "The very first time I saw you, I knew in the marrow of my bones you were dangerous. How I knew it, I cannot tell, but I did. And I was a fool to ignore it!"

Annan let his lids fall half closed. The bishop *still* didn't know how deeply they were all sunk in Gethin's treachery, still didn't understand how vast a web had been spun by his sins from long ago.

"But I will ignore it no longer." The bones of Roderic's sword hand jutted against his skin. "Your perfidy has come to an end, Sir Knight. Now it is your fate in my hand, and not the other way around. You *will* give me Matthias of Claidmore, and we will put an end to this."

In the corner, enveloped in the aureole of morning light, Mairead stirred.

Laughter, cold and bitter, rose in Annan's mouth. "Nay, Bishop. *That* battle is one that neither you nor the Baptist will win." He glanced to where Gethin waited in passive assurance.

Roderic flung his arm in Mairead's direction. "Deliver him to me, and I will spare the countess's life."

She didn't flinch, but her knuckles burned white within the blood-red folds of the curtain. She bit her lower lip, and Annan's chest tightened. "Matthias is dead."

Gethin folded his arms into his sleeves. "Nay. He is not."

Roderic hissed. "Mark me and mark me well." The skin of his face, grayer even than usual, drew taut across his cheekbones. "If Matthias of Claidmore is not on his knees to me—even as you are now—before the Christians have departed Jaffa, I will give your wife over to Lord Hugh."

Annan growled. "Lord Hugh's dead."

"Then I will kill her myself!"

"Nay, you will not!" His breath quickened.

"God help me, tourneyer, I will tempt you to ever hazard my wrath again!"

Annan levered his good leg under his body and lunged. Blood thundered in his head, blearing his vision, blocking his hearing, threatening to plunge him once more into darkness.

The bishop's sword flashed up defensively, and suddenly Mairead was between them. Her slender arm held Annan back as she faced the bishop. "Your Grace, I beg you! Don't do this! It is I you want—it has always been me! Let him go—"

"Silence! If you beg mercy, then look to your husband, not to me."

She turned to Annan, her warmth pressing against him. "Annan—don't do it. Not for me. Please." Her chin trembled.

"Mairead… I'm sorry—" Sorrier than he could ever tell. He had failed her. It was *his* enemies they had been running from all this time, had they only realized it.

Roderic grabbed her wrist from where it lay on Annan's shoulder. He jerked her up beside him and pointed to her with the sword. "Her life is nothing to me. Nothing." A tangle of veins throbbed in either temple. "I will kill her in an instant. Do you understand that?"

She stood with one arm close to her side, her lips parted, her eyes huge. And yet, she shook her head. She didn't even know what it was they wished to trade her life for, and still she shook her head.

His heart hammered in his ears. He loved her. He admitted it. He loved her enough to die for her without a second thought. But did he love her enough to surrender, at long last, St. Dunstan's and all its secrets?

He looked back to Father Roderic.

"Tell me where he may be found," Roderic said. "Once and for all, *where is Matthias of Claidmore?*"

Annan's every muscle tremored. The breeze, warmed by the rays of the morning, filled the curtains like sails, and the air caressed his face, soft and humid and taunting. Screams and shouts had joined the harried buzz of the besieged city. Saladin was breaking through, just as surely and inexorably as was the past.

The Baptist was going to win after all. And Matthias would be dead no more.

Gethin came a step nearer, just within Annan's vision. He whispered, his words barely rising above the clamor of besieged Jaffa: "Tell him."

Annan filled his lungs, feeling afresh the stab of every wound. His head bowed, and the breath slipped back out. He shook his head. "You have found him already."

Roderic's brows darted together once more. "What?"

"*I* am Matthias."

CHAPTER XXVII

RODERIC STAGGERED BACK, one hand groping for the arm of his chair. His eyes were huge in his face—gray slate against grayer marble.

Mairead stared at Annan. "But he's dead. You said he was dead."

Past the burn of strained tendons in his neck, Annan coughed. "He *was* dead. For sixteen years he was dead. And he resurrects now only because… I know no other way."

To the left, hovering at the edge of his vision, Gethin looked on, eyes hooded like a purring cat.

Annan's throat knotted. Aye, *he* was Matthias. It was *his* rage that had lit the fire of St. Dunstan's holocaust. In his desire to remove Father Roderic's iniquity, *he* had fomented the rebellion that had torn the Abbey apart and laid the peaceful brethren ripped and bleeding among the ashes. *He* had throttled Roderic and left him for dead, and it was only by some whim of Heaven that the bishop had lived.

He had left St. Dunstan's even as it burned—with smoke like black horses thundering into the heavens and the flames licking higher and higher—and he had known to the dregs of his soul that he was forever blackened in the sight of God. He had despised himself; he had wished the very fires of Hell down upon his own wretched head. And from that day on, Matthias of Claidmore had lived no more.

Gethin stepped forward, his hands digging themselves elbow deep into his sleeves. His eyes glinted with jubilation. "I whet My glittering sword, and Mine hand takes hold on judgment. I will render vengeance to Mine enemies, and will reward them that hate Me." The clamor of war and the frantic voices of the guards in the street punctuated the strains of his delight. "I will make Mine arrows drunk with blood, and My sword shall devour flesh; and that with the blood of the slain and of the captives, from the beginning of revenges upon the enemy."

"I don't—understand." Roderic fell against the back of his chair, his eyes still on Annan. "This cannot be…"

"Suffice it that I am he." Annan looked at Gethin. "But if he speaks of vengeance, Father, he speaks it upon my head. We will both of us die unforgiven. You, because even yet you bear the sins of bloodshed and whoredom. I, because I saw not the beam in my own eye and allowed myself to think it my right to punish those sins in kind."

A shudder passed through Roderic's limbs. "Yes. You *are* him. Eloquent, as ever." He rose from his seat. "And you are right. You *will* die. At last I hold the upper hand, and I will not squander it." He started forward, his gait stilted.

In the streets, people were screaming and running. The infidels were attacking the wall. Someone began pounding on the door.

Roderic hazarded not a glance at the interruption. "Lord Matthias, you will bow your head."

Mairead hurled herself at the bishop's sword arm. "Annan, don't let them do this. Tell them you are not Matthias. Tell them he's dead!"

"Enough!" Roderic cast her aside as a dog would a rat.

Behind Annan, the door crashed open. "Bishop! They are ordering every able man to the front lines! The king has barely fifty knights facing Saladin's cavalry. No one knows if the reinforcements from Caesarea will arrive! He begs your attendance."

Roderic waved as though shooing a fly. "I am occupied. Leave us."

The soldier hesitated, and Roderic whirled on him. "Leave us!" The door pulled shut, footsteps hurried away, and Roderic turned back. "Matthias of Claidmore. Bow your head."

"No!" Mairead struggled to rise from the floor.

Annan kept his head aloft. The pulse in either temple held steady.

Here, at last, was death. And before he went to face whatever was beyond, he would die as he had not lived. With honor.

Roderic lofted the sword in both hands. He would cleave Annan's head in half if he could not take it off. His eyes were dark and terrible. The sword fell.

With a motion like the well of the tide at equinox, Gethin shot forward, shrieking wordless nothings. From within his sleeve he had drawn a dirk the length of the bone between shoulder and elbow. The blade found a space between Annan and Roderic's sword and stopped the descent of execution with the crash of metal against metal. "*Veritas vincit!*" Truth conquers. He hammered his free hand into the bishop's face. Father Roderic staggered back, falling against the footstool. "*Judice regit!*" Justice reigns.

With the deftness of one of the Moslems' famed Ismailian assassins, he clutched Annan's shoulder, dragging him forward, and severed the rope that bound his hands. "*Vindicta esse ab noster!*" Vengeance is ours.

For all of a breath, Annan didn't move. The heart that had been ready to meet death in silence suddenly filled his chest with its pounding. Blood smashed through the veins of his aching hands. Fire surged into the throbbing depths of his brain.

He lurched for Roderic's fallen sword and rolled to his feet.

A wheezing Roderic scrambled, on hands and knees, to where Mairead still lay in the red-gold light of the window. He fell atop her, and when they rose together, he had pulled a dagger from some hidden pocket, the necessary caution of a man who had spent his life crushed beneath the killing weight of fear.

Annan froze.

"Stay yourself, Brother Matthias."

Mairead's veil of hair, smashed between her face and Roderic's palsied hand, shuddered with her gasping.

"If you kill her, do you think I would let you live?" Annan demanded.

"Her life for mine. It is just." Roderic's eyes bulged.

In the background, Gethin scoffed. "What does he know of justice?"

Annan stayed where he was, bloody and aching, before the face of this man he had despised for sixteen long years. Time and again, Gethin had urged him to kill him, and time and again, Annan had sworn that to kill him would be to unleash the mistakes of St. Dunstan's all over again. He swallowed past the ache of his throat and held out his left hand.

"Give her to me, and I will not slay you."

He could hear Gethin's start of surprise. Slowly, Roderic's grip on Mairead's throat slipped. Her hair fell away from her face, and he withdrew entirely. Uttering a cry, she staggered to Annan's outstretched hand and folded herself into his arm, face pressed against the hollow of his shoulder.

But Annan didn't heed. His gaze didn't falter from Roderic's. He watched, waiting until the tentative relief melted from the bishop's features, as Roderic realized what so many men upon the tourney field had realized when they had seen the same look upon his face.

Annan took a step forward, opening his arm to let Mairead go.

"Annan—"

Roderic staggered back. "But you said you would spare—"

Annan no longer wanted to spare. The man deserved death. How many times had Roderic tried to tear from Annan all that mattered? Would he not have killed Mairead even now had he the chance? He was filth in the sight of both God and man, and he deserved to die. Why shouldn't Annan finish what he had begun?

All the reasons that had been burrowing inside his skull for the past sixteen years fluttered away, chaff before anger's fiery wind. He would kill Roderic, pluck Marek from his cell, which would be but lightly guarded in the face of the Moslem attack, and then they would leave this place behind forever.

"Kill him." Gethin's words grated at the edge of his perception, shrill against the cacophony of battle noises. "He is evil. Evil must die. He murdered his own bride to gain a bishopric. He debauched his body and his office. He tried to silence me forever when I called for righteousness!"

"Annan, don't do this—" Mairead's fingers were cold against his arm, even through his sleeve. "Will breaking your word to him acquit you in the eyes of Heaven?"

He faltered. His sword arm quivered.

Her hand pressed against his jaw, trying to make him look down at her. "If you do this thing now, you will be truly lost! You are not yet too lost for redemption, no matter what you've convinced yourself to believe all these years!"

"If you shirk your duty, do you think you will be redeemed?" Gethin demanded.

"No!" Tears clogged Mairead's voice. "It is only your stubborn pride, your own shame that separates you from the forgiveness of God!"

Annan stopped, and a long breath shuddered in his body. Where would the killing stop? Where would forgiveness begin? If not now, then when? His hand trembled, and he closed his eyes.

"Oh God—" Mairead's hand dropped from his face to his chest, and he opened his eyes to see her bent head. "You can still begin anew," she said. "Please don't throw it away."

Annan looked up and found Roderic cowering in the light of the window. His shoulders slumped. "Take your life as a gift, Father. May you make better use of it now than you did the last time."

Then, pulling Mairead close to his side, he turned away.

"No!"

He didn't look back at Gethin's screams.

"No! You cannot go! You must kill him for what he did to me!" Gethin caught Annan's shoulder from behind and spun him around. His grip had the strength of talons as he clutched Annan's arm. "I will have justice!"

"Nay." Annan put a hand atop that of this one-time friend. "I am as much to blame for what happened to you as is he."

Gethin's fingers sank deeper, his eyes protruding in the distorted wreck of his face. "Kill him, I tell you!"

"His sins were not ours to avenge."

"Aren't they?" Gethin leaned away, and in the rabid depths of that intense gaze, Annan recognized the madness Marek had so often jested about. "If you have sunk so low you cannot do what must be done—" He stepped back, and one hand reached into his sleeve. "Then I must."

He whirled, short sword whipping once more from within his sleeve, and flung himself at Father Roderic.

Roderic had not even time to cry out. Gethin's dirk pricked above the heart and plunged as deep as the forte. Roderic clamped both hands on the wound and fell back against the window. Gethin stayed upright, only tilting the sword so that the bishop's body might slide off.

Annan's breath hissed past his lips. In the shadow below the window lay the prior of St. Dunstan's Abbey. But this time the weight of his blood did not rest upon Annan's hands.

"It is done," rasped Gethin. "You are weak."

Annan said nothing. Since their reunion in Bari, Gethin had not listened to him, and he would not listen now.

Eyelid quivering, Gethin limped a step forward. "He tried to kill me. He had them beat me like a dog and then cast me aside as dead. He had to die for that!"

"Not at my hand."

"It *should* have been at your hand!" He took another step. "Do you know why he beat me? Why he tried to kill me?"

"Because of me."

"*Yes!*" The word clawed the air. "Because I befriended you when you came to us, consumed with your guilt. Because I stood beside you when you cried for reform! Because I would not renounce you when you took the law into your own hands! I thought you strong then. But you are not strong! You have refused to finish what you started. And because of that, you will share in his sins!" The short sword flashed in his hands.

Reflex saved Annan. He snapped Roderic's blade before his face and caught Gethin's ringing blow.

"God will have His justice!" Gethin shoved hard with both hands.

"It is not *God's* justice you seek!" Roderic's sword was made to be wielded with just one hand, but Annan wrapped one fist on top of the other. The scabs in his palms cracked and split. New blood, sticky with clotting, seeped. Something wasn't right in his left shoulder; the arm was heavy, the joint thick.

"You do not know of what you speak, tourneyer!" Deadlocked against Annan's strength, Gethin strained, then broke free and struck again. In the Saracen prison camp outside Acre, Annan had admired the sword that had felled an infidel guard. Now, standing against the fervor and skill of the Baptist's blows, he had cause to admire the arm that had wielded that sword.

Gethin fought like some mad knight paladin escaped from Marek's minstrel songs. A strange, impassioned strength hummed in the lines of his crippled muscles. His fury astounded Annan. The body that had been destroyed at St. Dunstan's found new life in its anger. Without buckler or mail, and with the odds evened by Annan's wounds, they fought as equals, neither giving ground, neither finding an opening.

Annan faltered beneath a hammering blow, and the dam that had been their equality was swept aside. He took one halting step back with his wounded hip, and Gethin flooded through the breach.

Back, back, they battled, Gethin's breath gusting in huge, angry bursts. Annan gritted his teeth. Was this how his opponents felt? Suffocating with their exertion and hardly able to afford the distraction of any breath at all? White-washed daub closed in on either edge of his vision, and he braced for the impact of the collision. As his shoulders crashed into the wall, it yielded. Warm air wheezed against his neck.

His cheek quivered. He was leaning against a set of slender doors. He had seen them—painted red like the window curtains and barely as tall as his shoulder—when he had been dragged into the room. From the feel of them creaking behind his shoulders, they were made of only the lightest of woods.

He dropped his left hand from the sword and slammed his elbow into the crack between the doors. They clattered open, louvers crashing and splintering against the doorframe. He stumbled into the sunlight, leaving Gethin's blade to cleave only shadow.

Immediately, he was aware of two things: He was standing upon the city wall, which formed the back of Roderic's house. And the battle was right beneath them. The sound of it thundered in his head. The energy pumped in his veins.

Gethin burst through the door into the heat of the sun, sword cocked above his shoulder, teeth bared in the deep tan of his skin. Annan pushed himself up from where he had fallen against the parapet and turned to face him.

"What happened at St. Dunstan's was wrong." He held his sword before his face, the side of his left leg pressed against the rampart wall.

He backed away slowly, one step back for every of Gethin's steps forward. "It is my fault you have traveled the path that has led you here, and I am sorry."

Gethin spat. "It is a path you should have walked yourself! It is you who should have killed the bishop. Have you forgotten already what he did to the countess?"

Below them, an English voice shouted for the troops to hold steady. Annan did not risk the glance that would show him the crash of iron against flesh. "What the *bishop* did? Gethin, you have blinded yourself! It was *you* who twisted him and misled him and played upon his fears, just as you sought to play upon mine!"

"He was evil!"

"He was a weapon in *your* hands!"

Gethin struck like a snarling cat.

Annan met the blow with all the strength of both arms. Pain rattled through his bones. His left shoulder pounded. His vision blurred white, and he struck again. It was Gethin who had perpetrated all the atrocities against Mairead. It was Gethin who was responsible for Lord William's death. And Lord Stephen's death. And Lady Eloise's devastation. And Marek's wounds.

Was this the man who had been his dearest friend, his only confidante, his paragon of charity? Something squeezed in his heart, and he wanted to weep.

Gethin's blade smashed into his once more. This time Annan held it, screeching, against his own. Barely a span separated their faces.

"How far we have fallen." Annan's words were hoarse. "A long time ago, it was you who taught me of mercy. For all these years, I thought I had forgotten it. I thought that when such a moment as this came, I would be ready to leave a cruel world behind and my own cruelty in it."

The tendons in Gethin's neck stood out above the heave of his chest. His eyes fluttered like an ensnared kestrel.

"But God is still merciful, and I will fall no more. Let us end this."

With a roar, Gethin pulled away. He charged headlong, casting aside all thoughts of defense. Annan took one step back, braced, and swung to meet him. His sword connected just above the dirk's hilt. The force of the blow slammed Gethin's hip into the low wall, and his upper body swung out over the parapet.

Annan stepped back. The soles of Gethin's sandals slipped against the plank flooring. His eyes bulged, black pupil engulfing amber iris. Cavalry thundered in the plains below; a hundred archers added the twang and patter of their steadfast fire; an English voice roared the age-old battle cry of the Crusades: "God wills it!"

And Gethin the Baptist fell from Jaffa's ramparts.

Annan closed his eyes and listened as the scream was chopped short. He did not step to the wall to see the dusty heap of brown homespun that had fallen amidst all that remained of Christendom's greatest armies. He did not want to see. Turning away, he sank to his knees. Roderic's sword clanked against the planks, and at last he prayed. *Christ, have mercy... Save me.*

He slumped his head to his chest, utterly spent. He had been forcing punishment for St. Dunstan's upon himself long enough. The time had come to put it aside forever. His pride torn down, he could now accept the forgiveness he had so long shunned, the forgiveness that had never been his to earn, but only to claim. His punishment was at an end—at last.

He opened his eyes. For the first time in sixteen years, perhaps for the first time in his entire life, a glimmer of day flickered at the end of his dark path.

Behind him, painful, halting footsteps whispered. *Mairead.* He didn't turn around, even as she laid her hands on his aching shoulders. For a long moment, neither of them moved.

"It's over," she said at last.

"Aye." His throat grew thick, and he raised his right arm to hers. Aye, it was over. And, in that one word, he—undeserving, miserable man that he was—had been given a gift so great it overwhelmed him. The chance to begin anew. The chance to remember what it was like to serve a God who loved. The chance to push Death out to arm's length and keep it there. The chance to love this woman who was his wife.

"Stay with me," he whispered.

She sank down behind him, her fingers closing over the reopened gash in his forearm. Her arms slipped around him, her cheek against his shoulder. "Yes," she said.

He cradled her arms against him and looked out at the battlefield. Darkness was growing on the faraway horizon. It was the darkness of gathering troops. Probably the rest of Richard's army on their way from Caesarea to rescue the beleaguered city. Jaffa was saved.

And so was he.

CHAPTER XXVIII

ON OCTOBER 9, 1192, Richard Coeur-de-Lion, King of England, together with most of his army, left the Holy Land in the hands of the infidels and embarked for home. Far down the beach, near where he had held his first meeting with Brother Warin under the cover of moonlight, Annan watched the ships catch sail and begin their creaking way out to open sea.

Beside him, mounted on a little black Turkish mare he'd dubbed Lucretia, Marek lifted his chin from where he had propped it against his hand. "Well, this has been a right good waste of a Crusade, hasn't it? Here we were, hovering round for practically the whole rotten thing, and we've not an absolution to show for it among the lot of us. Complete and utter waste. 'Specially considering I had to spend a night in some cold, nasty cell."

"Will the Christians return?" Mairead asked over Annan's shoulder. She put her hand against his side, balancing as she shifted on the pillion.

"I don't know. Perhaps." He hoped not. Despite the Christians' escape at Jaffa, the Turks had soundly beaten the might of Christendom. Had it been a mission blessed of God, he could not help but think the outcome would have been vastly different. His eyes followed the retreating galleys. Did they even realize their mistake? Or would they come again, believing—like Gethin and Father Roderic and Hugh de

Guerrant—that they were wise enough and righteous enough to claim their swords as God's judgment?

Aye, they would come. It was the way of man.

The wind picked up, cold for the time of year, and swept across the sea, ruffling undulant silver into whitecaps. Mairead's cloak spread with it, and she leaned closer to Annan. "Will *we* ever return?"

"St. Jude." Marek sniffed. "Only a fool comes back to a place this bloody."

Annan half-turned, careful to balance his weight on his battered hips, and looked at Mairead. "Do you want to return?"

She met his gaze, then looked away, out to the sea. A strand of hair escaped from the braids atop her head and blew past her cheek. "Nay. But I think I'm afraid to leave." Her gaze flickered in his direction.

He turned away, and a smile tucked itself deep within the corners of his mouth. What had begun for them would not end here. His promise to Lord William had yet to be fulfilled.

He nudged his heel to Airn's side, and they started forward. "But *you're* ready to leave, are you?" He looked over at Marek.

"No more Crusades for me. I've better ways to waste my time."

"Such as?"

"Ha. Keeping you out of trouble doesn't allow me much time for the wasting, does it?"

"And what about Maid Dolly in Glasgow?"

"By now she probably thinks I died saving dusty old Jerusalem. Hope they gave me a proper eulogy."

"Would you like to find out?"

"Hmph. And how would that be?"

Annan swiveled to look him in the eye. "Ask her for yourself."

Marek raised an eyebrow, then suddenly his mouth dropped. "You mean I'm—you're letting me—?"

"When we get back to Scotland, you go find this Dolly of yours and tell her you earned an honorable freedom."

"I—" Marek stared. Then he dropped his reins onto his mount's neck, cupped both hands round his mouth, and yelled like he thought he had won the war single-handedly. Still yelling, he laid his heels into his mare's ribs and tore down the beach.

Mairead laughed. "He'll be in Constantinople ere midnight if he keeps up like that." Her hand rested on Annan's side. "Why did you do it?"

"He deserves it." He smiled at the sand spraying in all directions from beneath the black mare's pounding hooves. He was going to miss Master Peregrine Marek more than he wanted to admit. He chuckled, the sound so soft it was barely audible.

Mairead's fingers tightened in his jerkin. "I've never heard you laugh."

"I will laugh again," he said. "When we see the Cheviot Hills, I will laugh. When we make our home in their shadow, I will laugh. And when our children are born to us, I will laugh."

"What?" The word was breathless.

He reined Airn to a stop and turned to look at her despite the ache of his hips. Her teeth caught her lip. Another gust of wind flattened the loose strand of her hair against her face, and he lifted it from her cheek and feathered it against his forefinger.

"We're not going to Orleans." He dropped the hair and cradled her jaw. "Lord William wanted me to give you the name of Matthias. That was the name he thought would best protect you. And it is time I did that."

He kissed her, once on the lips, once on the forehead, then leaned away. His back was beginning to cramp, but before he turned around, he would say everything that needed to be said.

"I was afraid. Afraid to forgive myself, and even more afraid to ask Heaven to forgive me."

"But no longer?" Her eyes shone. He remembered that night in Brother Werinbert's earthen chapel, when she had knelt in the dirt and prayed for him. Those prayers had gone farther than she knew.

He nodded. "You were right. You learned from your suffering what I would not allow mine to teach me. Every dawn is a new beginning."

Two little tears glistened against the glow of her face. "Aye." She smiled and became radiant.

"Yaaaaaiiih!"

Annan turned to see Marek beginning his return trip down the beach, the sand flying just as furiously as on his departure. "Take hold." He laid his free hand over Mairead's where it crossed his ribs and closed his legs around the courser's girth. The horse jumped forward into a few trotting steps, then flattened its body, ears against its head and ran to meet Marek.

They passed him and kept on going. From the corner of his vision, Annan could see on the faraway eastern horizon, where the bone white of the sky met the pewter glass of the sea, a rim of sunlight, like the crease of an eye just waking from sleep. For sixteen years his world had slept.

But no more.

Afterword

I FIND MYSELF at the close of a story that has borne the brunt of some huge personal growing pains. Ironically, the theme of Marcus Annan's story—that each new day holds the opportunity to redeem yesterday's mistakes and begin afresh—was a lesson I faced on an almost hourly basis during the writing of this book. Although my representation of such an immense topic as redemption and grace must necessarily be flawed, I hope you will be able to see past the dross and take away a few flakes of the gold at the story's heart. And perhaps Marcus Annan and company will leave their impact on your life, as they most definitely have on mine.

Although I have tried to remain as true to the historical setting as possible, I have taken a few liberties I would like to point out.

No record exists of Saladin executing mass numbers of prisoners in retaliation for King Richard I's breach of promise, in which Richard ordered the deaths of some 2,700 prisoners from the garrison of Acre. After this incident, however, Saladin did adopt a strict take-no-prisoners policy, in which all surrendered Christian troops were summarily beheaded.

The timeline of the Crusade has been shortened to accommodate the necessities of Annan's story. In fact, the time that passed from King Richard's arrival in Acre on June 7, 1191, to his departure from the Holy

Land on October 9, 1192, encompassed almost a year and a half.

Finally, the languages found throughout the story are not representative of those spoken during the Middle Ages. English, French, and Italian did not exist as we now know them, and even in the forms in which they were found, they were largely fragmented into hundreds of local dialects. For obvious reasons of clarity, I have chosen to use primarily modern English.

The Crusades—especially the Crusade of Kings—are perhaps the most familiar symbols of the Middle Ages known to us in the 21st century. Gritty, gory, and often brutal though they may have been, their sense of the shortness of life and the realness of living is arguably unmatched. In lives so fleeting (Psalm 90:12), how can we afford to let even one dawn slip away without taking hold of the redemption found only through the blood and mercy of Christ?

K.M. Weiland
September 1, 2009

GLOSSARY

Absolution: Forgiveness for sins, given formally by the Church.

Anathema: Curse from a religious authority that denounces or excommunicates.

Baldric: Sash or belt worn from one shoulder to the opposite hip, used to support a sword.

Beatified: Statement by the Church, after someone's death, that he lived a holy life; first step toward sainthood.

Bellwether: Sheep that leads the rest of the flock; usually wears a bell around its neck.

Bodkin: A slender arrowhead, capable of piercing armor.

Bondman: Man who is enslaved or a serf.

Boon: A gift or favor from someone.

Buckler: Small round shield either worn on the forearm or held by a short handle at arm's length.

Bugbear: Monster invented to frighten children, traditionally in the form of a bear that eats those who misbehave.

Caparison: Ornamental cover for a warhorse.

Capon: Rooster castrated to improve its growth and the quality of its flesh for eating.

Cassock: Full-length, usually black robe worn by priests and their assistants.

Charger: Large, strong cavalry horse.

Charnel house: Building or vault in which bones or dead bodies are placed.

Charwoman: Servant woman employed to clean.

Coffer: Strong chest or box used for keeping money or valuables safe; also used as both a seat and a bed.

Couch: To lower (a lance) into attack position.

Courser: Swift horse, used for hunting; also refers to a warhorse, when destrier is used specifically for competitive mounts.

Courtier: Aristocrat who frequents a royal court or attends a king or queen.

Cowl: Hood of a cloak, particularly one worn by a monk.

Crenellation: Small open notches in a battlement.

Cudgel: Short heavy club.

Destrier: Warhorse, the most expensive mount; usually a stallion; similar to a modern heavy hunter.

Dirk: Dagger with a long blade.

Equipage: Equipment, particularly for equestrian use.

Ere: Before.

Eucharist: Symbolic or consecrated bread and wine consumed during the ceremony of Communion.

Fain: (to do something) With gladness or eagerness.

Forecastle: Raised deck at the bow of a ship.

Forte: Strongest section of a sword's blade, between the middle and the hilt.

Fortnight: Two weeks.

Frankish Syrian: European native of the Kingdom of Jerusalem, primarily of French descent.

Gauntlet: Glove with a long wide cuff that covers and protects the forearm.

Goodwife: Title of respect for a married woman who is the mistress of a household.

Great Hall: Main room in a castle, used for most of daily living, including eating, entertaining guests, working, and occasionally sleeping.

Great helm: Large, heavy helmet with faceplate which covers the entire face and neck.

Griffin: Monster with the head and wings of an eagle and the body and tail of a lion; a symbol used in heraldry.

Haft: Handle of a knife, ax, or other weapon or tool.

Hand: Unit of measurement, equal to the width of a man's hand, approximately four inches.

Hawser: Cable for mooring or towing a ship.

Hermit: Someone who chose to reject material things and live apart from the rest of society, in order to completely devote his life to God.

Hospitaler: Member of the Knights of the Hospital of St. John, a religious military order founded in the late 11th century by European crusaders to care for sick pilgrims in Jerusalem.

Inglenook: Recess for a seat or bench beside a large fireplace.

Jerkin: Close-fitting sleeveless outer tunic.

Jongleur: Wandering minstrel who sang the compositions of troubadours or recited epic poems in noble households or royal courts.

Ken: Knowledge (n.); know (v.).

Kirtle: Woman's long loose gown, often worn visibly beneath another garment.

Knave: Man who is considered dishonest and deceitful.

Lance: Long spear carried by cavalry in battle.

Larboard: Port (left) side of a vessel.

Lists: Area of combat in a medieval tournament, enclosed by a fence of high stakes; often used as an arena to settle private quarrels and matters of honor.

Livery: Identifying uniform worn by members of a group or trade, especially men and boys who are feudal retainers or servants of a household.

Lute: Instrument resembling a guitar but with a flat, pear-shaped body.

Mace: Heavy club with a round spiked metal head.

Maid: Unmarried woman.

Man-at-arms: Mounted, heavily armed soldier.

Matins: Dawn prayer service.

Mayhap: Perhaps.

Melee: Early form of tournament, in which teams of knights engaged each other; although varying rules of play were often instituted and holding prisoners for ransom was encouraged over killing, the contests differed little from real battles.

Mendicant: Member of a religious order such as the Franciscans, Dominicans, Carmelites, or Augustinians that forbids the ownership of property and encourages working or begging for a living.

Misericorde: Small dagger, often used to deliver the *coup de grâce*.

Mohammedan: Muslim.

Moslem: Muslim.

Nakers: Double drum.

Nigh: Near.

Norman: Native of Normandy, then under the rule of Richard I.

Paladin: Any one of the twelve legendary companions of Charlemagne.

Palfrey: Well-bred, easy-paced riding horse, often used by squires and women.

Penance: Sacrament in which a

324 – K.M. WEILAND

person confesses sins to a priest and is forgiven after performing an assigned religious devotion or duty.

Penitent: Someone performing penance.

Pike: Spear-like weapon used by foot soldiers.

Pilgrimage: Journey to a holy place, undertaken for religious reasons, often in search of absolution or miraculous healing.

Pillion: Cushion mounted behind a saddle, on which a second person, usually a woman, rides.

Poleax: Battle ax with a long or short handle, especially one with a hammer or spike opposite the ax blade.

Poniard: Small dagger with a slim blade, the cross section of which is triangular or square.

Postulant: Someone who applies to join a religious order.

Quarrel: Short, square-headed bolt or arrow used in a crossbow.

Quarterdeck: Rear part of a ship's upper deck.

Quarterstaff: Stout, iron-tipped pole, six to eight feet long, used as a weapon.

Quean: Woman of loose morals.

Retainer: Soldier or other person who fought under or was dependent on someone of high rank.

Saddlebow: Arch at the front of a saddle.

Saracen: Muslim who fought in the Crusades.

Scimitar: Turkish sword with a curved blade that broadens out as it nears the point.

Score: Twenty.

Scriptorium: Room in a monastery for storing, copying, illustrating, or reading manuscripts.

Shawm: Woodwind instrument with a double reed; predecessor of the modern oboe.

Siege tower: Rectangular, wheeled tower constructed to protect assailants while approaching the walls of a fortification.

Span: Unit of measurement, equal to the distance from the tip of the thumb to the little finger of a man's outspread hand, approximately nine inches.

Squire: Young apprentice who acted as an attendant to a knight.

Surcoat: Tunic worn over armor, often emblazoned with the wearer's coat of arms.

Tabard: Surcoat.

Templar: Member of a Christian military order founded in Jerusalem in 1119 to protect pilgrims after the First Crusade.

Tonsure: Shaved patch on the crown of a priest or monk's head.

Tournament: Sporting contest in which knights took part in single and mass combat; popular despite the Church's ban in 1130.

Tourney: Tournament.

Tourneyer: Competitor in a tourney.

Trencher: Large slice of day-old bread used as a plate, then given to the poor.

Troubadour: Writer or singer of lyric verses about courtly love.

True Cross: Believed to be pieces of the cross upon which Christ was crucified; captured by Saladin at the Battle of Hattin in 1187.

Varlet: Rogue or rascal; also, specifically, a servant.

Viand: Food, particularly in reference to provisions.

War hammer: Shafted weapon with a spiked hammer head.

Wedge tent: Triangle-shaped tent featuring two upright poles and one ridge pole.

Wimple: A cloth covering for a woman's head and neck.

Yeoman: Member of a class of commoners who owned and cultivated their own land.

About the Author

K.M. WEILAND'S FASCINATION with the Middle Ages began during childhood with stories of William Wallace and Robert the Bruce. A lifelong fan of history and the power of the written word, she enjoys sharing both through her novels and short stories. She blogs at *Wordplay: Helping Writers Become Authors* (wordplay-kmweiland.blogspot.com) and *AuthorCulture* (authorculture. blogspot.com). She lives in western Nebraska. Visit her website: kmweiland.com.

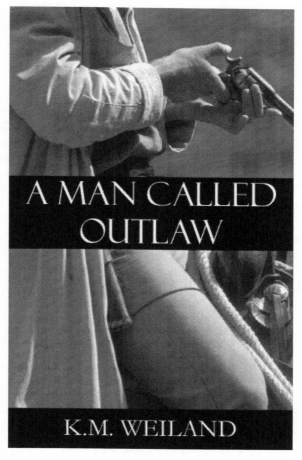

Made in the USA
Middletown, DE
18 March 2017